AND IF I DIE

AND IF
I DIE

John Aubrey Anderson

THE BLACK OR WHITE CHRONICLES,
BOOK THREE

NEW YORK   BOSTON   NASHVILLE

FaithWords
Hachette Book Group USA
237 Park Avenue
New York, NY 10017

Visit our Web site at www.faithwords.com.

Printed in the United States of America

First Edition: August 2007
10 9 8 7 6 5 4 3 2 1

The FaithWords name and logo are trademarks of Hachette Book Group USA.

Library of Congress Cataloging-in-Publication Data

Anderson, John Aubrey, 1940–
    And if i die / John Aubrey Anderson. — 1st ed.
        p. cm. — (The Black or white chronicles ; bk. 3)
    "John Aubrey Anderson artfully crafts the third in a series of stories of conflict between the natural and spirit worlds and of Missy Parker Patterson and Mose Washington, targets in the battle"—Provided by the publisher.
        ISBN-13: 978-0-446-57952-0
        ISBN-10: 0-446-57952-1
    1. Race relations—Fiction. 2. Texas—Fiction. 3. Spiritual warfare—Fiction. I. Title.
    PS3601.N544A84 2007
        813'.6—dc22   2006100712

To Nan

AND IF I DIE

CHAPTER ONE

Clear Creek County . . . northwest of Pilot Hill, Texas. 1968.

He stood in a thick stand of blackjack oaks, motionless and un-noticed, peering through the trees, camouflaged by their shade. Waiting.

He'd watched the house before, almost a year earlier. It was set back from the seldom-used gravel road, isolated. The woman was in the backyard—one hand propped on her hip, the other holding a garden hose—filling a small plastic wading pool. She was in her early thirties, casually dressed—flip-flops, cut-offs, and a denim shirt with the sleeves cut off—and every man who had ever seen her would testify she was attractive. To him, she was no more than a barrier. He continued to wait.

The pool was almost full when a three-year-old version of the woman—complete with oversize sunglasses and ponytail—flip-flopped through the back door of the house carrying an armload of pool toys. She arranged the toys on the ground by the pool then stood by, chatting and supervising, while her mother fin-ished filling the pool. The child had worn her brand-new pink bikini—complete with frilly skirt—day and night since the previous Saturday. On this day, when the afternoon's temperature moved into the nineties, she managed to talk her mother into letting her put her new swimming attire to the test.

The woman finished with the water hose and pulled it out of the way while the little girl placed her toys, one at a time, in the water. The child was stepping over the side of the pool and the woman was settling into a nearby lounge chair when the phone in the kitchen rang.

The woman jumped out of her chair, yelling something he didn't understand at the child, and the watcher's eyes tracked her as she jogged toward the house. When the screen door banged shut, he drew in a deep breath of anticipation and let it out in a long, audible sigh—the barrier was down. In the next moment, he was away from the cover of the trees and moving deliberately through the knee-high grass.

The woman would later recall she was in the house less than two minutes.

A short mile south of the wading pool, in a small house hidden behind a gentle swell in the grassland, an old man was waking from his afternoon nap.

"Hmm," he mumbled to himself. "That boy should've been home by now."

The Redbone hound by the sofa yawned his agreement and sat up to get his oversized ears closer to the man. The man raised his head enough to look at the kitchen clock while he rubbed the dog's ears. The hand that massaged the dog was black, and the eyes that checked the clock had seen their share of a hard life.

The little girl was sitting waist deep in the water with her back to him, herding her toys.

With the woman inside the house, the only thing between

the watcher and the colorful little wading pool was a five-strand barbed-wire fence—an inconsequential hindrance.

The air-conditioning unit by the house was humming loudly, masking the sounds of his approach, but the child somehow sensed his presence. He was over the fence and only two short steps from the pool when she whirled around, let out a startled screech, and scrambled to her feet.

"Mommy says you're don't supposed to be in my yard." She shook a stubby finger at him, more indignant than afraid. "Mommy says you don't behave nice!"

Her words were wasted. He moved closer, looming over her.

His size alone was enough to intimidate the girl, and she took an involuntary step away from him. When she moved back, he stepped into the water.

The child gave ground again and tripped when she backed against the side of the pool. She let out a short scream and tumbled backward over the edge; the sunglasses flew off when she hit the grass. He kept coming.

Inside the house, the woman placed the phone back on its cradle and glanced out the window in time to watch her daughter sprawl by the pool. Her first thought was, *Leaving that backyard was the stupidest thing I've ever done in my life.*

Her following thought was, *I'll kill him.*

He was centered in the small pool when the back door flew open and the woman bolted into the yard—a nine-foot bullwhip was coiled in her right hand.

On the other side of the barbed-wire fence a pickup truck was bumping its way across the pasture, raising a thick cloud of dust. The driver saw the woman closing on her adversary and pressed harder on the accelerator—punishing himself and the truck, rushing to get to the drama unfurling by the pool.

"I told you I'd take your hide off if you came back over here." The woman gave her wrist a practiced roll and played out the bullwhip. "Well, big boy, I meant it."

The interloper fixed deep brown eyes on her as she approached. If her threat generated any fear, his expression didn't show it.

Before she could get close enough to use the whip, the pickup skidded to a stop on the far side of the fence. Morris Erwin jumped out of the truck into the follow-on dust cloud, already yelling, "Just hang on, Millie, I'll take care of this!" The cowboy was leaning into the truck, reaching for the gun rack.

The woman heard the words but chose to ignore them. She was fed up.

When the dog got up and nosed the screen door open, the man gathered up his Bible and newspaper and followed him onto the front porch. The dog paused on his way to the steps and stretched thoroughly.

The tilt of the sun said it was midafternoon; the hound's sense of timing said the boy should be at the house in just a minute or two. In the southwest corner of the sky, a line of thunderstorms was using the day's warm temperature—expanding rapidly, gathering height, building energy.

The instrument of intervention Erwin was grappling for was trapped between the truck's gun rack and the man's haste, held captive by its leather strap. Adrenaline laced the man's system, and panic colored his anticipation of what might happen if he was too late.

The Redbone hound was getting gray around his eyes and muzzle, but his ears still worked. The dog was shambling toward the porch steps when the sharp report, weak but clear, came to him. He changed direction and moved to the north end of the porch, sniffing at the air coming from across the pasture. He cocked his head, trying to classify the faint explosion that didn't belong in the warm afternoon.

When the woman's whip cracked, the unexpected explosion lifted the adrenaline-charged cowboy off the ground and caused him to smack his head on the pickup's door frame. The blow dazed him and knocked his straw hat to the dust at his feet. He was a tangled knot of frustration, sweat, and profanity when he heard the whistle-swish that told him the whip was moving again.

The black man, whose ears were older than the dog's, studied the area where the dog's nose was pointed and saw nothing but trees, grass, chickens, and guinea hens. "What're you smellin' at, boy?"

The dog moaned in response to the question and squared himself to the north, leaning forward slightly. While the man watched, the hound cast his nose back and forth across the warm breeze and looked perplexed; the dozens of easily categorized smells the dog picked up did little to explain the harsh sound he'd heard.

When the answer to the dog's quest continued to elude him, he decided he had more important things to attend to. Instead of shrugging, he snorted to clear the uninteresting information from his nostrils and padded down the steps—he wanted to be standing by the car when the boy stepped out. The man lingered long enough to give the land on the other side of the trees a final inspection, then took a seat in one of the rocking chairs.

The whip cracked again before Erwin could get backed out of the truck.

"Dadgummit, Millie," the cowboy yelled over his shoulder, "I told you I'd handle him! If you cut 'im, he can't work."

Erwin won the tug-of-war with the gun rack and freed the looped end of a long hickory cane in time to turn and watch one of the best bucking bulls in the world sag to his knees in the wading pool. Stretching out wasn't as easy, and the animal's attempt was not unlike trying to load a ton of hamburger into a shopping cart. Before the bull could get fully reclined, the pool's perimeter collapsed under him and water cascaded over the sagging sides.

A minute later, the cowboy and his cane were across the fence. Erwin was busy dusting off his hat while the young mother threatened to barbecue the bull and his owner on the same spit. The bikini-clad girl had picked up a lime-green bucket with pink and white flowers for a handle; she was shaking it within six inches of the bull's nose and lecturing him on the finer points of pool ownership.

Millie Roberts was red in the face and waving her whip at the cowboy. "Dadgummit, Morris, he tore up a double handful of these pools last year."

The emergency was over and the bull was safe; Erwin's anxiety was flowing away faster than the water in the pool. The easygoing cowboy freed the whip from his young neighbor and coiled it as he spoke. "He didn't tear up but two, Millie, an' I went to town both times an' got y'all a new one."

"I don't want a new swimming pool every month. I want this good-for-nothing, pot-licking lapdog to stay out of my yard. When he's not tearing up the wading pools, he's stripping the fruit trees and eating my zinnias."

The bull ignored them all and groaned contentedly while reclining across the pool, apparently in an attempt to soak up as much of the escaping coolness as he could.

"Well, I can't afford a fence high enough to hold him, Millie, but I'll put Tony in with him when he's in this pasture. That should keep him on the ground." Tony was Erwin's favorite quarter horse—a chestnut paint. Tony and the bull had "grown up" together on the ranch, and they enjoyed each other's company; the bull would most likely stay where Tony was.

Millie said, "Well, if Tony can't keep him over there, you're gonna have to build him his own swimming hole."

"Where's AnnMarie?"

"Inside being exasperating."

"You reckon her an' Tony could kind of work together to keep him on my side of the fence?" Sweet Thing liked being with Tony, and Tony and AnnMarie liked being together.

"You'll have to ask her yourself; right now she's not speaking to me."

"What'd you do to her?" Erwin and AnnMarie often got along better than Millie and AnnMarie.

"Set her up for adolescence when I gave birth to her twelve years ago."

"Mm-hmm. Well, I'll call her this evenin'. Maybe her an' me can work out a deal."

"Your funeral," snorted Millie.

Erwin nodded absently as he prodded the bull gently with the cane. "Okay, Sweet, git outta the dadgum pool."

Sweet Thing didn't pretend to understand English—and didn't move. The most famous bucking bull in the Erwin rodeo string was three years older than the little girl. Docile as a drowsy kitten when he wasn't "working," his fame found its source in his ability to do his job when the bucking chute opened. The Brahma cross was mostly light gray that shaded to black around his neck and weighed just short of two thousand pounds. He'd been ridden twice.

The reluctant hostess of the pool party stepped closer to the animal and smacked one of his horns with her plastic bucket. "You know better than to be in my yard, you dumb bull! An' you're not sweet neither; you're greedy!"

The water in the pool was gone, and Sweet couldn't pretend he didn't understand the girl. He sighed again and rolled over to get his feet under him.

CHAPTER TWO

The man and dog were watching through the trees when the car came in sight; it was approaching the curve below the house—and, as usual, it was traveling too fast. Instead of slowing, the driver asked for more speed, and the old sedan gave it to him. Its rear tires sprayed gravel as it slid into a powered drift through the wide curve. The car straightened smoothly as it came out of the turn, and the driver let its speed bleed off in order to coast up to the house at a more sedate pace, thus keeping down the dust. The dog's front feet were dancing in place when the car pulled into the long driveway and parked beside the man's truck.

Bill Mann stepped out of the car, lifted a negligent hand at the man, then dropped to one knee by the dog; the hound pressed his head against the boy's chest to get hugged and rubbed. The boy said something to the dog, and the dog tried to lick his face. The boy laughed and stood. He reached into the car and brought out a box containing a three-layer chocolate cake—a present from his boss's wife. As he moved across the yard, he hooked his thumb at the curve in the road and smiled. "New record . . . fifty-four miles an hour."

"Mm-hmm." Mose Mann nodded. "An' I figure fifty-five'll

put you over yonder in Mr. Erwin's pasture, wrapped around one o' them live oak trees."

The boy smiled wider. "Fifty-four felt pretty smooth."

The man surrendered and returned the smile. "Looked smooth too." If the boy wanted to entertain himself by sliding around every curve in the country road, that was his own business; he'd paid for the car with his own money, he bought his own gas and tires, and, most importantly, he handled the car like a professional stock-car driver—the man would save his negotiating currency for more important issues. "You 'bout got things finished up at that school?"

"Getting close." The boy put the cake inside the front door and came back to slouch in the other rocker. The dog made a cursory check of the breeze at the north end of the porch, passed by the screen door to make sure the cake was safe, then settled on the floor by the boy's chair. "We start final exams in a couple of weeks, and I'll be finished before the middle of next month."

"You been up to the café today?"

"Had lunch there." He smiled and nodded at the unasked question. "Crowded."

"Sam seem to be doin' all right?"

"I guess he's as excited as Sam gets. According to him, they're bringing in more money than the bank can hold."

"That's the way I like to hear you testify."

Sam Jones, the man who talked the two men on the porch into moving to Pilot Hill, had been the cook at Nettie's Café in Pilot Hill for ten years.

Only eight weeks earlier, Sam had been sitting with Mose and Bill in his "office"—a back booth in the café.

During a lull in the conversation, Sam put his hands palm-down on the table. "Well"—he patted the Formica surface—"she's gonna lose the café."

Bill was surprised. "Miz Nettie is?"

"Yep. I knew things weren't going too good, and she finally told me about it a couple days ago." Sam shook his head at the sadness of it all. "Bud was sick a long time, and when he died, he left her with too many bills and no way to pay 'em. Money's tight . . . after she takes care of the overhead and the payments on the building, she can't scrape together enough from what's left-over to keep up. She could do better if the place was bigger . . . as it stands, it just won't seat enough customers to pay out."

Nettie Holton was the best cook in town and had turned her favorite pastime into a modest business. Over the last few years Nettie's Café on the square had become popular with folks from Denton to Sherman, some even as far away as Fort Worth. The evening meal would find people who had driven forty or fifty miles lined up outside the doors, waiting to enjoy Miz Nettie's pan-fried catfish or chicken-fried steak. Her pies and homemade cobbler were the best to be found between Waco and the Red River.

Bill looked around at the neat little café. "Does she owe much money on it?"

"Almost ten thousand, but that's not the problem—she needs a bigger place, and she can't afford it. I'd like to help if I could, but I can't come up with that kind of money. It's a shame because this town is primed to bust wide open, what with all the horse farms coming in. This could be a real moneymaker."

"What's she gonna do?" asked Bill.

Sam smiled wryly. "Work for somebody else, I guess . . . same as I am."

"What about the old dry-goods building next door?" Bill pressed. "It's in good shape, and it's vacant. She could knock a big hole in that wall and expand into it."

"She'd buy it tomorrow if she could, but she's caught be-tween a rock and a hard place," Sam explained patiently. "She'll never come up with the income she needs to expand, because she doesn't have enough cash coming in to keep this place going." He studied his big hands and sighed. "She's been to all the banks here and in Denton; they said they'd like to help, but restaurants are a poor risk. It's just a matter of time before she shuts it down."

"She needs a partner."

"That'd work okay, and she shopped around some. There's nobody willing to help that she can trust."

"She can trust you."

"Like I said, I just can't come up with that kind of money."

Mose held silent throughout the conversation, waiting. When Bill looked a question at him, the old man smiled and said, "We can."

Back in the fifties, Sam Jones and Mose spent time in Parchman prison together. It was a bad experience that generated a good friendship.

Sam looked from Mose to Bill and back to Mose. "You can loan her enough money for her to get herself out of this spot?"

The other two men shook their heads, each knowing what the other was thinking.

"No-no," said Mose. "Miz Nettie's a fine white woman, but she don't need to be knowin' 'bout our business. We'd loan the money to you."

Bill nodded.

Sam wasn't prepared for the offer, and the initial thought of borrowing that much money stopped his breathing. Then, because he was human, his mind filled itself with a dozen questions about the money's origin. Before any doubts could take root, his memory took him back to the years he spent on the Parchman prison farm with Mose . . . any money in Mose's hands would be as pure as a church collection.

He said, "We need to pray."

The sparse crowd of customers watched as the three black men bowed their heads. Sam and Mose bowed in supplication; Mann bowed out of respect for his friends. The two older men thanked God for His provision and asked for wisdom and guidance; Mann thought about how many more tables Miz Nettie would be serving.

Forty-eight hours later, Sam sat down with his boss and offered to put up enough money to pay off the note on the existing café building and pay half the cost of incorporating the dry-goods store into their operation. Within ten minutes they agreed to a fifty-fifty partnership. Because folks in town wouldn't understand about a white widow being in business with a black man, Miz Nettie would maintain "ownership" of the café; Sam would run the kitchen and be her silent partner.

So far, the café was generating more income every week.

"You gonna work down there at Pat's office this summer?" asked Mose.

"On and off. He and Missy are going to Mississippi for a couple of days as soon as classes let out; he said I can have all the work I want when they get back. And he's got a new guy—another undergrad student—who's going to be coming to work in June, so I won't be swamped."

"What you got planned for while Pat an' Missy is gone?"

"Well, I'll help out down at the feed store a little." The boy sat forward and brushed at the grass on his jeans. He had a tendency to choose his words carefully—this time he was stalling. "And Will's started back to doing some bull riding. I was thinking I might as well pick up where I left off."

The man was shaking his head before the boy finished talking. "Bull ridin'? Have mercy, boy, didn't that trip to the hospital teach you that bulls is dangerous?"

The would-be bull rider offered his easy smile. "So they say."

"You been talkin' 'bout fightin' in that war in Vietnam. You got to be alive to go to a war."

"Yes, sir."

The man's face twisted into a frown and he sat back to let the rocker work its magic on his reaction. Bill and the Pierce boy had been riding on and off since their senior year in high school. Bill took "that trip to the hospital" when he got tangled up during a dismount and ended up getting slung around like a rag doll. The result was some kind of elbow sprain and a badly split lip, both of which were healed in a few weeks. Mose had prayed the bull riding was behind them.

The boy waited. He knew what would come next, and he knew it would come quickly.

"Well, lemme see." The man patted his leg with the newspaper. "How old're you gittin' to be now?"

The boy smiled. "I'll be twenty next month." He would've winked at the man, but that wasn't in the script.

"An' man enough to make them kind of choices for yo'self, I reckon." The old man shook his head, smiled wryly, and admitted, "I have to tell you, boy, for a tall feller, you sho' do make ridin' one of them animals look easy. An' I ain't got nothin' better to do than spend some extra time prayin'.'"

"I appreciate it."

"Humph. Better save yo' 'preciation for when I has to bring yo' cake to the hospital."

Chocolate cake was a midafternoon ritual at the Mann house.

The boy sat forward in his chair. "You ready for a piece?"

"Every time," the man nodded. "An' there's coffee on the stove."

The boy pushed himself out of the rocker and walked over to the south end of the porch. "Looks like we might get some rain."

The man leaned forward and looked across the fence. "My weathermens say it ain't gonna git here." He pointed to the north side of the house where the chickens and guineas were roaming the pasture, foraging for insects. "Chickens wouldn't go that far out if'n it was gonna rain."

The boy took the man's words as gospel and went to cut the cake.

Minutes later, the young man made one trip to the porch carrying a slender wedge of chocolate cake and a mug of steaming coffee. On his second trip he returned with a quart container of milk, a plate holding a fourth of the cake, and a pair of hard-boiled eggs. He rearranged himself in his rocker and thumbed open the milk carton while he fed the eggs to the dog.

The man took a sip of his coffee before observing, "You already got that dog spoiled rotten. An' if you keep eatin' like that, you gonna git big as Aunt Jemima."

The boy pointed his fork at the dog and talked around a mouthful of cake. "He's the one that's gonna get fat. I eat the cake to keep my coat shiny."

"Humph. How much you weighin' now?"

The boy, who was more man than boy, fed a pinch of cake to the dog. "One seventy-five or one eighty with my watch on." He fooled with the dog for a minute, then tried to sound nonchalant when he asked, "How've you been feeling?"

"I been doin' just fine. Better'n any time since I had that little go'round with my heart." The man watched the line of thunderstorms in silence for a minute or two; they were threatening to make liars out of him and his chickens. He put his plate where the dog could get to it, then blew on his coffee and took another sip. "I got a question for you."

"Yes, sir?"

"You got any plans for what you gonna do when I die?"

The young man let his breath make a couple of round trips while he used his fork to push the last bite of cake around on his plate. Normally the kind of person who faced things head-on, he was stalling for the second time that day. "Shoot, Poppa, I guess I haven't thought that much about it."

"You got time for us to talk about it?"

The youngster glanced at his watch, a handsome piece with a blue and red bezel. "Will said he'd be right behind me."

There were some things the two men couldn't talk about where others might hear. The man said, "We can keep a lookout for his truck."

The boy knew what was coming. He took a second look at

his watch and said what they were both thinking. "Today's the fifteenth."

"Yep . . . eight years." The man nodded. The newspaper in his hand agreed with the boy's watch. The date was April 15, 1968, the anniversary of the killings. "Passes pretty fast, don't it?"

"Yes, sir." They rarely talked about the killings; it would serve no purpose. The boy put his plate on the floor so the dog could clean off the icing, then sat back and draped a leg over one of the chair arms. "Do you get lonesome for Mississippi?"

"Maybe a little." He had something he wanted to say, but he didn't want the boy to ever feel he was being pushed. "But I'll tell you this, I wouldn't trade a whole life in Miss'ippi for these few years God let me be yo' granddaddy."

The boy on the porch was young, but he had known for a long time his adopted grandfather's commitment to him was second only to the old man's allegiance to his God.

Of the three on the porch, only the dog was using his real name.

The old man was born Moses Lincoln Washington. His great-grandfather, old "Preacher" Washington, named him after two men who stood strongly on the side of oppressed people. The godly old ex-slave's choice for his great-grandson's name was, like so many major aspects of Moses Lincoln Washington's life, a thing of providence.

In 1960, on a wet night in Mississippi Delta backcountry, a gang of white men attacked a black woman and her son—and Mose Washington stepped in. In the middle of the twentieth century, for a black man to oppose the actions of a group of white men was dangerous—for him to face them down from behind a shotgun was courting death. A mysterious white man emerged from the darkness and allied himself with Mose in time for them to rescue the young boy. They were too late to save the child's mother.

That same night, in the predawn hours, Mose, Bill, and the

mysterious white man stood over the body of Bill's mother while Mose prayed. Mose and the woman's son vanished after the short funeral. Their white ally was gone as well, leaving no more trace than a figure carved in steam.

Law enforcement officers were on the scene before noon the next day. They found the bodies of the black lady and three white men, and because one of the dead men was the son of a powerful congressman, the FBI entered the picture.

Bill Prince, the boy who fled Mississippi with Mose, lost his dad in March, 1960—less than a month before the white men killed his mother. Major William L. Prince, one of the famed Tuskegee Airmen, fought and won aerial battles in the skies over Africa, Europe, and Korea, but he couldn't beat cancer. When he was on his deathbed, the Air Force fighter pilot gave his ten-year-old son and namesake four things—a handsome Rolex watch, a .45 caliber Colt automatic, a gentle dictate to be a man, and, most importantly, a commission to care for his mother.

When young Bill Prince disappeared, he left his mother, the Colt pistol, and his father's name in Mississippi. From his former life, the orphaned boy salvaged the watch, his dad's admonition to be a man, and a vow to himself that he would be a fighter pilot, just like his dad.

In 1962, two years after the killings, Mose Mann and his "grandson," William P. Mann, settled themselves in the middle of a wooded tract of land in the sparsely populated country outside Pilot Hill. Their home's location offered privacy; their nearest neighbors were the Roberts family, a mile to the north.

"Poppa?"

"Hmm?"

"You think they'll ever catch us?"

"Can't say for sure. Pat an' Missy say nobody ever comes

lookin' for us in Miss'ippi. That Wagner boy from the FBI says don't nobody ever mention us. An' that Bainbridge fellow from Washington is dead."

"Has anybody said anything about that last son of theirs . . . or that Mrs. Bainbridge? They say she's becoming a big woman in Washington." Bill wouldn't classify himself as a worrier, but it was his nature to stay abreast of his situation. The anniversary of the killings usually prompted a short discussion on the state of their circumstances.

"We under the protection of the good Lord, boy. We done all we can do; the rest is up to Him." The old man reminded his grandson more than once during the past eight years that they each had at least one guardian angel. "Evil folks—demons even—might come up an' stand on this here porch, but they can't never find us long as God don't want 'em to. If He let's them find us, they still got to git past Him an' His angels."

Mose Mann's assertions found their origins in his faith—and his faith was well-founded.

Three hundred years earlier, a man who thought himself clever offered as a point of speculation the number of angels that could dance on the point of a very fine needle. Had that intellectual wastrel been offered a glimpse of those who stood at the shoulders of the old black man and his grandson, he would've been disposed to spend the remainder of his earthbound days introducing more worthwhile questions. Clothed in brilliance and bearing swords in God's righteous cause, two angelic beings stood guard over the men on the porch.

The angels were seasoned veterans of an ongoing multimillennial war spanning the universe. God's ultimate defeat of the forces of evil was ordained in eternity past, but the ferocity of the battle would continue unabated until the day His Son returned to reign on earth. For now—for the two capable warriors—their given roles had to do with the protection of the two humans. That the younger man had no felt need for angelic protection did not diminish his guardian's vigilance.

"Mmm." The younger man had never been able to bring himself to care about God or His angels—if they were real, they'd stood by while a pair of deranged killers beat his mother to death. He watched lightning strike the ground in front of the widening squall line and changed the subject. "Are you sure about the chickens? Those storms are getting closer."

"And bigger." Mose let the conversation take the turn. "Guess we got the kind of hens what ain't scared of gettin' struck by lightnin'."

The two watched the storms in silence until Bill said, "What're the chances of us getting a tornado?"

"Can't say. They can come up sudden."

Bill thought he knew the answer to his next question, but he asked it to keep the conversation away from the things of God. "You ever see a tornado?"

"Mm-hmm . . . seen two."

"You never told me that." Bill sat up. He thought he'd heard everything that ever happened to the man. "When?"

"The first one was back when I was just a tad. I was livin' down in south Miss'ippi with my momma."

"I thought you were born and raised at Pap's house."

"Well, I mostly was, 'cept for that short spell with my momma."

"Did they come close?"

Mose smiled. "The first one couldn't've come no closer. I'd of been 'bout eight years old, I reckon—an' I can close my eyes right now an' see the inside of that funnel."

"The inside? You got sucked up in a tornado?" Bill was surprised, but only mildly. The story of the old man's life played out as a closely linked series of dangerous adventures and severe hardships. On top of that, he'd stood on the edge of, or played a part in, several shootings.

When Mose told the old stories to the boy, he did so in a matter-of-fact manner. In the instances where most men would paint themselves as heroes, Mose would give his God the credit for the outcome. From anyone else on earth, accounts like the man related might be suspect, but Bill knew people who corroborated what Mose said—people who were there.

The sound of Will's truck engine interrupted them, and Bill stood up. "Gotta go." He stopped at the top of the steps and asked, "Will you tell me about the tornadoes when I get home?"

"Mm-hmm." Mose glanced at the pickup coming down the driveway. "But don't be sayin' nothin' 'bout it to nobody. This is 'bout them other days, an' it'll best stay between you an' me."

"Yes, sir." Bill and Mose only talked about *them other days* with a few select people—people who were committed to helping hide and protect Bill and Mose Mann from the ones who wanted them dead.

Will Pierce stopped the truck and stepped out. He waved at Mose and knelt to greet the dog. "Howdy, Dawg. How you been doin', boy?"

When the dog was thoroughly rubbed and petted, the boys waved again and climbed in the truck.

As the truck was backing out of the driveway, Will asked, "Well, what'd he say?"

"About what?"

Will had been Mann's best friend for six years, and he knew when he was being baited. He also knew how to snap his black buddy back to the subject at hand. "About the earliest mention of Christ in the Old Testament."

Mose knew more about the Bible than lots of preachers, and Will liked learning from the old man. Mann, on the other hand, could be counted on to keep his distance from theological discussions.

Mann said, "He said what I knew he'd say." He dropped his

voice an octave and mimicked a past generation's dialect. "You man enough to make that decision fo' yo'self."

Will shook his head. "Boy, I hope you know that man is one in a million."

Mann looked at the coming storms without seeing them and told Will more than he'd ever told anyone else. "You don't know the half of it, buddy boy."

When Mose stood to watch the truck leave, a gust of wind blew dust across the porch and ruffled the pages of his Bible—a precursor of the coming storm. The chickens out in the pasture continued their bug hunt, oblivious to the impending opportunity to get struck by lightning or blown into Oklahoma. Mose looked at the chickens and frowned. "Ain't no different from most human folks—they more interested in eatin' than they is in gittin' to where it's safe."

The dog, because he was smarter than the chickens, trotted back to the porch and waited by the screen door. Mose let him in, and the dog curled up near the man's chair while Mose walked into the kitchen.

He was sixty-eight years old, and, to him, life was as fleeting as the gust of wind that had just blown across his porch. That was one of the reasons he invested more time praying than reflecting.

Dawg continued his afternoon nap . . . wind and thunder bore down on the house . . . chickens and guinea hens started a stampede for the protection of the small barn. The old man pulled his chair closer to the front window and divided his time between praying and watching the effects of the wind. The trees would bend, and some smaller limbs might break, but unless the storm got really bad, the house and trees would be standing in the morning.

CHAPTER THREE

The people who tried to burn the city achieved little more than the destruction of their own neighborhoods. Burned-out buildings, looted stores, and broken glass were all that was left of the area around the intersection of 14th and U Streets. The woman standing at the office window watched the tendrils of smoke rising from the destruction and felt a sense of triumph . . . she lost nothing in the riots, and seeing evidence that people's lives were in turmoil gave her pleasure.

She used the resources available to her as a member of the House Committee on Intelligence to locate the man she needed, ferreting him out the same way she had the others. As soon as she secured his contact information, she sent him a message—she wanted a meeting. Her only stipulations were that the meeting's location be remote and her identity be protected.

Within twenty-four hours of receiving her message he was on his way to Philadelphia. He took the bus from Philadelphia to

Baltimore where he bought an average-looking car. He set up housekeeping in a motel that rented rooms by the week.

Early on a Monday afternoon he called the phone number she'd given him—the private line in her office. "You'll receive a package at your office at one thirty tomorrow—be there. Tell your staff that you are the only one allowed to take it from the messenger." He was off the phone within ten seconds.

Tuesday afternoon found her standing at her office window, alternately checking her clock and watching smoke add itself to an already gray sky. Heavy showers had been coming and going for two days, helping to suppress the few lingering fires and knocking off most of that spring's cherry blossoms. The congresswoman wasn't looking at the cherry blossoms—she was waiting. The power residing in Estelle Bainbridge was far greater than that of an ordinary congresswoman, and she could've contacted the man sooner; she chose not to because the world was not ready to experience her full potential.

At one twenty-five someone tapped on her door. "Come in, please."

A young woman opened the door and said, "The messenger you told us about is here, Estelle. He said he has to put the envelope in your hands."

The congresswoman winked at her staffer to show they both knew couriers took themselves too seriously. "Thank you, Sam. Ask him to step in here, please."

"Anything else?" Sam knew the answer.

"Mm-hmm." Estelle's smile was warm. "Would you make sure I'm not disturbed?"

Samantha Dutton smiled and nodded. She had been chosen from hundreds of applicants for the opportunity to serve as an intern on Congresswoman Bainbridge's staff. The young woman had been in Washington four months, and she had discovered that Estelle Bainbridge was not only brilliant, she was one of the most gracious people the girl ever met—she had only one minor flaw.

*   *   *

Jimmy Palmertree graduated from Dunbar High School in 1958. Dunbar was arguably the finest all-black secondary school in the nation, and the teachers there did two things for the bright young man: they nurtured his diligence and they encouraged his uncanny ability to "read" people.

The day after graduation, Jimmy inaugurated his one-man courier service. His mother answered the phone, "Palmertree's. We deliver the goods." And that's what Jimmy did. Customers left instructions for pickups, and Jimmy called his mother every half hour to see where he was going next. The aggressive young entrepreneur stayed safe by avoiding the bad neighborhoods, and he kept his business healthy by culling customers who wasted his time. Now, after only ten years, he'd bought a small house in the suburbs, he'd hired a girl to answer the phone, and he'd brought his cousin in to help deliver the goods.

Black couriers in Washington attract no more attention than beige wall paint—and walls hear plenty. Jimmy saw Jimmy Stewart in *Mr. Smith Goes to Washington*, and after ten years of moving along the edges of conversations in the halls of Congress, it was obvious to him that Washington had long since sent James Stewart and his integrity back to Indiana or Nebraska or wherever they'd come from. The gifted appraiser of moral fiber was confident that every politician in the city would sell his own children to move one step up the ladder of power.

Being cheap walked hand in hand with being corrupt, and the tips Jimmy received when working in the vicinity of Capitol Hill were paltry compared to the rest of the city. The staffers didn't want to spend their money tipping him, and the politicians invariably made a show of patting their pockets before saying, "I'll catch you next time." For pickups and deliveries on the Hill, his quoted rates included a 20 percent premium.

When he stepped into the congresswoman's office, the messenger's heart stumbled.

If Congresswoman Bainbridge was miserly or corrupt, it didn't show on her face. The white woman was looking mighty fine in tailored slacks and a loose-fitting white blouse with a scoop neck—Grace Kelly with a traffic-stopping figure. When she stepped around her desk to take the envelope, he saw she was in her stocking feet.

Fine and *homey*, thought the young messenger.

"Afternoon, ma'am. I was told to put this in your hands." The scoop in the blouse's front was fairly deep, and he came to an immediate understanding with his eyes about where they were not allowed to linger.

Grace Kelly said, "Hi, I'm Estelle Bainbridge." She had a soft Southern drawl and a smile straight out of one of those toothpaste commercials. "Thanks for getting out in the rain to bring this. I was getting anxious."

Fine and *homey* and *warmhearted*, he thought . . . yet somewhere out on the rim of his consciousness, an alarm started to beep.

Jimmy ignored the alarm and managed to mumble, "Yes, ma'am." He wanted to say more, just to prolong the meeting, and struggled to force out, "Umm . . . we deliver the goods."

She supplemented the warm smile with a wink. "It looks like 'delivering the goods' keeps you in great shape." She reached for her purse. "Would you be offended if I tipped you?"

This country needs more women in politics. "That's not necessary, Congresswoman."

"Well, aren't you sweet." She turned her back on the purse and propped herself against the desk. "You're a believer, aren't you?"

"A believer?"

She was concentrating on his eyes, smiling softly and toying absentmindedly with the top button of her blouse—right where the scoop reached the bottom of its curve. "You know . . . a Christian."

A yellow light began to pulse in time with the steady beep in Jimmy's brain. "Yes, ma'am, I'm a Christian."

"I thought so." The button accidentally came undone, but she didn't seem to notice. "I was wondering . . . have you ever considered taking a job on the Hill?"

"No, ma'am, never have." He could feel sweat beading on his forehead, and the alarm changed to a steady squeal—the light was flashing red.

This'd be a real good time for you to boogie on outta here, bro.

"Please . . . call me Estelle." More smile. "Would you care to sit down while I dig through my purse?"

Jimmy's first choice was to move into the office and live there for the rest of his life, but the squeal from the alarm was moving up the scale toward intolerable. "Thank you, ma'am, but I'm rain-wet and sweaty."

Somethin' ain't right in here, boy! Don't say nothin', just cut 'n' run! Do it, boy, do it now!

"Nonsense." She picked up the purse. "My folks were Arkansas sharecroppers, and Daddy said sweating kept his heart clean."

She brought her purse over and dropped it in the chair next to him . . . and Jimmy saw the move coming from ten days away. When she bent over the purse, the scoop of her blouse fell away from her chest, but Jimmy Palmertree had his back turned; he was walking over to take a closer look at an antique bookcase.

If the lady was stung by his move, she didn't betray it. She straightened and held out a ten-dollar bill. "This is yours. And thanks again."

Jimmy took the bill and she offered her hand . . . and he took it.

When Jimmy's mother died, he'd stayed at the funeral parlor all night, sitting with her body. When they got ready to close the casket, he'd held her hand one last time—it was cold and dry, like Congresswoman Bainbridge's.

The messenger jerked his hand away from the white woman and stared at it, rubbing his fingertips with his thumb. When he realized what he'd done, he looked up at the woman. "I'm sorry, ma'am, I—"

The lady was picking at the second button of the blouse with a manicured fingernail; her smile was not from the girl-next-door collection. "You what?"

A cold drop of sweat escaped from his temple and traced a cool path to his jawline. The squeal became a steam whistle. *Last chance, boy . . . it's run-or-ruin time!*

Jimmy was talking as he backed toward the door. "I . . . uh . . . I better be getting on down the road, ma'am . . . uh, much obliged." He grabbed the door with an unsteady hand and jerked it open.

The lady's smile was gone.

So was Jimmy.

He pulled the door closed and leaned against it to catch his breath. The three young women in the reception area stopped what they were doing to stare at him. He tossed the ten-dollar bill in the direction of the nearest table, then wiped his hand on his shirt and left without saying anything to the office staff.

The three women looked at each other and their eyebrows went up.

"Well, well, well"—the one nearest the discarded money retrieved the bill and waved it at the others—"I guess we have to expect losses."

Her friends laughed.

Jimmy left the building and went straight to a park bench. He bowed his head and prayed, *Lord, that was w-a-a-a-y too close. I was thinking some bad thoughts in there, and I ask that You'd forgive me. And if it's all the same to You, I don't want another battle like that . . . I*

didn't do too good . . . and I didn't like it. If You're gonna throw me into
something else like that, I'd like some time to get my breath first.

While he prayed, sweat dripped from the tip of his nose and
splashed in a puddle of rainwater.

While Jimmy prayed, Congresswoman Bainbridge studied the
contents of the envelope. A single sheet—no greeting, no closing. The message was one paragraph long, typed in capitals. The
man gave her the location of a pay phone and told her what time
to be there. She looked at her watch, picked up her raincoat and
umbrella, and left the office through her private entrance.

When she got to the stipulated phone, he was watching
from down the street. He called and told her to go to a different
phone—on the other side of town. "Take a cab." He followed
and watched.

He shadowed her through the streets for several hours, going from
phone to phone by bus, by cab, and on foot. On the last call he
told her he would call her office again on Wednesday. "Be ready
to move around again."

He did that for several days, directing her from phone to
phone in downtown Washington while he watched for those who
might be following. She knew what he was doing, and she was
patient.

Early on Friday, because he felt assured that she was not trying to trap him, he closed the distance between himself and his
prospective employer. He'd worked for women in the past, but
this one was different; he wanted to see her up close.

Midafternoon found him plagued by thoughts of how unre-
markable the woman was. All people have traits that serve to dis-
tinguish them from their fellow humans. After following her for
five hours, he decided that, other than her stunning good looks,
she was the picture of an average woman.

Late on Saturday, he sent her to Baltimore. "Rent a car at the airport and drive west on West Lexington. Park the car at the North Amity intersection and walk south. You're looking for Boxer's Tavern. Be there at midnight. Sit at a table with your back to the door. I'll be close by."

The place he told her to park the car was in the middle of west Baltimore—black Baltimore; the recent riots had hit the area harder than Washington. The Baltimore Police Department had thousands of cops on the payroll, but not one of them, black or white, was brave enough—or foolish enough—to venture into the area alone at high noon. For a white woman alone at night, the odds of survival were infinitesimal.

Drizzle had been falling all evening—cloud-covered skies promised more of the same. The woman stood in the shadows across the street from a small concrete-block building. She was unrecognizable—disguised in a seedy-looking army field jacket, baggy pants, a wig, and a drunk's posture.

A grime-encrusted neon sign told the surrounding darkness the dingy little hut across from her was Boxer's Tavern. A block south of the bar, a trio of black men were hunched together beneath one of the few remaining streetlights, talking quietly and sharing a paper-wrapped bottle.

The woman waited until the three winos were facing away from her, then shuffled slowly across the street. She stopped again under the bar's awning and checked to see if she had been seen. A foul smell—somewhat moderated by the recent rains—testified that the bar was lacking a restroom. Lady patrons customarily sought privacy in the alley on the south side of the premises; gentlemen used the north.

She pulled the floppy brim of her hat lower and stepped through the front door.

There were two men in the bar, both black. The proprietor scowled at the woman; the stink of stale nicotine in the bar mixed with the odor from outside—the resulting stench was pleasant compared to the expression on the bartender's face. The other man, a customer, was too drunk to know she was in the room.

Boxer watched the woman take a seat at the only table in the room and shook his head disgustedly. The wig was arranged to hide the sides of her face, and the hat was pulled low, but a blind man could tell she was white. *If those fools find her in here, they'll burn this place 'til there ain't nothin' left of me but my teeth.*

He was getting ready to run her out when a second customer, a black man, came through the door and walked toward her; he was wearing thick glasses and a tattered Washington Senators baseball cap. The man's clothes were dirty, but his hands were clean.

Boxer didn't know what was going on, and he didn't care. Everyone who came into Boxer's Tavern was welcome, as long as they were black—white folks brought nothing but grief. The big man jerked his head at the woman and growled at the man, "I don't allow whites in here, or any nigger stupid enough to sit with 'em. Get out an' take her with you."

The man placed a large paper sack on the floor and spoke as if in response to an offer of service. "Bring me a bottle of beer. Whatever's warm." He lowered himself into a chair opposite the woman without acknowledging her presence.

Boxer got his nickname about the same time he quit fighting professionally—he was his own bouncer. He stepped around the end of the short bar and notched up the volume. "What's the matter, boy—you hard of hearing?" He had three inches and fifty pounds on the man at the table.

The man at the table said, "I'll open the beer myself." He pulled back his windbreaker to reach for his wallet and gave the bigger man a glimpse of a shoulder holster carrying a small automatic pistol.

The ex-fighter rethought his position—Baltimore cops didn't carry automatics, the feds wouldn't hire a man who wore thick glasses, and the dude didn't act like a pimp. He tried to save face by saying, "Come over here an' get it. I don't serve tables."

The Senators fan pointed his thick glasses at the barkeep; the lenses magnified the emptiness in his eyes. He patted a five-dollar bill that lay on the table and gave the bartender an out. "You carry it, and I'll open it."

Boxer put the beer bottle on the table and picked up the five. The man in the windbreaker lifted his hand to reveal a small stack of bills. "There's two hundred here."

The man in the apron straightened and stared at the money. "I got nothin' in here worth that kinda money."

"Get a couple of beers, and you and your friend take a thirty-minute break."

"That's it?"

"Outside."

Boxer looked at the bills and rubbed his cheek. The bar was on its last legs; if it weren't for his dope trade, he wouldn't take in a hundred dollars a week. He bought the joint when he quit the ring—and here he was on the ropes again. It would be five years before the area recovered from the riots, and when it did he'd be surrounded by package stores. He was willing to do what the man asked, but he stalled because he wanted to hear the words that would be spoken in two hundred bucks' worth of privacy. He jerked his thumb at the bar. "That guy can't hear nothin', an' I don't listen."

The windbreaker man shook his head. "All or nothing."

The bartender grimaced and told a partial truth. "My stash is in back of the bar, man, an' I can't be carryin' it on me."

Another head shake. "We're not here to steal anything."

The bartender had less than fifty dollars' worth of weed behind the bar, and he believed the man at the table. He took the folded money and counted it, then looked at his watch. "It's twelve fifteen. I'll be back in here at one to close up." He popped two beers open and used them to encourage the drunk to move outside.

When the front door closed, the man in the glasses used the edge of the table to pop the cap off the beer and said, "Take your clothes off."

The woman, who had yet to speak, pushed a thick manila envelope across the table. "You'll need this."

The man ignored the envelope and waved the woman out of the chair. "Clothes first."

She stood up and put a handgun—a .22 automatic with a Carswell silencer—on the table.

The average citizen has never seen a pistol with a silencer, much less carried one, but average citizens don't serve on congressional committees or set up meetings with professional killers. The man pulled the pistol out of her reach then ignored it.

Sheldon Aacock was two weeks away from his thirty-fourth birthday—a significant milestone for a man of his calling. His longevity was, in a small way, attributable to his physical makeup; his height and build were average, his face was ordinary and easily disguised. To an even greater degree, he was alive because he possessed an overwhelming personality trait, something far stronger than his physical and intellectual attributes, which served him well—he held all humans in contempt.

The woman started to disrobe. She wasn't wearing jewelry or carrying a purse; his orders had been explicit. "Everything?" she asked.

"Yes." He was watching her hands, making sure that she didn't try to palm or discard anything. Unlike Jimmy Palmertree, he didn't care that the woman was well on her way to being nude—men in his profession who allowed themselves to be distracted by women died untimely deaths.

For her part, the woman wasn't interested in trying to entice the man; he was already corrupted. The Jimmy Palmertrees of the world—the committed believers who might allow themselves to be tempted—were the ones she wanted to lure into her web.

When the woman was finished undressing, the man let

her stand by the table while he pat-searched every item of her clothing.

After he satisfied himself that there were no electronic devices sewn into her garments, he shook the contents of his sack onto the table—sweatpants, a sweatshirt, and a pair of tennis shoes. "Put these on." He waited until she was dressed in her substitute clothes and the others were sacked up and placed behind the bar then said, "Be assured of one thing . . . if this is a setup, I will kill your only surviving son. When he is dead, I will come to you . . . and I will make sure you plead for death long before I grant it."

The woman sat down at the table. "Save your threats for someone stupid enough to set you up. Let's get on with it."

The man made a mental note the woman was ten blocks from the nearest white person and she wasn't nervous. "How'd you find me?"

She could speak without fear; there was no one to whom he could divulge the truth. "I'm on the Intelligence Committee. I know people who know your name."

"That doesn't answer my question."

She told him what he already knew. "I am both crooked and evil, and I make it my business to associate myself with people who will tell me what I want to know in exchange for money. You don't need to know who they are."

The man was confident she was telling the truth, but there was something that didn't fit. "What do you want?"

"I want three people found and killed."

"And you picked me because . . . ?"

"Because you're black. I've used four men trying to get this done—white men—and they've all failed or been killed."

"Who killed them?"

"You don't need to know that either."

"And being black is going to make me more successful?"

"Two of those I want dead are black. Being black will let you go where the first four could not."

Things were beginning to make sense. The people Aacock relied on for information, those who were willing to market truth in the shadowlands, told him the woman possessed and demonstrated a hatred for all black people. He didn't care who the woman hated—whether or not he agreed to kill the men for her would ultimately come down to how much risk was involved balanced against how much money she would pay.

"You want the ones who killed your son," he said.

"I do." The woman wasn't surprised at the man's statement. He'd had ten days to look into her background.

"It's been eight years. What do you have on them?"

She motioned at the envelope. "Everything's there, and it's not much. Almost nothing is known of the white man. The ones who were present when my son was killed heard his voice, but he didn't have an identifiable accent. None of them saw his face, and he was described as about six feet tall with an average build. From what people have been able to piece together, he gave every indication of being familiar with firearms, indicating a military background, or possibly law enforcement, or possibly neither. Personally, I don't think we can find him, except through the two black men. Neither of the Negroes have any surviving relatives, but that old man has people—black and white—who are unalterably loyal to him."

"That's everything?"

She nodded.

What she had was next to nothing. He said, "Give me two weeks to look into this. If you haven't heard from me in fourteen days, I'm not interested."

"You should know that I will make this well worth your while."

Aacock wasn't interested in talking about money until he knew what the job entailed. He asked, "Do you want to change into your other clothes before I let those two back in here?"

"Yes."

He said, "You've got three minutes," and walked out.

* * *

When Boxer came through the door, the woman was dressed in her original clothes and sitting at the table with the sack in front of her.

The man with the gun had walked off down the street, and Boxer had the two hundred dollars in his pocket. He had nothing to gain by catering to the woman. "Your time's up. Get out before somebody around here sees you."

"Where's the other one?"

"Passed out on the sidewalk." He jerked a thumb at the door. "Now, git."

The woman moved her hand from behind the sack and pointed the .22 at the man's chest. "Come over here and sit down."

Boxer took one glance at the silencer and thought, *I ain't ever lettin' another white woman in here as long as I live.* He said, "I knew you were trouble."

"This is not trouble. This is just a precaution."

Boxer set his mouth and crossed his arms. "You won't shoot me."

She slid out of the chair. "I don't want to, but please believe that I will." She used her most winsome voice. "I can tie you up to make sure I'm not followed, or I can shoot you in the knee." She stood up and pointed at the chair. "Come on . . . sit down . . . make this easy on both of us."

Boxer cursed, but he sat down. *If I ever let another honky in this place, I'll save them the trouble and shoot myself.* "What now?"

She handed him a long strip of material she'd cut from the sweatpants. "Tie your right ankle to the chair." He groused and grumbled, but he did as he was told.

"Now the other one."

When he finished she had him put his hands behind the chair back and she tied his wrists together. Next she secured both of his elbows snugly to the chair.

"Look, lady, I don't care anything about followin' you. Just take whatever you want an' get out."

She took a small towel from the bar and said, "Open your mouth."

He swore again then said, "Don't be stupid, lady. I ain't gonna scream like some scared little girl, okay. Just leave me alone an' get outta my place."

"Open your mouth," she repeated. "The sooner I get this done, the sooner I'll be away from here."

Boxer sighed loudly and opened his mouth. She stuffed the towel in it then tied it in place with one of the makeshift ropes. She smiled the Grace Kelly smile and asked, "All comfy now?"

Boxer glared at her without trying to speak. The woman was nuts.

She cocked her head and gave him a flirtatious grin. "Do you still think I'm trouble?" She winked at him and said, "You have no idea."

Boxer glared at her without trying to respond.

He thought he was finished with her when she pulled her hat on and left, but she was back seconds later, dragging the drunk customer. When the unconscious man's hands were tied, she pushed him against the wall and straightened. "There." She smiled at Boxer again.

When the woman slipped out and dragged the drunk back into the bar, Aacock was well hidden in the rubble across the street. The killer wasn't afraid of being identified by the barkeep; in an hour or two the myopic baseball fan's persona would vanish forever. The woman, however, hadn't been as well disguised. Aacock was confident that the bar owner and his customer were as good as dead.

*　　*　　*

When the woman walked behind the bar and returned with an ice pick and a small knife, the expression in Boxer's eyes went from anger to anxiety. He fixed his gaze on the knife, and began to shake his head back and forth. Distorted sounds fought to push their way through the gag. The worst was still to come.

The woman waited until her captive was looking at her face—and tried to explain what she was. "This shell of a woman you are looking at belongs to us. She gave herself to us, and she resides in this body, but she hasn't made a decision in decades. Because we cannot allow you to tell anyone she has been here, we are going to kill you."

Boxer couldn't move for a long moment. He stared into the uncaring face and tried to find a glimmer of compassion. Reality finally fought its way past numbing shock, and he coughed when he tried to spit out the gag.

"It has been our experience that we will derive more pleasure from what we plan to do if we let you know precisely what you are about to experience," she said.

Boxer shook his head vehemently, and the sounds coming from his throat increased in pitch.

"You wouldn't tell anyone?" she purred.

Boxer tried desperately to make himself understood; a frenzy of head shaking accompanied the sounds.

The woman's hand moved toward him and he froze. She touched the ice pick to his face and used its point to trace a circle around one of his eyes. "It doesn't really matter, you know. The pleasure of seeing you die is not something we would deny ourselves."

The expression in Boxer's eyes reflected unrestrained panic.

The woman put the two implements on the table, then tilted the man's chair back until it was flat on the floor. She looked down at him and said, "You need to be thinking about what dying will be like. And you need to be aware that your fear of death will soon subjugate itself to the pain we are going to inflict upon you.

"Scientifically speaking, we have found people are most distressed when they anticipate pain in areas they can't see." The voice came from a face devoid of expressed emotion, pronouncing each word as if lecturing a class of first-year medical students. "We will, therefore, start with the bottoms of your feet."

Pictures of what the thing would do to the bottoms of his feet flashed on the screen of his mind. Boxer jerked and heaved, straining at the ropes, grunting and sweating, trying to rock the chair from side to side. Sweat poured from his face. The man's once-powerful body couldn't save him; years of tending bar had done nothing but weaken his physical condition. The gag wouldn't allow him to breathe well, and he was exhausted within seconds. He looked into the death mask and tears streamed from his eyes; a small, pitiful sound came over and over from the gagged mouth. "Eeee. Eeee. Eeee."

"Please? Please what?" the voice mocked him. "So you will know how fortunate you are, let me tell you that what is left of this woman's soul would gladly exchange places with you."

The woman stepped away from his face and began to unlace his shoes. When his socks were tossed aside, she ran her manicured fingernails across the bottom of his feet. Boxer watched the woman reach for the pick and began to whimper.

The voice said, "Now let's see if I can remember the words to that little rhyme." As it touched its victim's toes with the sharp tip, the monster whispered, "Eenie, meenie, minie, moe . . ."

The tip of the pick traced a casual arc from Boxer's toes to the back of his heel and paused long enough to allow the man to suck in his breath.

In one way, Boxer's choice to live a sedentary lifestyle stood him in good stead; his heart lasted only four minutes before it burst. However, had he any inkling of what was waiting for him in eternity, he would've chosen to spend ten thousand years being tortured by the demon.

* * *

Aacock had been in his hiding place thirty minutes when the grungy neon sign in the bar's window went out. Seconds later, the door opened and the woman shuffled out. She turned north toward Lexington. Aacock waited until the flames were showing through the window across the street and walked south.

The fire department arrived in time to watch the fire burn itself out, but they didn't linger. A week earlier, these same firemen had depended on the Maryland National Guard to protect them while they fought fires started by uncontrollable mobs—the residents of this neighborhood who hadn't shot at them threw bottles and bricks. The firemen sprayed a little water on what was left of the building, recovered two charred bodies, and beat a retreat back to friendly territory.

Daybreak found several shabbily dressed black men rummaging through the still-smoldering rubble of what had been Boxer's Tavern. The pickings were lean, but each of them had found at least one unbroken bottle of booze. All the searchers, with the exception of one, were combing through the wreckage near where the liquor had been displayed. The loner, who was apparently new at scavenging, was in the middle of the building. While the others were absorbed in their quest, the outsider pried up a charred tabletop and found a man's toe. The searcher, without attracting the attention of the others, flicked the toe into a pile of glowing coals. When he was sure the evidence was burned beyond recognition, he shambled away.

She picked up the private line and his voice said, "I'll do it."

"Good. Do we need to meet?"

"No. I'll tell you how to get the money to a drop."

She had to sound as if the money mattered. "How much?"

He quoted a figure ten times higher than what any of the previous four had asked. "That's exorbitant."

"I'll use half of it for bribes. Take it or leave it." Bribes would consume a portion of the money, but most of it would be used to allow him to hide in relative comfort where the woman could not find him.

The woman continued the pretense of negotiating. "Half now . . . the other half when it's done."

"No . . . all now." Nothing about his profession fostered trust in his fellow humans. "When this is over, I plan to disappear."

"How will we stay in touch?"

"We won't." Aacock could understand killing a potential witness and destroying the evidence, but staying in a dangerous place to torture a stranger made no sense. He had to assume the woman was demented, and therefore, grossly unpredictable . . . and unpredictable people were dangerous. "You'll hear from me when I find them . . . not before . . . and never again."

"How long will it take?"

"This Moses Washington has what it takes to stay quiet and not attract attention. If they're well hidden, it could take a year."

CHAPTER FOUR

Roosevelt Edwards was the overseer at the Parker Gin, and as such, he stood on the top rung of Allen County's black hierarchy, right alongside the black preachers.

Roosevelt's house sat beside the Mossy Lake road where it ran through the Parkers' woods, about a mile east of Cat Lake. On this day, as on most others, Roosevelt left his pickup at home and walked to the gin. Dawn's pink sky was at his back, and row after row of ankle-high cotton stretched as far as he could see on both sides of the road. He had a full Monday waiting on him at the gin—walking and praying comforted him.

He was approaching the Cat Lake bridge, enjoying the early-morning sounds, praying and planning his day, when he caught a whiff of smoke. On his left, a short way off the south edge of the road, a dozen century-old pecan trees stood back from the lake, offering protection to a cabin as old as they were. The cabin in the pecan trees belonged to Mose Washington, but Mose hadn't lived there for more than eight years. Roosevelt stopped and looked toward the trees.

In front of the cabin, near the lake, smoke from a small fire yielded to the stir of air and drifted toward the road. A black man was standing several feet from the fire, his hat in his hand, staring at three small gravestones.

In the Mississippi Delta, drifting black folks were a fact of life, but the ones who knew about that area's history stayed clear of the Parker plantation; the narrow strip of land running from Cat Lake to Parkers' Woods had a bloody history. In the fifteen-year span between 1945 and 1960, a dozen people had died violent deaths there.

Roosevelt had worked for the Parkers for fifty years. He hired on in the early days—back before Mose became Mr. Bobby Lee Parker's overseer—and worked his way up to be Mose's right-hand man. The two black men worked side by side at the Parker Gin for more than forty years. When Mose stepped down, Roosevelt took over as the operations manager.

Roosevelt felt blessed to be working for the Parkers; they were fine white folks—but they weren't receptive to having strangers stay on their land uninvited. The small handful of travelers who didn't know any better than to stop near Cat Lake were sent on their way by Mr. Roosevelt Edwards.

Mose was the finest man, black or white, Roosevelt had ever known, and when he disappeared the gin foreman adopted the little house as his responsibility; he turned off the road to see what was going on. As Roosevelt walked up, the man by the gravestones turned to watch him. When the big man got close, the stranger bowed slightly. "Mornin', uncle."

The gin foreman cut an imposing figure wherever he went. Except for a full head of white hair, he was as black as a steam locomotive and almost as big. He was dressed in accordance with his role at the gin—khaki shirt and pants, starched and ironed—just like a white man.

"Mornin'," rumbled the locomotive. "What're you doin' 'round here, boy?"

"Tryin' to git to Louisiana, uncle. Lookin' for work as I go."

"You got no call bein' 'round this here house." Roosevelt pointed at two nice homes on the west side of the lake and underlined his authority with the Parker name. "The Parkers is the white folks what owns this lake an' all the land 'round it, an' they don't take to havin' folks stayin' the night here 'bouts."

"Sorry, uncle. I was on the road an' just stopped where I figured I could get some sleep."

"Where you headed to?"

The smile came back. "Come from Detroit. Had me a job at that factory where they builds them automobiles—sweepin' out in the winter, yard work in the summer. I made it through this past winter but couldn't abide the thought of that cold comin' back. Told the fella I hitched that ride with I's comin' to a job down to Moorin'sport . . . it's out by Caddo Lake, over to Louisiana. I reckon he got messed up some, 'cause he dropped me off up yonder in that Moores Point town on Saturday night an' kept on goin'. I asked them folks in town where Caddo Lake was at, an' they sent me out here . . . so here I is."

"Well, you missed it sho' 'nuff."

"Sho' did." The man looked mildly troubled. "I'm powerful sorry, uncle. I didn't aim to bother nobody." He made a gesture at the lake. "I just had me some frog legs for breakfast. I didn't fool with nothin' else."

"Mm-hmm." Among black folks, Roosevelt was accustomed to getting his way; this would be no different. "Put that fire out an' git on down the road then."

"I'll do 'er, uncle." Roosevelt watched as the man dug in a burlap bag and came out with a battered coffeepot. He dipped it in the lake, poured the water on the fire, and went back for more. He poured the second potful on the fire and began to bank dirt around the ashes. As he worked he nodded at the houses across the lake. "You reckon them white folks got any day work they needs doin'?"

"Can you chop cotton?"

"Well, I might could, but truth be told, I ain't never done it. I'd hate to take a man's wages an' not do him right."

Honest black boys who would do what they were told to do

when they were told to do it were getting scarce. Roosevelt took a step closer to the man. "Do I know you?" The other man looked Roosevelt in the eye and shook his head. "I reckon not. I ain't never been 'round here before."

Roosevelt nodded. "I seen you in church over in Inverness last night."

"Well, yassuh, I was there, but I didn't see you."

"We was settin' in the back." A man who'd do like he was told and go to church on Sunday was rare enough. Roosevelt pointed across the bridge. "Stop by the gin yonder an' check with me after you git done here. Ain't nobody said nothin' 'bout no day jobs, but you can't never tell."

The man began to move more quickly. "Yassuh, I'll be right behind you."

Roosevelt went his way while the young man hustled back and forth to the lake, getting water to drown the fire. When he'd made sure the fire was out, he put the bag over his shoulder and moved off toward the gin.

The sun was up by the time Roosevelt got to the gin office. He stuck his head in the door and said, "Mornin', Mr. Glenn. Them gin stands gonna be here today?"

"Mornin', Rose." Glenn Hall ran the office for Mr. Bobby Lee Parker; Roosevelt was in charge of everything else. Hall was tilted back in his chair reading the Monday paper and waiting for the ankle-high cotton to get three feet tall and start producing. "The folks in Greenwood just called. Said they'd be here 'fore noon."

"Yes, sir." Roosevelt was pleased. "Well, I'm fixin' to go get ready for 'em."

"Just a minute, Rose."

"Sir?"

"Miz Susan just called . . . said they need somebody to come mow over at Miz Virginia's."

"Where's Lucas at?" Lucas Johnson was the Parkers' regular yardman.

"They took him to the hospital last night with a broke leg. Be in a cast for six weeks." Hall turned the page on his paper. "Pick whoever you can spare to go over there an' do whatever needs doin'."

Roosevelt frowned; he didn't have anyone he could spare. Picking season was short months away, and all the worthwhile men who lived nearby would be scattered around the area chopping cotton. He had three hand-picked men waiting to help him set the new equipment . . . but he needed all three, all day. He took his hat off and pushed his hair around while he mumbled to himself; he didn't have time for that fool Lucas to get his leg broke. Young Mrs. Parker, Mr. Bobby Lee's wife, was easy enough to please, but Old Mrs. Parker was persnickety about how her yard was kept. The fingers were making their third or fourth pass through the wiry hair when he turned around and almost ran into the young drifter from Detroit.

"Well, uncle, here I is." The man was holding his hat in his hand, looking expectant.

Roosevelt stared at the man without speaking for a moment, then took him by the arm and half-led, half-carried him out onto the gin's loading dock.

"What's yo' name, boy?"

"Lavert Jensen, uncle."

"You say you done yard work up there to Detroit?"

"Yassuh, sho' did."

He gestured across the road with his hat. "See them two houses yonder?"

The closest house was seventy-five or a hundred yards south of the road, a white antebellum; a sprawling ranch-style home was located on the far side of the older home. Lavert shrugged. "Yassuh, they looks real fine."

"M'Virginia, Old Miz Parker, lives in that big white one. The

Young Parkers, Mr. Bobby Lee an' Miz Susan, live on the other side of her."

Lavert nodded. "Yassuh."

"M'Virginia's a fine white woman, but she picky 'bout that yard . . . an' her regular yardboy went an' broke his leg. Can you mow that yard an' git it done today?"

The lawn of the plantation home was huge, and Lavert looked doubtful. "I'm gonna be usin' a push mower?"

"Uh-uh." Roosevelt shook his head. "Gas."

"Yassuh"—Lavert smiled—"I can finish it by this afternoon . . . do it pretty good, too."

"Well, that's what I'm countin' on." He nodded at a paint-deprived shed standing next to the gin. "The mower an' other tools is in that shed yonder. Take the mower over across the road first an' see Almeda. Tell her I said you was gonna be cuttin' the grass, but don't be startin' that mower 'til she says."

"That's it?"

"Git to it." Roosevelt put his hat on and walked away.

Lavert opened the doors to find a dust-covered old pickup taking up most of the space in the little building. Two narrow aisles worked their way down the sides of the truck, separating it from seventy-five years' worth of assorted clutter; additional junk was piled in the truck's bed. The lawn mower and most of the other tools Lavert would need were situated close to the doors. Lavert pulled the lawn mower outside and looked toward the gin—Roosevelt was talking to another colored man, pointing toward something in the gin. Lavert went back inside and picked up a yard rake and a well-used hoe and carried them outside. When his things were where he wanted them, he checked the gin again—no one in sight. He made another trip into the shed and opened the door of the pickup, being careful not to make any noise. The inside of the truck was well preserved; except for a small place in the middle of the seat—a small, dark handprint—the upholstery was spotless. The yardboy leaned into the truck to examine the stain on the seat and thought, *That's dried blood*. Seconds later, he was gathering up his tools and heading across the road.

He took his hat off and tapped on the back door of the big white house.

The black woman was frowning when she opened the screen door. "What you wantin', boy?"

He was ten years older than the young black woman. "You Miz Almeda?"

She was definitely Miz Almeda—and she was definitely the boss. "An' who's askin'?"

"My name Lavert Jensen, miss." He pointed over his shoulder. "That man at the gin say for me to come over an' mow this here yard, but to don't start 'til you said."

"He said right. M'Virginia still readin' her Bible, an' I don't want nobody makin' no racket 'round here 'til she finish."

"Yassum."

The man looked too thin. "Did you eat yet?"

"Yassum." He pointed at the lake. "Had me two frog legs."

"Mm-hmm. Wait here an' I'll git you some o' my biscuits."

She closed the door but was back in short order with four biscuits, as many sausage patties, and a tin cup full of hot coffee. She pointed at a nearby oak tree. "You can sit on these here steps if you gonna be quiet. If you gonna be hummin' or such as that, you sit out yonder under that tree."

"Yassum." He stayed where he was. "I generally don't make no noise."

"Good. When you finish, you wait here 'til M'Virginia come out to talk."

"Yassum."

"An' you be careful for her. She walks with a cane 'cause she ain't steady, so don't you be lettin' her hurt herself."

"No, ma'am."

"An' she hard of hearin', so she talk loud. You do the same."

"Yassum. You reckon she be hard to please?"

"Maybe some, but she fair. You do yo' job right, you gonna be doin' yard work here an' at Miz Susan's long as you wants. That good-for-nothin' Lucas Johnson was gittin' to where he was at that bottle too much—probably got drunked up last night an' laid down on the road somewheres."

"Yassum."

Miz Virginia came out after he finished his biscuits and told him what she wanted done.

He spent the rest of his day mowing and cleaning out Old Mrs. Parker's flower beds. When suppertime came, Roosevelt walked over and told him it was time to quit. "This here is ten dollars. You earned it."

"Much obliged. M'Virginia told me to come back in the mornin' an' do Miz Susan's yard, so I reckon I got me two days' work."

"Fine," said Roosevelt. "I unlocked that cabin over yonder where you was this mornin'. You can spend the night in there if you wants."

"That'd be real fine, uncle. I 'preciate it."

An easy chair sat in front of the cabin's fireplace. Except for a new rats' nest in the chair's cushion, the cabin was fairly clean.

Lavert checked in with Roosevelt at sunup on Tuesday morning and had his lawn mower and tools at Old Mrs. Parker's back door shortly thereafter. He ate biscuits and fried ham along with a cup of strong coffee while he waited on M'Virginia to tell him to start on Miz Susan's yard.

By midafternoon on Friday the yards and trees were neatly trimmed, every flower bed on the place was free of weeds, and Lavert Jensen was ready to be on his way. Roosevelt gave him a ride into town, and he walked from there out to Highway 82 to see if he could hitch a ride to Louisiana.

He'd just dropped his sack by his feet when an old black man stopped his car and pushed open the passenger door. "Come on, boy. I'll take you down the road a piece. Just put yo' sack on the floor back there."

Lavert had his head down, stowing his burlap bag on the floor behind his seat, while the old man was watching a car coming toward them from the west. Lavert never saw the approaching car's distinctive white-on-black Texas license plates, nor did he see the young white couple in the car, but the old man did; they were friends of his. The white couple turned south toward Moores Point.

When he was settled, Lavert said, "I'm mighty obliged to you for pickin' me up."

"You welcome enough, but it wasn't my doin'," said the old man. "The good Lord Hi'self told me to pull over an' pick you up."

"An' I 'preciate it. My name Lavert Jensen."

"I be Red Justin."

"How far you goin'?"

"Greenville."

Lavert said, "Mmm," then busied himself watching the cotton fields go by.

Minutes later, on the outskirts of Indianola, Lavert asked, "You from Greenville?"

"No, no." Red pointed over his shoulder. "I stays back there in Greenwood. I's just settlin' down for my after-dinner nap when the good Lord spoke to me an' told me to go to Greenville."

"That's good." Lavert smiled. "That'll git me on down the road some."

Red shook his head. "Oh, you ain't goin' to Greenville with me. The Lord say take you to Indianola . . . the rest is up to Him."

Lavert studied the old man. "Reckon why would He have you put me off?"

Red took his eyes off the road long enough to meet Lavert's gaze. "I reckon you'd know more 'bout that than me, son."

Lavert made a bad mistake when he said, "I ain't no trouble-maker, uncle, I'm a churchgoin' man. You can ask them folks out at Cat Lake."

Cat Lake, huh? Red nodded. *I reckon I'll do that.*

When they got to Indianola, Red let his passenger out and drove off. Lavert watched the car until it was out of sight.

Doe's was open when Red got to Greenville, and he was hungry. He bought half a dozen hot tamales and some iced tea and turned the ground under Doe's big cottonwood tree into a dining room. When he finished his supper, he knelt by the tree and prayed, "Lord, You was the one what wanted me in Greenville. An' if don't nothin' happen 'tween here an' Cat Lake, I may not never know why, but I reckon you do though . . . an' them hot tamales was sho' nuff fine."

Red headed back east—he'd be at Cat Lake before sundown . . . and Missy Patterson and her husband would be there. The timing of his arrival at Cat Lake would be perfect.

Pat and Missy were committed to spending their first hour "back home" sitting on the porch behind the brick house, visiting with her parents and soaking in the atmosphere around Cat Lake. The young couple's news that Pat had been selected as the new chairman of the philosophy department at North Texas State University was cause for a minor celebration, but fifteen minutes after the announcement, Missy started to fidget. Bobby Lee let her squirm awhile then said, "Baby, why don't you take Pat over an' check on the cabin 'fore it gets dark?"

She was out of her chair and pulling on Pat's hand before her daddy finished his sentence. "Hallelujah, I was about to go nuts. C'mon, Pat."

The Young Parkers' favorite—and only—son-in-law stood up and smiled. "It's good to be back."

"Don't be late for supper," Susan Parker called after them. "We're eating at Granny's."

Missy lifted a hand to show she heard, but her track record for adhering to other people's schedules had never been good; she was holding her husband's hand, dancing and tugging like a frisky colt on a short lead. The two were across her grandmother's backyard and almost to the road when they saw Roosevelt walking down the gin steps with Red Justin.

When they got closer the two black men lifted their hats and spoke in unison, "Evenin'."

"Hey, y'all." The fact that she was "home"—back at Cat Lake and among people she loved—was almost too much for Missy. "It's really good to see y'all."

"Howdy, Rose. Red." Pat shook hands with both men.

"Where's Emmalee?" asked Missy. Roosevelt's daughter, Missy's first disciple, had just graduated from college.

"She's took the bus to Washington. My boy, Milton, is in the Marines up there, an' she gone to see him."

"Tell her I asked about her. Okay?"

"Yessum." Roosevelt nodded. "She gonna be sorry she wasn't here."

"Me too. You tell her I said she's special."

"Yessum, I'll do it."

She turned the smile on the other man. "Red, what brings you to the lake?"

"Just a visit, I reckon. I was wantin' to talk to Rose here, an' I came to check on y'all two."

"On Missy and me?" asked Pat.

"Yessuh."

Pat glanced at his wife before asking, "How'd you know we were here?"

Red ignored the question and asked his own. "Y'all goin' over to Mose's place?"

Pat nodded. "Mm-hmm."

"Let me an' Rose walk along with y'all. I ain't got to talk to him yet, an' this way I can tell y'all all at the same time."

The four walked abreast onto the bridge. Red told the other three about God's sending him to Greenville and how he'd picked up the hitchhiker at the precise moment they were turning into Moores Point. The three with the old man listened and believed; Red Justin had a reputation for being the next thing to a prophet.

They were getting close to the cabin when the old man finished, and Rose spoke first. "How come him to say somethin' 'bout Cat Lake, you reckon?"

Pat said, "Because God wanted Red to hear it."

Red and Missy nodded agreement, and Rose said, "I just wanted to see did y'all believe like me. Somethin' ain't right 'bout his bein' here."

"Amen to that." Red nodded slowly "Same reason he claimed to be a churchgoin' man."

"Why did he say he was here?" asked Pat. He and Missy exchanged a look; conversations about strangers being around the lake could lead to words about Mose Washington. Rose and Red were unalterably trustworthy, but Mose's safety would not be enhanced by their knowledge of his whereabouts.

"Well, he said he was tryin' to get to Louisiana an' needed a little work." Roosevelt grimaced. "I hired him to do the yard work at the houses, an' I let him stay in the cabin here."

Missy was listening quietly. She had spent the past few weeks looking forward to their trip to Cat Lake, anxious to be where so many of her favorite memories were anchored. What she was hearing from Red and Roosevelt reminded her of things best forgotten. Her first words were a question. "Where's Lucas?"

"He got his leg broke when somebody run over him in—" Roosevelt's speculations interrupted him. "Have mercy . . . you reckon he would run a man down just to git his job?"

Each of them thought their own thoughts for a moment and

came to the same conclusion. Any man looking for Mose would be sent by the Bainbridges, and any man sent by the Bainbridges would be utterly ruthless.

"We best take us a look inside," said Red.

Roosevelt was trailing as they mounted the stairs to the cabin's porch, thinking back over the past week. If Lavert was looking for Mose Washington, he hadn't heard anything during the last few days that would help him in his search . . . nobody at Cat Lake would ever say where Mose was, even if they knew. He said, "'Fore we goes in, I needs to say somethin'." The other three stopped on the porch, and Roosevelt spoke as if he'd read the Pattersons' minds, "I don't know where Mose is at, an' I don't know if any of y'all do. What I'm sayin' is, Mose is as fine a friend as a man could have, but if any of y'all knows, you needs to be careful I don't find out."

Red, for his part, knew if only one person in the world knew where Mose was, it would be the white girl standing at his elbow. He said, "Rose is right. I'm gettin' on up in years, an' I seen too many old folks accidentally blab out stuff they didn't even know they was sayin'. The less I know 'bout Mose, the safer he is."

She'd been born and raised across the lake—the crown princess of the Parker family. In June of 1945, she'd been a skinny little seven-year-old with long eyelashes and a short temper—and the target of an assault by a congregation of demonic beings. The demons had set out to kill her, her best friend, and her brother.

The demon at Cat Lake, the leader of those who purposed to kill the children, chose as his means of destruction a gigantic cottonmouth water moccasin. His plan called for his underlings to harvest their own moccasins and use them to drive Missy to him; he intended to kill her in front of a crowd of people—people who knew her.

*   *   *

In those days, if you could factor the three "Parker" children out of the mix, Cat Lake's environs were the picture of peace—its quiet waters were surrounded by rich cotton land, moss-draped cypress trees, and gentle people. However, because children don't lend themselves to being "factored out," the folks on the Parker Plantation welcomed all newcomers and visitors with the admonition that they "best watch out for them Parker children, 'specially that black 'un an' that girl." Bobby Parker, a typical twelve-year-old, was the group's acknowledged leader. Mose Junior Washington, eleven years old and fairly easygoing, was the most adventurous. Missy Parker was born tough, spoiled rotten, and followed her own rules.

On a warm June day, the three kids were playing near the Cat Lake bridge. Missy and Junior were taking turns jumping from the bridge, and Bobby was nearby in their homemade boat when the first water moccasin surfaced near the girl. Local folks still tell the stories about the events that took place in the next few minutes—they call what happened on that Sunday afternoon "The War at Cat Lake." And that's what it was.

Bobby and Missy survived—Mose Junior gave his life to save theirs.

In the months that followed, what had been a casual friendship between the girl and Mose Junior's parents became a bond unlike any the people in the Mississippi Delta had ever witnessed. With the Parkers' blessings, Mose's wife, Pip, met with the child to pray and study the Bible. Missy confounded the white community by frequently referring to herself as "Mose's almost-daughter."

Missy stopped on the porch and the men waited.

Under the pecan trees in the front yard, what had been bare dirt was covered with grass. The cats were gone, giving the redbirds, sparrows, and doves unrestricted access to the grounds in front of the cabin; from somewhere in the tops of the trees, a mockingbird warned others of his kind not to intrude into his portion of the world. There'd never been a daylight hour when a person couldn't hear a bird's song from the front porch.

Missy looked at the manicured area around the tombstones and said, "Y'all go on in. I'll be there in a minute."

The men went inside, and Missy walked back to the top of the steps and sat down.

Nothing had changed, and everything was different. The same cypress trees guarded the banks of the lake, their soft clusters of Spanish moss moving like thick tassels of ash-colored hair, conversing with the late-afternoon breeze. The surface of the lake glittered black and beautiful, the birds in the yard were lively and colorful, the coo of a dove offered warmth to her heart . . . and the scene filled her with dread. Red's words reminded her that, in the vicinity of Cat Lake, abundant peace had been known to portend tragedy.

In her short lifetime, three men had been shot within fifteen feet of where she sat. All three were, in some way, victims of demonic attacks. All three died.

She bowed her head. "Lord, please keep me reminded that You're in control. Amen."

When she stepped into the cabin, Roosevelt said, "We was just lookin' 'round without movin' nothin'. I don't see nothin' different from the last time I was here, 'cept for that big hole in Mose's chair."

Missy looked at the chair. "Rats did that," she observed.

"Mm-hmm." Red peered at the hole though his bifocals. "Somebody just cleaned out the nest."

"Well, let's rummage around and see if we can find anything he might've left," said Pat.

They didn't—not so much as a stray piece of paper.

They were back out on the cabin's porch, when Pat said, "He left it clean."

Missy nodded. "Maybe too clean."

"Maybe." Pat shrugged and turned to Roosevelt. "Where else would he have been by himself?"

"Nowhere," said Roosevelt. "He was either outside workin' in the yards or in the house here. I could walk out on the loading dock any time of . . ." He paused, then looked across the lake. "The shed over at the gin . . . that's where he went to get the yard tools an' sharpen the mower blade."

The other three followed his gaze. Missy said, "Let's take a look."

The interior of the shed was pretty much unchanged. Red stood outside while the others edged down the sides of Mose's old pickup.

On the night Mose fled Cat Lake, Bobby Lee and Mose came to this shed and swapped Mose's truck for the Mercury left there when Old Mr. Parker died.

"What was in the truck?" Missy asked.

"Nothin'," said Roosevelt. "I cleaned it out myself."

Pat nodded. "I went through it too . . . with a whisk broom . . . glove compartment, under the seat, ashtray, everything. The license plate's at the bottom of Mossy Lake."

Missy pulled open the passenger door and wrinkled her nose. "There's a rats' nest in the seat."

Roosevelt opened the other door, and Pat looked over Missy's shoulder. When they saw the rats' nest, the two men looked at each other. Pat said. "Let me get closer."

"What?" said Missy.

"Just a minute," said Pat.

He and the big black man leaned into the cab from opposite sides, and Pat lifted the rats' nest and put it on the floor of the truck. A saucer-sized segment of the seat's upholstery and the padding underneath it were gone.

Roosevelt straightened from examining the seat. He shook his head. "That ain't good." Pat was nodding agreement.

"Tell me what ain't good, Rose" she said.

"When I cleaned out this here truck, they was a bloody

handprint in the middle of the seat . . . one what that young boy made that night."

Missy stretched across the seat and sniffed at the hole where the nest had been. "It doesn't stink bad enough. A two-legged rat put that nest here."

Roosevelt pursed his lips and shook his head again. "I should'a washed out that spot."

"I missed it too, Rose," said Pat. "Don't worry about it."

"You'd be right to don't worry 'bout it," said Red.

"Yep." Missy sidestepped back to stand by Red and brushed off her jeans. "What's done is done."

"No, no," said Red, "not like that. I mean it ain't in our hands."

"I don't understand," said the girl. Pat and Roosevelt made their way to the tailgate of the truck.

Red pointed at the cab of the truck. "That feller was most likely lookin' for Mose, right?"

They nodded.

"He come here an' snooped around some without nobody knowin', right? Now," he pointed to the west, "I ain't bothered to go to Greenville in a year, but the good Lord come near speakin' out loud . . . tellin' me to go today." Red pointed at Missy and Pat. "An', I don't pick up no hitchhikers, but y'all two drove within twenty feet of that same feller, an' he missed seein' y'all 'cause I got prodded to pick him up in my car. You wrap all that in what we lookin' at here, an' you see where we at."

Red's audience responded to his revelation with blank looks. Missy touched Red's arm and said, "I'm sorry, Red, but I still don't see what you see."

Red smiled. "Mose been gone for eight years without bein' found 'cause that's how God wanted it; can't no demon, nor no man, find him what God wants to hide . . . not ever. An' if the bad folks is still lookin', that means Mose is alive an' still hid. But . . . you take what we seen today, an' folks what's payin' attention would be lookin' to see things change." He took the girl's hand in his and patted it. "God had Mose an' that boy behind a veil . . . an' now He's fixin' to lift it up."

The faces around Red were no longer blank. Roosevelt rested his hand on the truck and bowed his head. "Lord, have mercy on us all."

Pat and Missy were able to avoid looking at each other, but they were both thinking the same thing: Mose needed to be warned.

Red could see their consternation. "Lemme tell you young white folks somethin'."

Missy reached for Pat's hand. They waited.

"It ain't never mattered where Mose was at; if God wanted him hid, he was hid. He could've stood in the middle of that bridge yonder for eight years an' couldn't no bad folks have seen him . . . an' if God's fixin' to let bad folks or demons peek behind the curtain, runnin' ain't gonna change nothin'." He nodded to himself. "Was I him, I'd be expectin' to be found, an' I'd pray that God would git plenty of glory from whatever comes."

When Red finished his pronouncement, Missy was trembling, and Pat pulled her close. Red noticed and said, "We better pray." He and Roosevelt took off their hats and he said, "Father, Yo' Word says, 'The Lord is my light an' my salvation; whom shall I fear? The Lord is the strength of my life; of whom shall I be afraid?' We come askin' for Yo' strength an' Yo' protection, an' we begs You, Lord, to let us honor Yo' name by how we trust You. Amen."

Missy wiped her eyes and tried to smile at Red. "I'm still scared."

Red nodded, then took a bandana out of his pocket and dried his own eyes. When the cloth was back in his pocket, he took the white girl's hand in both of his and said, "God'll be yo' strength when the time comes."

Pat and Missy both repeated, "When the time comes?"

"Mm-hmm. Looks to me like the time's comin'."

"What time?" asked Pat.

"Hard to say, I reckon." The old man seemed distracted. He looked at the setting sun and said, "I reckon I best be gettin' on to Greenwood."

Missy took Red's arm. "What time are you talkin' about, Red?"

"Well, when it comes right down to it, I ain't for sure . . . but you'll know when it comes." He waved his finger back and forth at the two of them. "Both o' y'all gonna know. God brought y'all all the way to Miss'ippi so's y'all could know things was gonna happen. Was I you, I'd be on the lookout." He put his hat on and walked to his car.

Pat and Missy walked with Roosevelt till they got to the middle of the bridge. They stood by the remains of the old ladder and looked down the length of the lake. The tops of the trees stood still in the warm air; the surface of the water was a black mirror, reflecting clouds turned red by the sunset.

She leaned forward and looked beneath them. "The float's gone."

"Yessum," said Roosevelt, "it got too rotten for folks to be on, so I had 'em tear it up."

The girl didn't respond, and Roosevelt murmured his good-byes and ambled away to get his truck.

Missy thought out loud, "We spent a lot of time on that old float."

Pat smiled. "Are you wishing you were a kid again?"

She shuddered and said, "No, thanks." All of her childhood memories were not good ones.

This was where she'd had her first experience with demons. Junior was on the float when he stopped the water moccasin from killing her. No sooner was she safe, than Junior intervened to take a snake strike meant for Bobby. When the battle was over, her daddy and A. J. Mason brought her friend up the ladder. She watched him die minutes later, right where they were standing.

Pat said, "Sorry, hon. I didn't mean to—"

"Shhh, shhh . . . it's okay. I spent a million summer days playin' on that float with Bobby an' Mose Junior—built it ourselves." She smiled. "We tore up a pretty good cotton wagon to get the lumber, an' when our parents found out about it, they tore up our backsides. A few months after Junior died, I knelt in this very spot with Mose an' prayed to receive Christ, an' I got to watch you do the same thing . . . prayin' right here with Emmalee."

"And I proposed to you here."

"An' it was wonderful." She traced her fingers along the railing, remembering Mose's words. "We called it a memorial bridge after Junior died . . . I guess that's even more appropriate today than it was then." She smiled again, more softly. "It would be a shame to let that all sift down to one horrible memory." She looked up at him. "It's a wonderful place."

He agreed. "It's certainly special to me."

She took a deep breath. "Do you think Mose is in danger?"

He thought for a moment, frowning. "I think we should assume that he is, yes."

She took his hand. "Are you as scared as I am?"

"Yes . . . and no." The gin's pigeons made a last sweep over the lake before going in to roost. Pat looked around him; the treetops stirred, water rippled around the bridge pilings—the clouds overhead were changing from red to dark gray. "God always does what's best for us."

Missy was twirling a strand of her hair; her eyes were looking without seeing. "Mmm."

He looked out at the lake. "Do you think God brought us here so Red could warn us?"

She didn't hear him. "What're we gonna do?"

"Well, the second thing we need to do is get back to Texas."

"The second?" she said.

Bobby Lee opened his back door and looked out. "Wonder where the kids are."

Susan was pulling a roast out of the oven. "They were standing on the bridge the last time I looked."

"Yep. They're still there . . . an' look at that."

"Hmm?"

"Well . . . they just got on their knees." He watched the young couple for a few seconds then said, "Looks like they're prayin'."

Susan looked over her husband's shoulder. "Hmm . . . right in the middle of the bridge." She tossed her pot holders on the counter. "If they need to stop where they are and pray, then you and I should be doing the same."

Pat and Missy walked off the bridge hand in hand and met her parents at the back door of the big white house.

During supper, Pat, who normally carried the conversation, spoke only when spoken to. Virginia Parker cooked a dozen extra rolls for him; he took one and ate half of it. Susan Parker watched her daughter push her food around on her plate and worried that youngsters had been arguing. Bobby Lee talked some about the farm and gin, then swapped to baseball; he came close to talking to himself.

After an exceptionally long lull, Missy said, "Pat an' I are going back home in the mornin'."

"Well," Susan said, "knowing that beats the living daylights out of thinking you two are fighting."

Her grandmother pushed her plate back. "Well, I guess that explains why Pat's acting like this is a funeral instead of supper."

"Sorry." Pat winked at her. "I'll do better next time."

Granny was tapping the edge of her plate with a fingernail, looking at Missy. "And I suppose it's safe to assume that this has something to do with Mose?"

Missy picked up her coffee cup and walked over to open the back door. After checking outside and satisfying herself that no one outside could hear her voice, she refilled her cup and brought it back to the table. "Yessum, it sure does."

*   *   *

The aliases of Moses Lincoln Washington and William L. Prince Jr. were known to fewer than a dozen people—their whereabouts, to half that many. None of the Parkers knew where the two men were, and by unspoken agreement, they never broached the subject with Missy. Over the past eight years, Missy spoke of Mose every now and then, but no more than any close friend might. No one ever said it, but the girl's parents and grandmother all knew if they wanted to find Mose they'd start their search near the girl.

Missy took a sip of coffee then put the cup down. "Red Justin was just here." She picked up her dessertspoon and traced a design in the tablecloth. "He thinks things are fixin' to start happenin'."

Virginia Parker was eighty years old, but she was sharp as a rose thorn and had a nose for trouble. "Tell me what we know about that man who worked in my yard this week—that Lavert Jensen."

Pat said, "Mr. Jensen is the rub." He related the afternoon's discoveries.

"Anybody figure out what Red means by this *time* he's talkin' about?" asked Bobby Lee.

"Nah." Pat picked up the remainder of his roll and lectured with it. "You know how some prophets are . . . long on warnings, short on specifics."

"But you believe him." Bobby Lee wasn't asking.

"Oh, yeah." Pat was sober. "Sure as sunshine."

"Y'all want us to come with you?" asked Bobby Lee.

Pat and Missy shook their heads at the same time. She said, "Better not."

"Baby," said her grandmother, "nobody here can make Mose safer by knowing where he is, and you already know you can call on us if you need us. Let me take a moment, though, to tell you that God has put you in a special place."

"How's that?" asked Missy.

"If it weren't for Mose, you wouldn't be here."

Missy patted her hand. "Granny, you mean Mose Junior."

"Humph," her grandmother sniffed. "Honey, the day's coming when I won't remember what I take in my coffee, but it's not here yet."

"Then I don't know what you mean."

"There's no reason why you should." Virginia turned slightly in her chair so she was facing her granddaughter. "The long and short of it is . . . God singled Mose out sixty years ago. That means you're standing in a unique, God-chosen place because of your relationship to him."

"Sixty years ago? Mose would've been eight years old, Granny."

"Mm-hmm, but he was called on to do a man's job, and he did it."

"What job?"

"That's Mose's story to tell, not mine." She waved away the question. "Now, let me finish. Sixty years ago, God made it abundantly clear that He had chosen Mose to play a special role in His plan. Over twenty years ago, when Junior died, you pledged yourself to know God and make Him known, and you're following through on your promise. When you couple those facts with Red Justin's pronouncements and Mose's advancing years, you have to assume that it's possible, if not probable, that God is planning something significant in the near future."

No one spoke.

Virginia had said her piece. She got up to fix dessert while she let her guests mull over what they'd heard; she could predict their reactions.

The two couples at the table continued to turn Virginia's words over in their minds; their individual conclusions ran along parallel lines—everything she said made sense.

Bobby Lee and Susan raised the girl to make her own way, and, with her husband's help, that's what she'd do. Missy's response would be directed at protecting Mose; she was as stubborn as a concrete column, but she probably wouldn't do anything stupid. Pat tended to plan more carefully than his wife, but he wasn't as pliable as he pretended to be; he wouldn't hesitate to help Missy make her decisions.

Missy said, "It's startin' again, isn't it?"

The last time Satan's angels attacked someone at Cat Lake, two men died in the backyard of the house where they were sitting. No thinking person could live through what the people in the kitchen had seen and assume God was always going to bring peace into a Christian's life. Based on what they'd heard that afternoon, it was safe to believe something cataclysmic was looming in the near future.

Bobby Lee looked at his daughter and said, "You still don't think your momma an' I ought to follow y'all out to Texas."

"Mmm." Missy was thinking. She turned to Pat. "What do you think?"

"Uh-uh. Our leaving after such a short visit will attract some attention. Taking a caravan back with us would be worse." He stood up to go start packing.

Bobby Lee nodded; the boy was right. "Maybe we'll come later in the summer."

Pat thought that over and answered carefully. "Let's wait and decide that later. Give us a week or two to make some plans." Everyone in the room knew he wanted to talk to Mose before making any decisions.

When the sun came up Saturday morning, Missy and Pat were crossing the Mississippi River bridge at Greenville. On any other day Missy would've been commenting on the view—she didn't seem to notice. They stopped in Texarkana at lunchtime and walked into a cafeteria under overcast skies. Thirty minutes later they had to sprint back to their car in a downpour. Being soaked to the skin added irritation to anxiety, and Missy's mood turned darker than the weather.

Late that afternoon, when they pulled up in front of Mose's house, the rain had slacked off to a sprinkle and the skies were trying to clear up—Missy's mood wasn't.

CHAPTER FIVE

The old man stepped through the front door carrying a slender stick in his hand. He didn't depend on the makeshift cane as he walked over and stood by one of the white rocking chairs to wait for his visitors, but he kept it close; the porch could be slick when it was wet. The dog left his side and sauntered closer to the edge of the porch. He stopped there to stretch thoroughly, timing his moves so he could meet Pat and Missy on the top step. If he stayed close to the porch he didn't have to expose himself to the fat raindrops falling on the steps from the porch's overhang.

Pat stopped to pet the dog; Missy crossed to where Mose was standing. "Hi."

"Mighty quick trip," Mose observed.

She linked her arm in his and spoke her day's first soft words. "Mmm . . . too quick."

She wasn't ready to talk, and Mose never pushed. When Pat stepped onto the porch, Mose asked, "Y'all thirsty?"

They weren't.

"Well, it probably ain't gonna rain no more. Why don't we sit out here for a spell?" He motioned at the porch swing and rocking chairs with his walking stick. "Sit wherever you please, an' tell me what got y'all in such a hurry to get back here."

Pat and Missy chose the swing. When they were settled, the dog sat so he could put his head on Missy's knee.

Pat waited for Mose to sit down and asked, "Where's Bill?"

"Should be here any minute. Him an' Will Pierce went over to that Collin Turner's place after they got off at the feed store. Summer's comin' an' they figure to make some money on weekends . . . ridin' them bulls at the rodeo. Bill figures Mr. Turner can teach him stuff he don't know."

Pat sighed and shook his head. "We put in our two cents' worth on the rodeo thing a couple of times. It didn't take." He pointed at Mose's walking stick. "Are you okay?"

"Just old. My joints don't take to this wet weather." Hundreds of tiny pockmarks covered one end of the stick; the surface around them was polished to a high sheen by years of use. Mose ran his fingers across the slick surface and smiled. "I had this ol' sawed-off hoe handle long as I can remember . . . an' Pap had it 'fore me."

As Mose spoke, Dawg's head came up. The man pointed at his old friend and said, "He just heard the car."

The three turned to watch Bill's car approach the curve below the house while the dog—braving wet grass and leftover drops falling from the oak trees—went to the yard to wait for his boy. The car was coasting when it got to the curve. The freshly cleaned air carried reverberations from the car's radio to those waiting on the porch; Little Richard was screaming words of accusation at an elusive woman named Lucille.

Pat noted the car's sedate pace and observed, "Looks like we're not going to set a new record today."

"Mmm," Mose agreed. "Maybe the road's too wet . . . or might be that radio's drainin' all the power off'n the motor."

Bill and Little Richard pulled into the driveway, and Bill took his time getting out of the car. He stooped to pet the dog and straightened slowly when he finished.

Pat had to smile. "Looks like he's learning the hard way."

"Humph," Mose grunted. They watched as Bill let the dog

lead him around the puddles in the yard; the bull rider was favoring his right leg. "For some things, there ain't no easy way."

"Hello, buddy boy." Pat grinned and gripped Bill's hand without shaking it. "You look like you just went a couple of rounds with some bad hombres."

Bill gave Pat change for his grin and lowered himself gently into the empty rocker. "That'd be my first choice, I guess. Collin Turner spent the last hour working us on a mechanical bull . . . he says I'm too tall and too heavy. I think he's wrong."

Mose didn't smile. "You looks stove up as a ol' man."

"Well, I came out better than Will." He touched his side and grinned. "On my last go-round, I think I pulled an ab trying to get back in the middle, but it only hurts when I breathe. I twisted my right knee a little the ride before that, but I hardly notice it 'cause my left shoulder feels like somebody dropped me off a short building."

"What about Will?"

"He tried to hang on too long, and the machine busted his lip. That probably won't make Ella Claire too happy. Anyway, that's when we decided we'd learned enough for today." He took in Missy's frown and his grin spread. "It's been my experience that the real thing's always gonna be easier."

"Right." Missy was tired, worried, irritable, and in no mood for jokes. As far as she was concerned, Bill Mann couldn't have chosen a worse time to be involved with something as dangerous as bull riding. "An' everybody knows a real bull is gonna have a better disposition."

"I've been well, Mrs. Patterson." Bill winked at her. "And you?"

"Humph." Missy was on the back side of a sleepless night and a long car ride. Since meeting with Red, she'd been tormented by memories of past encounters with bad people and worse demons. In her short life, she'd stood in the center of three pitched battles with unbelievably wicked beings, and the prospect of a fourth conflict was looming. One overriding thought circulated in the center of her memories, and she was frustrated because she spent the last twenty-four hours fully anticipating her "almost-brother" would turn a deaf ear to their warnings. A tear formed in the corner of her eye, and the dog resumed his station near her knee. She petted the dog with one hand and waved the other at Pat and Mose. "Sorry. These two are always gonna be more patient than I am."

Mose nodded. "'Specially when you carryin' bad news."

Pat wasn't too surprised at Mose's ability to see past Missy's mood. "Am I going to be able to read minds when I'm sixty-eight?" he asked.

"If the Lord don't tarry, you ain't gonna have to worry 'bout it."

"Why's that?"

It was Mose's turn to smile. "'Cause He could come back any day now, an' you won't never make it to sixty-eight."

Missy sat back and said, "Well, He can come right now if He likes. I'm ready."

Mose shook his head. "Not just yet, child. We needs to see a few more folks in the fold first."

Missy understood immediately and nodded. "You're right."

The "few more folks" Mose wanted to see "in the fold" were embodied in one person—Bill Mann. But Bill steadfastly refused to have anything to do with the things of God.

Bill could see where the conversation was going and chose that moment to underline his lack of interest by sliding forward in his chair and moving to get up. "Well, I think I feel a prayer meeting coming on, so if y'all will excuse—"

Pat motioned for him to wait. "Hang on a second. You'll want to hear this."

Bill allowed his skepticism to show. "Hear what?"

Pat looked at Missy. "Do you want to tell them?"

She spoke without taking her eyes off the dog. "You better do it."

So Pat told it. He didn't have to embellish what they learned on their trip; someone was looking for Mose and Bill, and a reliable old man in Mississippi was convinced they were going to be found. Each of the four people on the porch was a veteran of at least one deadly encounter with the demonic realm, and each of them had lost at least one loved one. While Pat talked, Mose and Bill drew their own mental pictures of what might be in store.

"Well, I'll be," said Mose when Pat finished. "You know, I ain't got a impatient bone in my body, but I reckon I wouldn't be surprised if we was to get found out real soon."

"You sound mighty relaxed for a man who knows what demons can do." Missy's dread wanted company.

Mose's eyes were on the trees in the front yard, unseeing. "Relaxed ain't a good word for how I feels, but I got better things to do than to start frettin' over somethin' that I ain't got no control of."

Missy chewed the inside of her cheek while she frowned at Mose. Finally, she said, "I've been in the middle of three of these things . . . an' I lost a friend in every dadgum one of 'em." She shuddered when she took a breath. "We never have kept the demons from killin' people . . . good people."

Mose's gaze moved out to the trees in the Erwins' pasture; his voice was gentle. "You takin' that up with the wrong person, child."

"Yes, sir. I guess you're right." It wasn't her nature to give in, but Mose was practically quoting the Bible. She went back to petting the dog.

Mose turned his full attention on the girl. He didn't smile. "Now, I ain't sayin' I want to be in the middle of no fight, child. I'm gettin' old, an' slow . . . an' I been waitin' a long time to see what God's fixin' to do. If I'm on His side, I reckon there ain't no way I can come up short, an' I reckon them demons or bad folks wouldn't be the only ones what gets to see what God's got

planned . . . I might get a little peek myself. All I got to do is figure where I want to be when it comes."

"I agree," said Pat. "I don't know how much help we'll be,
but I like the thought of having you standing near us."

"I been thinkin' 'bout that," said Mose, "an' you might be
right. At the same time, I hates to see y'all get drawed into it."

Missy and Pat were both shaking their heads. Missy said,
"You've already said that if we're on God's side we can't lose."
She reached out and touched her old friend's arm. "You an' I have
stood too close for too long to start thinkin' about lettin' ourselves
get separated."

Bill's chair was on the edge of the circle and so was his interest; he'd been massaging his knee and listening halfheartedly
while Pat talked. The cool air was encouraging his sore muscles
to stiffen. When the discussion started between Missy and Mose,
he began to shift back and forth in his chair, trying to get comfortable. During a lull in the conversation, he said, "If God is supposed to be protecting us, why would He let these demons or the
Bainbridges find us?"

"For the same reason He does everythin' else," said Mose,
"to bring glory to Hi'self."

Mann didn't try to contain his exasperation. "By getting people killed."

"It ain't somethin' we called to understand . . . an' we won't
'til we gits to Heaven," explained Mose. He made a wide, sweeping motion with his hand. "God sees all the tomorrows at a
glance . . . every minute of 'em. Me an' you can't see nothin' but
now an' yesterday."

"Then what about me?" asked Mann.

Missy looked up. "You?"

"Yeah . . . me. If there's a decision to be made about where
Mose and I go and what we do, shouldn't I get to have an
opinion?"

"Sorry, Bill," Pat said. "I don't think we intentionally left you
out. You've got as much say-so here as anyone else."

"Good," he grumbled, "because I think it's obvious that old man in Mississippi is just guessing, and I'm not interested in planning a fight with goblins. Besides that, if we have to change our identities again, my entry into the Air Force could be delayed." He shifted in his chair again. "I say we stay here."

Bill's mild flare-up shifted Missy's mood in the wrong direction. Her brow furrowed, and she scooted forward in the swing, glaring at the youngest member of the council. "Well, there you are, folks. We've just gotten a short course in spiritual warfare from a man who starts raisin' Cain every time somebody says the name of Jesus in his presence. I swear—"

Mose held up his hand and said, "Here, now . . . let 'im speak, baby. He's a growed man, an' God ain't called us to tell him how to think."

"He's not grown," she snapped. "He's a hardheaded, eighteen-year-old brat who—"

Pat touched a finger to his lips and shook his head. "Easy, hon. Let's not start throwing the furniture."

Missy wasn't amused. "You and Mose can act calm an' cool if you—"

Her husband touched her arm and quoted part of one of her favorite Bible verses, ". . . yet with gentleness and reverence."

Missy clamped her mouth shut and glared at her husband. She knew he was right, but she didn't have to like it.

Bill waited until Missy sat back, then addressed himself directly to her, mirroring her frown as he spoke. "The first time I met you and Pat, I told you I wasn't interested in anything about God, and y'all said you wouldn't try to cram this religion stuff down my throat. If you've changed your mind, you need to say so."

Over the past two years, when Missy and Bill argued, Pat stood between the two strong-willed almost-siblings and tried to teach them both how to make their points with light, not heat. Bill's naturally even-tempered demeanor made him the more adept learner, and his inherent bent toward composure was the catalyst that kept their verbal encounters civil. On this occasion, his willingness to give his emotions a more relaxed rein fired Missy's righteous indignation.

Her brows came together and she said, "Spoken like a man who hasn't seen the destruction a demon-possessed man or animal can unleash." The hound eased to the side to get out of the line of fire.

"Missy, when I was ten years old, I shot and killed two white men who were beating my mother to death, and the three of y'all think they were being influenced by demons. People who aren't too narrow-minded to see reason might think that makes me a veteran."

"You banter that *narrow-minded* phrase around pretty freely, but you're the one who refuses to hear the truth about demons or angels, an' you aren't interested in what we have to say about God. If anyone's narrow-minded an' stubborn, it's you."

"You're saying that because you're mad; you're dodging the issue, and you're turning a discussion into a fight," Bill scolded. "I've been telling you for two years that I'm not going to depend on supernatural forces to bail me out of anything."

"The Supernatural, as you call Him, will be our only ally in a war with demonic forces."

"You're presupposing something I don't believe in, Missy—I have no reason to. If God exists, then He and those angels you talk about stood aside eight years ago and let those two men beat my mom to death. As for demon-possessed people"—he made a dismissive gesture—"that's why Colonel Colt made big handguns. If Poppa believes we can hide here as well as anywhere, then I'm staying here. When it comes right down to it . . . I go where he goes."

While Bill made his short speech, Missy sat back on the swing and took a deep breath. When he finished, she said, "I did this all wrong, an' I'm sorry. Maybe I'm gettin' cantankerous in my old age."

Bill's frown faded by half. "If that's an apology, I accept."

"That's as close as you're gonna get today, bud." She didn't smile, but her voice was softer.

Mose let the two catch their breath, then said, "This'd be a good time to drink a cup of coffee. Let's go in the house."

They were preparing to move indoors when a Sheriff's Department car rounded the curve and slowed in front of the house. When the driver saw who was on the porch of Mose's house, he pulled into the driveway and parked behind the Pattersons' car. "Howdy, folks. Y'all been seeing if you're waterproof?"

They all spoke, and Pat beckoned with his hand. "Have you got time to come in for a minute?"

"Yep." The man shut the car off then stepped out and took off his yellow rain slicker. Deputy Sheriff Clark Roberts was one of eleven people who knew Mose's and Mann's real identities and why they were living in Clear Creek County; if this group wanted to talk to him, he needed to listen. Missy followed the dog into the house. The men stayed on the porch long enough for Patterson to catch Roberts up on their speculations.

When Patterson finished, they moved into the house. Roberts was saying, "I like your plan. Stay where you know the people, keep to your regular routine, and I'm right down the road if you need me." He'd been in the house on several occasions, but this time he was paying closer attention. "Where do you keep your guns?"

Mose gestured at the hall leading from the living room. "We each got one in our bedrooms."

"Judging from what you've told me about those Bainbridge folks, I'd want one in every room." Roberts rubbed his hand across his mouth while he thought about worst-case scenarios, then pointed at a table by the front window. "I'd put another one closer to the front door and hide one in the kitchen."

"That might be good." Mose nodded. "Me an' Bill'll give it some thought."

Mose and Bill trusted the deputy, but they kept silent about their arsenal. The two had let their past experiences guide what measure of protection they might need in the event of another encounter with the Bainbridges, and they turned the home into a small fortress. In addition to a scattering of shotguns and rifles, there were two handguns already stashed in the living room—one in a hidden cubbyhole in the fireplace mantel and one concealed behind a framed Scripture passage on the opposite wall; there were two more in the kitchen, two in each of the bedrooms, and one each in their vehicles—all with rounds in the chambers. Mose supplemented their preparations by praying every day for the Lord's continued protection; Bill checked the guns every Sunday morning to make sure they were ready for use.

Roberts said good night and Bill walked out with him. The rain was all but gone and Roberts could make it to his car without getting wet. They were standing by the deputy's car when Mann pointed at Roberts's waist and said, "Looks like you're carrying a new gun."

Roberts pulled the new revolver and handed it to Mann. "Yeah, a guy in town made me a deal on it . . . .44 Magnum." He looked back at the house. "Come to think of it, I bought it when I was kind of following up on something your granddaddy said."

"Yeah?"

"Mm-hmm. He was looking at that Browning I used to carry . . . asking me if it would stop a man on drugs, that sort of thing. It got me to thinking about what we're hearing from the West Coast, and I decided to shop around a little."

"Well, it definitely looks like it would stop anybody around here—or maybe a train." Bill held the gun at arm's length, pointing it across the road. "Good gosh! The thing must weigh ten pounds."

"Just short of three." Roberts grinned. "Come down to the house and I'll let you try it out. It bangs louder than a shotgun."

"Thanks, anyway." Mann jerked his thumb toward the house. "I'll stick with something I don't have to haul around in a wheelbarrow."

Roberts chuckled. He slipped the pistol back into its holster, fastened the snap, and said, "Call us if you need us."

"Thanks."

Roberts paused with the car door open and said, "Bill."

"Sir?" A breeze moved tree limbs overhead and cold drops of water splashed on the men and car.

"That's a savvy old man in there—and you ain't no slouch yourself—but if I were you I'd assume the worst. I'd figure that fellow who's been prowling around over in Mississippi is real slick, and I'd plan on having him show up where he's least expected."

Bill was too polite to tell Clark he was being overly cautious. "I'll be watching. We both will."

"Well, like I said, I'm here if you need me"—he slid behind the steering wheel—"but I figure anything that happens is going to be over before you can pick up the phone."

"Yes, sir."

Roberts gave his next words some thought then said, "You know about me being in that gunfight a few years back."

Mann said, "I do."

"Well, for what it's worth, I found out a man can do a lot more than he thinks he can, even after he's been shot—he just has to take care of first things first. Remember that."

"Yes, sir." Mann felt cool sweat break out on his brow. "Thanks."

Roberts drove away and leftover rain fell from the trees as Mann hobbled back to the house. When he stepped through the door Missy said, "Okay, Mose, there's nobody here but family now, an' I've got a question. Granny said I wouldn't be here if it wasn't for you . . . why's that?"

Mose took a seat in his chair and leaned the hoe handle against the wall by the fireplace. He said, "How come her to bring that up?"

"It all started when Red told us he thought you might be in trouble. She was tellin' us about how God had picked you for something special, an' that whatever happened to you when you were little had something to do with it. Anyway, she wouldn't tell us what it was—said it was your story."

Mose glanced at the walking stick. "An' she wantin' me to tell it?"

"Well, she didn't say one way or another, but I could use something to take my mind off of all this mess. How 'bout if I make us some fresh coffee an' you tell us the story?"

Mose was tempted, but the rain was gone. He wanted to sit and enjoy watching the woods come back to life—the fireflies would be coming out . . . and maybe the deer. "Well, it's a lot went on in my life you don't know 'bout, an' Bill been wantin' to hear 'bout a tornado I seen once. I figure it might be rainin' again tonight; that means it's gonna be too wet to do anything outside tomorrow." He put his cup on the table by his chair and passed his hand through a short stubble of gray hair. "Why don't y'all come over here after church tomorrow, an' we'll eat some fresh tomato sandwiches an' I'll see can I recollect some of what happened."

Pat picked up on the old man's desire to be alone and stood up. "Good, 'cause I feel like I've been rode hard and put away wet. If there's nothing else we can solve tonight, my wife and I are heading for our house."

Bill pushed the screen door open and stepped out to hold it for Missy and Pat. The dog walked past him and plopped down by a calico cat. Missy stopped and used her finger to tap her almost-brother on the chest. "You're too stubborn." She had yet to smile.

As she stepped past him, Bill stooped his shoulders and copied Missy's drawl. "Sorry, boss lady, I reckon I gits it from my sister."

She looked him in the eye and warned, "I'm mad at you right now 'cause you've been actin' like a jerk, an' I don't feel like jokin' around."

Maybe he was tired, or sore from the falls he'd taken, or maybe just careless—for whatever the reason, Mann missed the warning signs. He had known Missy for two years, but he'd never seen her fully express her frustration. He followed her onto the porch and took their conversation into a minefield. "And that's supposed to scare me?"

The calico was the most perceptive; she was through the closing door and trotting for her sanctuary under Mose's bed before the dog could get his feet under him. Inside the house, Mose was pushing himself out of his chair.

Pat, who was standing by while the exchange was accelerating rapidly in the wrong direction, made a halfhearted attempt to rescue the younger man. "Better leave her alone, ol' buddy. She has what it takes to be . . . umm . . . volatile."

Bill's tone was sharper than he intended when he said, "Really? I thought all you Christians were supposed to be perfect."

Mose was moving toward the porch. When he pushed the screen door open, the dog met him, heading in the other direction. The old man, who had known Missy for thirty years and had seen where her anger could take her, was holding up his hand and warning, "Pat's right, boy, ain't no need to get nobody riled up here."

What had been a verbal altercation could've ended right there, but it didn't happen that way.

Bill turned to Mose and snapped, "I don't need anybody to tell me how to act."

The kid's rash words sounded the opening bell for round one . . . and Pat stepped out of the ring.

Missy's husband was backing a step as her left fist was leaving her side. She was eight inches shorter, sixty-five pounds lighter, and twelve years smarter than her opponent.

Bill, for his part, caught the movement from the corner of his eye and almost smiled—Missy was quick, but she was just a girl. He turned toward the threat, almost negligently, and raised his arm to block the incoming blow. In that same instant—and way too late—he noted that the little athlete shifted her right foot.

*   *   *

Several forces were aligned against Bill Mann. Had any one of four ingredients been absent from the mix—if he had kept his mouth shut, or if he had not spent a few hours getting thrown from Collin Turner's mechanical bull, or if the porch's wood flooring hadn't been rain-slick, or if a spirit being he stubbornly refused to believe in had not been present—he could've been spared a generous dose of humiliation. However . . .

Missy's real target was on the boy's left, and while he was distracted by the feint from his right, she was putting her one hundred and ten pounds of petite pique behind a roundhouse swing at his sore shoulder.

Bill, slightly out of position to his right and fully aware of what was coming from his left, was involuntarily starting to flinch. In a too-little-too-late move, he tried to twist away from her, and pain from the pulled muscle in his abdomen stabbed him so hard he gasped; her tiny fist smashed into his arm a millisecond later and stars exploded behind his eyes.

The punch, and the anticipation of its effect, rocked Bill sideways, and he moved his foot to catch himself. The porch was wet, his heel slipped, and his knee popped loudly and collapsed. He tottered for a long moment on the edge of the porch, windmilling his good arm, and was close to saving himself when an invisible being, bright and beautiful, poked him in the chest. He sailed off the porch and landed in a neatly kept, but soggy, bed of day-lilies.

Somewhere in the world a screen door slammed.

When he got his breath, he groaned; cold drops of water were falling on his face from the edge of the roof. He opened his eyes; Pat and Mose were looking down at him from the porch. Pat had his arms crossed, shaking his head. Mose was saying, "My, my, my." The dog chose that moment to reappear and sit down by Mose's leg; he was withholding comment.

Mann got his good elbow planted and managed to push himself up slightly before he heard the screen door slam again. Three seconds later Missy was standing by the flower bed pointing the sawed-off hoe handle at his chest. "You an' I need to decide if this is over yet."

Bill grumbled a string of curse words, followed by, "You could've hurt me."

"I *did* hurt you, sonny boy"—she stepped closer and prodded his chest hard with the hoe handle—"an' I *will* hurt you. The last twenty-four hours have been wearin' on me, an' I may be a little testy, but you an' I need to get one thing real clear, real quick. I've spent the last two years treadin' lightly around you . . . makin' sure I didn't offend your tender sensibilities . . . but on my best day . . . in my most forgivin' mood . . . I'm not gonna put up with one syllable of you sassin' that man standin' up there on that porch. Do you understand me?"

Bill looked up. Mose, Pat, and the dog looked back.

Pat's eyebrows were raised as if to ask, *Well, dimwit, are we learning anything yet?*

Mose almost smiled and said, "Pat tol' you to leave her alone."

The dog covered his contempt with a yawn.

Bill closed his eyes and took a breath. When he opened them, he looked at Missy. "You're right, and I was wrong. If you'll promise not to hit me with that hoe handle, I'll be respectful for the rest of my life."

Missy wasn't ready to be friends. "Tell him you're sorry."

Bill let himself sink back into the mud because his good arm was getting tired. He looked up from the muddy flower bed at the finest man he knew and said, "Poppa, I'm sorry for acting stupid. I may not always do the right thing, but I'll always be thankful that you're my granddad, and I'll try not to ever make you ashamed of me." He rolled his head toward Missy. "And I'd appreciate it if you'd tell this bully not to hit me with that stick."

Missy didn't wait for Mose to speak. "I guess that'll do."

Mose nodded and smiled; Missy went back into the house to put the hoe handle in its place, and Pat walked down the steps to help Bill out of the flower bed.

When he got the bull rider on his feet, Pat made a pretense of brushing off his young friend's shirt while he confided, "If you ever use profanity in front of her again, I'll tell the other profs in our department that you let a girl sucker-punch you. Fair?" He wasn't smiling.

Bill grimaced. "Sorry 'bout that." He thought for a moment then asked, "Has she ever knocked you into a flower bed?"

Pat remembered sitting on a porch in Mississippi ten years earlier. "The only time I was ever foolish enough to provoke her, she had ten or twelve bruised ribs, but she gave it her best shot."

Bill digested that, then posed his next question. "Am I really as stupid as I feel right now?"

"Well, for a college kid, I'd say you color inside the lines better than most"—Pat had to smile—"but when you decide to stray, it's usually pretty spectacular."

"Is that an answer?"

"Not really."

"Why not?"

"'Cause you ain't ready for the truth, amigo."

Bill dropped the subject because, for Pat, any discussion about truth usually included talking about Christianity.

Missy chose that moment to walk back out on the porch. "Who's ready to go home?"

"Put me down for a couple of those," said Pat.

Bill waited for her to get to the bottom of the steps and said, "I apologize for cussing."

"I forgive you." She stood on her tiptoes to kiss him on the cheek, then looked him in the eye. "I'm gettin' too old for this kind of stuff, an' so are you."

She was right. He said, "I second the motion," and followed the couple to their car.

Pat was opening the door for Missy when he remembered

something. "By the way, our new guy—the undergrad who's gonna be helping out in the office—will be checking in on Monday or Tuesday. Plan on showing him the ropes."

"Yes, sir," answered Mann. "I'll take care of it."

Pat put out his hand. "We'll see you tomorrow after church."

"Yes, sir."

The Pattersons left, and Mann limped back to the house.

He found Mose in the kitchen, standing by the stove. "You need me for anything, Poppa?"

"I reckon not. You goin' to town?"

"Planning on it . . . haven't seen Ella Claire for a while. I'll probably be home before midnight."

"Mm-hmm. Well, I reckon I'll just sit here an' think on my storytellin' for tomorrow."

When Mose's cup was filled, the dog followed him as he carried it back to the living room and picked up his stick. The two took their places out on the porch, and Mose bowed his head. "Lord, You say in Yo' Book that man is born to trouble, an' I reckon I'm proud You sent me my share. I pray, Lord, for what time I got left, that I'll live it good. It ain't in me to know how You gonna use me tomorrow . . . but there ain't nothin' keeps me from believin' that every one of them things You done in my yesterdays was to git me ready for watchin' over this boy today . . . an' I 'preciate it." When the man opened his eyes, his gaze fell on the old sawed-off hoe handle resting by his chair. The stick was as old as he was, and almost as dark . . . glossy from years of use. The man leaned forward to pick it up and ran his fingertips over it, remembering. After a long moment he put it back on the floor and said, "An', Lord, I reckon I'll wait right here an' keep on watchin' till You calls on me. In the meantime, I'd 'preciate it if You'd touch the hearts of them young folks what's gonna hear this story—that they'd hear Yo' voice . . . an' know why You put 'em here."

The dog slept.

The birds were in their nests; the woods were after-rain quiet.

The calico came out of hiding and curled up against the dog.

The fireflies were out in abundance—a hundred points of light, blinking quiet poems of peace.

And Mose sat back with his coffee.

The memories of his distant yesteryears were as bright as the fireflies. He'd lived sixty-eight years under God's guarding wing, watching the events of his life—and of the lives around him—order themselves like a flight of geese . . . moving forward, well aligned, pointing toward one purpose.

In the fall of 1899, his daddy was killed while helping build a gin over in the Mississippi Delta. After the funeral, his momma left the little town of Moores Point and moved five miles south to Cat Lake to live with the only kinfolk she had left—her husband's granddaddy. She'd been a widow for two months when she became a mother.

CHAPTER SIX

He was born right there in that tiny cabin on the east side of Cat Lake. His great-granddaddy helped birth him and named him Moses Lincoln Washington after two great men. He said Moses led his people from the captivity of a nation; Mr. Lincoln led his from the captivity of war. Folks called his great-granddaddy Preacher Washington; Mose called him Pap.

Mose was learning to crawl when Boone Finley came through Moores Point. Boone was a soft-spoken man with wide shoulders and a wider smile. The Yazoo and Mississippi Valley Railroad—the Yellow Dog—was building its way south toward Yazoo City, and Boone was helping lay the track. He attended church on his first Sunday in Moores Point and made the acquaintance of Mose's momma. Two weeks later, when the track was ready to take the steel-driving man south, Boone asked the young widow to go with him.

She sat at the small kitchen table, cradling the child and having a difficult time painting sadness over her excitement. "He's got a good job, Pap, an' the folks on the railroad know he's a steady man. I reckon I just can't let him go."

Pap wasn't trying to act sad; he thought he could see what was coming, and he was praying. He spoke matter-of-factly, "Boone's got what it takes to be a good man, baby, but he ain't quite there yet. Till he gits there, he's gonna be fiddle-footed." He shook his head at the thought of her leaving. "An' the end of the track can be a hard place for a baby boy."

"I was comin' to that, Pap. Boone's lookin' to have steady work through the end of next year. Is it okay if I leave the baby here—just till me an' Boone gets settled?"

"I think that'd be real fine, baby." Pap's prayers had been answered. "The good Lord will see to it that me an' young Mose an' this here dog'll come out on top of whatever comes our way."

Mose's momma was packed and gone inside an hour. She was off the porch and halfway to the road when she remembered she hadn't kissed her baby good-bye.

Preacher Washington was fairly well off for a black man. After the surrender, Major Parker came home from the war and made him a free man. The Major gave Preacher the fine little cabin on Cat Lake, a good mule, and forty acres of prime cotton land; Cat Lake and Pap's piece of ground sat smack in the middle of the Parker plantation. Preacher lived in the tree-shaded cabin by the lake and farmed his forty acres. He outlived his former owner, and he outlived the owner's children. Now, the resident Old Mr. Parker, grandson of the Major, lived in the big white home on the west side of the lake and ran the plantation. Old Mr. Parker's son, Mr. R. D., ran the Parkers' gin in Moores Point.

Preacher firmly believed all men should own a good dog, and when his boy turned three, the old man brought home a Walker coonhound pup. She was mostly white, with black and tan markings. Except for Sunday church, the little tricolor female rarely left Mose's side.

Mose was tall for his age, and by the time he was five, he was picking his share of their cotton and driving his great-granddaddy's wagon a little. In the fall of his eighth year, on a warm Saturday morning, Pap was busy overseeing the picking of the small crop and asked Mose if he thought he and the dog could take a load of cotton to the gin by themselves.

In years past, when the wagon went to the gin, the boy and dog clambered up and rode in the back, playing on top of the cotton or napping in the sun. Ten minutes after Pap asked his question, the barefoot boy and his dog were on the wagon seat. The boy sat with the reins loose in his hands, straight and relaxed; the dog was alert, expectant. They were waiting on final orders from the boss.

"Folks here 'bouts know who you belong to, so they won't be botherin' you. If you come on any troublesome strangers, you let 'em talk to the dog."

"Yessuh." Mose nodded, and the dog sneezed.

"It's Saturday, an' there'll be boys at the gin. You doin' a man's job today, so don't be lettin' 'em pull you into no shenanigans; you ain't got the time."

"Yessuh."

Pap put a sawed-off piece of hoe handle on the floor by the boy's feet and a Bible on the seat. "Just let the mules alone an' they'll take you across the bridge an' straight to the gin." He touched the Bible. "You can get in some readin' while you on the road."

"Yessuh." The boy reached over and put the Bible on the floor by the makeshift club.

"Mr. R. D. Parker'll be at the gin, an' he knows me. If you got any questions, you ask him."

"Yessuh." Mose knew what R. D. Parker looked like. Mr. R. D. and his wife lived with the Old Parkers in the big house across the lake.

Pap pointed at the hoe handle. "An that ain't for fightin', it's for sho' 'nuff bad trouble. Understand?"

"Yessuh."

"You ain't full growed yet, boy, but you doin' a man's job. If the trouble's bad enough for you to pull out that stick, don't be holdin' back. Understand?"

"Yessuh."

"You need anything else?" Pap asked.

Mose smiled because he knew the answer. "No, sir. I got this dog, an' this here stick, an' I got God."

Pap smiled back. "An'?"

"An' I always got my guardian angel."

Pap reached up to pat him on the leg. "God sho' done me a good turn when He let me have you for my boy."

The Parker Gin was five miles from Cat Lake and a world away.

Two hours after they left the quiet of the lake, he and the dog pulled into a long line of wagons waiting to have their cotton sucked into the gin. A confusion of what looked like two dozen workers, all of them black, circulated in the gin area. Those who were operating the machinery or moving the cotton bales were preoccupied with their jobs; the rest were constantly yelling at each other. Every surface within a hundred yards was coated with a thin snowfall of white lint. The drivers of the other wagons, seemingly heedless of the noise and activity, napped here and there in the shade or stood in small pockets and visited while they waited their turn to unload their cotton. The wagon stopped and the dog stood up and stretched. When her boy didn't climb down to mix with the other boys, the dog went back to her nap.

Several ramshackle saloons backed up to the alley across from the gin. They were payday-busy; their back doors were open, and noisy music competed with the machinery from the gin. Black men and women came and went through the doors—talking too loud, laughing louder.

An hour or so later, Mose's wagon was sandwiched between the gin's loading platform and the back door of a whiskey joint called The Delta Belle; Mose was immersed in reading his Bible. He caught the movement of the wagon in front of him and clicked at his mules without looking up. The mules were leaning into the harness when a man stumbled out the back door of the Belle, bumped into the mule on the right, and went to his knees in the dirt. Mose held the team and waited while a skinny white man with a full beard struggled to get to his feet. When the man got up he slapped the mule with his hat and cussed at Mose.

The dog sat up and growled at the shabby-looking white man.

Mose shushed the dog and did like Pap taught him; he ducked his head while saying, "Sorry, boss."

The white man didn't reply, and Mose raised his eyes to watch the man stagger over to stand by the stairs to the loading platform; he was drinking a clear liquid from a Mason jar. The jar disappeared inside the folds of a soiled coat, and its owner lurched up the steps. The dog was standing on the wagon seat—trembling slightly, her hackles up—tracking every move the man made.

The drunk's unsteady foot was on the top step when he found himself confronted by a black wall in the form of a certain Willie Edwards. Willie was Mr. R. D.'s head man at the gin for at least three reasons: he was smart, he knew how to handle men, and he was only slightly smaller than a pair of draft horses. The big black man said something Mose couldn't hear, and the white man started yelling and cussing loudly enough to be heard over the racket surrounding them.

Being this close to a quarrel between grown men, especially between a white man and a Negro, made the boy uneasy. He wanted to get off the seat and move away from the confrontation, but Pap had trusted him with the wagon. He looked to see what the other drivers were doing.

Every man in sight was staring at the two men on the loading platform; if anything, they were more troubled than the young boy. A cluster of drivers near Mose's wagon watched the action and talked in hushed tones about the white man. Mose heard one say, "That there's one of them trashy Pommer folks. He been bad drunk since yesterday."

Mose didn't know that he'd ever seen any Pommers, but he'd heard the talk. Folks said they were a "nest of po' white trash what lives in them shanties out to Mossy Island." The same folks said the Pommers were moonshiners.

The white man tried to push the black giant out of his way and lost his balance. Edwards caught Pommer's arm to save him from falling, and the drunk's cussing got louder.

One of the other drivers laughed nervously. "He ain't gonna git by Willie."

Pommer was waving his arms and yelling, working himself up to take a swing at Willie, when a young white man Mose recognized stepped out of the gin office.

Mose leaned toward the group of drivers. "What'll Mr. R. D. do to that man?"

If the man who turned to answer him was surprised to see a seven-year-old boy driving a wagon, he didn't show it; colored folks grew up early in cotton country. "Whatever it takes. His poppa owns this here gin."

"Mm-hmm," a second driver agreed. "An' folks knows Mr. R. D. totes a mean gun."

R. D. Parker had Willie step back and spoke to Pommer without raising his voice. Pommer turned his anger on the young white man and continued his ranting. Each time the drunk paused for breath Parker would say quiet words and point at the stairs.

When Pommer backed a step and moved a hand inside his coat, one of the drivers said what every man there already knew. "Uh-oh! He goin' for his knife."

Willie Edwards was as quick as he was big. Before Pommer could slip the skinning knife from its scabbard, the giant grabbed the white man by his greasy collar and the seat of his britches, swung him out like a sack of cotton, and dropped him face-first off the platform. The man landed on the ground by the front wheel of Mose's wagon—the sound of breaking glass accompanied his impact. The pocket of men next to Mose's wagon retreated to the far side of the alley.

Parker and Edwards stood on the edge of the platform and watched as Pommer used the front wheel of Mose's wagon to pull himself up, climbing the spokes like a ladder, cussing as he climbed. The air around the man was saturated with the stench of sour sweat and moonshine-soaked clothing.

Mose didn't want to be within reach of the man's knife, and he wanted to get away from the smell. He was sliding to the far side of the wagon seat when Pommer's fingers grasped the side of the wagon; his face came into view a second later. The fall from the platform had cost the belligerent drunk part of a front tooth; blood from his nose and mouth was dribbling into the thick beard, mixing with a thick crust of dried snuff.

"What're you lookin' at, boy?"

Mose fastened his eyes on the floor of the wagon. "Nothin', boss."

Pommer's smile transformed his face into a mask of wickedness. "I think you're lookin' at my face, boy. I reckon maybe you'd think I's prettier if'n you didn't have no eyeballs."

Mose's knees were trembling. He kept his eyes fixed on the floor of the wagon— and saw the wooden club. "No, suh, boss."

Parker watched the man by the wagon and knew instinctively where he would focus his meanness. He started down the steps two-at-a-time, saying, "Hold it there, Ced."

Ced Pommer muttered garbled profanity at Parker and reached for a handhold on the wagon seat . . . and everything seemed to happen at once.

Pommer pulled his knife.

Mose dove for the club.

A man nearby yelled, and Parker vaulted the stair railing.

The dog growled and went for Pommer's throat.

Mose dropped the club and grabbed for the dog.

Pommer screamed and tumbled backward, taking the boy and dog with him.

CHAPTER SEVEN

Pommer's beard probably saved him from a bad mauling.

Mose was spraddled on top of the pile, trying to pull the dog off the man. The hound had a mouthful of the greasy hair, snarling and shaking it like she would a boar coon. The drunk was fighting the dog and wrestling to get on top of his attackers, trying to bring the knife into play. He made one swipe with the blade, cutting the dog's ear before Mose got his arms around his bodyguard and rolled clear.

Pommer was on all fours, scrambling after Mose, when Parker kicked his hands out from under him and stomped down on his arm; the gin man was holding Mose's sawed-off hoe handle. "You can put up the knife, Ced, or I can break your scrawny neck. You choose."

Pommer couldn't move his arm. He nodded.

Parker stepped back to let the man up. "I don't have time to mess with fools, Pommer. When you get drunk, you stay clear of the gin."

Pommer got to his feet and propped himself against the loading dock. The drunk confirmed that alcohol can always be depended on to erode good judgment by saying, "Next time, I might be seein' how high an' mighty you an' that big buck'll be if'n I bring one of my brothers with me."

"You do that, bub." Parker leaned the hoe handle against Mose's wagon and smiled at the thought of something that would plant a seed of horror in the man's heart. "Come on a Saturday, Ced, an' every colored man in town can watch while I let Willie beat the both of you like a pair of borried mules. Now scat, before I decide to start the show today."

Pommer tried to sneer at the staring faces around him—not an easy thing when your nose and lips are split and bleeding. As he passed by Mose he growled, "I'll be seein' you an' that dog again."

The dog growled back. Mose held his arm around her neck and told her to hush.

Pommer shuffled down the alley, weaving from side to side, and turned toward Main Street.

Parker waited until the drunk was away from the gin and turned his attention to Mose. "You all right, boy?"

It was the first time a white man ever asked Mose a question. He released the dog and stood up. "Yessuh, we fine. He cut Lady's ear some, but she been done worse by a bad coon."

"What's your name?"

"Moses Lincoln Washington, boss."

"Mm-hmm." Parker stroked his cheek while he studied the boy and his companion. "You're Preacher Washington's boy?"

"Yessuh. His great-grandson."

"How old are you?"

Talking to Mr. R. D. wasn't much different from talking to Pap. "Goin' on eight, boss."

"Seven? How'd it happen that you brought that wagon to town by yourself?"

Mose stood straighter and almost smiled. "Pap sent me, boss. He busy with the pickin'."

Parker thought for a moment then said, "Tell Preacher I said

I don't want you bringin' the wagon up here by yourself. Tell him to send a regular driver an' hold you back for a few years."

Mose's shoulders sagged; the white man didn't think he was man enough to do the driving. "Yessuh, boss, I'll tell 'im."

Parker said, "Tell Preacher I don't want to risk havin' the team get away from you."

Mose kept his eyes on the ground. The mules were both well trained and steady, but he knew better than to argue. "Yessuh, boss, I'll tell 'im."

Parker turned back to the steps, but the arrival of a new Packard motorcar stopped him. A young woman wearing a bulky duster and riding boots jumped down from the driver's seat and ran toward him. He braced himself, and Young Mrs. Parker, the former Virginia Allen of Indianola, shocked her audience by tackling him around the neck and letting him lift her off the ground. When she kissed the man on the lips, Mose got busy looking at something else.

"It's wonderful!" she squealed. "And it's faster than the train, and it doesn't blow cinders!"

Parker laughed at her. "Happy anniversary."

"How long will it last?"

"Hopefully, for several more anniversaries." Her husband was not surprised that a key person was absent. "I thought I told Henry to drive you."

Virginia Parker stepped back, held one arm out, and parodied a fashion model's pose. The duster she wore fit her like a tent—the bottom six inches drug the ground, the tips of her fingers were peeking out from under the rolled-up sleeves. "I'm the driver now, 'cause Henry's a scaredy-cat." She was laughing with every breath. "I can walk faster than he makes it go, so he can just stay at home."

The young woman's husband enjoyed the sound of her happiness. "You're the boss." He looked toward the new automobile. "Who's with you?"

"Evalina and her baby. I'm taking them by the doctor's." She wrapped her arms around one of his and started back to her new car. "You want me to come back by and give you a ride to the house?"

"Better not." He pulled out a gold pocket watch. "I'll see you back at the lake—probably after dark."

She mounted the seat, blew him a kiss, and laughed again. "Your loss."

Parker did not think of himself as a romantic, but when he looked at his wife, he knew why men wrote poetry. He watched her wrestle the vehicle into a turn, narrowly miss colliding with a cotton wagon, experiment with the levers and controls until she could make it go backward, then experiment again to get it moving forward. She grinned throughout the entire maneuver.

She waved and drove off; the expression on her face was a mixture of stern concentration and childish delight.

Parker thought, *They ought to tell men that if they buy their wives an automobile, everybody in the whole house will be happy. They would sell hundreds.*

He turned to mount the steps and his eyes fell on Mose. The boy sat with his dog by the wagon wheel; the child was as sad as Parker's wife was happy. He made a detour, and the boy and dog both stood as he approached.

Parker picked up Mose's stick and dropped it in the wagon. "Time'll pass fast enough, Mose. You'll be drivin' plenty."

"Yessuh."

The man put his hand in his pocket and pulled out a penny. "This might help. You can go to the store an' get you some striped candy. It'll help you grow faster."

Mose backed a step. "I'm much obliged, boss, but I reckon me an' Pap'll be makin' some m'lasses candy this fall."

Parker was mildly surprised by the boy's response. He nodded and was turning away when Mose's Bible caught his eye. "Is that Preacher's Bible?"

"No, suh. It's mine."

"Aren't you a little young to be readin' a Bible?"

"I don't know, boss." If he wasn't old enough to drive the wagon, Mr. R. D. might want him to stop reading. "You want me quit readin'?"

"No, no, boy." Parker smiled and picked up the tattered book. "I was just askin' if you're old enough to know how to read."

"Yessuh. I been readin' for long as I been rememberin', just like everybody else."

Seven-year-old colored boys who were able to read were a rarity, and Parker decided a test was in order. "How about readin' me a verse?"

"A verse, boss?"

"Mm-hmm." Parker let the Bible fall open and handed it to Mose. "Read me one of those verses."

When Mose looked at the page without saying anything, Parker misread his hesitation and smiled. The boy kept his eyes on the page and asked, "I can just pick the one I want, boss?"

Parker said, "That'll be fine."

"This here is one of my favorites; it's Ephesians, chapter six, verse twelve." The boy held the book close to his chest and followed the small print with his finger. " 'For we wrestle not against flesh an' blood, but against principalities, against powers, against the rulers of the darkness of the world, against spiritual wickedness in high places.' "

Parker had been wrong—and he surprised himself by feeling relieved. The little boy was smart, and old Preacher Washington was teaching him well. "Well, Mose, it sounds like you might be plannin' on goin' to war against those rulers of darkness."

Mose didn't know the man was kidding him. He said, "We already in the war, boss. The Book says it real clear."

Parker smiled down at the boy. "An' you're plannin' on fightin'?"

"Already am, boss—every day—everybody is."

"Well, I guess you might have to fight for both of us then, 'cause I've got my hands full with this gin." Parker had wasted enough time with the child. He waved a casual finger at the boy's stick and spoke as he walked away. "If you get the chance, throw in a good lick for me."

While Mose was reading to the white man, Pommer was watching Virginia Parker drive down the street and stop in front of the doctor's house. When the woman climbed down from the Packard, he watched every move she made. She stood by the automobile and removed the too-big duster; beneath it she was wearing a white blouse with lace at the throat, tan jodhpurs, and polished riding boots—and she was beautiful. A black woman carrying a baby got out of the back of the car and followed the white woman up the gravel path. The man would not be interested to know that the visit to the doctor was to confirm something the woman already suspected.

When they were inside, the man stood looking at the doctor's house and thinking of the woman. He wondered what the high and mighty gin boss would think if he found that pretty little wife of his with her throat cut. The man took his time and walked around the car, looking at it up close. Minutes later he was on his way out of town, walking south on the lake road, becoming more sober and more determined with every step.

The next hour or two went slow for Mose. He read his Bible, and he and the dog dozed. When they finished getting his cotton into the gin, he took the ticket and turned the mules toward Cat Lake. The trip home would be faster; the wagon was lighter, and the mules knew they were on their way to the barn.

Trees on the west side of the road shaded the wagon and its crew. Mose had the reins across his arm and held his Bible in his lap. The noisy motorcar passed him when he was a couple miles south of town; otherwise, traffic on the road was sparse. The late-afternoon temperature was warm; a red-tailed hawk drifted aimlessly on the last of the day's rising air. The rhythmic crunch of the mules' hooves on the gravel and the jingling from the harness eventually lulled the boy to sleep. The boy's angel stood near, watching, guarding—waiting for the appointed moment.

The wagon was nearing Cordy Brake when the angel leaned close and whispered to the dog. The dog sprang to her feet and growled, waking Mose in time for him to watch her spring from the seat and land on the red mule. In the blink of an eye, she nimble-footed her way down the length of the mule's back and launched herself at a point out in front of the team. Mose looked past the dog and saw two women about two hundred yards down the road. It was Young Mrs. Parker and Mrs. Evalina Daniels; they were pulling a log out of the road so their car could pass. The women got the log out of the way and straightened.

Mose was trying to figure out why the dog would get so excited, when Pommer stepped out of the woods between him and the women. The man was facing the women, holding his knife behind his back; he was moving slowly, sneaking closer to the women when they saw him. At that same moment Mose clicked at the mules and said, "Hup, there, Red! Hup, now!"

The mules started to jog. Mose watched the three people near the car. The dog was sprinting toward the man, raising a small trail of dust, straining for more speed.

When the man with the knife reached in the car and took out a small bundle, Evalina Daniels covered her mouth in an effort to stifle her cry. Her reaction made the man laugh. The dog was mere seconds from the scene, running hard and quiet.

Mose could hear Pap saying, "If the trouble's bad enough for you to pull out that stick, don't be holdin' back. Understand?" He got a hand on his club and slapped the mules hard with the reins. "Yah, mule! Yah!" The mules began to run.

Pommer stooped over and put the bundle on the ground. He straightened in time to see the women's mouths drop open—they were looking at something behind him. He turned in time for a tricolored blur to ram into him, hitting him just above his belt buckle. The man's explosion of breath mixed with his yell, and the dog's momentum carried them to the ground in a tangle of long ears, flailing arms, and angry sounds. Evalina Daniels scurried past the fight to get her child; Virginia Parker was turning in a tight circle, searching the ground desperately for something she could use for a weapon.

The boy's club felt heavy in his hand, the mules were galloping, and the man was getting the better of the dog. He didn't close his eyes, but he prayed, "Lord, please take care of my dog, an' just help me to make You proud."

In the next instant, he hurled himself off the wagon—leading with his bare feet—and crashed into the fight—temporarily disarming the man and knocking him off the dog. The boy rolled and skidded in the gravel. When he gained his feet, he had his stick back, ready to strike.

It was hard to tell who was getting the worst end of the fight. The dog bayed and yipped and growled; Pommer was snarling and yelling cusswords. The man had his hand on his knife when Mose hit him in the shoulder with the club—the blow didn't faze him.

Pommer left trying to pin the dog and was on his feet in the next instant, crouched and moving in on Mose when the dog came in from the man's left, snapped at his arm, and got his sleeve. The man twisted his hand, caught the dog on the back of the neck, and pinned her to the ground, yelling, "Gotcha!"

Mose Washington was going to be a baseball player when he got big enough. The club he was holding was his practice bat, pitted and nicked from the thousands of pebbles the boy had tried to knock across Cat Lake. From the edge of the water in front of their cabin, it was three or four hundred feet across the lake, and Pap said Mose was "gonna knock enough gravel out there for folks to walk from one side to the other on dry ground." The youngster hadn't hit any rocks as far as the middle of the lake yet, but he came closer every day.

*　*　*

R. D. Parker left the gin early, and, in an effort to get home before dark, he was letting his horse have its head; the gray had been corralled for three days, and he was moving along well. They were north of Cordy Brake when something on the strip of road through the brake attracted the man's attention. As he watched, a person jumped from the seat of a fast-moving wagon and landed on something in the road. The wagon kept traveling, giving him a clear view of the scene. His wife's car was stopped in the middle of the road. He could make out his wife standing by the ditch on the left; people who looked to be fighting were rolling around near the car. He kicked the horse with his heels and spoke once. In three strides the big gray was stretched out, and Parker was leaning out along the horse's neck. "C'mon, boy, we need to be gettin' there."

Evalina was whining with frustration. She couldn't leave M'Virginia to handle the man by herself, but there was no safe place for her to put the baby; the baby had gone from crying to screaming. She watched the boy's club bounce off the man's shoulder and came to the realization that the three of them would all fight together or the man would kill them one at a time.

"Lord God in Heaven, save us!"

She put the baby on the ground by the car and went back to the battle.

Young Mrs. Parker watched Evalina put the baby down and move toward the man holding the dog down.

The young colored boy had a long stick, but he was no match for the man. The man pinned the dog and raised his knife.

The boy squared himself at the man, spread his feet apart, and took a batter's stance. The dog was yipping and growling, fighting desperately to escape the man's grip. The baby was screaming in the background.

Parker could see the knife suspended over a form in the road. He wanted to yell, but he was too far away to be heard.

Pommer held the knife poised over the struggling animal; the two women and the boy froze as he looked up—grinning and triumphant—making sure they would see what he was going to do to the dog. He leered at Virginia Parker and said something that was drowned out by the dog's yelping—but the woman read the message in his eyes. When Pommer turned to face the young black boy, the hoe handle was already closing on its mark.

An angel can move across the universe in the time it took for the slender baseball bat to travel those last few inches. Pommer managed to turn his head.

The gray was back on its haunches, sliding to a stop, when Parker left the saddle, running when he hit the ground.

His wife was on her knees by the side of the road. He ran to her and knelt to take her by the arms. "Are you all right?"

The woman seized him and held on, pressing her face against his chest, clinging to him. Both were out of breath; Parker couldn't tell which of them was trembling. "Are you hurt?"

She managed to shake her head. "I'm not hurt."

He pried her loose and held her at arm's length so he could look at her. She was too pale.

She said, "I need to sit down."

He took her hands and stood up. "Let's get you to the motorcar."

She shook her head and stayed on her knees. "Not there . . . here. I just want to sit here."

He helped her sag sideways until she was sitting with her feet tucked next to her. She looked past his shoulder and said, "See about them."

Parker stood up and surveyed the scene around him.

Evalina had followed her mistress's lead and was sitting in the roadbed. She was rocking back and forth, cooing to the baby; her face was wet with tears. The baby's cries were subsiding.

The cotton wagon had slowed some, but its team was still headed for the barn.

Ced Pommer was splayed on his back in front of the automobile.

The boy was kneeling in the road. He held his dog close, whispering to her—the hoe handle was near his hand; when Parker looked at him he stood. Parker moved in their direction and the dog took a step forward, positioning herself between her boy and the white man. When Parker kept coming the hound growled.

Parker stopped. "What's her name?"

The little boy rested his hand on the dog. "Lady, boss."

The man squatted down and held out his hand. "C'mere, Lady. Nobody's gonna hurt anybody here. C'mon, girl, every-thing's okay now."

Mose nudged the dog, and she sniffed at the man's hand.

When the dog was placated, Parker looked at the boy. "How're you doin'?"

Mose was looking at Ced Pommer. "I guess I ain't doin' too good, boss. I ain't ever hit nobody with a stick before."

"You had it to do, Mose." He waved a hand behind him. "I could see it from back yonder. If you hadn't stopped him, he would've killed somebody—maybe everybody here. Lady would be dead for sure."

"Yessuh, he sho' would've done that." Mose sank slowly back to his knees, and the dog moved closer to him. "Sorry, boss. I reckon my legs was gettin' weak."

"I understand." Parker looked at the body behind him then turned back to the boy. "Mose?"

"Yessuh?"

"We're the only people who know what happened here." Parker motioned with his hand. "I'm gonna tell my wife and Evalina to keep this all a secret, an' I'll talk to Preacher. Can you keep it a secret till we get this sorted out?"

"Yessuh."

"This is the most serious thing that's happened around here in a long time, Mose. Don't even tell your best friend. Okay?"

"I understand, boss. I won't tell nobody."

"Good."

R. D. Parker left Mose and leaned over the man by the car. Ced Pommer had a depression an inch deep in his left temple. Parker said, "Small loss," and drug the man's body off the road and several yards into the woods. When he got back to the others he started giving directions to get people into the car. Evalina Daniels and the baby went in first. The boy hesitated before putting his foot on the running board and asked, "Can Lady ride with me?"

Young Mrs. Parker offered him a weak smile and answered, "Lady is welcome to do whatever she likes."

Parker walked his wife to the car. "Are you gonna drive home?"

"Uh-uh." She shook her head. "Let the gray go by himself. I'll show you how to drive."

Mose rode on the back seat with Miz Evalina and her baby; Mr. R. D. and his wife sat up front talking quietly. At one point, when the white lady leaned close and whispered in his ear, Mr. R. D. came close to running the automobile off the road.

Preacher Washington came out on the red mule and met them when they were almost to Gilmer's Grove. Parker got the car stopped and said, "Everything's fine, Preacher. Follow us on up to the house, an' I'll tell you what happened."

Old Mr. Parker joined them when they got to the backyard of the big white house.

The two white men and Pap visited; Mose and Lady sat in the grass under one of the big oaks; Red was content to crop grass along the lake bank. Every now and then, one of the men would turn and look at the quiet boy. While the three men conferred, Evalina Daniels came out the back door of the Parkers' house and brought Mose a big ham sandwich, a piece of apple pie, and a cup of cold milk. The dog was served the finest plate of scraps she'd ever eaten.

The sun was dropping behind the trees and the katydids were starting to sing by the time the men finished talking. R. D. Parker walked with Preacher to where Mose and the dog waited. They both stood up, and Parker said, "Mose, I just told Preacher you're man enough to drive your mules to our gin any time he wants you to."

It was the best news Mose ever heard, but he wasn't ready to smile yet. "I'm obliged to you, boss."

"It was a hard thing you did."

"Yessuh," the boy agreed. "It wasn't what I wanted."

Parker nodded. "I know."

Preacher heard something in the boy's words Parker missed. The old man touched Mose's shoulder and said, "I don't understand."

"I was gonna try to knock his knife loose 'cause I reckon I couldn't bring myself to kill a man over a dog." He touched his best friend and sighed. "Not even Lady."

Preacher nodded. "But you changed your mind."

"Yessuh." Mose held on to the dog with a trembling hand and looked at the ground, stirring grass blades with his toes. "When he was holdin' Lady in the dirt an' laughin', that man looked at M'Virginia an' said, 'I got somethin' special waitin' for you.' " The little black boy's eyes brimmed over with tears when he looked up at Parker. "I tol' you at the gin we was in a battle, but you said you was too busy to fight. You tol' me if I got the chance, to throw in a good lick for you. When that man said them words, I know'd that's what I had to do."

Parker opened his mouth, but no words came out. After a long moment, he took his hat off and stood without moving, unable to take his eyes off Mose. When his first tear came, he wiped his cheek and knelt in front of the boy.

It was a struggle, but the man managed to croak, "I appreciate that, Mose." He wanted to say more, but the words were trapped behind his emotions. Finally, he shook his head, stood up, and walked back to the big house.

Pap put his arm on Mose's shoulders and started for home with their mule and the dog. When they got to the middle of the Cat Lake bridge, Pap stopped.

He looked down at his boy and said, "You done a good thing, Mose."

"Yessuh."

"Mr. R. D. just told me his wife's gonna have a baby. I figure you saved 'em both."

Mose nodded. "Yessuh."

"I hate to tell you this, boy, but you need to go see yo' momma for a while."

"My momma? How come?"

"Boy, the good Lord knows you done a needed thing when you hit that white man in the head, but them sorry Pommers won't see it that way. Folks might remember that you were in that set-to at the gin today, an' they might get to blabbin' about it. We need to give 'em time to forget."

Mose couldn't remember a time when he talked back to the man. "I ain't wantin' to go, Pap."

Preacher knelt in the dust on the bridge and put his hand on the boy's shoulder. "The good Lord knows I don't want it either, son, but we ain't got a choice. Me an' you will pray every day for

God to bring you back home soon, but in the mornin' we gonna be on that southbound Yellow Dog."

"How long you reckon I'll be gone?"

"The Lord'll decide that, boy."

Mose dropped to his knees by the man. "Lord, Jesus, I'm obliged to You for protectin' me an' them other folks today. I ain't wantin' to be away from Pap, Lord, but if I got to be gone, I ask that You'd keep me mindful of You. If You'd see fit, I'd 'preciate it if You'd bring me home right soon. Amen."

Pap said, "Amen."

True to the man's word, Preacher and his boy were on the train to south Mississippi the next morning. Lady traveled in the baggage car.

They rode for two hours through the Delta, stopping at every little town they came to. When they got to Yazoo City the train started up the first hill. They changed trains in Jackson, and five hours later they were standing on the station platform in Purvis, Mississippi.

The boy stood still and held on to his dog while Pap talked to his momma. The sky was a deep blue, but it was hard to see because there were so many trees.

When Pap's train was ready to leave, he knelt by the boy and said, "I'll be prayin' for you."

"Yes, sir. Me, too."

"I want you to be brave."

"I will, Pap."

They say Ced Pommer turned up missing sometime during the fall of '07.

Nobody cared.

CHAPTER EIGHT

Purvis, Mississippi . . . mid-April . . . 1908.

Still, hot air surrounded a desperate struggle.

Three white boys were piled on top of a black one—all three trying to cuss, beat, and kick him at the same time; so far, the cussing was the only thing they were managing to do effectively. A young white girl stood at the edge of the conflict, her eyes squeezed shut, her head bowed over tightly clasped hands. Grunts and harsh words coming from the tumbling boys conspired with thick dust in the street to muffle the sounds of an approaching horse.

The white boys were on the verge of getting their attack organized when the air above the miniature battle was rent by a harsh *Sweesh!* punctuated by a sharp *Whap!*—the sounds of fast-moving leather meeting denim-covered flesh. The biggest white boy squealed and abandoned the fight; his two cronies rolled over to see what had happened to their leader and came to rest squinting up at the sole of a man's riding boot.

"Would someone care to tell me what's going on here?" The answer to the girl's prayer was a slender man riding a bay mare. He sat straight in the saddle, his right fist resting on his leg—on the hottest day they'd seen, he was wearing a starched, collarless shirt, buttoned at the neck.

The white boys got to their feet and became interested in their bare toes. All three boys wore their hair long; the biggest boy's hung over his eyes.

When no one answered him, the rider rested his quirt on the tallest boy's shoulder and drawled, "Would you be the oldest?"

Every facet of the man, from his steel-rimmed spectacles to the pistol on his belt, spoke of severity. The stout thirteen-year-old pushed back his hair and eyed his companions first, then peered over his shoulder as if wishing for someone to rescue him from any coming wrath. The quick search informed him he was on his own. He rubbed the material on the seat of his overalls up and down while he answered, "Yes, sir, I reckon."

Cold gray eyes appraised the boy; the impatient quirt began to tap the side of the rider's boot. "Then answer my question."

The boy moved back in an effort to distance himself from the whip's reach and jerked his head at the black youngster. "We was just teachin' this here nigger some manners, Mr. Gilmer."

The colored boy had rolled over and made it to a kneeling position before stopping to catch his breath. He looked to be four or five years younger than his adversaries.

"Mm-hmm." Gilmer let the whip dangle from its wrist strap and stepped off the horse to watch the black child get to his feet. A trickle of blood came from the small boy's nose and he had a cut under his left eye, but he had given as good as he got.

"How about that, boy?" The man didn't smile. "Are you in need of a lesson in manners from three fine gentlemen who outweigh you by thirty pounds apiece?"

The black boy was eight years old and hadn't spent much time around white folks. This white man had a face like a hawk—quick and hard—but his words sounded fair. He recovered enough of his breath to straighten. "I don't reckon, boss, an' I'm obliged to you for steppin' in."

Gilmer nodded. "What's your name?"

"Moses Lincoln Washington, boss. Folks calls me Mose."

"Well, Mose, if you don't need a lesson in manners, who might?"

If he told the truth, the white boys would catch him when the white man wasn't around and exact their revenge, but his great-granddaddy told him a million times, *It's no matter if he's black or white, boy—if a man ain't got honor, he ain't got nothin'.* He took another deep breath and nodded toward the surly white boys. "Them three was sayin' unseemly things an' pluckin' at that lady's dress."

Harley Crawford forgot about the hot spot on his backside and yelled, "He's a bald-face liar!" The other white boys chimed in on the chorus and started shouting accusations against Mose.

Jacob Gilmer held up his arm and Mose noticed for the first time that the man's cuff was sewn together at the wrist. The white man was missing his left hand, but none of his sway; at his signal, the mouths of the three white boys clamped shut.

The man turned to the girl and spoke too crisply. "Well, miss."

The frightened girl flinched at his words. Her hands were intertwined tightly at her chest, her head bowed. Her thin cotton dress was faded but clean; the hem trembled in time with her shoulders. She looked to be eleven or twelve.

"Yes, sir?" As she spoke, she moved one foot back slowly and let her knees bend in a small curtsy—a simple gesture steeped in natural charm.

The girl's ladylike deference startled the man and opened the gates of his memory to thoughts of yesteryears—of gracious ladies in sweeping gowns, attended by men who valued honor above life. His cheeks turned a deep pink, and he reached up and removed his hat. "It appears that I have forgotten myself. Speaking harsh words to a lady is too close to being a sin, ma'am, and I apologize. If you would be kind enough to forgive me, I would be long in your debt."

The earnest quality of his words and the change in tone

attracted the girl's gaze to the man's face. A full mustache, dark red sprinkled with white, accentuated a naturally stern expression, but the gray eyes had softened. He stood relaxed, holding the white Panama hat under his shortened arm, waiting patiently for her response. Her whispered words were as grace-filled as her curtsy. "I forgive you."

"Then I am, as I said, in your debt." All four boys stared as the man saluted her with a shallow bow. "Would it suit you to tell me what happened here?"

Her eyes went from the man to the three boys. Harley Crawford had started in on her at recess that day—and he had the worst reputation of any boy in town. The other two, Roscoe Weems and Dee Henry, weren't too bad when they weren't with Crawford. "I don't want to get in any trouble."

Gilmer's eyes followed hers to the boys. "I can assure you, ma'am, there will be no trouble. Ever." His last word sounded like the prelude to a death sentence.

The girl's thin chest rose and fell. "It was like that colored boy said—they were waitin' here in the street when I was comin' home from school. I tried to run, but they caught me an' started in to . . . uh . . . pester me."

Gilmer shifted so that he was facing the three white boys. "Pester you?"

Dee Henry, the smallest of the three white boys, paled and his lower lip began to tremble.

"Yes, sir." A slender finger escaped the twisted hands at her chest and pointed at Mose. "That one came along an' told 'em to stop, an' when they didn't, he picked up a stick"—the finger moved to point at Crawford—"an' jumped on that one."

The Crawford boy stepped close and sneered, "Why, she ain't nuthin' but trash. An' besides that, she—"

In his haste to defend himself, the boy forgot what he should've remembered about Mr. Gilmer. Harley Crawford was on his back in the dust before his senses told him that the back of the man's hand had put him there.

* * *

In the fall of 1863, Jacob Gilmer was serving in the Army of the Confederacy—a thin, bookish-looking, nineteen-year-old lieutenant in Walthall's Mississippians. At the Battle of Chickamauga, during a bitter fight near Reed's Bridge Road, a Yankee minnie ball cut a wicked groove across his palm. Compared to the carnage around him, the wound was insignificant. The lieutenant tied his scarf around his hand and carried on, but the wound continued to bleed. An hour later another bullet cut his scalp. In due course, exhaustion and blood loss took his consciousness, and a drunk surgeon took his hand. When he returned home after the war, the citizens of Purvis found that—along with the hand he left in Georgia—the austere young officer had buried any disposition to suffer fools.

Gilmer stepped close to the boy in the dirt, planted a polished boot in the center of his chest, and leaned over him. "Be good enough to tell me your name, sir."

"Harley Crawford, sir."

"And you are how old?"

Tears cut the dust at the corners of Crawford's eyes. "Near fourteen, Mr. Gilmer."

"And, decidedly, too old for nonsense of this sort." He stepped back. "On your feet."

Crawford wiped his hand across his cheek and looked to see if his fingers had blood on them. The blow apparently dazed him because his next words found no root in reason or wisdom. "My momma don't take to other folks layin' their hands on me."

When Crawford's companions heard their leader's words, the pair backed to the edge of the street and tried to stand stock-still; they were certain that Gilmer would be dealing out retribution and were praying earnestly that he might somehow overlook them. In spite of Dee Henry's intense desire to secrete himself against the landscape of houses and trees, his body was shaking and his teeth were beginning to chatter.

Gilmer was distracted by a sound and looked over his shoulder. The black boy was walking to the opposite edge of the street. He picked up a cloth-wrapped packet and dusted it off.

"Is that yours, boy?"

"It's my Bible, boss."

"Your Bible?" Crawford was momentarily forgotten. "Why do you have it with you?"

"My Pap, boss—my great-granddaddy—he gave it to me when I was just a tad."

"And why do you have it with you *now*?"

"I take it back and forth to school with me, boss, so I can read in it. I laid it there when I was called to step up for the lady."

"You can read?"

"Yessuh, boss. My Pap says I talk too much like the field hands. Pap says the Book'll teach me how to talk—an' how to walk."

More thoughts—memories of words long forgotten—came to the man. He stared at the Book—remembering and thinking—then murmured, "My own great-grandfather told me much the same thing." When he faced Crawford again, he sounded distracted. "Tell your father I will be stoppin' by this evenin' to visit with him about what happened here."

Crawford was getting his senses back. He said, "Yessuh, I'll tell 'im."

"And Crawford"—Gilmer rested his hand on the boy's shoulder and spoke almost as gently as he had to the girl—"tell him, when he says his prayers tonight, to thank a gracious God that I chose not to hang you, because you came near."

The words emptied Crawford's lungs and his vision blurred.

A gentle man by nature, the former lieutenant was willing to be harsh when confronting those who would commit flagrant evil—in the years since the war, Jacob Gilmer had killed four men; two were shot to death, two hung. The number of dead might've been greater were it not for the fact that bad folks made sure to give the soft-spoken man a wide berth.

The man looked at Mose. "What would you say the Bible says about your actions today?"

Mose was on solid ground. "It says real clear that men got the job of standin' up for them that can't stand up for themselves."

"Excellent commentary." Gilmer turned to the young lady. "May I ask, ma'am, if you have any brothers at home?"

"No, sir." The girl shook her head. "It's just me an' Momma."

Gilmer almost smiled. "Then it would seem that providence has favored you. You now have three faithful champions—bodyguards, if you will—at your service. These young gentlemen"—waving his quirt at the white boys—"will see to it that any man who crosses your path grants to you the honor that befits a lady."

The three boys looked at the man, the girl, and each other. The girl stared at the man.

Weems raised a tentative hand. "Uh, Mr. Gilmer? Bodyguards?"

"Precisely. You three have earned the right to protect this lady. In so doing, it is conceivable that you will learn—as has this colored gentleman—to embrace the privilege God granted to men in the Garden. If you give your life defending this lady, or any other worthy soul, you will have died a noble death. Should God allow you to live out your natural lives, your reward at the end of the day will be the assurance that you lived as true men. In the meantime, until this young lady chooses her husband, you will gain a reputation as the men who stand between her and any casual or indecent act or word by man or boy."

It took the last reserves of Dee Henry's strength to hold his hand up. "What if he's bigger'n us?" he whispered.

Gilmer looked at Harley Crawford. "Would you care to answer that?"

"Yes, sir." The thirteen-year-old had what it took to be a good man, and he had matured appreciably in the few moments since he heard the reference to a hanging. He met the man's eyes and said, "It means we do whatever it takes to get the coon."

"Well said." Gilmer nodded. "But mark this . . . you are not ruffians, and you are not a gang. You are gentlemen. You shall resort to violence only on those occasions when diplomacy fails to turn distress from the lady's path. If it takes more than one of you to do the job, then you join forces. Do you understand?"

Dee Henry wasn't sure. All three boys nodded and said, "Yes, sir."

The stakes were high, and it was important to Crawford that he begin his new job well. He tried to look at the girl, but his eyes dropped. He chewed on his lip before asking, "What do we do first, Mr. Gilmer?"

Gilmer looked deliberately at Mose, then back at Crawford. "Were I you, I would find a man who values honor above his own well-being, and I would seek his counsel."

Crawford studied the black boy. "Yes, sir."

"That should do it, then." Gilmer settled the Panama in place and swung his leg over the mare's saddle. The horse backed a step and Gilmer touched his hat brim. "By your leave, ma'am." The gentleman reined the horse around and touched her with his heels.

The three white boys were looking at Mose. The girl was looking at the horseman. Mose found his stick and moved to stand between the boys and the girl.

"You won't be needin' that," said Crawford. "None of us are gonna be botherin' you."

Mose looked at the girl. "What about that lady?"

"Mr. Gilmer told us to be her bodyguards. That means we got the job of takin' care of her from now on."

Mose hated to call anyone a liar. "What if you don't?"

"Do you know Mr. Gilmer?" Crawford asked.

Mose shook his head. "I don't know no . . . uh, any white folks in this town."

Crawford cut his eyes at the departing figure. "That there's a real bad man, an' he don't carry that six-gun for show. He'd just as soon shoot one of us as whistle 'Dixie.'"

Mose was unsure. He looked at the girl. The young lady hadn't taken her eyes off her departing hero. "Ma'am?"

"Hmm?"

"You reckon these here are gonna bother you again?"

"No." She shook her head. "Never. That was Mr. Jacob Gilmer. Momma says people do like he tells 'em to."

Two of the white boys nodded. Dee Henry had escaped with his life and was trying not to bawl.

The girl added, "Momma said he's a gentleman."

The boys didn't comment.

The girl turned and continued down the dusty street toward her house. What had begun as a dread-filled journey was now a quiet stroll home from school.

Crawford looked expectantly at the other boys. When they shrugged, he called after her, "You reckon it would be all right if we was to walk with you to your house?"

She didn't look back. "I guess."

Crawford looked at Mose. "You wanna go?"

Mose didn't care. "I reckon. My momma stays down that way."

The young lady walked slowly, humming to herself. Mose tossed the stick in the ditch, and the four boys followed silently in the girl's wake.

The houses toward the west edge of town were smaller and less attractive than those closer in. As the little parade approached the girl's house, an attractive woman straightened from her chores to watch their arrival. When she saw the boys following her daughter, the woman left her washtub and walked to the top of the steps, drying her hands on her apron before she rolled down the sleeves of her dress. The girl waved and smiled. The woman shaded her eyes and waved back.

When the group gathered in the shade of a tree near the

porch, the girl grinned at her mother, then turned to her entourage. "These gentlemen walked me home."

The lady's cheeks and forehead were red from heat and exertion; tendrils of light brown hair escaped from her scarf to soften the outline of her face. "Did they, now? Well, thank you, gentlemen." She walked down the steps, studying the boys. According to the talk, the Crawford boy was bent on trouble, but if he was with her daughter, something had changed. The colored boy had dried blood on his face, the youngest white boy had been crying, and young Harley Crawford had a knot over his eye the size of a hen's egg. The three white boys all needed haircuts.

The colored boy's inclusion sparked the most interest in her. "You go to the white school, boy?"

Mose thought he could get by without lying. He pointed down the street. "No, ma'am. My momma stays right down yonder, an' I was just walkin' with these here folks."

The lady smiled and decided not to press the point—more often than not, what happened between boys was better kept between boys; when she and her daughter were alone, the girl would let her know. She included the colored boy when she said, "Well, it just so happens that I have a pan of gingerbread cooling in the kitchen, and we have milk in the icebox. Is anyone hungry?"

Mose spoke first. He was hungry, but he had somewhere he needed to be. "I 'preciate it, ma'am, but I best be gettin' to my house. I ain't allowed to take my dog up to that schoolhouse, an' she ain't seen me all day."

When Mose turned down the treat, Crawford decided to join him. "Thank you, ma'am, but I reckon I'll walk a piece with . . . uh . . . Mose here, an' . . . uh . . . see his dog." He looked at Mose. "If it's all right."

Mose shrugged. "That'll be fine."

Having one boy put his business ahead of her gingerbread was a new thing for Elise Austin—having two turn it down heightened her curiosity about the events that inspired their choices. She said, "Very well, gentlemen, do what you must."

Mose stood spraddle-legged, put his fists by his legs, and bowed stiffly. His effort didn't quite reflect the polish of Mr. Gilmer's, but he had been practicing it in his mind and he thought maybe it turned out pretty good.

Resentment—and panic—attacked Crawford. He jerked one arm across his waist and the other behind his back and snapped over so abruptly he lost his balance and almost went to his knees. He recovered in time to see the ladies' elegant curtsies.

Crawford looked at the younger white boys then at the woman. "Ma'am, is it okay if these two stay 'round here till I get back?"

Could the situation become any more bizarre? "Certainly."

"Thank you, ma'am." Crawford gave the two appointees a meaningful stare and pointed at a spot under the lady's chinaberry tree. "You two stay in this yard till I get back."

"For how long?" Henry whined.

"For as long as it takes," Crawford hissed. He jogged to catch up with Mose.

The girl's mother looked at their remaining guests. "Well, gentlemen, there's gingerbread and milk for those who are so inclined."

The younger boy didn't want anything on his stomach for fear that it would cause him to throw up. He said, "No, ma'am, thank you."

Weems was too timid to eat by himself. "I reckon not, thank you, ma'am."

The shock of having four adolescent boys refuse her gingerbread was nearly too much, but a background permeated by an emphasis on refinement stood her in good stead—she was spared the embarrassment of having her mouth fall open. Background aside, when she turned to mount the steps, she smiled to herself and whispered, "Lord, send us help."

And He did.

*　　*　　*

Out in the dirt street Crawford was walking and seeking counsel. "What do you reckon we ought to do next?"

"Do what that Mr. Gilmer says, act like gentlemen."

They walked several more steps before the white boy said, "What if we don't know how?"

The boy's words stopped Mose. "You don't know 'bout bein' a gentleman?"

Crawford shook his head.

Mose resumed his trek, thinking as he went. Finally, he said, "It's like that Mr. Gilmer said, the Bible says God gave us men the job of lookin' out for ladies."

"I don't know nothin' about the Bible." What Crawford was discovering about what he didn't know was beginning to make his chest hurt.

Mose could see it coming. "Lemme ask you this. If that white man kills you, will you go to Heaven?"

"I don't aim to have him kill me, 'cause I'm gonna do like he told me, or I'm gonna run off."

"Well," Mose needed to be patient, "if you was to die from a snakebite, would you go to Heaven?"

Crawford shrugged. "I reckon."

"Did you ever become a Christian?"

Crawford shook his head. "I don't guess."

"To go to Heaven, you gotta be a Christian. To be a Christian, you gotta ask Jesus to forgive you for your sins an' be yo' Savior. Did you ever do that?"

Another head shake.

Mose had never thought he'd be telling a white person about Jesus, but here it was. Mose prayed, and God answered. The boy smiled at Crawford. "You wanna see a fine-lookin' coon dog?"

There wasn't a boy in the world who didn't think his own personal coon dog was the finest in the world, and Crawford knew it. "I guess."

The last place on the east side of the street was set off by itself; a small shack standing at the front edge of what had been the old livery yard. The corral behind the house was spread across the level top of a small hill. Rotting posts were all that was left of the corral fence; the only part of the property that didn't look like it was ready to fall down was a stand of trees behind the dilapidated barn. On the opposite side of the street, Mr. Saucier kept a few milk cows in a narrow pasture. The pasture sloped westward down the hill to a wide expanse of scattered trees; the woods along Big Black Creek were visible in the distance.

Crawford watched Mose put two fingers to his lips and whistle. Ten seconds later the boy was almost knocked down by a Walker coonhound. The boy laughed while the tricolor dog greeted him—nuzzling, whining, and wagging her tail.

When the dog quieted, Mose pointed at Crawford and started building a bridge to the white boy. "Lady, this here's Mr. Harley Crawford."

Lady presented herself to Crawford by sitting down and offering her right paw.

Crawford had never seen anything like it. He laughed out loud and squatted down to shake her paw. "Pleased to meet you, Lady." He grinned up at Mose. "She's awful smart."

Mose grinned back. "Naw, she just friendly."

Both boys laughed. The dog pretended to be disgusted. The eight-year-old boy prayed.

Crawford was petting the dog. "How old is she?"

"Five. I was three years old when I got her, an' I named her Gal."

Crawford cocked his head and looked at the dog. "I thought her name was Lady."

"Uh-huh. It is now. My Pap said we needs to be thinkin' 'bout respect when we thinks about women. That's why Pap got me to change her name—to remind me to show respect."

Crawford stood up. "Well, I'll be . . . that's real good . . . sorta like rememberin' to be a gentleman."

The boys followed Lady into Mose's big backyard. A large round water trough, its concrete perimeter long since cracked, its interior littered with trash, stood at the foot of an old windmill. The boys sat on the lip of the trough and raked their toes through patches of grass. Mose thought maybe it was time to start talking. "Pap says a man can't be a for-sure gentleman without he's a Christian."

Crawford considered that then said, "You reckon Mr. Gilmer's a Christian?"

In years past, Mose had prefaced almost all of his important pronouncements with the words "Pap says." But he was eight years old now, and he was expected to act like a grown man—and if the words he spoke were true, it didn't matter who said them first. He said, "I reckon that ain't for another feller to call—that's 'tween Mr. Gilmer an' God. The only person I can know 'bout for sure is me."

"How come a feller has to be a Christian?"

Mose thought for a minute then said, "I better read you somethin'." He unwrapped the Bible and thumbed through it, praying the whole time. Lady rested her head on Crawford's leg to be petted. "All right, this here is two verses out of Ephesians, chapter five. One says, 'Husbands, love your wives, even as Christ also loved the church, an' gave Himself up for it.' The next one says, 'So ought men to love their wives as their own bodies. He that loveth his wife loveth himself.' "

Crawford stroked the dog's ears and grimaced. "I'm not wantin' to marry that girl, I just want to know how to be her bodyguard."

All a boy had to do was stay around Pap for a month or two, and he'd hear the answer to any question that was going to come up—Mose had spent seven years with the wise old man. He tapped the words in the Book and lectured, "The good Lord knows we need to get our minds set on how to treat womenfolk before we get married, not after. We can't start off right, if we don't know where we're headin'."

"That's it! That's what I said!" Crawford stood up and jabbed his finger at the Book. "I need to know how to start."

Mose was praying and thanking the Lord for the boy's reaction. He couldn't keep from smiling when he said, "Then I got somethin' else I needs to read to you."

"What is it?" Crawford was too excited to sit down. There was a chance—maybe a good chance—that he would live to be fourteen.

"This here is the answer." Mose found the verse and held up a finger for attention. " 'For God so loved the world, that He gave His only begotten Son, that whosoever believeth in Him should not perish, but have everlastin' life.' "

The day's first warm breeze stirred splotches of April-green grass in the barnyard. Crawford watched dry leaves circulate in the bottom of the water trough. "Not perish? Does that mean somebody can't kill me?"

"No-no . . . not like that. It means a Christian's soul goes to Heaven right when he dies . . . his life don't ever stop. Everlastin' life means forever an' ever."

The old fan over their heads turned slowly; the greaseless gears in the windmill registered a shrill, off-key complaint. Crawford looked up at the blades and said, "Have mercy."

Mose waited a moment before he asked, "Are you prayin'?"

The blades of the windmill turned; its mechanical parts continued their high-pitched protests. Crawford was neither listening nor watching. Without looking at Mose, he said, "That man knew you'd tell me about this."

Mose nodded. "Could be. But comes right down to it, it don't matter what he knew . . . the good Lord wants everybody to be a Christian. Now, you got to decide what *you* want."

Crawford pointed at the Bible. "I want to do like it says. Can you tell me how to be a Christian?"

"I can"—Mose held the Bible up—"but this ain't about keepin' that man from killin' you. This is about somethin' in yo' heart."

"My heart?"

"Mm-hmm. Lemme read you somethin'." He searched the

Book for a moment. " 'That if thou shalt confess with thy mouth the Lord Jesus, an' believe in thine heart that God hath raised Him from the dead, thou shalt be saved.' That's from the book of Romans."

"I believe God raised Him from the dead, but I ain't sure how to believe it in my heart."

"But you believe God raised Him from the grave?"

"I've always believed that."

"Do you know you're a sinner?"

"Uh-huh. I 'spect everybody but the preachers sin a little."

"The Book says real clear that preachers are right in there with the rest of us," corrected Mose. "Do you know He died for your sins?"

"Yep." Crawford nodded. "I reckon everybody knows that."

"Then all you got left to do is to pray an' ask Him to be your Savior."

"What about believin' in my heart? How does that happen?"

"Well, I guess I ain't for sure, but I think it means it's more special than just knowin' in your mind . . . it's a thing that changes how you feel about Him . . . an' about yo'self. You'll see."

"Do I pray right here?"

"If you decided you want to be a Christian, you best pray as soon as you can."

"What do I say?"

"You tell God you know you're a sinner, an' you thank Him that He died for your sins." He thought for a second, then added, "An' you ask Him to be your Savior."

Crawford pointed at a spot by his feet. "How 'bout right here?"

"Good as any."

The two boys dropped to their knees, and Crawford worked his way through a prayer . . . confessing, asking, and thanking. When he finished he looked at Mose. "That's it, ain't it?"

Mose said, "Yep. I reckon."

"You reckon this'll make any difference to Mr. Gilmer?"

Mose hesitated, then said, "Maybe, maybe not. Mr. Gilmer seems like a fine man, but what he thinks comes a good piece behind what God thinks."

"How come?"

"Lemme read you what counts to God." Mose took his seat on the water trough and hunched over the Bible. "This is Second Chronicles, the sixteenth chapter. 'For the eyes of the Lord run to an' fro throughout the whole earth, to show Himself strong in the behalf of them whose heart is perfect toward Him.'" He closed the book. "Me an' you are young, but you're a Christian now, an' you pretty much know what's right. Puttin' what Mr. Gilmer thinks in front of what God thinks is trouble."

He might not make it to fourteen after all. "He's liable to kill me."

"Not if God don't want him to. You got a guardian angel now—one that don't do nothin' but watch out for you every minute of every day. All we need is for God to help us make our hearts to be like He wants 'em . . . He'll take care of the rest."

"Is my angel here now?"

"Right this very minute, an' every minute from now on."

Crawford took his place on the lip of the trough, and the two boys were silent for a while. Finally, Crawford said, "Bein' a Christian is gonna be a little harder than I thought."

Mose nodded. "You sho' got that right, but it beats the dickens outta what's easier."

Crawford sighed and stood up. "Well, I guess I need to go tell those other boys what happened."

"That'd be good, 'cause time's gettin' short."

"How's that?"

"The Bible says a time of great trouble's comin'."

Crawford's hand went involuntarily to his backside. "More trouble?"

"Real, sho' nuff, like in the Bible, trouble." Mose talked for five minutes—telling the white boy what the Bible said about the

Great Tribulation that loomed on history's horizon and the events that would precede it.

When Mose finished, Crawford felt both relief and guilt because he had narrowly missed the coming years of suffering. His next thought was for his friends. "If I can't explain what you told me to Dee an' Roscoe, you reckon you could help me?"

Mose considered that for a moment. "I'm colored. You reckon they'd want to hear about Jesus from me?"

Crawford hadn't thought about that. "Does it make any difference if a Christian's black or white?"

Mose thought it shouldn't, but he knew different. "It don't make no . . . uh, any difference to God an' me, but it does to some."

Crawford knew that would be true. "Can I come back down here an' see you?"

Mose rested his hand on the dog's head. "Come see us anytime." The dog and her boy walked their visitor to the street.

Crawford walked a few steps and looked back to wave. Mose was kneeling, one arm holding on to the dog and one holding his Bible.

The white boy would likely see Mr. Gilmer before he saw Mose again. He stopped and said, "I was wonderin' . . . are you sure my angel's here right now?"

"Yep."

"Did you ever see yours?"

Crawford had hit Mose's weak spot. He took a deep breath and shook his head. "No. I been lookin', but I never did. I'll tell you this, though. My pap an' the Bible both say he's here, an' ain't neither one of 'em ever gonna be wrong."

Mose Washington's angel was standing at his boy's right shoulder, listening to the argument for his presence. His counterpart was standing by Harley Crawford.

When Crawford walked away, Washington's angel lifted his

sword and held it across his chest. *I implore You, Lord, in these terrible moments soon to come, that You would grant us the privilege of glorifying Your great and awesome Name.*

His fellow warrior raised his sword and said, *For Him Who sits on the throne, and for the Lamb. Amen.*

CHAPTER NINE

The young man who walked up the street to the Austins' house was not the same boy who left there earlier.

As he approached the house, he could see Mrs. Austin rinsing out her wash. Julia stood beside her, wringing out the finished pieces and stacking them in a basket for their trip to the clothesline. The designated guards had abandoned their post under the shade tree and moved to a point down near the street corner. Crawford motioned for them to come back, but they shook their heads and beckoned earnestly for him to come to them.

When she saw Crawford, Elise Austin straightened, dried her hands, and left her sleeves where they were. A buggy whip was propped against the wall by her wash bench.

Crawford gave up on his helpers and walked to the porch. He took a deep breath, and said, "Mrs. Austin?"

Mrs. Austin didn't bother to reply . . . anger deepened the color in her complexion. She took her time coming down the steps, leaving the whip where it was to keep it out of reach of her emotions. When she reached the bottom step, she spoke without making any attempt to mask her contempt for the boy. "Julia has told me what happened this afternoon, and I've chased off those other no-goods. You're next."

Words that would fully express her disgust would never find their way to her lips—she could only say, "Young man, it burdens me to tell you that I find your conduct to be despicable in the extreme. Now, you mark this carefully . . . should you ever speak to my daughter again, your trouble will not be founded in Jacob Gilmer's quirt. *And . . .*" she raised a hard finger and spoke her words one at a time, "if, at any time in the future, you are foolish enough to lay your hand on her, you will not live out that day. Do I make myself clear?"

Well, there it was. Julia had told her mother what happened, and the whole town would likely hear about it. Crawford ducked his head, the hair fell in his face. "Yes, ma'am."

"Well, don't just stand there. Get off this property."

He pushed the too-long hair back and ventured a look at the woman. "Uh . . . Mrs. Austin?"

"You have nothing to say that I want to hear. Now, you will get yourself out of this yard immediately, or you will take the beating you have already earned."

He looked at the ground long enough to take another deep breath. The prospect of having the woman hit him with the whip bothered him less than his failing to do what needed to be done. He looked into the lady's eyes and said, "No, ma'am. I got somethin' I need to say."

Elise Austin turned to her daughter. Her voice trembled as she said, "Julia, get me that whip."

The girl left the washing and picked up the whip.

Dee and Roscoe saw what the girl carried to the edge of the porch and took off for town.

Crawford didn't want the lady to use the whip on him, and it passed through his mind to follow his friends, but he had a job that needed doing. He said his first uncoached prayer—*God, I'd appreciate it if my angel wouldn't let her hit me too many times*—and stayed where he was—a man with a purpose. The girl took her time coming down the steps, watching Crawford watch her mother.

When her mother extended her hand for the whip, Julia held it out of her reach and touched her mother's arm. When Elise turned her frown on her daughter, the girl answered with a gentle smile and the first two words from one of her mother's timeworn phrases: "Patience, dearest."

The woman took a moment to reclaim control of her choices and reached for the whip again. The girl continued to smile, holding the whip away and completing the phrase. "All in God's good time."

The woman wanted her hands on the whip, but she was too wise to let her anger overrule the girl. She paused to take a longer breath then addressed herself to the boy, "Well, what is it?"

He thought over what he wanted to say, but getting the words out wasn't easy. "I need to make an apology to Julia."

"Mm-hmm. And what, may I ask, brought on this instant contrition?"

He thought he could just step up to the porch and say his words to the woman and her daughter and things would be better. His task was getting harder by the minute. "Umm . . . I don't know what that word means, ma'am . . . the 'cahtrition' one."

Mrs. Austin sighed then said, "Why have you decided to make an apology?"

He wanted to look at the ground, but he couldn't take his eyes off hers. "That colored boy . . ." he pointed back down the street without turning, "uh, Mose . . . he told me how to be a Christian. He read me lots of different things in the Bible, an' then he told me how to pray. There was a piece in there that said somethin' about God watchin' out for what my heart does." He didn't have any reason to cry, but the tear came anyway. He brushed at it with his hand and said, "Those words said God would be standin' behind me if my heart's doin' right."

"You said he told you how to pray. Did you pray?"

"Yes, ma'am."

"And you would have me believe you've become a Christian?"

The girl cleared her throat and barely whispered, "Momma."

Crawford used his fingers to comb back his hair for the hundredth time. "Mose said nobody could tell but me an' God. I guess that means I could lie about it. I reckon God would know if I did, though," he said as he shrugged and expressed his newly found fear, ". . . an' I reckon He wouldn't stand with me."

Mrs. Austin took her time considering the boy and his words. She and her daughter exchanged a look, and the girl nodded. Mrs. Austin said, "Well, in that case, speak your piece."

He faced the girl and pointed up the street. "We done a bad thing back there . . . a shameful thing . . . an' I'm powerful sorry. I promise I won't ever do it again."

It was the girl's turn to be ill at ease. Her face turned a pretty pink, and she said, "I forgive you."

"I'm much obliged."

The woman fanned herself with her apron and watched the youngsters fidget for a moment, then said, "Mr. Crawford, I'm good with a pair of scissors, if I do say so myself."

"Ma'am?"

"If it pleases you, I'd be more than happy to trim your hair."

The conversation's sudden shift caught him off guard. His eyes went to the girl. She gave him the suggestion of a smile and an encouraging nod. He said, "That'd be real nice, Mrs. Austin, if it ain't any trouble."

"If it's *not* any trouble," corrected the lady. "Julia, put up that whip and get my comb and scissors while I finish rinsing out this load of wash."

"Yes, ma'am." She turned to the boy. "I'm gonna have a piece of gingerbread. Would you like some?"

He nodded. "That'd be real fine, thank you. I feel like I'm near to starvin'."

"Sit here on the steps, then," she directed. "I'll be right back."

The boy said a proper, "Thank you," and took a seat.

Elise Austin looked up when her daughter came back through

the door carrying two plates. The girl's helping was half the size of a deck of playing cards; the boy's was as big as a skillet. Because the woman had her back to their visitor, she could roll her eyes without offending him. The girl chose to ignore her mother's rude behavior and sat down to have dessert with her guest.

The woman stayed at her washtub, rinsing and wringing, humming to herself. The young couple ate gingerbread while the girl chatted and the boy nodded at all the right times.

Three invisible warriors watched the scene. Waiting patiently.

One of the guardians said, *They have come far.*

The second angel agreed, *And their hearts are strong.*

And so shall they need be, for the time is soon coming. The third member of their group looked at the cloudless skies. *We would be wise to pray now, while He offers this interlude of peace.*

———

By eleven o'clock Friday morning the temperature in the school auditorium was ninety degrees and the air was thick with humidity. The men came in wearing collars and ties and blotting at their faces with handkerchiefs; the ladies wore hats and fanned themselves with their fingers—all were praying for short speeches. At one fifteen, the men were dripping sweat, the ladies were fanning themselves with their hats, and the high school graduation ceremony was over.

Julia and her mother walked out of the school building to find Jacob Gilmer standing by the flagpole with Harley Crawford. Harley had his back to them.

"Good afternoon, gentlemen."

Gilmer lifted the Panama and said, "Ladies."

When Harley turned to speak, the Austin ladies, and every other person leaving the ceremony, could not fail to note that he had a brand-new black eye and his lips were swollen.

Elise understood that boys and black eyes went together, but Harley had walked Julia home from school every day since their encounter with Gilmer—if he was going back to his old ways, she wanted to know about it. "Harley, have you been fighting again?"

The boy had been steeling himself for the meeting with Mrs. Austin. It hadn't helped. "Yes, ma'am . . . kind of."

"Kind of?"

Gilmer had already heard the story behind the boy's battered face. "Call it an altercation," he prompted.

Harley shrugged. "I reckon I got in an altercation with Mr. Henry."

"Mr. Henry?" The normally unflappable woman was aghast. She looked at Gilmer, then back to the boy. "You got yourself into a fight with a grown man?"

Harley wasn't happy about it. "It didn't seem like a fight at the time."

For the last ten days Elise Austin had hoped against hope that the boy wouldn't backslide into his old ways; his news brought disappointment, frustration, and anger. Julia, however, spent the better part of an hour a day walking home from school with him and observing his somewhat unorthodox attempts to live well; his fervent efforts nourished an unlikely friendship.

The lady stepped close to Harley and said, "Young man, do you not have any—"

For the second time in two weeks—and in her short life—Julia rested her hand on her mother's arm and said a gentle, "Momma."

Gilmer underlined the girl's word with an almost imperceptible headshake.

Elise turned to her daughter, and the girl's composure worked itself across the silence and into the woman's heart. The child had been a chubby three-year-old when her father passed. The man left his wife a small home with a large mortgage and a fledgling business that was worth approximately what it owed the bank;

his legacy to the child was his eyes and smile, his wisdom, and his gentle nature—the woman embraced the girl's interruption. She turned back to Harley and said, "Forgive me, Mr. Crawford, the heat in the auditorium seems to have gotten the better of me. Would you tell us about your altercation with Mr. Henry?"

"Yes, ma'am." He took a deep breath. "Me an' Roscoe went to see Mose day before yesterday . . . Roscoe was wantin' to hear about how to be a Christian like me." If he was concerned that people leaving the school building were eavesdropping on his testimony, it didn't show. "Dee said he didn't want to go, but he tagged along anyway. Roscoe ended up prayin' just like me, an' it made Dee mad. He said some bad things to Mose an' started in to whip him. When me an' Roscoe made him quit, he said he was gonna tell his daddy. Well, Mr. Henry came down to Mose's house yesterday when just me an' Mose was there." The boy was a past master at helping people's notions get the better of them, and he knew it. In Mr. Henry's case, however, Mr. Gilmer had already assured him he was innocent of any transgression. He took a breath and continued. "When he started in on Mose, I tried to pull him off an' he turned on me." He touched his finger to his swollen lips, remembering. "I reckon he should'a waited 'til that dog wasn't around. Lady bit him on the back of the leg an' chased him off." The boy pointed toward the courthouse. "I saw him up on the square just now an' he cussed at me a little. He was limpin' some an' sayin' how he was gonna get his shotgun an' go back out there this afternoon after he closed the mercantile . . . said he was gonna shoot Lady an' anybody that got in his way."

"And Mr. Henry is the one who hit you in the face?" But for the slightest crinkle at the corners of her eyes, the woman's facial expression was bland.

When Harley said it was, Elise looked past him toward the town square. "Well, if you gentlemen will excuse us, the church ladies are hosting a small luncheon for our graduates, and Julia and I are on the way to help out."

"It happens that I have business at the courthouse," said Gilmer. "May I accompany you as far as the square?"

"Please do."

When Harley fell in behind the trio, Gilmer stopped and said, "You might not want to cross paths with Henry while he's heated up."

The boy shrugged. "I reckon I can't let other men decide where I walk."

"I'm afraid I have to agree with you there. At the same time, though, I think it would be wise for you to allow Mr. Henry time to think through his actions."

"Yes, sir, that'd be good, 'ccpt I need to see him before he closes the store. I figure to take the blame for him gettin' bit, that way he'll lay off of Mose an' Lady."

Nash Henry was a mouse of a man who allowed his wife to bully him, then took his frustrations out on his store clerks. Gilmer said, "Henry won't be inclined to listen, son. He's not a strong man, and what happened with that dog shamed him. He's likely to blame some of that on you and still seek to penalize Mose and Lady."

"I don't mean to argue with you, Mr. Gilmer, but I got my guardian angel with me, an' God's watchin' to see if my heart's doin' like He'd want it to. If I could hear God talk, I think He'd tell me to stand by my friends, black or white." The boy's decision to go against the man was a hard one. "You're a good man, Mr. Gilmer, an' I'm beholden to you for how you treat me, but I figure God'd want me to listen to Him."

During the past week or so, while the ladies were watching the new Harley Crawford emerge, Gilmer had spent his time being astounded by the boy's rapid transformation. "Well, on those past occasions when I've argued against God, I've invariably come up a poor second." He held out the horse's reins. "Would you be good enough to lead the mare?"

"Yes, sir," Harley nodded. The bay wasn't happy about having a stranger lead her, but Harley won her confidence with a gentle hand and soft words. He and Julia walked in the street, leading the horse; the adults strolled along the sidewalk in front of tree-shaded homes.

The sky, except for darkening clouds in the southwest, was clear. The sun was warm, the air still. A flock of bluebirds passed over their heads, hurrying eastward. Mrs. Crayhill stood on the front porch of her big house, overseeing the pruning of her rosebushes. The banker's wife interrupted her business in order to note the couple's passing; her careful observation would lend nothing in the way of accuracy when she recounted the matter. Gilmer touched his hat, Elise Austin nodded. When the couple was out of sight, Mrs. Crayhill hurried over to her neighbor's house.

Gilmer and the woman had no reason to be anxious about walking a few blocks together; only the most notorious gossips would comment. Gilmer's wife fell victim to the fever back in '85, and he was thirty years older than Mrs. Austin. For her part, Elise Austin had been a widow for ten years, and her reputation was above reproach.

The gossips couldn't know that Gilmer watched the young widow from a distance, admiring her ability to meld her no-nonsense attitude with an innate sense of propriety. For her part, she drew pleasure from the company of a Christian gentleman who consistently came down on the side of right; that he was intelligent multiplied his appeal. Between the two of them, they didn't give a tinker's hurrah what people might have to say about their choosing to walk together.

They parted ways at the square. Gilmer went into the courthouse; the ladies went to their church.

When the others were out of sight, Harley walked across the square and sat down on the bench in front of the mercantile. Almost all of the people in Purvis knew the Crawford boy, and most knew his reputation. While passersby watched, he bowed his head and prayed.

Across the street, two old men sat on a park bench and scattered crumbs on the sidewalk while they conferred about the absence of the courthouse pigeons. The skies southwest of town were darker.

Two unseen figures stood by the boy on the bench—one on either side—listening to him ask God to make him brave enough to go into the store and to please make sure his guardian angel stayed close.

The messenger at the boy's right hand watched the people going about their business on the square, some staring in amazement at the boy on the bench. He said, *The children of this world are too often the leaders. In ten of their days he has discovered more about our Lord than many of these have learned in their lifetimes.*

The taller figure smiled on the boy. *So he has. And in these coming moments, he faces an opportunity to learn about himself.*

The first angel pointed his sword at the people who scurried around the square, most of them under the impression they were on important errands. *And some of these will soon be given a wonderful chance to praise God for His bounty.*

The taller angel was somber. *And for some, I fear, that time has already passed.*

Too true, old friend, too true.

The two watched the boy rise from the bench.

It begins, said Harley's angel.

So it does. Let us pray, for the sake of young Mose, that young Harley Crawford chooses to embrace his coming lesson.

When Harley stepped through the front door, a bell tinkled.

A wide center aisle separated the dry-goods side of the store from the food and hardware. The pungent smell of coal oil was softened by the fresh scent of linen and perfumed soap.

The store's office area was situated in the dim recesses of the store. Nash Henry was perched behind a slightly elevated desk with a napkin stuffed in his collar, eating his dinner. He poked a piece of roll in his mouth and talked around it. "You've got no business in here, brat. Get out."

Harley walked as far as a table stacked with bolts of flowered material. "I need to talk to you about yesterday, Mr. Henry."

In the best of times, Henry's round face was fixed in an expression of distaste. "I just told you to get out, boy. You've got nothing to say that I want to hear."

Harley moved to the low railing that enclosed the office area. "It was my fault you got bit, Mr. Henry, an' I'm sorry. Mose's dog was just standin' up for me."

"That mutt is as good as dead." The man pointed at the double-barreled shotgun propped against the railing. "I'm going out there before supper and take care of that myself."

When the man spoke, Harley smelled whiskey. "Mr. Henry, that dog is practically Mose's best friend. If you kill her—"

Henry put the rest of his roll on the plate and stood up. "Boy, I cuffed you yesterday for interfering in my business. If you came here for a second helping—"

The little bell over the door interrupted Henry's threat.

Harley and the store's owner watched as a tall man wearing a dark suit made his way down the aisle. "Good afternoon, gentlemen." An aura of wealth radiated from the customer.

"Afternoon," answered Henry. "May I help you, sir?"

"It happens that I find myself in need of a set of wine goblets. Have you any in stock?"

Nash Henry almost laughed out loud; he had two dozen crystal goblets that had been taking up storage space in his loft for nearly a decade. Ten years earlier, he let a smooth salesman convince him he and the Purvis Mercantile could lead the state's retailers into the next century. Southern Mississippi was poised for growth, the man predicted, and a merchant with vision could position himself to ride the crest of the new prosperity. The plan was simple, said the salesman. "You sell one stem of crystal a week and you'll double your yearly income. People will begin to hear of your reputation and sales will increase." Henry was left holding twenty-four fancy wine goblets and high expectations for his future—his store was sure to become the flagship of a chain spreading rapidly across the South.

Within a year of the salesman's departure, the would-be merchandising giant was forced to take the crystal pieces out of the display case because his wife was using them to point out his gullibility to every customer who came through the doors. For the past ten years, his life had been one letdown after another, and he could trace every disappointment to the goblets. Nowadays, performing the store's annual inventory always refreshed his wife's memory, and he had to spend a week listening to the shrew carp about the money he had wasted on "those fancy gewgaws."

His hands shook as he pulled the napkin out of his collar and pointed over his shoulder at the back loft. "Well, I believe I still have some up in the warehouse section. How many do you require?"

"Two dozen would suit me nicely." The man's accent did not come from anywhere in the South.

Henry looked up at the storage area then glanced down at the new shirt he was wearing. Digging through that mess in the loft would be hot work, and his helper wouldn't be at the store till after two o'clock. "If you can come back in an hour or so, I'll have my boy pull them down."

The man pulled out an ornate gold watch and consulted it. "Mmm. The time is now one forty-five." He shook his head. "I'm terribly sorry, but an hour from now I will be otherwise engaged."

The henpecked storekeeper decided he would rather ruin a drawer full of shirts than subject himself to another round of his wife's bleating. He pushed through the little wooden gate and limped toward the stairs. "In that case, I'll have them down here in a jiffy."

Henry was at the top of the stairs when the man in the suit said, "Perhaps I could provide some assistance."

The storekeeper was disappearing into the stacks of boxes. "You might. Just watch your step on the stairs."

"I'll be right there," the man answered. He paused to glance at Henry's shotgun, then looked straight into Harley's eyes. Seconds later he was mounting the stairs.

Finding the goblets was harder than Henry expected, but minutes later he stacked two large wooden crates on the floor by the office railing; the store owner's shirt, socks, and pants were sweat-soaked. Now was the time to open the negotiations for the crystal. "I should have told you sooner . . . these goblets are fairly expensive."

"Of course."

Henry put one of the crates on his desk and started working at the lid with a small pry bar. "I don't remember seeing you around here before," he said.

"I have been in town on several occasions recently, but you and I have never met."

"Mm-hmm." Henry's mind was on making money, not friends, and the pry bar needed careful handling. "Quality like this comes priced pretty high, you know."

The customer smiled warmly and said, "I am quite confident that price will not be a hindrance to the sale."

Henry took time to return the smile and came close to offering the gentleman a drink.

When the lid came off the first crate, Henry made a choking sound and turned as pale as paste. Harley and the man in the dark suit watched as the distraught merchant fell to his knees by the remaining crate. He worked the pry bar quickly, jerked the top off, and lifted some of the packing material. Small pieces of glass, none larger than a child's fingernail, caught the light as they sprinkled from the shredded paper. The contents of both boxes, all twenty-four stems of crystal, had been completely pulverized. Nash Henry moaned and doubled over as if someone had kicked him in the stomach. There would be no redemption for him on this day.

The man in the suit had seen enough. He said something about having other things he needed to do, turned abruptly, and made his way back down the aisle. The little bell tinkled, and he was gone.

"How could this happen?" the storekeeper whispered at the broken glass. The largest sale in the history of the Purvis Mercantile evaporated before his eyes. All the nails, hammers, stick candy, and milk buckets in the store weren't worth as much as he'd just lost. He stared at the tiny pieces of sparkling debris and began to weep; he could already hear his wife screeching at him, calling him a foolhardy dimwit. Tears of anger mixed with the sweat on his face and dripped into the box of broken ambitions.

Crawford watched as Henry lurched to his feet and kicked at the box, missed it, and almost fell. Harley reached to steady him, and the man screamed a string of profanity heard by people out on the square. He turned on the only other person in the room. "Who did this?"

Harley had never seen a grown man look so desperate. He shook his head sadly and said, "There ain't no tellin', Mr. Henry."

The troublemaking Crawford boy was standing there shaking his head, pretending he was sad, but Nash Henry wasn't fooled. As soon as he got outside, the boy would be laughing and spreading the word about how he watched a grown man cry over some broken glass.

Harley thought having the boxes out in the open was making things worse for Mr. Henry. He stooped over and picked up the crate from the floor, saying, "I can move these boxes out back for you, Mr. Henry."

Henry drew back his hand and struck the boy full in the face. The unexpected blow spun Harley around, and he collapsed under a shower of shredded paper and broken crystal.

Henry was taking up his shotgun when the little bell over the front door jingled. A man in a Panama hat was silhouetted against the gray light from the store windows.

"Is everything all right in here, Henry?"

Outside the store, the day was growing darker, even as the man spoke.

CHAPTER TEN

Gilmer stood with his back to the front door, waiting for his eyes to adjust to the dim interior of the store. Fast-fading daylight came through the skylights and glinted on the shotgun in Henry's hands.

"Where's the boy, Henry?"

Harley stood up behind Henry. "I'm right here, Mr. Gilmer." He was holding a hand to his nose—blood leaked from between his fingers.

"Step over here by me." Gilmer was moving down the wide aisle.

Harley nodded. "Yes, sir."

"You just hold it right there." Henry took a step forward—the gloom in the building magnified the sound of the shotgun's hammers snapping back. "Just because your family left you a lot of money doesn't mean you can walk in and start giving orders in my store."

"That's true, Nash."

Henry was drunk, or insane, or both. Gilmer wanted to get himself and Harley out of the store alive, but Henry could trigger both barrels of the shotgun before he could touch his pistol. He said, "I propose that we send Harley outside while we discuss whatever it is you have in mind."

"Well, *I* propose," sneered Henry, "that you get out of here and mind your own business. This boy and I will stay here and mind ours."

"May I ask what Harley has to do with this?" The odds were weighed heavily against him, but he wasn't going to leave the boy in the store with a crazy man.

"No, you may not." Henry raised the gun to his shoulder and looked at Gilmer over the barrels. "I'll give you till the count of five to get out of my store. One."

In his lifetime, Gilmer had been called on to use a gun in one-on-one gunfights and pitched battles, at close quarters and in wide fields, while knee-deep in water and from the back of a running horse; while Henry might know how to shoot a shotgun, the one-armed man understood about gunfighting. He didn't have to think—he only had to let his mind and body do what they had trained themselves to do.

"Two."

Harley was almost directly behind Henry. The part of Gilmer that would dictate his moves in the fight was taking over. He took a step to his left so that the boy wouldn't be in his line of fire. Harley saw this and moved to his right; he was still behind Henry, but now well clear—the hand he'd been holding over his nose went into his pocket.

"Three."

Father, prayed the warrior, *I desperately need a miracle.* His left foot moved back slightly, and his body turned sideways to present less of a target.

Harley Crawford's bloody hand came out of his pocket. He opened it and held it out so that Gilmer could see what he was holding.

"F-four!" stammered Henry.

The boy was crying, his head bowed, his hand shaking; a pair of 12-gauge shotgun shells were nestled in his bloody palm.

Gilmer moved his arms away from his sides. "Don't shoot. I'll leave."

Henry lowered the shotgun slightly. "Then do it," he wheezed.

Gilmer said, "Put your hand in your pocket, Harley, and go wait for me outside."

Henry snatched the gun's stock back to his cheek. "If he takes a step, I'll cut you in two."

Harley hesitated.

"Go ahead, son." Gilmer motioned at the door. "I'll be out in a minute."

Harley moved slowly at first, keeping an eye on Henry. The store owner gripped the shotgun with trembling hands; his eyes were squeezed shut. A high, pain-filled cry—the sound of an animal in agony—came from somewhere inside him. When the boy got to the door, he looked back in time to see Mr. Henry crumple to the floor by his office gate; scattered around him, a thousand points of light sparkled from tiny pieces of shattered dreams. Mr. Gilmer was walking up the aisle toward the front of the store.

The little bell over the door sounded its musical note, but Nash Henry didn't hear it.

On the sidewalk, Gilmer handed Harley his handkerchief. "Did he break your nose?"

Harley touched the cloth to his nose then examined it. He had his mind on something else. "We come out alive."

"We *came* out alive."

"Ain't that the gospel truth." Harley stared at the bloody handkerchief, rubbing it between his thumb and forefinger, caught up in his own thoughts.

Gilmer walked to the corner of the store and looked up at the sky. "Well, you saved some lives in there, son. How'd you manage to get your hands on the shotgun?"

The boy followed Gilmer to the edge of the walkway without knowing it; the handkerchief was back at his nose. "It was my angel . . . my own personal guardian . . . walked in there big as all outdoors." He was talking to himself more than to Gilmer. "He came right in that store an' fixed it so Mr. Henry would get busy doin' somethin' else. He even gave me the idea about unloadin' the gun." A wide grin showed from behind the handkerchief, and he jerked his head at the bench. "I sat right there an' prayed for him to go inside with me, an' he did. He practically broke open that shotgun an' handed me them shells." The boy was shaking his head in wonder. The grin stayed, but the tears came; Gilmer was forgotten again. "God, You did it just for me . . . just me."

Harley had the man's full attention. "Can you remember what he looked like?"

"Who?" asked the distracted boy.

"The angel, son. Can you remember what he looked like?"

"To tell the truth, Mr. Gilmer, he looked a whole lot like you." Harley looked up at the man. "That's how I knowed he was my angel."

"You *knew* he was your angel."

"Yes, sir." Harley barely heard him. He was remembering his angel. "I knowed it for sure."

Gilmer almost smiled.

The boy got most of the blood off his face, thanks to the water pump at the courthouse. Gilmer was taking a closer look at his nose when Julia and her mother walked up.

Elise Austin was clearly astounded, but she was learning. "Mr. Crawford, I beg you to tell me that you were injured while performing an heroic act."

The two men looked at each other and smiled, then Gilmer laughed. He didn't laugh often, but when he did he enjoyed it. Harley, who had never even seen Mr. Gilmer smile, joined in because the man was laughing and because he was vastly relieved no one was killed.

Julia Austin smiled. Her mother crossed her arms and waited.

Gilmer recovered and said, "Forgive us, ladies, but Mr. Crawford did, in fact, save someone's life."

"And you find humor in this?"

Gilmer's smile lost none of its liveliness. "I suppose I have that right, ma'am. The life he most assuredly saved was my own."

Both women looked at the boy. There was a courthouse bench nearby and Elise took a seat. "I would like very much to hear about this."

A sharp gust of wind blew across the square and Gilmer said, "Perhaps we should retire to the courthouse."

Dark gray clouds, black and bulbous on their underside, advanced on the town. Fat raindrops splattered here and there in the dusty street. Elise stood up. "Let's."

Harley thought otherwise. "I better go see Mose. He'll want to know about this."

"You're gonna get all wet," warned Julia.

Harley was thinking about angels, not thunderstorms. "It'll just be a sprinkle." He was turning away when Gilmer said, "Harley?"

"Sir?"

"Without those shotgun shells, he couldn't win. What made you show them to me?"

A long roll of thunder came from the advancing line of storms. Harley looked up at the darkening sky, then across the street at the Purvis Mercantile. His small audience was learning he would often take a breath and let it out before he spoke. "You needed to know he didn't have a chance. Mose says, as long as a man's breathin', he still has a chance to pray to be a Christian . . . so Mr. Henry still has a chance. I knowed . . . uh, I knew you wouldn't want to take his last chance."

"Of course," Gilmer nodded. "I thank you for giving me the privilege of sparing his life."

"Yes, sir. I gotta go now. I gotta tell Mose Mr. Henry ain't gonna shoot his dog."

Gilmer held up an arresting hand. "Harley?"

The boy tried to stand still, but his feet wanted to get moving. "Sir?"

"Mr. Henry hasn't said he's not going to shoot Mose's dog."

"Oh." He considered that for a minute then said, "Well, then me an' Mose'll have to pray, I reckon. My angel's gonna be right by me, an' Mose's'll be right by him. They'll be standin' up for us, sure as shootin'."

Gilmer and the ladies watched the boy jog off in the direction of the approaching weather.

The chimes in the courthouse tower told the town it was two o'clock. Mr. Gilmer escorted the ladies up the walk and into the building.

Harley beat the rain to Mose's house, but barely. Mose and Lady were standing in the doorway of the lopsided barn, watching the sky turn a greenish color. Lady saw Crawford first and loped across the deserted horse lot to greet him. Mose followed. The three gathered by the old water trough.

"We need to pray," said Harley.

"Okay." Mose didn't ask any questions. "C'mon over here in the barn."

They sat in the dirt at the barn's door to watch the rain work its way toward them, and Harley told him what happened at the store. Mose showed a rare smile when he heard about the real live angel. When Harley told him Mr. Henry was acting crazy, Mose stopped smiling.

"You reckon he'll come down here an' try to shoot Lady?"

Harley shrugged. "Hard to say. I don't think Mr. Gilmer trusts him, even a little bit. What'll you do if he comes?"

"Well, like you said, we needs to pray." Mose sat up straighter. "An' I reckon this'd be a good time to start, 'cause that's him right yonder comin' down the road."

And it was. Nash Henry was two blocks away, walking in the

rain, coming right down the middle of the street. He was carrying his shotgun.

Harley jumped up and Mose followed. Without consultation the two boys bowed their heads. Mose said, "Lord, we in a bad spot here. We ain't got much time to pray, an' we need Yo' help right quick. Amen."

Harley was next. "That's the truth, Lord. I thank You for lettin' me see my angel an' for gettin' me an' Mr. Gilmer outta that scrape just now, an' I ask that You'd do the same for me an' my friend right now. Please protect us. Amen."

When they looked up, the man was a block away and still coming. He was leaning into the wind, carrying the shotgun in front of him like a soldier in a skirmish line. The wind was getting stronger; even as they watched, it blew his derby hat off and rolled it back up the street. The man didn't turn or slow. Out by the water trough the windmill was spinning, its gears squealing.

Mose looked around the interior of the barn and said, "He ain't seen us. You reckon we oughta hide in here?"

Harley shook his head. "Can't. It's the first place he'd look, an' he'd have us trapped for sure."

The wind was starting to howl; hay blew from the recesses in the loft and swirled around the boys. Lightning flashed on the far side of the creek, thunder followed. Lightning flashed again, then again, closer. The windmill fan was a blur. A deep roar could be heard from somewhere west of them.

"What's that sound?" asked Harley. The roar became a rumble—deepening, resonating. A line of lightning moved toward them, the rumble was beginning to drown out the sound of the thunder.

"I ain't ever heard one, but I bet it's a cyclone."

"That's bound to be what it is," yelled Harley.

The ground was beginning to shake; dust spilled from the old rafters to be blown out of the barn. Shingles, one or two at a time, were being torn from the roof of the house. Henry stopped in the street; he was facing southwest.

Harley looked up and watched holes appearing in the roof of the barn. Patches of gray daylight were ticking into the roof faster than he could count. "We can't stay in here." Harley looked at the little shack. "An' most of the house'll be gone 'fore we get there."

"My momma ain't here. She went over to the railroad station, an' I better get over there in case she needs me."

"If you try to get past him, he's liable to shoot you."

"Can't be helped." Mose pointed over their heads. The roof was disappearing before their eyes. "Can't stay in here either. The sides'll go next an' it'll fall in on us."

Harley pointed at the water trough. "The wind ain't gonna blow away that concrete. Let's get in there."

Mose shook his head. "You stay there. I gotta go make sure my momma's gonna be all right."

The rain was holding off, but the force of the wind was increasing. They looked through the door—Henry was on the move again.

"I'm gonna circle around the house an' get behind him, then run up the street." Mose was having to yell. "He won't ever see me."

"Follow me as far as the water trough," yelled Harley.

Mose nodded.

Harley yelled something and ran from the barn with Mose and the dog at his heels. The bigger boy had taken only a few steps when the wind knocked him backward into Mose. They rolled a few feet, then got to their hands and knees and started crawling. Mose yelled something Harley couldn't hear.

Small pebbles and sand were blowing across the yard, stinging their faces and making it difficult to see. They moved side by side, almost on their stomachs. The dog was out front, head down, going for the trough. They could see Nash Henry in a ditch by the street, one arm wrapped around a medium-sized oak, the other hand holding on to the shotgun. Mr. Saucier's cows broke through the fence on the far side of the pasture and were running headlong down the slope toward Big Black Creek.

The weather system moving toward them spawned four major tornadoes. One went through the middle of Natchez, tearing up everything it touched along a path seven hundred yards across and a hundred miles long.

It wasn't the big one.

The largest of the four twisters would, in years to come, become known as The Great South Mississippi Tornado. It hit Amite, Louisiana at midday and came close to wiping out the town. It crossed the Pearl River between one thirty and two o'clock, moving northeasterly into Mississippi, gaining energy by the second. Within fifteen minutes of crossing the Pearl it was cutting a swath of destruction two and a half miles wide and coming up on Big Black Creek.

The boys and dog made it to the trough and peeked around the side, trying to locate the source of the loud roar.

They huddled in the limited protection offered by the trough. Mose put his mouth against Harley's ear and yelled, "I can make it from here."

Harley twisted so he could yell back. "You can't even stand up." Harley didn't want to threaten his friend, but he'd use force if he had to. "I'm bad sorry, Mose, but I can't let you do it. I'm bigger'n you, an' I'll hold you down 'fore I'll let you get blown away."

"Don't do it." Mose shook his head forcefully. "If you try to stop me, Lady won't know not to bite you, an' it might be bad."

Harley yelled his prayer in Mose's ear, "Lord, don't let him do this here thing; he'll get hurt for sure. An', Lord, I'd sure like to come out of this without gettin' bit too bad."

Lady was on her belly, tight against the side of the trough.

When Harley finished his prayer, he looked at the dog and yelled, "Don't you bite me, Lady." The dog opened one eye as the white boy grabbed Mose around the neck and pinned him to the ground.

Before Mose could react, Lady abandoned him and made a leap for the inside of the trough. The wind caught her at the apex of her jump and flipped her over the low wall. She scrambled up, braced her feet against the side, and barked at the boys. The wind blew her back into the tank.

Dust filled the boys' open mouths as they stared first at where the dog had appeared and then at each other.

Harley tried to spit out the dirt and got saliva blown into his face. He yelled, "God wants you in that tank, Mose!"

"Amen!" yelled Mose.

They fought the wind and followed the dog, grunting and clawing their way over the low wall.

Lady was pressed against the west side of the tank, hunkered down as low as she could get. They crawled on their bellies to where she was and peered over the side.

The rain wasn't as heavy as it was going to get, and they could see the dark outline of the trees that followed the creek. The tornado chose that moment to explode through the edge of the timber; the rain and mist parted like a curtain, and the thing started up the slope. Mose gasped, "Have mercy."

Both boys had heard old-timers talk about tornadoes, but nothing could have prepared them for the monster moving toward them. The funnel wasn't hanging from a thunderstorm; it *was* the storm. The body of it was undulating slowly, almost casually; the lower edge seemed to boil the dirt, turning it into an angry eruption of reddish-brown steam. Full-grown trees by the thousands were being uprooted or broken off. Some were cast aside; others were hundreds of feet off the ground, circulating in the edges of the rotating cloud.

Fighting their way from the barn to the tank sucked out the

boys' energy; the sight of the storm emptied their hearts. It was less than two miles away and coming fast.

Harley dropped to the bottom of the tank on his stomach, his hands pressed against his ears, his eyes tightly closed. Mose heard a high whine from somewhere above him and looked up in time to see the first blade depart the windmill, cleaving the air like a blunt arrow. In the next instant the unbalanced fan came apart, shedding wooden shrapnel in all directions before the boy could think to protect himself.

A constant barrage of lightning stabbed at the air from the sides of the tornado. Mr. Saucier's cows had vanished.

Flying barn doors and wagons were visible now, mixing with the trees—tumbling, spinning. The sound became a physical force, a demonic howl beyond deafening. A huge oak landed at the back edge of the yard and rolled down the hill behind the barn. The little water trough was centered in the storm's path.

The funnel was halfway up the hill when Nash Henry turned loose of the tree and pointed the shotgun at the cloud. Two silent spurts of flame and smoke belched from the shotgun. As Mose watched, the wind seized the poor man and rolled him down the street, slamming him into a lamppost. He wrapped his arms around the post, clinging to it, his mouth open in a soundless scream. In the next instant, the gale lifted him off the ground, then snatched him away from the post.

Mose pressed himself against the far side of the trough, looking up at the savage black mass. It was coming up the hill too fast, closing on the edge of the pasture across the street. He held his hands tightly against his ears but couldn't keep out the wind's scream. His momma's little wooden shack flew apart as if bursting from fright. His mouth moved as he watched the storm, but he couldn't hear his own words. *Lord, I'm close to dyin', an' I can't think of what to pray. I know You're close, but I'm scared. If I die, please take care of my momma and my Pap. Amen.* A tenacious strobe of lightning clawed at the barn, ripping huge sections off the sides and top. An instant later, the wind tore away what the lightning had left.

When it reached the top of the hill, the lower edge of the funnel continued following its upward trajectory and moved into the air above the corral. The crushing roar became a hissing sound and the ground stopped shaking. When it came over the water trough, the bottom of the tornado was more than a hundred feet above them, still moving eastward. Harley hadn't moved. Mose was on his back, scrooched down as far as he could get; he took his hands off his ears and wrapped his arms around Lady. The opening in the bottom of the funnel was passing directly over him.

The nightmare overhead swallowed the daylight and the world was midnight black.

The feeling he was looking into a deep well gripped him—it was accompanied by the sensation of spinning slowly in space, falling into the black pit. He felt dizzy and wrapped his arms more tightly around the dog. He wanted to scream, but he was too terrified—the storm might hear him and pluck him away.

The inside of the storm was a portrait of evil in motion—a horrible masterpiece offered by a demented artist. Lightning flashes worked their way up and down the interior walls and pulsed from side to side. The thousands of bright electric veins appeared like cracks in shattered mirrors, illuminating the depths for a long heartbeat while their Designer prepared a million more to feed the sucking void.

Clusters of small tornadoes, angry at being held in check by the monster storm, whipped and snapped from the lower fringes of the rotating column. The hissing sound was coming from these miniature killers.

The dreadful opening was past the crest of the little hill within seconds, descending as it moved, seeking the ground. The earth resumed its quaking when it touched down. The trees on the back side of the lot were tossed into the air like a splash of dark green liquid.

A thick curtain of rain followed on the heels of the black cloud, eventually obscuring the tornado and muting its roar.

It was headed for downtown.

Quiet came to the tiny round refuge.

The leaves and accumulated trash in the trough were gone.

The dog stirred first. She pushed herself to a sitting position, and the boys sat up with her. The three peered over the edge of the trough, looking toward the creek, surveying the approach path of the storm. Holes in the fast-moving cloud cover allowed rays of sunshine to highlight the destruction.

Lady jumped over the concrete wall and shook herself. The boys stood up, looked long at each other, then turned in a slow circle.

Nothing was left of the little house or the barn. As far as they could see not a single house remained. The trees were gone; the ground was bare. All that was left was their water trough.

Harley looked at his hands. Every trace of the dried blood from his nose had been polished away by blowing dust, even the residue under his fingernails was gone.

The unnatural silence was almost as frightening as the maelstrom.

Mose tried to speak, but his throat was too dry. He finally managed to croak, "I better get down to the train station. My momma might need me."

"I'll go with you." Harley was hoarse too. "I can go on home from there."

Mose put out his hand. "If it wasn't for you, I'd be dead."

When they shook hands, Harley could only nod.

A suggestion of warm drizzle was all that was left of the storm. The air around them smelled of freshly cut grass.

*　　*　　*

The roof was damaged on the new courthouse, and the windows were blown out. The remainder of the business district was completely obliterated. The small handful of homes that hadn't flattened or carried away were severely damaged.

The railroad depot had been rolled across the tracks, leaving little more than an unrecognizable scattering of lumber. Boone Finley, Mose's mother, and two other black people had sought refuge in a railroad boxcar. The car was thrown a hundred and fifty yards, killing all four.

Harley Crawford's family survived.

Gilmer, Elise, and Julia Austin were among the dozens of people who had sought refuge in the courthouse. They, along with the three horses taken inside by their owners, were safe.

Mr. W. B. Allsworth and Mr. F. J. Calhoun rode their horses ten miles to Richburg to tell what happened. Four hours after the storm hit, an N.O. & N.E. train arrived from Hattiesburg carrying doctors, nurses, and medical supplies.

The courthouse doubled as a hospital and morgue.

Trains came and went around the clock on Saturday—along with a steady stream of wagons—bringing tents, food, and rescue workers from as far away as Jackson. The badly injured were moved to the two hospitals in Hattiesburg. The trains and wagons kept coming. Two days earlier the population of Purvis had been two thousand; by Sunday evening thirty-five hundred people were living and working there.

Rescue parties started combing through the devastation before the storm was out of sight; the efforts went on day and night. Somber, mud-covered men came too frequently to the square—bringing wagons burdened with the lifeless bodies of men, women, and children. The workers would stay long enough to take a few bites of food and drink a cup of coffee before going back out. For the first two days the sound of weeping and wailing never ceased.

By Monday the area was taking on the appearance of an orderly refugee camp. The National Guard and Army set up bivouac areas; row after row of white tents were spread in all directions. Wagons loaded with blankets and clothing were stationed around the courthouse. Food lines were open all day. Dozens of small fires dotted the tent city. Women and children huddled by the fires in small groups, talking and praying in low voices. The men and boys dug through pile after pile of rubble, all hoping to find one more survivor.

Monday evening the sky was black and moonless. Hundreds of kerosene lanterns moved to and fro through the town; that many more hung from poles among the tents. A thin layer of smoke hung low over the area, casting back a reflection of the glow from the fires. Every few hours, the night's peace would be cut by a plaintive wail—the signal another body had been found.

Just east of the courthouse, a small black boy and his dog lay in the mud by one of the small fires; a white boy, equally un-mindful of the mud, lay on the other side of the fire. The boys had spent the past three days doing men's work—the dog was fairly clean, but the boys were muddy from their ears down. The fire they used for comfort wasn't near their regular tent, but the tents all looked alike at night, and they weren't sure where theirs was . . . and they were too tired to care.

A suggestion of a breeze, barely strong enough to stir the open flames, drifted through the encampment from the southwest.

South of the courthouse, just west of the Pass Christian Road, an old black man was moving slowly through a collection of tents pitched on the ground where "The Quarters" had been. He was looking for a black boy and his mother, and it made sense to start his search in the colored section of the temporary town. The old man was dressed for church; he wore a brown suit and hat and a loose-fitting white shirt with a tie. He walked with the help of a thick walking stick, picking his way carefully through the mud, stopping here and there to ask a few questions.

*   *   *

The boy didn't stir when the dog lifted her head. She stood up and sniffed the air, then moved to the other side of the fire. The wind confirmed what she suspected, and she blew through her nose to wake the boy. When he didn't move, she trotted off by herself.

A group of bone-weary black men sat around a fire, eating stew out of tin plates and drinking lukewarm coffee. One or two looked up when the old man stopped near their circle. He had to be the only man in town wearing a tie, but he didn't look out of place.

The stranger said, "Good evenin', gentlemen. I'm lookin' for a young colored boy name of Mose Washington. Wondered if any of ya'll might know him?"

The men looked at each other, then shook their heads and went back to their food.

"The boy would have a coondog with him, a fine little Walker female."

All of the men looked up. One of the younger men asked, "Does him an' that dog run with that Crawford boy?"

The old man shrugged. "I haven't seen them lately. They might."

The man who asked the question put down his plate and stood up. He wasn't much more than a boy himself. "Young boy . . . acts polite? Dog knows what he's thinkin' without that boy sayin' nothin'?"

The men in the circle were nodding.

The old gentleman smiled. "I 'magine that would be them."

"I know that dog, an' I know them boys. Them two been right in amongst all this here work—us diggin' folks outta all this here wreckage an' all. Folks here 'bouts done taken to callin' 'em Salt an' Pepper."

"Hmm. It's not like him to get in the way of folks workin'."

"No-no, I don't mean it like that," said the young man.

Tears seemed to be a part of his life these days, and they came while he spoke. "That little Walker hound found two babies this mornin' . . . twins . . . an' them young boys dug 'em out. Folks said them little ones was near to dyin' . . . said them three saved they lives."

"That's real fine then."

"Uh . . . uncle?" the man hesitated. "I been 'round that little colored boy for the better part of two days now, an' . . . uh . . . an' I ain't heard him talk yet."

The old man considered that, then asked, "Do you know where they are right now?"

The man smiled for the first time in three days. "No, suh, I don't know where them boys is at, but I betcha I know somebody what does."

"And who might that be?" asked the man.

The man pointed over the old stranger's shoulder. "Why, I reckon it'd be that dog comin' yonder."

The boy wore a man's cast-off hunting coat that fit him like a sleeping bag; the rubber galoshes came to his knees.

Pap bent over him and touched his arm. "Boy?"

The boy opened his eyes and stared at the fire first, then rolled onto his back and looked up at the man. His expression was bland, his voice even. "Pap?"

"That's right, boy."

"I was dreamin' you came an' got me." The boy didn't move. "This ain't a dream, is it?"

"This ain't a dream, son. I'm right here."

The boy took his time getting to his knees. He was afraid to move too quickly—Pap might disappear. "I'm wantin' you to take us home, Pap . . . back to *our* home."

"That's why I'm here, son."

The boy looked smaller than when he left the Delta. He

knelt in the mud, making no effort to move toward the man. "Momma's dead."

Pap nodded. "They told me."

From somewhere in the camp, a woman's pain-filled cry told the night another loved one had received "some bad news." The man watched as the boy looked in the direction of the heart-piercing sound.

His eyes came back to the man, and he said, "That's what folks do when they find out somebody's dead." He looked at the ground and began to shudder. "It happens a whole lot."

The man said, "I understand, boy."

The boy sat back on his heels and hung his head. The wailing continued, and he moved his head slowly back and forth. "It's been bad here."

There was nothing the man could say to help.

The child's arms hung limp at his side; his shoulders sagged. "It's been real bad." He took a breath and looked up at the man, his eyes shiny with tears.

The man knelt in the mud and reached out to rest his hand on the boy's shoulder. Words were useless, but he said, "I know, son, I know. But I'm here now."

The boy took the man's arm and wrapped both of his around it. "Are you gonna take us home?"

"God willin', son, that's exactly what I'm gonna do."

The shuddering was getting worse. "An' we ain't ever gonna . . ." His body jerked as he struggled for breath. ". . . have to leave again?"

"Not ever again, son, not ever."

The child's hands climbed the man's arm, tugging on it until he could get his arms around the old man's neck. The forlorn little figure pulled himself as close as he could get and held on. Quiet sobs racked his body; a mewing sound came in concert with the tremors that passed through his body and added itself to the wailing from the nearby tent. The man held the muddy child close and patted his back.

When he recovered to the point where he could almost talk, the child put his mouth against the man's ear and managed to whisper, "I was brave . . . just . . . like you said." Another torrent of tears followed, and he pressed his face to the man's chest to muffle his sobs. The man gathered him up and held him close.

The sky was turning pink in the east, and men were up and moving. The old man sat on a small stack of firewood, rocking gently and humming a soft hymn. The little boy wearing the man's coat was curled against his chest.

The dog stood and stretched, then walked over and nosed the boy awake. Mose's eyes sprung open and he jerked up. When he realized where he was, he took a deep breath and sagged against the old man's arm. "I was scared maybe I dreamed it."

"If it's a dream, boy, we both in it." Pap smiled and said, "I reckon we ought to go see can we find us a cup o' coffee."

"Yessuh, I know where it's at." Mose climbed out of the man's lap. "The coffee ain't always hot, but they do the best they can." He pointed at the white boy and spoke to the dog. "Wake him up, so he can meet Pap."

The coffee was good, and hot.

For breakfast they sat on a tree trunk and ate sausage patties wrapped in white bread. Word got around about the hound and the two boys, and people stopped by to visit and offer the dog their meager leftovers. Lady wagged her tail at the offerings, and Harley thanked the folks. Mose sat next to Pap and sipped at his coffee.

During a lull in the visiting, Mose spoke without looking up. "I guess me an' Lady better not go home just yet."

"Oh?"

Mose traced the rim of the tin cup with a mud-flaked finger.

"No, sir. They ain't got another dog like Lady here, an' she might find some more people. I reckon we best stay a few more days."

Pap nodded. "That's the choice a man would make, boy, an' I'm proud of you."

Mose was saying, "Yessuh," while Harley was saying, "Yonder comes Mr. Gilmer."

Gilmer stepped off the mare and ground hitched her at the end of the tree trunk. As he approached, the three on the log stood up, and he said, "Morning, gentlemen."

Harley and Mose said their good mornings; Pap took his hat off and smiled at the man. "Good mornin' to you, Cap'n Gilmer."

Gilmer hesitated for the briefest moment then stepped closer and peered at Pap. He compared what he saw in the old man to Mose's upturned face, and said, "It surprises me that I didn't see it sooner."

The two boys were looking from one man to the other, mystified, when Gilmer added, "He's a fine man, Preacher. Your grandson?"

"My great-grandson, Cap'n," said Pap. "It's a God-given pleasure to see you again."

Tough times and fatigue tend to bring emotions closer to the surface. Gilmer put his hand on Mose's shoulder and spoke quietly. "I came on him a week or so ago in a situation that was not unlike the circumstances of my first meeting with you. You'll be pleased to know that he . . ." He had to stop and clear his throat before finishing. ". . . that he is cut from your cloth."

Mose and Harley had no reason to cry, but they almost did.

"Thank you, Cap'n," said Pap. He turned to Mose. "Cap'n Gilmer had an occasion to come by an' visit Old Major Parker some time back—be 'bout forty years ago now. He was kind enough to pull me out of a tight spot."

It rained on and off all that week. Pap helped out around the food lines; the dog found a young married couple on Tuesday and a small child the next day. On Thursday and Friday she came up empty-handed. Saturday morning Pap, Mose, and Lady got on the train to go home. Mr. Gilmer had a word with the conductor, and Lady rode in the passenger car with Pap and Mose.

The head porter on the Hattiesburg-to-Jackson train was a slender black man with white hair and a deep voice. When they got to Jackson, he led them through the big depot telling black folks to "Step outta the way, there," and white folks to "Move aside, please." Preacher and Mose were embarrassed by the extra attention; Lady was growing accustomed to it. Their escort told the head porter on the Yellow Dog about what Lady and the boy had been doing down there in Purvis, and Lady climbed up in the passenger car just like everybody else.

It was after dark when they got home to Cat Lake. Pap left Mose and Lady on the porch of the cabin and went to bed. When he got up Sunday morning, they were still there, listening to the sun come up and looking at their lake.

Pap brought two cups of coffee to the porch, and they sat in their rocking chairs while Mose told Pap about the tornado. When he finished, the boy asked, "You reckon that's what hell's like, Pap?"

The old man thought for a minute then said, "Some, I reckon, 'cept for the noise an' all. When the Bible talks 'bout 'the outer darkness,' I think it means a place where there's nothin' but emptiness. Folks who're spendin' their time on earth wantin' God to stay away from 'em are already choosin' hell on earth. It makes sense to me that when those folks get to hell they gonna be where they wanted to be while they were here . . . out in the darkness, all by theyselves . . . forever."

They stayed home from church to give the boy time to get reacquainted with the place. Pap walked out on the porch after Sunday dinner and threw a handful of crumbs under the trees for the birds. The three—Pap, Mose, and Lady—sat on the front porch of the cabin to watch the lake and listen to the birds, and Pap got Mose caught up on what had happened while he was gone. Two of the cats, the momma and a young tom, acted like they resented having the dog back. The momma cat marched out and plopped down in the middle of the yard so the birds couldn't congregate there; the mockingbirds perched in the nearest pecan tree and complained; the redbirds took their business elsewhere. The dog pretended to be asleep.

Mose told Preacher how he happened to meet Mr. Gilmer, and Preacher told the boy how Gilmer's Grove got its name.

CHAPTER ELEVEN

The commissary sat on the north side of the road, centered between Gilmer's Grove and the Cat Lake bridge. A man could sit
on the porch of the store and look south across the road at the
Parkers' big white house.

"That ol' commissary was practically brand-new back
then," said Pap. "Ol' Major Parker built it pretty soon after The
Surrender. The Major had a feeble, old white man name of Percy
runnin' the place, an' all of us traded over there an' settled up
after our crops came in.

"I walked over there just 'fore noon on a day pretty as this
here to get somethin'—cornmeal or whatnot. Anyways, I got my
business done an' came out the front door right when the Major's
daughter was comin' across the road from they house. Cap'n
Gilmer had come out here to visit with the Major, an' he was
comin' along a little piece behind Miss Sarah.

"There was one of them sorry Yankee carpetbaggers, a white
feller, been hangin' around there, drinkin' from a jug an' tor-
mentin' folks." Pap worked his mouth and spit into the yard, just
missing the momma cat. The old man was pretty careful of his
manners, but talking about Yankees put a bad taste in his mouth.
"When Miss Sarah stepped up on the porch, he reached an' took

ahold of her arm. She was tryin' to git free, an' I was standin' right there . . . when he didn't turn loose, I drew back an' laid him low with my fist."

He paused to remove his glasses and took out his bandana. He cleaned the glasses and shook his head slowly. "Well . . . things happened right quick like after that."

He fixed the glasses in place and took his time stowing the kerchief. "That feller come off the floor yellin' an' cussin', reachin' for his gun an' sayin' what he was gonna do to me . . . callin' me a nigger an' all . . . an' next thing you know, Cap'n Gilmer was on the porch. The Cap'n stood right there between me an' that white man an' said, just as nice as you please, 'You may reach for your pistol, sir.'

"Well, they ain't no man in his right mind wants another man to go to hell, but seems like some folks won't let theyselves be turned away." A fish splashed near the lake's bank, but Preacher didn't hear it. He was looking across the lake, remembering the day a white man stepped between him and death. "That fool Yankee was grinnin' 'cause he already had his hand on his gun . . . an' I reckon he thought he had the bulge on a man with one arm. He went to unlimber that shooter, an' soon's he twitched, Cap'n Gilmer shucked that Navy Colt. Mmm-mm . . . I believe the thing I recollect most is the ratchetin' sound of that pistol's hammer comin' back." He paused for a moment, listening to the forty-year-old memory, then shook his head and sighed. "The Cap'n blowed that no-good Yankee carpetbagger right through that porch railin', an' clear to kingdom come."

Pap stayed quiet for a long time, and Mose finally asked, "An' ya'll didn't git in no trouble?"

"Could've, but didn't." Pap almost smiled. "Cap'n Gilmer sent a man to tell, an' a whole troop of Yankee horse soldiers came that next day an' found that carpetbagger's body danglin' from a rope in one of them oaks up by the store. Had a note pinned to his coattail sayin', 'He laid his hand on a lady an' threatened a brave man.' "

Mose was wide-eyed. "How'd they come to let ya'll off?"

"Cap'n Gilmer was visitin' at the big house 'cause he was in the war with Ol' Major Parker. When the Yankees rode up, the Cap'n stepped out in the yard an' talked for a while with that bluebelly officer. After a bit that officer spoke up nice as you please, sayin', 'Sir, it sounds like you did what any good man would do.' That Yankee shook Cap'n Gilmer's hand like a regular gentleman an' told those horse soldiers to leave the body where it was at . . . said it might remind menfolk that they was called to be respectful to womenfolk." He shrugged. "I reckon it worked, 'cause any trashy folks comin' 'round after that kept shut."

Mose was looking across the lake at the trees in the grove. "An' that's why they calls it Gilmer's Grove."

Preacher nodded and smiled. "Ol' Major Parker started in callin' it Gilmer's Grove right off, an' they been callin' it that ever since. Every now an' again, when I ride by there, I thank the good Lord for what Cap'n Gilmer did for me. From now on, I reckon those trees'll remind me to thank Him for what he did for you."

Mose was frowning, thinking. "It don't seem likely that the same white man'd pull me an' you both out of a tight spot—I mean, what with him not knowin' us an' all."

"If I was you," said Preacher, "I'd think some on that . . . a boy an' his great-granddaddy, forty years apart an' spread out by two hundred miles, an' the same white man steps in an' saves their bacon."

"God done it?"

Pap smiled. "Sho' as He made little green apples."

"Reckon how come?"

"If I was you, I reckon I'd do me some prayin', an' I'd ask myself that same question. I figure the answer's gonna end up bein' mighty important."

Mose took the man at his word.

* * *

An hour later they were still on the porch, rocking and watching the sun sprinkle itself on the lake. An occasional fish would make a splash in the water. The momma cat was curled up by the dog; the tom was in Mose's lap. The birds came and went, pecking in the dirt under the pecan trees.

Pap was dozing off when Mose said, "For the eyes of the Lord run to an' fro throughout the whole earth, to show Himself strong in the behalf of them whose heart is perfect toward Him."

"Mm-hmm."

"That's what I needs to be thinkin' about. I needs to make sure my heart is perfect . . . God'll do what needs to be done after that. Does that sound right?"

"You sho' can't go wrong if you lookin' to make yo' heart perfect, but it don't take you to why He chose to single me an' you out."

The boy shook his head and sighed. "It don't make any sense that He'd be doin' it for somethin' special."

"Why's that?"

"'Cause ain't nothin' ever happened out here. Ain't nobody out here but me an' you."

The boy had been spending too much time around folks who didn't use their words properly, but this wasn't a good time to start turning him back. Preacher said, "Folks are still alive 'cause of you."

Mose picked at a loose thread on his overalls. "Lady done that."

"Lady's a good dog . . . but mostly 'cause of you. An' she didn't tell those two white boys down at Purvis 'bout Jesus."

Mose watched his fingers fool with the thread while he asked, "Whatta *you* think?"

"God wants me to know Him an' make Him known—an' He wants the same from you. I'm nigh eighty years old, an' sittin' on this porch an' lookin' back, I can't think of but one reason why He'd keep me around here this long . . . an' it's to take care of you. I believe God let Cap'n Gilmer step in 'cause He's tellin' us that you're next. He's got somethin' special lined up He wants you to do—maybe He's got somebody He wants you to look out for."

Mose didn't think so. "Cap'n Gilmer didn't save my life. Them boys might've beat me up some, but they wouldn't've killed me."

"That's true. But you never would've gotten to tell Harley about Jesus, would you?"

"Probably not."

"An' if Harley hadn't've been yo' friend, he wouldn't've been there to keep you from goin' out in that tornado."

That made sense. "I guess."

"Well, then," said the old man, "if it was me, I'd set my heart on gettin' to know God better every day . . . an' I'd make Him known to anybody I could. I reckon that's as perfect as you can get yo' heart. After that, you just wait to find out what God wants you to do."

"But there ain't nothin' ever happens out here, an' I ain't never gonna leave again."

"Watch out, now. God's liable to snatch you outta here so fast you'd forget yo' ears."

That was possible. "If you was me, would you be scared?"

"Scared? Boy, gittin' to raise you is 'bout the finest thing ever happened to me. If I was you"—he pulled himself forward in his chair and tapped its wooden arm with a crooked old finger—"I'd be watchin' close. I'd figure God was plannin' for me to do somethin' that'd stop this here ol' world an' make 'er run backwards, an' I'd want to be ready. When the time hits—an' you can know it will—you wants to be squattin' to jump."

The days passed in peace. Except for trips to the gin and church, Mose and the dog stayed close to Cat Lake. Days became seasons. Cotton was raised, and picked, and planted again. Years passed.

* * *

In 1912, four years after Mose came home, they lost money on the farm; 1913 was worse.

The next year they used the last of their cash money to buy cottonseed.

Their crop came up strong, and it was all but ready to pick when a late-summer hailstorm put every smidgen of it on the ground. Pap stood at the edge of the muddy field and surveyed their loss. "There may've been folks that went broke bigger than us, boy, but I don't reckon any of 'em ever did it any faster." He was eighty-five years old that year, and the loss took a lot out of him.

Mose made a little money picking cotton for other folks, but spent the biggest part of it on medicine for Pap. They had no money left for food, but they wouldn't starve as long as they could eat fresh dock for greens and go fishing. By the end of September, they had a few teaspoons of coffee left, less sugar, no salt, and precious little cornmeal.

Pap spent the last week of September in his old bedstead. Late on a Friday afternoon, he said, "Moses."

Mose came to the side of the bed. He was thirteen years old, and Pap had never called him anything but *boy* or *son*. "Yessir?"

Pap was propped up a little. He motioned the boy closer. "You ain't very old, son, but you're as good a man as ever I've known. The good Lord knows what He wants from you, an' He can get it without me bein' here." The old man's eyes smiled. "I'm fixin' to leave you here on this earth, but you're not by yo'self. You understand me?"

Mose had known all day his great-grandfather was dying. He wanted to plead with him to stay, but it wasn't Pap's choice to make. He nodded. "I understand, Pap. God's here."

"He *is* here, Moses; He says so." He closed his eyes and rested. His chest rose slightly and fell . . . and rose again. He opened his eyes and reached for the boy's hand. "You needs to get closer to Him, son. Me an' you talked about this . . . He wants yo' heart to be completely His. An' you needs be listenin' real careful. He's gonna speak yo' name, an' you got to go be ready when He calls."

"I'll listen, Pap." He gripped the man's hand with both of his; tears welled at the edges of his eyelids. He waited quietly while Pap rested.

"I wrote you some things on a sheet an' put it in the Bible yonder. You keep my words, son. An' you tell 'em to yo' children."

"I will, Pap. I promise." The boy's lower lip wouldn't stop trembling. He was almost a man—he shouldn't be crying like a young child.

"The devil's here on this earth, son." The eyes closed. The chest rose and fell.

"I know, Pap." He spoke quietly. His eyes filled, and the tears brimmed over his eyelashes and onto his cheeks.

The old man kept his eyes closed. His voice was raspy with exhaustion. "Now, you listen to me. You can tell things about people most folks can't. You've got a gift. You . . . you know things." He stopped to breathe. He paused for so long the boy grew anxious. The chest rose again. "You spend yo' life like I'm tellin' you. You study God to know Him . . . an' you train yo'self to hear when He calls . . . an' you raise up yo' sons to do the same." Another rest. The ragged voice was earnest with conviction. "You got to have a good woman an' a good job. Don't go 'round with a foolish woman, an' don't work for a man that'll cheat you."

Mose nodded. Tears slipped steadily down his cheeks and dripped from his chin.

The old man pulled his hand from the boy's grasp and said, "Come close, son." Mose leaned close, and Pap rested his hand on the boy's stiff, short hair. "I was blessed by God when He gave me you. I named you Moses Lincoln 'cause those men stepped up to save they people. It comes to my mind now that maybe God has somethin' bigger in mind for you." He closed his eyes again. "Moses Lincoln Washington, I bless you in the great an' mighty name of God. I want you to be in prayer for that day when God will offer you the privilege of takin' that bold step for the cause of Christ." Pap's hand came back to rest on the boy's. "I'm leavin' you that book," he said, nodding at the Bible that lay by his side, "that old shotgun, that mule, an' you got that dog. The rest is up to you." He smiled and patted the boy's hands. "You'll do fine, Moses. You always have."

He and the dog slept by Pap's bed that night and stayed close all day Saturday.

Late Saturday afternoon he helped Pap out to the porch to watch the sun go down. Pap drank the last of the coffee out of his beat-up old china cup, and the two talked about Heaven and angels and living right. When the sun went down, Pap lectured him gently. "Boy, you need to do two things for yo' whole life. You got to know God better every day, an' you got to make Him known. If those two things cost you food an' shelter, then go hungry an' sleep in the cold, but you spend every day of yo' life knowin' Him an' makin' Him known . . . an' you bring up yo' babies to do the same."

Mose said he would.

"I reckon you will, boy. I reckon you will." After he finished speaking, Pap settled himself comfortably in his rocker and died.

Sunday morning Mose and Lady buried him by the rosebush on the south edge of the yard.

After the funeral the boy spent the rest of the day on the porch with the dog and cats. He prayed and cried, and he asked God not to let him miss His call.

Mose was up early Monday morning. He didn't have time to catch and cook a fish so he did without. The coffee was gone, but he had plenty of water. He let the dog follow him to the far side of the bridge, then sent her home and told her not to get too far from the house.

Cat Lake was five miles south of Moores Point. The road,

mostly gravel and some dirt, turned back and forth to wind its way past the cotton fields. Mose walked for a while until a Klondike Plantation cotton wagon came along and the driver gave him a ride to town.

When they got to the Parker Gin, Mose jumped down and found a spot in the grassy area out of the way of the wagons. The scene around the gin was familiar to him, but today he was seeing it from a different perspective—he was looking for a job. He reasoned if he was going to work at the place, he'd better know what went on there.

Mule-drawn wagons moved slowly toward a two-lane covered area where the sucking tubes were. When a wagon pulled under the shed, a quick-moving black man scrambled back and forth over the white fluff, using the big tube to send the cotton to the gin machines. The man would empty that wagon, the next wagon would pull up, and the man with the tube would start over. Inside the gin, after the big gin stands got the trash and seeds out of the cotton, the pressing machinery took the cleaned cotton and packed it into five-hundred-pound bales. When the bales were fully compressed, they were wrapped tightly and released to slide down a shiny steel incline to the gin floor. A lean black man wearing a tattered undershirt and baggy blue pants stood at the foot of the steel ramp. He sang a silent song and nodded to himself while he waited for the next bale to slide down to him. When the cotton got to him, he'd pick it up on a big dolly and roll it out onto the dock to wait for the train.

Willie Edwards saw the young boy get off the wagon and move over to stand behind the Busy Bee. Willie was probably the strongest—and close to being the smartest—black man in Moores Point. His position as Mr. R. D. Parker's overseer at the gin was almost a sure guarantee Willie would be able to feed his family year-round. The overseer made two unnecessary passes up and down by the outside row of gin stands while he watched the boy watch the gin. The boy stood in one spot with his arms crossed, feet unmoving, and studied what he could see from his vantage point. When he left the grass and began to wend his way through the wagons, making his way toward the loading platform, Willie moved up to the front of the gin.

Mose mounted the short set of stairs running from the ground up to the loading-dock level, and Willie intercepted him midway. They met under a gray board with faded white letters declaring they were outside the "GIN OFFICE."

Willie Edwards had the height advantage. He stood on the same step with the youngster, and peered down a full foot into wide-set brown eyes . . . calm eyes. "Where you goin' to, boy?" The man's voice sounded like it came from deep within a cavern.

The slender thirteen-year-old took his time and weighed the question while he measured the eyes of the man who asked it. Pap was right—Mose could tell about most people . . . what they felt and thought. He saw nothing in the eyes to warn him off so he decided to answer the big man. He moved up a step to bring equality to the conversation and responded without smiling. "Mornin' to you. I reckon I'll be seein' about gettin' me a job," he gestured at the office wall to show the big man who the deciding authority would be, "with the bossman here." He didn't bother to smile 'cause Pap said, *God gave us village idiots to stand about an' smile for no good reason.*

The boy was thinner than was good for him, but times were tough. He wore a long-sleeve khaki shirt, buttoned at the neck; it was frayed around the edges, but clean, and showed evidence of being ironed. Hand-me-down khaki pants had been taken up to fit him; the needle handler who did the tailoring job was careful but not experienced. The pants were too short to cover the fact that he wore no socks . . . but no one did; a trimmed-down belt held up the pants. High-top shoes, each boasting enough surplus space to accommodate a small rabbit, finished out the wardrobe.

Willie, still five inches taller in spite of the younger man's maneuver on the steps, continued his thorough appraisal of the boy. "You're Preacher Washington's boy, ain't you?"

"Was. His great-grandson," said the boy without changing expression. "Pap died Saturday night."

Death was an accepted companion of the Delta's black folks. Willie's expression reflected concern, but the frown that came was bidden by curiosity, not sadness. "I didn't hear nuthin' 'bout no funeral."

The older man's offhanded inquisition wasn't really a transgression of privacy, and the boy was patient with it. "Pap didn't want none," he said. "I buried him out by the lake yesterday mornin'." The boy offered no further explanation.

While Willie studied the boy's face, the boy turned his gaze slightly, looking past the older man's shoulder to follow a handful of pigeons circling over the gin. The multicolored birds landed, arranged themselves on the ridgeline of the tin roof, and began to preen their feathers. Their cooing was lost behind the noise from the gin.

Willie turned his head to see what drew the boy's attention. The two stood silent and contemplated the birds for a moment while Willie was making up his mind about something.

The boy was still looking at the roof when the overseer turned to face him. The big man took some of the khaki shirtsleeve material in his fingers and tugged slightly. Mose followed Willie's eyes as he looked directly above their heads at the open window of the gin office . . . the office where the white men worked. Willie jerked his head and motioned silently with his hand for Mose to follow him. With the boy trailing, they moved up the stairs and away from the office to a point about halfway down the big loading platform. White bales of cotton, wrapped in brown burlap netting and black steel bands, were arranged in groups around them. The cotton-picking season was running at its peak, and the machines in the gin told everyone within a radius of two blocks they were trying to keep up with the steady influx of loaded wagons.

Willie feinted casualness while he glanced back in the direction of the office and turned to Mose. "Cain't hear nuthin' 'round the machines less folks is yellin'," he explained. Then he told Mose why he drew him away from the office. "Mr. Hoot Washburn, he runnin' the gin while Mistah R. D.'s gone, an' he don't take to hirin' no boys. He's—"

"I ain't no boy, I'm—"

Willie frowned and made a chopping motion with one of the huge hands. "Hush now."

The man's hat, his eyebrows, and the stubble on his face were frosted gray-white with the lint from the gin. The white-covered stubble on his cheeks moved back and forth as he shook his head. Willie was more insistent than Mose, and considerably bigger, so Mose waited. Willie said, "You lookin' at the head nigger o' this here gin, boy. I'm tryin' to help you 'cause I thought yo' gran'daddy was a fine Christian man. Now, step over here an' pay attention."

Willie turned and moved to a line of cotton bales, looked around furtively, and pushed at a bale as if to rearrange it. The headman was nervous about taking so much time with the boy because if Mr. Hoot caught him standing around there'd be a ruckus. Willie was the overseer and stood around some because he was the boss; he just didn't want to have Mr. Hoot see the boy standing about today and come back next week and find him working there. It was too easy to keep things simple.

Mose followed and Willie spoke without looking at him. "You needs to talk to Mr. R. D. Parker. Mr. R. D. an' his daddy owns this here gin, an' he ain't here today. You come back on Saturday . . . Mr. R. D.'ll be here, an' Mr. Hoot won't. Mr. R. D.'ll hire you for the day 'cause he know'd yo' gran'daddy . . . an' he's a fine white man. He'll work you some an' see how you turns out. If'n you works hard, he'll be havin' you back. If'n you don't, we ain't got no time to mess wit' you. You understandin' me?"

Mose looked around him at all the men working at the gin. These men would earn money for five days while he waited at the cabin to ask for a job. He couldn't hide his impatience. "I reckon I do, but I'm needin' me some money right now."

Willie nodded. "We all needin' some money, boy, but there

just ain't much of it. You do like I say . . . you go on back home an' pick cotton, then you come in here Saturday mornin' at first light."

Mose thought for a moment then made his decision. "I reckon I will. I reckon I'll work too." He looked at Willie for a moment then stuck out his hand. "I'm Mose Washington."

Willie was surprised by the move, but recovered. "They calls me Willie." Mose's hand disappeared into the hard fist of the big man, and they shook hands. Or at least Willie moved his fist up and down, and Mose's hand went along for the ride.

When Mose turned to leave, Willie spoke again. "Wear you a hat when you comes back."

Mose turned back with a question. "How come?" There was the mildest hint of distrust in the words. He was becoming weary of being told what to do by a man he didn't know. He tried unsuccessfully not to frown.

Willie was tolerant of the boy's attitude. He could remember being thirteen years old . . . and he had been twice this boy's size. He knew that under the same circumstances he would have reacted more forcefully. "So's you can take it off an' show respect when you sees Mr. R. D. He notices such as that."

"I ain't never worn no hat, 'cept in the field. I don't plan on bein' in the field."

"If'n you wants a man's job, you best wear a man's hat." He touched a large finger to his own hat brim. "Have you got one where you stay at?"

"I don't know." There was a short stack of delapidated brown felt hats in the old chifforobe in the bedroom. Pap was never outside the house without one. "I reckon Pap'll have one somewhere around."

"I'll be gettin' here to the gin come daylight Saturday mornin'; Mr. R. D.'ll be here soon after. You can come an' find me before you goes up to the office, an' I'll show you what to do. Now you git on off from here 'fore Mr. Hoot say somethin'."

The boy nodded and turned away.

"Hey!" The big man stopped him. "You got any money, boy?"

Pap's words came to him as Mose turned around: *Don't be tellin' other folks yo' business, boy. You keep yo' counsel with the Lord, an' let others do the same.*

The headman didn't wait for an answer. "Here, now." Willie's hand was coming from his pocket as he spoke. He looked down at a hand holding two dimes. "You take this here." He held one of the coins out to Mose and put the other one back in its hiding place.

The long fingers looked almost stubby because of their breadth. The wide palm of the man's hand was almost completely calloused from edge to edge. Mose stared for a few seconds at the single ten-cent piece resting like a small island in the middle of the brick-hard palm. He told his eyes to stop looking at the money that could take away his hunger and nodded his thanks at the man. "I'm obliged to you, but I got all I need." The man who would give up half of his pocket money to a boy he didn't know kept the hand extended. Mose knew he would be hungry during the coming week, but he also knew he would eat. He shook his head again.

Willie nodded and put the dime back with its lonesome twin.

Mose watched every inch of the money's journey back to the man's pocket, then looked at the man's face. "I reckon I won't never forget you offered." The boy was nodding to himself as he turned away.

Mose Washington went back out to the cabin on Cat Lake to pick cotton for the Parkers and wait for Mr. R. D. to get back to the gin.

When Willie Edwards got to the gin Saturday morning, Mose was waiting. Willie took him behind some cotton bales and showed him how to take his hat off and hold it by his side and how to stand still and say "Yessuh" while he was being given instructions. "An' don't be wearin' no hat while you talkin' to a white man," he repeated for the tenth time.

The overseer had the boy go through the motions several times, continually reminding him how important it was to show Mr. R. D. that he knew how to be polite. "If I'm gonna show you to Mr. R. D., you needs to make sure I don't come off lookin' bad. You make sure you speak respectful if he says somethin' to you, but you don't need to be askin' him no questions," lectured Willie. "Anything you needs to know, I'm gonna tell you after."

Mose already knew about having manners, but he endured the lessons because Willie was trying to help him.

They were waiting by the office door when R. D. Parker mounted the steps.

When he saw them, the white man broke stride, hesitated a moment, then walked to where they were standing.

Mose, who until that minute was relaxed and confident, felt his mouth go dry. This was the first time he'd seen Mr. R. D. up close since the day he had to hit Ced Pommer with the hoe handle. His knees started shaking.

Willie took off his hat and greeted the boss. "Mornin', Mr. R. D."

"Mornin', Willie. Who's this?"

"This here Mose Washington, boss. He lookin' for a job."

"I thought that was you, Mose." Parker nodded solemnly. "I guess I haven't seen you much in the last few years."

Mose wanted to say something, but someone had stuffed cotton in his mouth. He ended up just nodding his head.

Willie nudged him and he realized he was still wearing his hat. He snatched it off too fast and dropped it. Fumbling the hat put him in a quandary because he didn't know if he should pick it up or leave it where it was. He cut his eyes at Willie, and the big man frowned and nodded for him to pick it up. By the time the boy got his orders from Willie, Mr. R. D. had stooped over and retrieved it.

When Mr. R. D. handed Mose his hat, the boy stared at it for a moment, then put it back on his head. He didn't bother to thank the white man.

Willie Edwards put a big hand over his eyes and groaned out loud.

Parker was smiling. "Mose knows how to do a man's work. Show him what to do."

The giant uncovered his eyes. "Suh?"

"I reckon you picked the best man in town, Willie. Get him started." Parker left the overseer with his newest hand and went to the office.

Seven years later, just before Mose's twenty-first birthday, Mr. R. D. tore down the old commissary out at Cat Lake and built a new gin on the site. Mr. R. D.'s big white house was right across the road from the gin; Mose's cabin was in a thick stand of pecan trees on the far side of Cat Lake. Mr. R. D. ran the office, and Mose ran the gin. Willie Edwards's son, Roosevelt—a nineteen-year-old version of his daddy—was Mose's right-hand man.

CHAPTER TWELVE

The knee sprain Mann picked up during his session with the mechanical bull—aggravated by the twist it took when Missy knocked him into Mose's daylilies—was bothering him when he woke up on Sunday. He skipped breakfast and subsisted on a diet of coffee and aspirin. Patterson and Missy showed up at the front door an hour or so after lunch. Missy was carrying a chocolate cake.

The cake thing was a tradition—initially started by Mann's mother when he was in the first grade. On his first day of school, the six-year-old was nervous about the prospect of spending all day in the big building, and his mom bribed him by promising him a slice of chocolate cake every day when he got home from school. Thereafter, for the next five years, until his mother was killed, he had chocolate cake every afternoon for his "school snack."

Missy found out about the practice when Mann was a freshman in college and reinstituted the custom.

She carried the cake into the kitchen, and Mose followed to help pour the coffee. Patterson and Mann stayed in the living room.

"Any better?" Patterson sat down and pointed at Mann's leg.

"Sore." Mann was trying to get comfortable on the couch. "It'll straighten out in a couple of days."

"You want to take off from work for a few days and rest up?"

"I guess not, thanks. The other bull riders might make fun of me."

"You're still bent on riding bulls then?"

Mann shrugged. "Only the tame ones."

Patterson rolled his eyes. "Wise choice."

Missy and Mose came in with the cake first, and Mose took a seat in his easy chair while Missy brought out the coffee. When everyone was served Mose said, "This ain't a meal, but it seems like it'd be a good idea to pray 'fore I tell y'all these ol' stories."

Missy took a seat on the couch with Mann. They bowed their heads and Mose said, "Lord, You an' me know how You've blessed my life, an' I 'preciate it. I reckon I'm the last person livin' what knows about the things You've done in my life . . . all the different ways You've worked to bring us to this day. My prayer, Lord, for all of us is . . . don't let us take a breath in vain. Give us to come to You well used. Amen."

The old black man started with the death of his daddy and told it the way he remembered it.

Missy knew the people in Mose's story and stopped him once or twice in the beginning to ask questions about the old gin in town and her great-granddaddy. Her questions stopped when Mose got to the part about what Ced Pommer tried to do—and what happened when Mose intervened.

Mose talked most of the afternoon; Patterson, Missy, and Mann listened. Missy or Patterson would get up every now and then to refill the coffee cups. At suppertime, they all moved to the kitchen table for tomato sandwiches. An hour later they were back in the living room with fresh coffee and more cake.

The sun was down when Mose finished his story.

Mann shifted to try and make his leg comfortable. Patterson

was staring out the window. Missy had the dog's head in her lap. No one spoke.

Mose removed his glasses and rubbed the bridge of his nose before putting them back. "Things out at the lake stayed quiet 'til '45. After them demons attacked, I figured we was back in a sho' 'nuff fight." He looked at Mann and Patterson. "You two came in late, but you know 'bout what went on. When it comes right down to it, God's been bringin' us all along, like puttin' us all in one of them funnels. We all been swirlin' 'round some, but we all headed for the same spot."

He paused, then said, "The Lord give me a good life; I just hope I finish it good."

No one spoke until Patterson stood up and stretched. "If y'all will excuse me, I've got some things I need to think about."

Missy came out of her reverie and slid to the edge of her seat. She picked up the few dishes on the coffee table and started into the kitchen. "Me too. I'll be ready to go in half a sec."

When she came back through the living room, Missy knelt by Mose's chair and took his hand. "You saved my life before my daddy was ever born. Thank you."

He patted her arm, and she kissed him on the cheek. "G'night."

The pain in Mann's knee started paying higher dividends late Sunday night, and on Monday morning he was operating on twenty-four hours without sleep. He eventually gave up trying to get the upper hand on his discomfort and lurched into Nettie's Café just after sunup. He seated himself away from the diner's morning traffic and was taking his first sip of coffee when Collin Turner stepped through the front door.

His bull-riding coach winked at him, and Mann watched him walk back and join several ranchers gathered around a table in the back of the room. The prospect of having to be civil to a crowd of old men who would want to make him the butt of their bull-riding jokes prompted his decision to get to work early.

Nettie Holton understood why Mann pushed himself out of the chair and limped toward the cash register; he didn't want to put up with a lot of guff from a pack of foolish old men. The boy was outgoing enough, but he wasn't the kind to let others squander a desire for privacy.

Over the past few years, Nettie and her only regular black customer had developed their own mutual admiration society. He didn't know why the tough old lady liked him, but she obviously did, and that suited him. She was one of his favorite people because she didn't ask anything in return for her friendship.

For the woman's part, her affinity for the young black man had nothing to do with his being her cook's—and silent partner's—cousin. Nor did she have any way of knowing that the financial windfall that kept her café in business came from Bill and Mose. She was fond of Bill because, unlike so many of the young people who were coming up in Pilot Hill, she saw in him a measure of dignity. She expected great things of Bill Mann, and bull riding wasn't one of them.

He put his coffee mug by the cash register and dug in the pocket of his jeans for some change. Nettie said, "It's on the house."

"Thanks."

"Mmm." She frowned up at him. "Sam said you hurt your knee."

"The truck was bigger than I was."

Inhibitions regarding the guidance of other people's lives, especially this motherless boy's, did not burden Miz Nettie. "You try aspirin?"

"Roughly four an hour for the last ten days."

"I think you're an idiot . . . so is anybody else that gets on the back of a bull."

"I'll have my secretary make a note of that."

"Everybody loves smart-alecky kids." She rummaged around

in a drawer beneath the cash register and pulled out a small brown bottle. "This is a little something that'll stop the pain—and you. Take one every twelve hours for a day or so."

He took the bottle and rolled it back and forth in his palm. Nettie's name was the only word printed on the label. "What is it?"

She shrugged. "I can't pronounce it."

"Where'd you get it?"

She motioned toward the kitchen. "I scalded my arm a while back . . . doctor brought this by, saying it would stop the pain. He was right." She tapped the bottle. "There's ten pills left in there, but don't get smart and take more than one every twelve hours. If you take more than that, you'll wake up sometime next week. Understand?"

He took the bottle and started to open it.

"Not now, cowboy"—she shook her head—"wait'll you get to where you're going. You don't want to be driving while you've got this stuff in your system."

He put the pills in his pocket and picked up the mug. "I'll bring your cup back later."

"See that you do . . . and any of those pills you have left over."

"Yes, ma'am."

"You might want to say 'Thank you.' "

"If they don't work, I'll have my lawyers sue you for malpractice."

"You're welcome."

Mann walked—or hobbled—out. Collin Turner and his friends watched and smiled.

The beginning of summer school was two days away, and the North Texas campus was all but deserted when Bill got there. He parked in a space reserved for faculty members, washed one of the little pills down with the last of his coffee, and took a few minutes to reread the Sunday paper's sports section. The throbbing in his leg began to fade, and he was limping across the marble terrace in front of Cartwright Hall at seven o'clock.

The unconditioned air in the old building's vestibule was nighttime cool, but that would change by midmorning; white-orange sunlight came in level streaks through the east windows, warming everything it touched and highlighting the building's emptiness.

The offices of the philosophy department were on the second floor of the building. Mann paused in the center of the lobby; brightly lighted dust particles drifted near him as he divided his attention between the tall staircase and the elevator, deciding. The welcome beginnings of relief granted him by the pill boosted his confidence, and he decided the short climb might help loosen his knee.

By the time he got to the tenth step, the brief rush of relief granted by the pill was evaporating like steam, and the pain in his knee had graduated to agony. When he reached the top, he was gritting his teeth and cursing himself. Nettie was right; he *was* an idiot—especially for letting her prescribe medication for him.

The door to the philosophy department was approximately a mile from the top of the stairs; a water fountain marked the halfway point. He made it to the fountain, sweating and panting, and stopped to catch his breath. He washed down two more of the ineffectual tablets, desperately hoping they might help him finish his journey. Somewhere along the way he acquired a broom and used it for a makeshift crutch.

The door to the department's outer office was standing open, and the reception area was empty. As Mann drew close to Pat's personal office, he could swear he heard someone snoring.

Because Pat was the head of the department, he had the choice office, and he'd scraped out a corner near the windows to give Mann his own area; the path to the small table and chair allotted to the assistant was blocked by a guy Mann had never seen. The intruder had shoved Mann's neatly arranged office furniture out of the way and was sprawled faceup on the floor in front of Pat's desk. He was dressed in a dirty Hawaiian shirt, wrinkled khaki pants, and deck shoes—no socks; a mustard-colored sport coat served as his pillow. The sleeper's face was completely concealed behind an unkempt mop of surfer-style blond hair; the snoring sounds came from somewhere beneath the bleached tangle.

Mann propped himself on the edge of Pat's desk and touched the guy's shoe with the end of the broom. "Rise and shine, amigo. Surf's up."

A muffled grunt came from somewhere under the hair, but the man didn't move.

Mann tapped the guy's shoulder with the broom handle and said, "Better get a move on, ol' buddy. The boss likes to get here early."

The man reached up with one hand and dug through his hair until he managed to uncover a squinting eye. "I had a rough night," came from an unseen mouth.

"Yeah, and you're finishing it up in the wrong place." Mann jerked his thumb at the door. "Time to shake, rattle, 'n' roll."

The man's head came up slowly. He pulled a handful of mane out of the way and took in his surroundings. The young black guy standing over him was slouched against a large desk, hunched over a broom—sweat ran down his cheeks and dripped from his chin.

"Listen carefully, Jack." The disturbed sleeper employed the meticulous diction of the completely inebriated. "I am the new peon in this department, and where I finish my nights is my business, not the custodial department's. Now go push your broom someplace else while the academic types get some much-needed rest."

Acute impatience helped mask what three worthless little pills couldn't, and Mann forgot about the pain in his knee. He straightened and said, "Son, I don't know how well you understand English, but you're in my way, and I've got work that needs doing."

"Judging from your conduct, I can only assume janitors are granted tenure at this illustrious institution." The fellow was sitting up as he spoke, turning toward Mann.

Mann pointed at his chair and table. "You're in Poppa Bear's way, Goldilocks, and he's ready to sit down."

The long-haired vagrant gathered his coat and got to his knees. He appeared to be about Mann's height, with a lean build. Most of the hair was out of the way, and he was struggling to focus badly bloodshot eyes. When he dropped his coat and bent over it, Mann expected him to pick it up. Instead, he lowered himself to the floor and curled up eighteen inches from his original spot—still blocking Mann's access to the small work area.

"Remind me when I wake up to take issue with your attitude," mumbled the intruder. Seconds later, he was snoring again.

The drunk guy was too big for Mann to drag out of the way, and to try to step over an unpredictable drunk while his knee was messed up would rank right up there with deciding to climb the stairs. He used his crutch to work his way around to Pat's chair and sat down to consider his alternatives.

When Dr. Patrick Patterson, newly appointed chairman of North Texas State University's philosophy department, entered the department's outer office at eight o'clock, his receptionist greeted him with a suppressed giggle and said, "Good morning."

"Morning, Anna. Did I miss the joke?"

"You'll wish you had," she laughed. "It's waiting in your office." Anna Gibson had been the department's receptionist for two years. She was young, attractive, and unflappable; Patterson described her as effervescent.

Technically, the two men in his office weren't waiting. A scruffy surfboard jockey he didn't recognize was passed out on the floor; Bill was sacked out in Pat's chair with his arms loosely wrapped around a broom.

Pat put his briefcase down and moved over for a closer look at the fellow with blond hair and no socks.

"Who's this guy on the floor?" he asked the doorway.

"I've never seen him before," Anna called back, "but he's kinda cute in an unconscious sort of way."

"How can you tell what he looks like without knowing if he has a face?"

Anna left her duties to come stand in the doorway. "I'm the seventh son of the seventh son."

Pat was stooping over for a closer look; Rip Van Winkle needed a bath. "I've got a nickel that says you've met him."

"Johnny and I are never wrong."

"Johnny?"

"Rivers," she explained.

When Pat's face remained blank, she feigned sadness. "You're too old to understand."

"I think I'm glad." Pat pulled back enough hair for Anna to see the guy's face. "And I think you know Mr. Hugh Griffin."

The girl's mouth fell open. "Good gracious! What happened to him?"

"Ask Johnny."

The man passed out on the floor of his boss's office was a *cum laude* graduate of Stanford University and had recently received his master's degree in philosophy from the same institution. Six months earlier, when Griffin applied to North Texas, Pat's predecessor, Dr. Charles White, invited Pat to sit in on the interview. All three men wore dark suits for the meeting; Griffin's hair had been browner and shorter. Dr. White, with Pat's approval, offered Griffin a job commencing the first semester of summer school, and the young man accepted it.

Pat nudged the surfer with his toe and got a muffled grunt for his trouble.

Dr. Patterson smiled to himself then turned to Anna. "Get me the number for the university barbershop."

The girl whirled around and practically skipped to her desk. She was giggling again.

When Griffin awoke, he pushed himself up so he was reclining against the nearest wall. Pat was in his place behind the desk; Bill Mann was nowhere to be seen.

Pat leaned forward and said to the doorway, "Coffee, please."

Griffin worked his way up the wall until he was standing.

Anna was in the room seconds later. She gave Griffin a cup of coffee, two aspirin, and a bright smile; he gave her a frown. Neither spoke.

Griffin reached up to pull his hair aside but it wasn't there. He put the cup and aspirin on the windowsill and ran both hands along the sides of his head. When he looked a question at Pat, Pat said, "You got your hair cut. I talked a friend of mine into making a house call."

Griffin frowned. "That wasn't my decision."

"You weren't here."

Patterson caught Anna's eye and she left the room.

Griffin glanced out the window. "What time is it?"

"Almost too late." Pat leaned back in his chair and propped his feet on the desk. "When you came here for your interview, you passed yourself off as a reasonably well-groomed, well-mannered man. If you aren't the man you professed yourself to be, you need to apply somewhere else."

Griffin put the aspirin in his mouth and sipped the coffee. "Most places would give a new guy a chance to settle in."

"I'm willing to give most men three chances myself," said Pat. "I'm letting you have four."

"Generous of you." Griffin didn't sound grateful.

"I think so, and you've used the first three." Pat pushed his chair back and sat up. "One . . . you came in here drunk. Two . . . you look and smell as if you selected your wardrobe from a garbage heap. Three . . . and most importantly . . . you failed to thank the sweetest girl on the campus when she brought you that cup of coffee."

"You're cutting it close, aren't you?"

"My prerogative."

When Griffin didn't respond, Pat stood up. "Be back here tomorrow morning at eight o'clock, and we'll show you the schedule."

After Griffin left, Pat walked down the hall to check on the other half of the joke. Bill Mann lay corpselike on a couch in the faculty lounge; a note pinned to the inert man's shirt asked people to check with Pat before trying to rouse him. Tracing the cause of Mann's stubborn refusal to wake up had been easy enough; the doctor said to expect him to sleep the clock around.

The receptionist entered her office at five till eight on Tuesday morning and found a handsome vase full of red roses in the center of her desk. A card tied to the vase said, "Thanks for the coffee and aspirin. Sincerely, Hugh Griffin."

Pat walked in a minute later; Hugh Griffin was seconds behind him.

Pat's eyebrows went up when Anna showed him the card, and he looked at Griffin. The new man was decked out in a gray blazer and navy slacks; he was wearing socks.

Pat nodded. "There may be hope after all."

"Let's hope so." Griffin's eyes were bloodshot, but he'd had a bath.

Anna smiled.

Griffin took a surreptitious second to note that Anna Gibson's figure was doing astounding things for a plain straight skirt and starched blouse. Griffin liked his women slender and thought she'd look better if she lost five pounds—ten and she'd look pretty fair in a bikini.

Pat beckoned to Griffin. "Walk over here with me and we'll get a cup of coffee and check on my friend."

Mann was sleeping on his side, and Pat took that as a good sign. He bumped the couch with his knee, and Mann's eyes came open.

"You planning on working today?"

It took Mann a full thirty seconds to prop himself up. When he was semi-vertical, he looked around. "How'd I get in here?"

"I hauled your sorry carcass over from the office."

"What time is it?"

"Eight o'clock Tuesday morning. Nettie said she warned you not to take too much of that painkiller."

"They were placebos." He was staring at the floor, slowly massaging the back of his neck. "Do you need me for anything?"

"Not till Friday. Missy wants you and Hugh to come to the house for dinner."

"'Kay." He stretched out on the couch again and closed his eyes. "Who's Hugh?"

Pat pointed at Griffin. "New instructor. Hugh, this is Bill Mann."

Mann lifted a hand without bothering to open his eyes. "H'yah doin', Hugh."

Griffin forced a smile. "My pleasure."

Mann moved his shoulders to a more comfortable position and said, "Wake me up in time to eat."

Pat and Hugh filled their coffee cups and stepped into the hall.

When Pat excused himself and stepped into a nearby office, Griffin went back to the reception area to complete a more comprehensive appraisal of Anna Gibson's figure. If she met his standards, he might take her to lunch.

He swore mildly to himself when he found her sitting behind

her desk; the assessment would have to be postponed. *But I might as well start laying the groundwork, just in case.*

He kept his voice low when he asked, "That black guy that's sacked out over in the lounge . . . is he on staff here?"

"Student . . . helps around the office." She had a soft drawl.

"Oh."

Anna flashed her trademark smile and added, "He may be the nicest guy I've ever met."

Griffin didn't care if the black guy was St. Francis of Assisi; he was captivated by Anna's drawl and wanted to prolong the conversation. "He gets invited to dinner at Dr. Patterson's house?"

"Teacher's pet." She smiled more brightly to allay any assumptions that she might harbor malice toward Mann. "Dr. Pat's wife treats him like one of the family."

Griffin was genuinely perplexed and mildly offended. "I'm not sure I've ever heard of a gofer socializing at the department-head level."

"That's 'cause you've never met Missy Patterson."

"Is she supposed to be different?"

Anna, who had seen Missy in action more than once, was attacked by a fit of giggles. She tried to contain it, became more tickled, and ended up bursting out laughing.

Griffin watched her laugh, noting that her propensity for merriment was far from irritating—it was infectious. When Anna recovered to the point of being able to hear him, he smiled and said, "I can only assume the good doctor's wife is a bit eccentric."

"That's not it." Her smile probably seemed brighter because it reached all the way to her perfectly shaped molars. "Eccentric people are weird; Missy's different because she's . . . umm . . ." She tilted her head back and searched the ceiling for the word she wanted; straight brown hair fell back from her face, revealing a pair of tiny gold earrings. ". . . genuine."

Griffin abandoned the conversation to watch how her dark tresses caught the light . . . not unlike iridescent silk.

Without thinking, he voiced his observation, "Unpretentious."

And she misinterpreted it. "That's a good word."

"What's a good word?" asked Pat as he came through the door.

"Unpretentious," Anna answered.

"Ah, yes," said Pat. "Good for what?"

The girl shook her head, and the soft brown silk fell smoothly into place. "Sorry . . . can't tell. Shoptalk among the underlings."

Patterson looked at Griffin.

Griffin actually blushed and looked at his shoes.

Kids! thought the thirty-four-year-old department head. He started for his office, beckoning as he went. "C'mon, Griff, you'll want to know how your life is going to shape up this summer."

Patterson's phone rang before he could sit down. "Hello." He was smiling as he collapsed into his chair. He slipped off his shoes and propped his feet on the desk.

Griffin took one of the chairs in front of the desk.

Patterson waited for the other person to finish talking then said, "We managed to get a few words out of him before he rolled over and went back to sleep."

Another pause, then Pat laughed and said, "Fairly normal, I'd say. He told me to wake him up in time for dinner."

Pause, smile, wink at Griffin. "Yep, he's sitting right here. What's on the menu?"

Griffin watched Anna walk in to put a stack of mail on Pat's desk. By the time she turned forty, she'd be bulging in all the wrong places, but for the next year or two she was definitely deserving of a place in his little black book.

Pat listened to the phone then looked at Griffin. "You're invited to lunch today . . . our house. Interested?"

"Most certainly. Thank you." Griffin's stomach was beginning to recover from the abuse he'd subjected it to thirty-some-odd hours earlier. He was starving.

"Good choice." Pat held his hand over the mouthpiece. "Sandwiches . . . cold roast beef or chicken salad?"

When Griffin hesitated, Anna drawled, "One of each, he probably hasn't eaten since yesterday."

Griffin half-smiled and kept his mouth shut; Pat gave the order to the phone.

Anna walked back to her desk as Pat was saying, "Me too, sweetheart."

With the phone conversation over, Pat pulled out a copy of the pending schedule and passed it to Griffin. "You get one class each semester. It's a reasonably light load, and it'll give you a chance to get used to Texas."

Griffin looked at the sheet. He would be in the classroom only ten hours a week for the entire summer. He wondered how far it was to the nearest lake.

Pat interrupted his thoughts. "C'mon. We'll take a look at your office and give you a Cook's tour of the campus."

Griffin's office was larger than he expected, and it had a window. Pat let him look over the office, then told him to leave his jacket and took him out to show him around the campus, pointing out a few of the classroom buildings, making small talk as they went. At the student center, Pat left Griffin on his own and told him they could meet back at the office just before noon.

Griffin bought a cup of coffee and sat down at an outside table to survey the coed crop. Thirty minutes later, the sun reminded him of his lingering hangover, and he went back to explore his office.

Patterson drove past the Denton Country Club and turned down a street that paralleled one of the fairways.

Griffin was impressed with the neighborhood; most of the homes they drove by would tax the income of a family making three times as much as a North Texas professor. His host pulled into a circular drive at the end of the street. The Pattersons' home was not the smallest on the block.

Patterson reached into the backseat to pick up some papers then said, "Come on in."

Griffin was on the front walk when the home's front door opened and a petite lady in white tennis shorts and an NTSU golf shirt came down the walk toward them. She had skin the shade of a South American surfer girl and black hair, cut short. "Hey, y'all. Hungry?"

"Hi, kid." Patterson took time to kiss her on the lips. "This is Hugh Griffin. Griff, this is my wife, Missy."

The lady put out her hand and Griffin took it.

"Hello, Griff. Welcome to Texas." Her voice was reminiscent of Lauren Bacall with a genuine Southern drawl.

"Hi," Griffin said. "My pleasure."

The California native, who had seen more than his share of movie stars, was comparing Missy to Anna Gibson while he mentally patted himself on the back for being cool enough to avoid drooling. Anna's attractiveness might go unnoticed for a few seconds if a man were distracted—or badly hungover; Missy Patterson's beauty was the lightning-strike variety. Her blue-black eyes, unlike any he'd ever seen, were appraising him calmly when he realized he was still holding her hand.

Mr. Cool grimaced and croaked, "Sorry."

In a situation where Anna Gibson would be beaming, if not laughing out loud, Missy Patterson was barely smiling. If she cared what measure of effect she'd had on him, it didn't show.

Griffin glanced at Patterson to get his reaction.

Patterson was standing by his wife, waiting patiently.

Griffin got control of his voice. "I guess it happens every time."

"Blind men only have to deal with the voice," Pat said. He was impressed by Griffin's rapid recovery. "You came back more quickly than most."

Missy, who was no more impressed with her own looks than

she was with anyone else's, saw where the conversation was going and led the way up the walk. "Okay, you two. Dinner's waitin'."

Griffin would've been content to skip lunch and stand in the sun—heat, hangover, and all—while they talked about how beautiful his boss's wife was. He settled for allowing himself to say, "Wow."

"Well said," agreed Pat.

The mansion's interior presented itself as a home, not a showplace—a blend of antiques and quality furnishings encouraging guests to come in and visit. The pervading aroma of freshly baked bread was an invitation to dine.

Missy went straight to the kitchen. Pat and Griffin trailed along behind.

"Who wants iced tea?" asked Missy.

Pat raised his hand, and Griffin said, "Two, please."

Missy pointed at a pitcher by the refrigerator and told Griffin, "Make yourself useful. Plastic tumblers are in that cabinet."

When everyone had a glass, Griffin took a sip and exclaimed, "It's sweet!"

"Oops, sorry," Missy laughed. "It's a Miss'ippi thing, an' I forgot to warn you. Would you rather have something else?"

He took another sip, licked his lips, and pronounced, "Never again. I can't believe I wasted my youth on unsweetened tea."

"Well, there may be hope for California yet. Y'all sit, an' I'll bring the plates to the table."

Griffin told himself he could get used to the way Texas women talked, especially if they all sounded like Anna and Missy. The professor's wife was easier to watch than any coed he'd seen that morning—or any other time—but he busied himself by taking in his immediate surroundings.

Lunch would be served in an atmosphere spanning the gamut from formal to picnic—chilled peaches in cut-crystal compotes, plastic tumblers for tea, sterling silver flatware, and paper towels for napkins. A fine china soup bowl holding pieces of a pale green condiment, wooden salt and pepper shakers, and homemade mayonnaise in a plastic container collaborated to make up the table's centerpiece.

Missy put a paper plate holding what appeared to be two loaves of bread in front of the guest. "One chicken salad an' one roast beef."

She pointed at the soup bowl in the center of the table and told Griffin, "Those are watermelon rind pickles. Help yourself."

Griffin took a bite of the roast beef sandwich, and an involuntary *Mmm!* escaped from behind a mouthful of warm homemade bread.

"Good?" Missy asked.

"Oh, my gosh." He knew he was talking with food in his mouth. "This is unbelievable."

The best sandwich he'd ever tasted was on his plate, and the sweet tea changed what he would choose to drink for years to come. He was convinced anything the lady served him was worth a try.

Missy saw him eyeing the pickles and reached over to spear one. She put it on his plate and said, "My grandmother put these up. Nobody doesn't like 'em."

She watched his face while he shaved off a thin sliver and put it in his mouth. He closed his eyes when he tasted it and said, "In my next life, I want to be born in Mississippi."

When he opened his eyes, Pat and Missy were smiling at him. His hosts had yet to take a bite.

"California's loss," said Pat, and took Missy's hand. Missy motioned for Griffin to hold hers.

When Griffin caught on, Pat nodded at Missy. "Your turn."

Missy already had her head bowed. "Father, nothing comes into our lives without Your sanction. Our hearts are grateful to You for our home, for our food, for this opportunity to fellowship, an' for our new friend. Amen."

Pat said, "Amen," and glanced up at Griffin.

Griffin's mouth was hanging open slightly; he was staring at Missy's hand as she pulled it away. After a long pause, he sat up straighter and frowned at Pat. "This is wrong."

Pat was preoccupied with wrapping his hands around one of his sandwiches. "Yeah? How's that?"

The guest's eyes went to Missy. "I'm sorry," he said stiffly. "You've made a mistake."

Missy didn't understand. "I said the blessin' wrong?"

"No . . . no." He folded his paper towel and put it by his plate. "I don't believe in prayer."

Missy looked at Pat then back at Griffin. "You're offended 'cause I prayed?"

"No." Griffin pushed his chair back. "I'm offended because I was allowed to waste my time driving two thousand miles to take this position."

"I think I'm a little confused, Griff." Pat put his sandwich down. "Can we back up and start at the beginning?"

"Nobody said anything about God during my interview." Griffin was letting his anger bleed through. "I could have told you I don't believe in God—I'm an atheist."

"And?"

"And I don't want to spend my time at this university being badgered by a bunch of Bible-thumping fanatics."

"Bible-thumping fanatics?" Pat nodded slowly, unperturbed. "You mean like Missy and me?"

Missy, as if she were watching a slow-motion tennis match, was letting her attention move back and forth while the men talked. When Griffin stopped to consider the significance of Pat's question, she offered him a disarming smile. "I think you people from California are right."

Missy's irrelevant comment failed to register because it collided with Griffin's staggering realization that he had let the remnants of his hangover trigger an overreaction that could cost him his job.

He looked at Missy, then Pat, then back at Missy. "What was that?"

Pat shook his head and spoke in a soothing tone, "Missy."

She ignored her husband and leaned forward to prop her arms on the table. She fixed the midnight-blue eyes on her guest; the smile was no longer on display. "I *said* . . . I think you people from California are right."

Griffin was half angry, half convinced that he was already out of a job, and completely confused by Missy's comment. He made the mistake of saying, "Right about what?"

"I think the dolphins *are* as smart as you."

Griffin's mouth fell open.

Pat bowed his head and sighed.

Missy took a bite of her chicken salad sandwich.

CHAPTER THIRTEEN

Griffin was speechless. He watched Missy chew her food while his memory went back to a beautiful brown-haired girl wearing tiny gold earrings. She was smiling and saying, *Missy's just . . . uh . . , genuine.*

Pat touched his napkin to his mouth, shaking his head at his wife.

Missy reached for her tea glass.

Griffin hated to apologize, but he didn't want to be fired in his first week on the job. The couple's short track record told him he wasn't expected to grovel, but the flavor of humble pie was repulsive to him. After fifteen seconds of piercing silence, a single drop of cool sweat was forming in the center of his forehead. *What the heck*, he thought, *I don't have to mean it.*

He held a hand in the oath-taking position and said, "You're right, of course. Maybe I got a little carried away."

"Maybe?" Missy set her glass down and reached over to pat him on the arm. "*Maybe* you're an impudent imbecile."

Her words emptied Griffin's lungs—his mild-mannered boss was married to a one-hundred-pound piranha with dark blue eyes.

He looked at Pat, and Pat testified to the blatantly obvious. "Diplomacy hasn't always been Missy's strong suit."

"Humph," sniffed Missy. "Diplomacy is—an' always will be—where the guy with the big stick tells the guy with the little stick how the cow's gonna eat the cabbage."

Pat made a surrendering sound and addressed himself to Griffin. "She's right. And you were wrong."

Griffin looked first at Pat then at Missy. Patterson had already made it clear he wouldn't put up with disrespectful conduct in the philosophy department; his wife was apparently unwilling to tolerate it anywhere else.

He weighed the few courses of action open to him and took the one that might save him a walk back to the campus in the sun . . . and salvage his job. "Agreed. So . . . are you going to fire me because I don't believe in God?"

"Of course not." Pat sat back in his chair. "You were hired because we thought you were borderline brilliant, not because of your religious beliefs."

Griffin caught Pat's use of the past tense. "You thought?"

"People who are genuinely intelligent wait until they've been on the job a week or two before verbally attacking their boss and his wife in their own home."

Missy picked up her tea glass and propped her elbows on the table while she watched the tennis match.

"Good point." Griffin passed his napkin across his forehead and glanced at Missy. "Are you going to fire me because I'm an impudent imbecile?"

Pat shook his head. "Nope."

"So what do we do now?"

"Easy. In whatever order you think appropriate: we finish our lunch and get back to work; you have a serious talk with yourself about decorum; you apologize to me, and . . ." he pointed at Missy, ". . . you beg that lady's forgiveness for your rude behavior."

Griffin knew the way to the man's heart. He turned to Missy

and said, "You were dead-on right; I'm an impudent imbecile. Would you forgive me?"

She didn't smile. "I have . . . an' I *will*."

His brow wrinkled. "Will?"

She put the tea glass down and gave his arm another reassuring pat. "You're probably pretty smart, Griff, but you're young an' foolish. I'd bet my dessert we're gonna get to catch your act again."

He let out a long sigh. "Boy, I hope not."

"Hear, hear," said Pat.

Griffin looked at his boss and spoke man-to-man. "I apologize."

"And I accept," Pat said. "That leaves two sandwiches and your self-reprimand."

For the next thirty minutes they ate sandwiches and pickled watermelon rind while Missy and Pat filled him in on what to expect from the university and Denton.

When they finished lunch, Griffin helped Pat clear the table. Missy brought out a three-layer chocolate cake, and the three of them ate half of it with their coffee. Missy wrapped half of the remaining half in wax paper and put it aside for Griffin to take when he left.

At one o'clock, Pat stood up.

Griffin followed. He surprised himself by thanking Missy for the most enjoyable meal he could remember, and she invited him to come back on Friday night. She walked them to the car and put a box holding a second chocolate cake in Pat's hands. "You be careful with that."

Pat kissed her good-bye and said, "That's what you said last time."

He placed the cake gently on the floor behind his seat and straightened in time to greet a pair of men who pulled into the circular drive on their golf cart. Introductions were made all around before Pat and Griffin had to excuse themselves.

The golfers took time out of their crowded schedule to stay and visit with Missy until their tee time called them away.

Back in the car, Griffin said, "You married an exceptional woman."

"Thanks. I couldn't agree more."

"And she cut me down to size without being mean."

"Ah, yes. Meanness isn't in her makeup, but intolerance is not something she battles to overcome."

The men were quiet on the way back to the campus—both content to think their own thoughts. They were on the stairs in Cartwright Hall when Griffin told Pat one of the things he'd been thinking about. "I know this can sound false coming from a guy who is hanging on to his job only by the good graces of his boss, but I enjoyed that meal more than any I've had in a long time."

"Thanks. As a matter of fact, I believe you."

"Good." Griffin was interested in whether or not he was going to get seconds on dessert without having to eat his leftovers. "Are you taking that cake to put in the lounge?"

Pat made a snorting sound and said, "Not if I want to sleep at my house tonight. It's for Bill to take home."

"That black guy?"

"Yeah. Missy thinks she's his guardian."

Missy, thought Griffin; she was the second thing he had on his mind. They were passing the water fountain when he cleared his throat. "Can I ask you something personal?"

Pat stopped. "Is it important?"

Griffin cleared his throat a second time. "Well, not really . . . and it's none of my business."

Pat started moving again. "Okay, how about we agree you

get to ask *one* none-of-your-business question each afternoon between one and one thirty."

"I like that."

"I like it better." Pat winked at the new kid and slapped him on the back. "Starting Thursday, I have a class scheduled between twelve thirty and two."

Griffin had to laugh.

They walked through the empty outer office without slowing. Pat stowed the cake on a shelf and sat down behind his desk. Griffin walked over and propped himself against the windowsill. What he'd seen of Pat's easygoing nature gave him the courage to work up to his question. "When we drove out of your driveway, those two guys were still there."

He paused, and Pat prompted him, "And?"

Griffin plunged in. "Chief, you and I both know your wife is a bona fide traffic stopper . . . she could very well be the most striking woman in the world. Does it bother you to drive off and leave her talking to a pair of men who probably stopped at your house just so they could look at her up close and listen to that voice?"

"Call me Pat. And, no, it doesn't bother me. If it did, I would've gone off the deep end years ago."

"What about when you introduced me to her . . . don't you ever get tired of watching guys like me get turned into zombies when they meet her?"

"Nope."

"You're serious?"

"I'm serious."

"Why doesn't it bother you?"

"You wouldn't understand."

"Why?"

Anna Gibson's voice smiled at them from the outer office. "I'm back, y'all."

Pat motioned at Griffin and said, "Shut the door."

When it was closed, Griffin pulled one of the visitors' chairs up and leaned close to the desk. "Why wouldn't I understand?"

"Lots of reasons, but the main one is rooted in your world-view . . . you don't believe God exists."

Griffin sat back, crossed his arms, and sighed deeply. "You're using my question as a springboard to try and convince me that God exists."

"Yes and no," Pat confessed.

"Yes?"

"Imagine this." Pat tilted his chair back and put his feet on the desk. "I'm like the man who takes his boat out to pick up people who've been forced into the ocean because of a ship-wreck. I pull my boat close to you, but you refuse to get in. You're helpless . . . your survival is totally dependent upon your willing-ness to get into the boat, but you've got your fingers in your ears and your eyes squeezed shut—I touch your shoulder, and you pull away. What would you have me do?"

"I've heard that analogy before, and the premise doesn't apply. I'm not in danger of drowning, because God doesn't exist. There's no ocean out there, and I'm not in it."

Pat held up his hand. "One thing at a time. The main reason I used that story is to show you that the man with the lifeboat has a responsibility—that's me, and what *you* would have me do does not factor into my choice. I can't pass a man by because he doesn't believe he's in danger of drowning. I cannot and I will not."

"Fine," answered Griffin, "as long as we're clear on my position."

"That's my second point. You're adhering to a position that is suffering from a lack of proof."

Griffin didn't like being told he was wrong. "The concept of God is archaic, Pat. He was invented by man as a method of conquering fear."

"That doesn't weaken my point."

"Of course it does. Thinking people have known for years that God does not exist."

"Okay. Let's use Missy to make my point," Pat said. "You said she might be the most striking woman in the world. Right?"

"I did." Griffin shrugged. "So?"

"It's easy enough for me to assume she's the most beautiful woman in the world; I've seen how men, including yours truly, conduct themselves when they first meet her. However, for me to prove she's the most beautiful woman in the world, I have to start traveling; I'd have to see the face of every woman on the globe . . . all two billion."

Griffin was thrown off balance. He frowned at Pat for a moment then said, "I don't follow you. What has that to do with the existence of God?"

"It's simple when you think about it. Only the man who has seen all the women can know which one is most beautiful—he has all the facts. A person would have to be possessed of all the knowledge in the universe to say that God does not exist."

Someone chose that moment to tap on the door.

"Come in."

Bill Mann pushed the door open and stood on the threshold in his sock feet; Pat's note was pinned to his chest. He slumped against the doorjamb and massaged his bad shoulder. "What time is it?"

"One thirty. You hungry?"

"What day is it?"

"Still Tuesday," Pat said. "You and I talked this morning."

"Mmm. You got anything that needs doin'?"

"Not today," answered Pat. He motioned at Griffin. "This is Hugh Griffin, the department's newest instructor."

"'Kay. I'm goin' back to sleep." He pushed himself off the jamb and shuffled toward the outer door.

Pat motioned at Griffin. "Make sure he can find his way to the lounge."

Passing students nudged each other as they watched the shoeless guy with a note pinned to his shirt weaving slightly as he crossed the hall.

When Griffin caught up with him, Mann said, "You must be the new guy."

"Yeah. Been on the job almost five hours."

Mann nodded wisely. "Pat probably fired the other one. Whatta bum."

"I wouldn't know." Griffin didn't like being called a bum by a student assistant.

Mann sat down on the couch and tilted to one side, unconscious.

Griffin figured Pat would be checking on his pet, so he picked Mann's feet up and arranged him lengthwise on the couch. When he turned around, he found Anna Gibson standing in the doorway. The expression on her face was a mixture of soft surprise and interest.

She said, "You didn't strike me as the compassionate type."

He looked back at Mann and shrugged. "I was just making sure he didn't hurt his back; I don't want to have to do his work and mine too."

She cocked her head to one side, frankly appraising him. "Mm-hmm."

Her steady gaze, a study in innocence, was unlike anything he'd ever experienced, and it unnerved him slightly. When she refused to speak, he finally said, "If you're thinking about buying me, I have to tell you that I'm not for sale."

The spell was broken, and her smile returned. She patted the pockets of her skirt and said, "I'm glad to hear it, because I don't have anything smaller than a quarter."

She went back to her desk, and he went to his office and closed the door.

There was a wide expanse of grass and oak trees between Cartwright Hall and the library, and it seemed to attract the coeds who wanted to spend their spare time congregating in the sun. When Griffin finished rearranging his furniture, he only had to swivel his chair to take in the landscape. Denton wasn't much of a town, but surely there was a store where he could pick up a pair of binoculars.

At three o'clock he decided he'd already put in a full day and walked out to see if anyone else was leaving for the day. Anna was behind her desk; Patterson and another man were standing nearby. When Griffin approached, Patterson said, "Hugh, this is Mike Epstein. Mike, this is Hugh Griffin . . . newly arrived from Stanford."

"My pleasure." Griffin extended his hand. Epstein was medium height and on the lean side; a pair of Buddy Holly glasses and a dark mustache covered the biggest part of his face.

Before Epstein could respond to Griffin, Bill Mann limped through the door; he was carrying a pair of penny loafers in one hand and Patterson's "Do Not Disturb" note in the other.

"Afternoon, Bill," said Patterson.

Mann ignored his audience and concentrated on negotiating his way across the uncluttered reception area. As he disappeared into Patterson's office, he mumbled, "Coffee."

Griffin's mouth fell open for the second time that day—a new record. Patterson smiled, and Anna came out of her chair, laughing her infectious laugh. Epstein was noncommittal.

When she recovered, Anna excused herself and left the room, still smiling to herself. Patterson followed Mann into the choice office.

Griffin looked at Epstein; Epstein shrugged. The two trailed Patterson into his office and found their boss behind his desk. Mann was slumped in one of the visitors' chairs with his belongings in his lap.

Anna came in with the coffee, and when he stood to take it the shoes and sign spilled onto the floor. He nudged the litter aside with his toe and said, "Thanks."

"You're welcome." She smiled. "Are you okay?"

"Mmm . . . downright feisty, I guess." He looked at Patterson. "I miss anything?"

"A couple of introductions. This is Hugh Griffin; he's fresh out of California."

Mann shook hands and wrinkled his brow. "Haven't we met?"

"Once or twice"—Griffin held up two fingers—"but you were running a little behind at the time."

"Mmm."

Patterson pointed at the newest man. "And this is Mike Epstein."

Mann put out his hand. "Super Jew, huh?"

"That's me," said Epstein.

"Super Jew?" Patterson didn't understand.

"Baseball player," Mann and Epstein answered together.

When Mann sank back into the chair, Griffin turned to Epstein. "We didn't get a chance to visit earlier. Are you on staff in the department?"

Epstein's smile was dry and partially masked behind the thick walrus mustache—naturally curly black hair spilled over his collar. "Maybe in a year or two. I'm working toward the grad program."

Griffin cooled. Patterson needed to start separating the worker bees from the faculty.

"Mike will be taking some of Bill's load," explained Patterson.

What load? thought Griffin. He said, "Well, at least I'm senior to one of the assistants." It came out wrong.

Epstein's smile was no longer touching his eyes. "I think *lowly* assistant captures the connotation more clearly, don't you?"

Anna cleared her throat and backed out of the room.

Griffin looked at Patterson's expression and grimaced. "I'm sorry. My mouth has been getting the better—"

Mann bent over to pick up his shoes. Maybe having the extra blood flow to his brain helped, but for whatever the reason, he chose that moment to recover something from his memory. He straightened and pointed his right penny loafer at Griffin. "I know who you are. You're the surfer."

"Surfer?" queried Epstein.

"Uh-huh," Mann frowned, struggling to bring a fuzzy picture into focus. "Monday morning . . . you were in here passed out on the floor."

Griffin turned down an offer from a small college in South Dakota to come to Texas; now he was having second thoughts about the wisdom of his choice.

The thought of the pompous new teacher passed out on Patterson's floor struck Epstein as funny. "You showed up for work bombed?"

The would-be professor turned on Epstein. "Look, *friend*, I don't have to put up—"

Patterson made the "T" sign with his hands. "Time-out, gentlemen."

Griffin, Epstein, and a more alert Mann looked at their boss.

"Mike," Patterson ordered, "you take Bill home in his car. I'll follow in a minute or two and bring you back to the campus."

He pointed at the chair vacated by Mann and told Griffin, "Grab a seat."

Mann and Epstein were out of the office in seconds.

When they reached the downstairs vestibule, Mann propped himself against the wall to slip into his loafers. A couple forced to detour around him stopped, and the guy looked back.

The man was big; the girl with him was attractive and aloof.

"You're Bill Mann," said the man.

"That's right." Mann studied the man's face, searching his memory. "I overdid it on some pain pills . . . either yesterday or maybe the day before . . . do I know you?"

The speaker was about six-three and probably weighed two hundred and twenty pounds. He put out his hand. "Homero Gonzales . . . San Antone."

"I remember you." A smile spread across Mann's face and he shook Gonzales's hand. "You played a good game."

"Thanks. You didn't do too bad yourself."

"Can we do this later, Homer?" Mann pointed down the hall. "I gotta make a stop in the little boys' room pretty quick. I'll see you around the campus."

"Sure." Gonzales watched him limp away and said, "I'll buy you a beer."

When Mann went into the restroom, Gonzales turned and looked down at Epstein. He took in the long hair, mustache, and glasses. "You a friend of his?" He sounded skeptical.

"We work together." Epstein offered his hand. "Mike Epstein."

Gonzales shook his hand and introduced the girl. She wasn't interested in men shorter than six-three; Epstein missed her mark by at least five inches.

Epstein was curious. "How'd you know who he was?"

"Process of elimination. Not many black kids up here. None like him."

"He's different?"

"A little." Gonzales had a voice like a prophet—deep and clear. "I played against him in the high school all-star game two summers ago. He's tougher than he looks."

Epstein looked back toward where the sleepy guy disappeared. "That guy right there?"

"That's the man." The big guy followed Epstein's gaze and spoke matter-of-factly, "I was a pretty-well-thought-of running back—bigger and faster than most. He was a skinny unknown that played in the North's secondary."

Gonzales paused, remembering.

"And?" prompted Epstein.

The former football star stabbed his finger slowly in the direction Mann took and winked. "And the South lost."

Epstein was a pacifist. He shrugged. "I probably won't try to pick a fight with him then."

"Neither will anybody else around here, if they're smart," spoke the prophet. The girl turned away and Homero followed. "See you around, Ep."

When they were in the car, Mann leaned his back against the seat. "Do you know where Pilot Hill is, Super Jew?"

"I can find it."

"That's the promised land," said Mann as he closed his eyes. "Take me there, then wake me up."

"I was thinking," said the driver, "what with me being Jewish and you being black, we might ought to form our own Anti-Defamation League."

"An Anti-Defamation League for Jewish people and blacks?"

"More selective than that . . . for one black boy and a left-handed Jew."

"You've been dipping into my pain pills, haven't you?"

"You don't like the idea."

"I don't like being awake. Put a lid on it and take me to my house."

"You got it. And if I'm going to be your chauffeur you can call me Supe."

"Whatever you say, Supe."

"Sounds good." Epstein smiled. "And I'll call you . . ." He thought for a second. "I'll call you Coon."

Mann didn't bother to open his eyes. "Not if you want to live long enough to eat supper."

Epstein chuckled. "How about Rastus?"

Mann pointed his face toward Epstein and forced one eye open. "How about less talking and more driving?"

CHAPTER FOURTEEN

Mann woke up when they passed through Pilot Hill. He was inclined to stop at Nettie's for a cup of coffee, but he wasn't ready to listen to the lecture.

They were a mile from town and going farther into the country when Epstein asked, "Your folks got a farm out here?"

"It's just me and my granddad. Five acres, no farm."

"Lots of big trees." Epstein was enjoying watching the countryside roll by. "Did you grow up out here?"

"Chi-Town . . . I'm a Yankee," said Mann.

"Where's your granddad from?"

"All over." Mann thought about the recent warnings out of Mississippi and turned the conversation. "How about you?"

"I was brought up in University Park. We moved to Denton a few years ago."

"We?"

Epstein slowed to let a squirrel cross the road. "My sister's five years older than me. We moved up here when our parents died—a money thing."

The two talked about University Park until Mann's house came in sight.

When he turned in the long driveway, Epstein said, "Well,

bro, it's not like I'm into poetry and trees, but if I was choosing between University Park, Chicago, and this place, I'd pick this."

"Thanks. We like it."

Mose was sitting in one of the rockers; Dawg had taken up his station by the driveway.

"Pull up right there by Poppa's truck." Mann pointed. "Go slow . . . and watch out for the dog; he's getting old."

The black man on the porch stood up. He was wearing starched khakis and carrying a long stick; he wasn't smiling.

Epstein watched the man with the stick move toward the steps and said, "Uh . . . your granddad doesn't look too happy."

"He usually doesn't start dancing till folks get out of their cars."

Epstein looked to see if Mann was serious. "I mean . . . I haven't been around all that many old black guys . . . uh . . . practically none. Does he like Jews?"

"I guess," Mann sighed. "He cooked the last two and ate 'em."

Epstein wasn't comforted by the humor. When the car stopped, the dog moved up to stand just outside his door.

Epstein eased the door open and the hound drew close enough to sniff at his ankles. When he didn't register the expected scent, Dawg backed slightly and leveled an unblinking stare at the stranger.

"This dog looks like he doesn't like me."

"For cryin' out loud, Epstein. Is this some kind of all-new decision to have a persecution complex?"

"I mean it. Does he bite?"

"Only morons." Mann got his door open and used it to help him stand. "Get out of the car or I'll clue him in on your IQ."

The dog heard Mann's voice and trotted to the other side of the car. Mann bent over carefully and rubbed his ears. "Hey there, big boy. Miss me?"

The dog leaned against his boy's leg and moaned.

The black man with the stick was at the bottom of the porch steps. He said, "Afternoon, gentlemen. Come an' set."

Mann straightened. "Poppa, this is Mike Epstein. Mike, my grandfather, Moses Mann."

"Mr. Epstein." Mose inclined his head. "I'm pleased to meet you."

Epstein put out his hand and used his new name. "My friends call me Supe."

"Sho' 'nuff?"

"Yes, sir . . . short for Super Jew."

"Mm-hmm. One of the chosen people."

The absence of humor Epstein imagined in the old man's countenance wasn't a hint at the presence of anger; it was dignity. Before Epstein could comment, Mann headed off any talk about God's chosen people. "Supe's the new guy Pat was talking about hiring."

"Mm-hmm. So . . . you reckon you gonna be a philosopher, boy?"

"Yes, sir, that's the plan." Mose took his time going up the steps. Epstein followed. "Another year of college, then graduate school."

The old man said, "Move that cat an' sit in that chair by me."

Epstein put the cat on the floor.

Mose took the other rocker; Mann managed to take a seat in the swing without capsizing. The cat wandered down the steps and sat under the nearest tree to wash her face.

While Mose and Epstein were getting acquainted, the dog was using his nose to examine the area around the swing.

"What're you doing?" Mann asked him.

Mose chuckled. "He ran out of cake yesterday . . . an' you didn't bring none."

Mann watched as the dog whuffed and left the porch. "I guess I made him mad."

"No-no," said Mose, "he hears somethin'."

The dog was standing out by the driveway again, wagging his tail.

A few seconds later Pat Patterson's car came around the curve below the house. He pulled in and parked behind Mann's car; the dog greeted him warmly. Patterson took a cardboard box out of the backseat, and the dog escorted him to the porch.

The professor brought the box up the steps and said, "I forgot to give this to Bill."

"I'll take it." Mann pushed himself out of the swing. "Have we got coffee going, Poppa?"

"No, but the water's on the stove."

Mann hefted the box and looked at the three men. "Who wants some?"

Mose and Patterson did. Epstein looked his question at Patterson, who answered, "Chocolate cake."

"Me, please," said Epstein. "You need any help?"

"Keep your seat," said Patterson. "I know my way around."

Epstein watched Patterson follow Mann into the house and wondered at the relaxed friendship between the head of a university philosophy department, a black office boy who referred to his boss by his first name, and an old black gentleman. He sat back in the chair and thought, *Maybe it's more amazing they'd include me.*

A mockingbird took offense at the cat's close proximity to her nest and perched on a lower limb to complain. The cat continued her bath. The first mockingbird was joined by two more and a redbird.

Epstein said, "I used to live close to Mockingbird Lane in Dallas, and we wouldn't see three mockingbirds in a whole month."

"That right?"

One of the mockingbirds left its perch and swooped low over the cat.

"Wow!" Epstein exclaimed. "That was close."

"Mm-hmm." Mose nodded. "An' that cat's been known to be mighty quick."

A second bird joined the attack.

While the two men watched the air show, the dog came over and put his head on Epstein's knee.

"Well, now," declared Mose, "I wish you'd look at that. He don't take to just anybody."

Epstein winked at the old man. "Maybe he thinks I'm special."

"Well, he'd be right about that, boy." Mose nodded somberly. "Dead right."

"I think he's mistaken this time, Mr. Mann." Epstein massaged the dog's ears gently and grinned. "I'm just a twenty-year-old kid who stopped in for free chocolate cake. There's nothing special about that."

"You a Israelite, boy; folks don't hardly get no more special than that."

The first mockingbird was gaining altitude to make another bomb run on the cat. Epstein was watching without seeing.

"You know," he said, "that's what my granddaddy used to tell me."

Mann was back on the porch ten minutes later carrying two slices of cake, one thin, one not. He found Mose apparently dozing in his chair. The mockingbirds and their friends had reclaimed the ground out under the trees. The dog was resting his head on Epstein's knee. The Jewish kid who stopped in for free chocolate cake was holding an open Bible in his lap. Epstein's finger was resting on the print, but he was leaning back in the chair, his eyes fixed on something in the distance.

Mann said, "Your cake's here."

Epstein's mind was busy elsewhere.

Patterson came through the door saying, "Hot coffee," and the spell was broken.

Epstein looked at the men with the food and tapped the page. "This is the book of Isaiah, chapter fifty-three."

Mose's eyes came open. Mann and Patterson waited.

Epstein looked at Mose then let his eyes drop to the Bible. "This was written by a Jewish prophet seven hundred years before Jesus was born"—he paused to take a breath—"and it describes His crucifixion in detail."

No one said anything.

Epstein looked at Patterson. "Did you know this?"

"Mm-hmm."

"Did you?" he asked Mann.

Mann handed him the larger slice of cake. "Probably."

The rank indifference in the response stopped Epstein. He studied Mann's face then asked, "Why don't you care?"

"It's a long story." Mann went back to get his own cake and coffee.

Epstein was baffled. "What did I say?"

"You didn't do nothin' wrong, boy." Mose took his coffee from Patterson. "It goes back a long ways, an' it's 'tween him an' God."

"He only has two years of college left." Patterson was looking at the empty doorway. "I wonder about when he'll turn around."

Mose pictured Mann's frequent attempts to set a new speed record on the curve below their house. He said, "You try to git things goin' too fast, an' you end up in the ditch, boy. If I was sayin' what I think, I'd say that boy's got a far piece to go, but the wide, wicked world is gonna know it when he gets there. God says me an' you been picked to stand by his side an' wait."

"Yes, sir. You're right . . . as usual."

Epstein stopped petting his new friend and looked up. It wasn't the choice of words; it was Patterson's tone. The learned chairman of the university's philosophy department was content to defer to the wisdom of the old black gentleman.

*   *   *

Patterson and Epstein were heading for Pilot Hill when Epstein asked, "Do you know much about Jesus?"

"Some. What's your question?"

"I'm not sure." Riding was better than driving, and he watched the landscape pass for a minute or two. "How about if you just tell me what you know?"

"How about if we go to the source," suggested Patterson. "You find yourself a Bible, and we'll spend a couple of lunch breaks looking at what it says."

When they drove past the square in Pilot Hill, a black man was standing at the curb in front of Nettie's Café. He was relaxed—one hand in his pocket, the other wielding a toothpick. They didn't notice him, but he recognized Patterson's car.

Mann was inside the house continuing his all-day nap. Mose was at his station on the porch when the dog stood and murmured deep in his chest.

Mose couldn't see anything moving, and compared to the dog he was deaf. "What's got you up, boy?"

Without answering, the dog trotted down the steps and moved off across the yard at a fast lope.

Mose shrugged and followed. The dog got to the road and turned north; in seconds he was beyond a small rise and out of sight. By the time Mose reached the road, the dog was on his way back; he topped the rise escorting Clark Roberts's three-year-old daughter—or she him.

The old man smiled as the two drew near. "Afternoon, Miss Trudy. You out for yo' evenin' constitutional?"

"No, I'm walking by myself."

"Seems like you quite a ways from home."

"I am. I never walked this far by myself before." For her pilgrimage ensemble the girl chose blue jeans, lime-green flip-flops, and a sleeveless pink blouse with white buttons.

"Well, I have to say you doin' a right fine job of it."

"Is this your dog?" She squatted by the dog to pat him on the back.

"Kinda. He stays here with me an' my grandson, but I don't rightly know as he's mine."

"What's he named?"

"We jes' calls him Dawg."

"Hmm." She took the dog's face in her hands and held it so they were nose to nose. "That's a good name. Does he like to walk?"

"Now you mention it, he likes walkin' long as he got some-body to keep him company."

"I'll keep him company if he'll behave."

"Well, he can behave pretty good, but he don't like to walk nowhere 'cept on the road 'tween here an' yo' house."

Trudy looked back up the road. "My sister's not behavin'."

"You don't say."

"She was riding Tony and told me to stay in the yard."

"Mm-hmm."

"I told her not to boss me, and she did anyway."

"You don't mean it?"

"Mm-hmm. I figure to go tell my daddy."

"Where's yo' daddy at?"

She thought about the question for a bit, then turned her attention back to the dog. "Does he like to swim?"

"Some."

"Well, he can go swimming in my pool if he won't knock all the water out."

"If I was to guess, I'd say he won't knock out a single drop. You wantin' to go right now?"

"Maybe." Trudy looked back where she'd come from then

looked at Mose's house. "I think we better get something to eat before we go."

"You might be right. You like chocolate cake?"

Ten minutes later, AnnMarie Roberts came down the road on Tony and found her sister in one of the rocking chairs on the front porch; her timing was perfect. Trudy was finishing up her chocolate cake and feeding every other bite to the Redbone hound. The girl rode the paint up to the porch and leaned on the pommel; Mose stood up and removed his hat.

AnnMarie nodded at Mose. "Trudy, I told you not to leave the yard."

"I was coming back."

"You can't be running off like that."

"You're too bossy."

"One of us is." AnnMarie took a breath. "Thanks, Mr. Mann."

Mose smiled and made a gesture that took in the dog. "Our pleasure. You want some cake?"

"No, sir, I gotta get back to the house and take Sweet Thing up to the barn." She glared at Trudy. "It'd be nice if I could get it done before he gets in the yard and tears up *somebody's* wading pool."

"It's a *swimming* pool." Miss Trudy did not seem inclined to leave.

"Whatever it is, Momma'll kill me if he tears it up." The thirteen-year-old was bearing the weight of the world. "C'mon, Trudy. Get up behind me."

"I'm busy."

"I'm in a hurry, Tru."

"You're too bossy, an' my name's not Tru."

"Well . . ." Mose was watching the little girl feed the last of her cake to the dog. "I was jes' thinkin' I needed a little exercise. How 'bout if me an' Dawg walk back up that way with Miss

Trudy soon's she ain't too busy. Maybe you can git to Sweet 'fore he gits to the pool, an' me an' the dog can git us a little stroll."

"Thanks," said AnnMarie. She pulled the paint around and galloped off to rescue the wading pool.

Clark Roberts pulled into his carport and found Trudy in her pool with the dog; the dog was behaving. Mose was sitting nearby in a lawn chair.

"Howdy, Mose. You get roped into lifeguard duty?"

"Yassuh." Mose stood up. "An' enjoyin' it."

"Where's AnnMarie?"

"She taken Sweet up to the barn. I 'spect she be back here directly."

"Is she on Tony?"

"Mm-hmm."

Roberts pulled off a good-looking straw cowboy hat and wiped his brow. "I'd give a week's pay if that girl got along with me as well as she does those two animals."

Mose remembered his own daughter's early teens. "She be awright soon enough . . . maybe a year or two."

Roberts put the hat back on. "If Millie lets her live that long."

"Miss AnnMarie's a fine girl, Sheriff; I watched the way she handle that paint . . . an' that bull. She got a right gentle hand."

"She gets along with Morris."

"Yassuh, but he don't never tell her to do somethin' she ain't wantin' to do."

Roberts exhaled loudly. "How many years?"

"Two at the outside." Mose took his own hat off and ran his hand through his hair. "But she jes' practice."

"What?"

Mose waved his hat toward the pool. "That'n there is the one."

"How's that?"

"She the one what's gonna teach you how to be a daddy."

Roberts watched Trudy fill a plastic bucket and pour the water over the dog's head. The dog sat still and behaved. Roberts groaned, and Mose smiled.

———

The pattern of summer school established itself at NTSU, as did the lunchtime meetings of Patterson and Epstein. They met on Tuesdays and Thursdays for sandwiches. As often as not, because the sandwiches were plentiful—and made by Missy Patterson— Griffin would wander in during their discussions and help himself to the food. Epstein asked questions; Patterson showed him where to find the answers; Griffin spent most of his time looking out the window. Mann ate somewhere else.

In mid-July, on a Thursday, the clock was moving toward twelve thirty when Epstein patted his Bible and said, "Dee's started watching over my shoulder while I study this thing."

Patterson knew about Delores Epstein from her brother. She was only twenty-five and had been responsible for herself and her brother for the past five years. During that time, she finished college, earned her CPA certification, and provided the lion's share of the money for her brother's education. What Epstein felt for his sister bordered on worship.

"And?"

"And . . . the gal ain't too keen on the New Testament."

"The New Testament in its entirety, or some passage in particular?" asked Patterson.

Epstein had crammed a handful of potato chips in his mouth. "Mofwee meewahcuz."

"Miracles?" asked Pat.

Epstein nodded and swallowed.

"All of them, or just selected ones?" asked Patterson.

"She didn't say."

"Mm-hmm. Okay, we'll take the one by which all others can be measured. The Resurrection is the hinge point of the

Christian faith—if it didn't happen, then we have no reason to believe anything else the Book tells us—none of it would matter." Patterson looked at his watch. "I've got a class in two minutes. Get with your sister—if she's interested—and write down all the objections y'all can come up with and bring them back here next Tuesday. We'll start there."

CHAPTER FIFTEEN

When Patterson got home that afternoon, Missy surprised him at the door with the news they were meeting someone for supper.

"Well, I suppose it's safe to assume it's someone at the Cabinet level or higher, because you don't get this spiffed up for the common folk."

She grinned and flipped her fingers at her hair. "All I did was get my hair cut."

"Remember, dearest, your nose gets longer if you lie." He grinned back. "That's a new blouse, those are new slacks, and you've got on earrings and lipstick."

She couldn't hold it any longer. "Bobby called from some place in Tennessee at one o'clock. We can pick him up at Carswell an' take him out for supper."

Patterson understood her excitement . . . and shared it. Except for their not getting to see him often, the couple thought Bobby was near perfect in his roles as brother and brother-in-law. The fighter pilot had returned from Southeast Asia the previous October, and this would be the first time they'd seen him in almost two years.

Missy's brother entered the Air Force Aviation Cadet program as a teenager and was flying jet fighters in Korea before he was twenty-one. His superiors in the fighter pilot community, most of whom were general officers, were acquainted with him and his reputation. For Lt. Colonel Robert L. Parker Jr., promotion to a higher rank would always take a back seat to the well-being of his troops, and getting the job done well was more important than getting the credit—and his putting seven MiGs in the bag would never hurt his résumé. If he stayed on his current track, he was destined to be the youngest general in the air force.

Patterson delayed their departure for Ft. Worth as much as he was able, but it finally came down to leaving with Missy or watching her drive off by herself. They drove onto Carswell Air Force Base an hour early and were standing on the flight-line side of Base Operations when Bobby led his formation of F-4s screaming in over the runway at four hundred knots. Half a dozen student pilots and their instructors—teams from the training wing at Reese Air Force Base who were out on navigation hops—took a moment away from their flight planning and weather briefings to come out and watch the "real airplanes" taxi in.

The hulking camouflaged fighters parked in a line facing a row of sparkling white T-38s . . . battle-ready broadswords, confronting dress daggers.

Parker dismounted from the lead airplane. He took a minute to stow his G-suit and helmet in the cockpit, then walked across the ramp to hug Missy and greet Patterson. "Let's get inside where it's quiet."

They stood near a flight-planning table and made small talk while Parker waited for his GIB (guy in back) to get on the phone and make arrangements for their overnight stay.

The other spectators were back at their tasks, planning their flights back to Reese; the room was a swirling collage of colorful unit patches plastered on a background of olive-green flight suits. A student pilot standing a few feet away sported a shoulder patch depicting the roadrunner cartoon character wearing flight boots and carrying a helmet. The stenciled nametape on the kid's chest read ASHBAUGH. He was staring at Parker.

Patterson watched as a light came on in the young officer's eyes.

Ashbaugh grabbed a scrap of paper and wrote "MIG KILLER!!!" on it with an arrow pointing at Parker. He nudged the kid standing to his left and eased the note over to him. The other student was engrossed in his paperwork and pushed the note out of his way. Ashbaugh elbowed his friend and shoved the note back. The recipient didn't appreciate the interruption and pushed back—too hard. The would-be messenger lost his footing, grabbed for the table, and missed. He let out a loud *Whoop!*—thereby attracting the attention of every airman in the room—windmilled his arms enough to prolong the moment, then augered in. He hit his head on Parker's flight boot when he landed.

The young instructors were shocked that one of their charges would attack a field-grade officer. The other student pilots laughed out loud. Ashbaugh turned lobster red.

Parker bent over, offering a hand and smile to the wreckage. "I see you've learned the first lesson."

Ashbaugh wasn't sure he'd heard right. "Sir?"

Parker said, "You can't learn anything when you're flying straight and level."

Ashbaugh let the lieutenant colonel pull him to his feet and nodded seriously, "I won't forget, sir."

The MiG-killer winked. "Daggum right, you won't."

The dinner guest wanted Mexican food, so the three went downtown to Joe T. Garcia's.

They swapped news and gossip over beef enchiladas, and Bobby seemed more pleased about Pat's elevation to chair of the department than he was about his own good news—he was on the colonel's list and would pin his eagles on in late September.

He waited until they were dropping him off in front of the Visiting Officers' Quarters before sharing the news about the assignment change that would come with his promotion.

He stood by the open passenger's door and said, "Scuttlebutt says I'll probably be heading back to Thailand before Christmas."

"For what?" asked Missy. Her brother was a veteran of two years in Korea and one in Southeast Asia.

"Some wing-weenie role, no doubt. Pushing a pencil and inventorying toilet paper."

The last time he'd gone to Udorn Royal Thai Air Force Base "to fly a desk," he'd logged a hundred and ninety-one missions— a hundred and eight of them over North Vietnam. "You've already been over there once. They can't send you back."

"Are you sure?"

"This isn't fair, Bobby."

"I told them you'd say that."

"This is not funny." Tears were threatening.

"I know, kid." He leaned into the car and kissed her on the cheek, then stepped back. "If I'm proud of anything, Missy, it's being your brother—I always have been, I always will be. I'm convinced that God has singled you out to do something really special . . . and I'm anxious to see what it's going to be." He smiled at her and shrugged. "He called *me* to drive fighters."

Patterson and Missy drove back to Denton in silence.

When Patterson stopped in their driveway, neither of them moved to get out. Patterson said, "We all have our own calling; his is to lead men who protect our nation."

"War," she sighed.

"Speaking of which . . . did you hear what he said?"

"What?"

"He said, 'God has singled you out to do something really special.' You and I are starting to hear a lot of people use words to that effect."

"I've been hearin' that all my life," she said. Her eyes were on a groundskeeper on the other side of the fairway. He was staying late, working near one of the cart paths.

Patterson took her hand. "You want to pray here or in the house?"

"Both."

They bowed their heads and prayed for her brother.

The man who'd been standing in front of Nettie's Café pretended to scrape at some dirt out on the golf course.

The kids who lived near the golf course called the groundskeepers "greenies," and stayed out of their way. Greenies were bad about using their little maintenance carts to chase people who were caught playing games other than golf on the manicured course.

Two angels, hidden from all eyes in the physical world, watched while the greenie stayed at his task for a few minutes after the couple went into their house. When he'd waited long enough, the worker started his maintenance cart and drove back to the groundskeeper's shack.

Patterson's guardian angel said, *He has seen neither the old man nor the boy.*

True, said the angel who had been standing at Missy's side since before her birth, *but the time soon comes.*

A line of thunderstorms passed through Denton on Tuesday morning, and small showers were continuing to make things messy at lunchtime.

Someone's shoes made squishing sounds in the outer office, and Epstein stuck his head into Patterson's office at eleven thirty; the sandwiches were waiting. "Morning, boss."

"Hey, Supe." Patterson waved at the box of goodies. "Help yourself while I go wash my hands."

Epstein stepped back to let a young lady precede him, and she met Patterson in the doorway. "Hi."

Epstein said, "Sis, this is Dr. Patterson. Boss, this is Dee Epstein, my mouthpiece."

"Very funny," she said to her brother. She offered her hand to Patterson. "My brother tells me you're a good man to work for."

"Thanks. He speaks well of you too."

She was wearing a yellow plastic poncho. Her hair, black and curly like her brother's, was rain-plastered to her head.

"May I take your raincoat?"

"I'll just put it on the floor. Do you allow females to barge in on your bull session?"

"By all means."

Hugh Griffin was down the hall when he heard a woman's voice and chose that moment to saunter into the office. He helped Dee out from under the poncho and said, "Hi, I'm Hugh Griffin."

"Hello," she said. "Dee Epstein." She didn't offer to shake hands.

"My pleasure," said the cool philosophy instructor from California.

Patterson returned in time to complete the introductions. "Griff came on staff this summer."

As far as Griffin was concerned, Dee Epstein had everything it took to warrant his attention—Bambi eyes and a beautiful face, dark skin, and a body that would do justice to a bikini. The woman was definitely doing her share to uphold the Texas tradition. He decided to sit in on the theology discussion.

While the others got settled, Dee leaned close to her brother and said, "Supe?"

"My namesake's a baseball player—a real slugger. Mike Epstein—Super Jew."

"Boys," she said and rolled her eyes.

Minutes later, hands were washed, introductions were complete, and sandwiches distributed. Patterson said, "We can look out the window and tell what the weather's like, it's too soon to predict who's going to win the World Series, and the presidential election is in the far distant future. I propose we use the whole hour to talk about our chosen question. C. S. Lewis said, 'If Jesus Christ rose from the dead, all other miracles are incidental.' So . . . did He?"

Dee put her plate on the floor, picked up a paperback book, and pulled out two sheets of typed notes. "Who goes first?"

Patterson knew the answer. "The ladies, of course."

"It's interesting you phrased it that way"—her smile exuded confidence—"because it touches the basis for one of my questions. The Biblical account says two women discovered Jesus was not in the tomb. No one in that culture gave any credence at all to a woman's word . . . no one would've believed them, so why should we?"

"That's a great start," said Pat, "and in one sense, you're correct. Too often in that culture, ladies were thought of as little more than chattel. However, the writers who recorded the Resurrection account appreciated that fact more than you or I . . . and they told it like it happened. Had they been more interested in deceiving their readers than in communicating God's truth, don't you think they'd have told us the empty tomb was discovered by a handful of trustworthy men?"

Epstein looked at his sister.

She looked at Patterson while she absorbed the logic of what he said. After a moment she looked at her notes, then said, "I got these questions from a book that makes a good case against the Resurrection. The writer is a scholar who has obviously done his homework."

"I understand." Patterson nodded. He'd read the book she was holding. "But I think it's fair to ask why—if he has done his homework—he allowed himself to reason to a wrong conclusion?"

She looked up and wrinkled her nose. "He missed the point about the women, didn't he?"

"He did."

"How about this, then . . ." She looked back at the papers and stated her second argument. "He says it's likely that Jesus' disciples came and stole the body."

"What about the guards?"

"It's obvious." She rested her fingers on the book and papers—her evidence. "Either the disciples bribed them, or the guards were asleep."

Patterson shook his head. "Roman soldiers were some of the most disciplined fighting men in the history of warfare. A willingness on their part to accept a bribe—or going to sleep at their post—would've put them in danger of being executed."

"But it is possible."

"Granted, but consider the counterpoint." He slid forward. "Ten of the twelve disciples, those whom your scholar says stole Jesus' body, were later executed. Those men died cruel and painful deaths professing with their last breaths that they saw and conversed with the risen, wounded Christ. Any one of them, or all of them, could've saved themselves had they recanted their faith. Would you allow yourself to be skinned alive, crucified, or burned at the stake to perpetrate a hoax?" He shook his head slowly. "I submit that a man will readily abandon a lie that can profit him nothing, if by doing so, he might evade a hideous death."

She looked at her pages again. "You've read this book."

"Yes, and many like it." He pointed at the book. "And that author uses the shotgun approach to put forth a diverse collection of weak arguments against the Resurrection because he doesn't have one strong one—nor does anyone else." Patterson continued, speaking softly, "Jesus didn't faint. He wasn't drugged. The witnesses did not accidentally go to the wrong tomb, and it wasn't an episode of mass hallucination. When those women arrived at the tomb, the stone—a very heavy stone—was rolled back, and the tomb was empty. Jesus had been raised from the dead."

"You can't prove that."

The lingering light rain transformed the campus sidewalks into active flower beds of brightly colored umbrellas. Griffin turned away from the window and sat down to hear Patterson's reply.

"That's true, but if we weigh the evidence on an unbiased scale, we have to conclude that the Biblical account is more plausible." He pointed at the book. "That gentleman offers a dozen weak ropes that will help you climb a tree in order to believe a lie, while the Bible provides you with an opportunity to stand on the ground and embrace the truth."

Her brow darkened. "You're besmirching a man's reputation because he doesn't agree with you."

"Only indirectly," Patterson reasoned. "That man and I understand that the Resurrection is the linchpin of the Christian faith. He wrote those words knowing that any seeds of effective doubt he sows in the minds of his readers will grow into trees obscuring their view of the truth. When a man brings his argument to the public forum, he opens himself up to rebuttal."

The solid reasoning behind Patterson's statements attracted the young Jewish woman, but a heritage of misunderstanding held her back. She was glancing down at her notes when her brother said, "I wouldn't."

She turned to look at him. "What?"

Epstein had moved from his chair to stand at one of the windows; his sandwich lay half eaten on the plate by his feet. Tiny specks of drizzle joined forces on the other side of the glass and continued their pilgrimage as fat raindrops. His eyes traced one drop's path as it answered gravity's siren call. "I wouldn't die for a lie."

Something cold invaded Dee Epstein's body. "Michael."

Her younger brother turned from the window, and they became the only people in the room.

Michael said, "He's right."

The import of his words—and her feeling of foreboding—

propelled her from the chair. She extended her hands toward him, her fingers splayed, as if commanding him not to take the issue any further. Had she been able to make a sound, she would've screamed a warning.

When she could speak, she said, "Michael! You have to stop this!"

He shook his head. "You're yelling."

"I don't care!" she whispered a scream. "This is crazy!"

"No. It's not." Her book had fallen to the floor at her feet. He pointed at it and said, "*That* is crazy."

In January 1963, Delores Epstein was a college sophomore living with her family in a nice section of University Park. She was on Christmas break from SMU when a drunk driver ran the stop sign in front of their house and crashed into her parents' car. Her father died instantly; her mother lived long enough to tell her to take care of her brother. In that single, awful instant, the twenty-year-old college girl became the mother of a fifteen-year-old boy.

She stared at her brother, and a million thoughts assailed her. She had neglected him . . . she should've sent him to a college where he would've been protected . . . she should've arranged for him to meet with a rabbi until he fully understood their faith . . . she should've taken him and moved to Israel when their parents died; he would've been safe there. But she didn't do any of those things, and he was turning his back on their beliefs . . . and her.

"Michael, just slow down. This isn't something you can—"

Epstein was shaking his head again. "Dee, I come in here a couple of times a week because I want to hear reason . . . you can't hear because your mind's already made up."

"Of course my mind's made up." The tears in Dee Epstein's eyes were put there by anger. "We're Jewish."

"So was Jesus, Sis." He walked over and took her hand. "Walk out in the hall with me."

"Y'all take the office." Pat stood up. "C'mon, Griff. I'll buy us a cup of coffee."

Epstein emerged thirty minutes later, and Pat met him in the main hall; Griffin had wandered off. When they walked back into Patterson's office, Dee Epstein was taking her turn at the window, drying her eyes.

She sniffed and told Patterson, "He said I couldn't accuse you of proselytism because all you did was show him where to find the answers to his questions."

Patterson could only imagine what the woman was thinking. "Are you okay?"

Had she been a snake, she'd have struck. Her eyes became slits and she leaned toward him. "Have you ever lost a younger brother, Professor Patterson?"

He didn't want to retaliate, but he wanted to let her know he'd had his share of extreme pain. "Yes—nine years ago this past spring. He was murdered."

Her brother watched her digest the words. Her anger faded to empathy, and a lone teardrop started down her cheek. "It hurts."

He nodded.

She folded her notes and placed them in the book. "I'm going to . . ." She stopped to breathe. "Excuse me . . . may I sit in on your lunchtime get-togethers?"

Patterson thanked God for what she was asking and said, "You'd be more than welcome. In fact, if you're here, my wife will have an excuse to come, too."

"So you can sic her on the Jew girl?" She spat the words.

"Sis!" warned Epstein. "You promised."

"Gently, Supe," cautioned Patterson. To Dee he said, "You're going to like my wife, and she you. That's a promise."

Dee Epstein was not going to like Dr. Patterson's wife or any other Christian—not ever again. She gathered her purse and poncho from the floor. "I have to get back to work."

Epstein moved to follow her out, and she said, "I'll see you at home later."

Patterson waited until she was gone before saying, "It sounds like you've made up your mind about accepting Christ as your Savior."

Epstein nodded. "Already done it. I asked her to stay with me while I prayed."

Patterson was surprised. "And she did?"

"Yeah. I prayed and she cried." He grimaced. "She doesn't know what's going on, but she loves me."

"You can say that again, brother." Patterson sat down behind the desk. "What now?"

Epstein spread his hands as if to say, *Isn't it obvious?* and said, "We start answering her questions."

CHAPTER SIXTEEN

Weeks passed.

Patterson, Epstein, and Dee met at lunchtime every Tuesday and Thursday; Missy was there more often than not. When Dee was there, the three Christians tried to answer her objections to Christianity without offending her; the conversations encompassed points of reason, philosophy, and Old Testament theology. On those rare days when she was absent, Patterson and the other two visited about doctrine and theology. On Monday, Wednesday, and Friday, Epstein took his Bible outside at noon and sat under an oak tree to feed the squirrels and study.

Griffin met enough people to help him occupy his free time and slowly pulled away from the little noontime study group. It was not unusual for him to sit at his window during lunch; it interested him that the skinny Jewish kid's willingness to read his Bible in public seemed to attract an inordinate number of girls. The girls treated the goofy-looking little guy as if they took him seriously. Amazing.

Mann's knee eventually healed itself, and he picked up bull riding where he'd left off.

* * *

In late August, Mann came in from working with Collin Turner and found Epstein's ancient Fiat parked in the driveway . . . again.

Super Jew was sitting on the porch with Mose. The dog was at his post in the driveway.

Mann shut the car door and knelt to confer with the four-legged welcome committee. "Hey, big dog. You having another one of those action-filled days of yours?"

The dog snuffled and whined while he tried to lick Mann's face.

Epstein was spending more and more time at the Manns' house, and he held on to the arms of his chair and cringed every time he watched Mann's car slide around the long curve in the gravel road. Mann was reserved and somewhat distant for the most part; however, when bringing his car around the bend in their road, he was a maniac. He called to Mann, "Hey, bro, how fast were you going when you came around that turn?"

Mann stood up and started for the porch. "Ask Poppa. I got a quarter says he can tell you within a mile an hour."

"A mile an hour?" Epstein looked from Mann to Mose and back to Mann. "Nobody can do that."

Mann took his ballpoint and wrote something on his palm, then took a quarter out of his pocket and held it up. "Put up or shut up."

Epstein looked at Mose. "Can you tell how fast he was going?"

"I been watchin' him come 'round that bend for a long time," said the old man. "If'n I was you, I wouldn't bet."

"Humph," Epstein grunted. He turned to Mann. "I got a buck that says it can't be done."

Epstein had no business losing a dollar and Mann knew it. He said, "I can't risk a buck. Two bits or less."

"Okay." Epstein pulled out a handful of change and scraped together three nickels and a dime. "How fast?"

"I'd say 'tween fifty-six an' fifty-seven," said Mose.

"That's two different numbers," said the gambler-turned-lawyer. "You're supposed to pick just one."

The old man thought for a second then said, "Fifty-six an' a half."

Mose's exactness distracted Epstein for a second. When he looked at Mann, the race driver was grinning, holding out his right hand for his money while displaying his left—three characters and a decimal point written in blue ink on the pink palm . . . *56.5.*

Mose gave the Jewish boy an I-told-you-so look and said, "Yo' granddaddy would tan yo' britches if'n he saw you throw yo' money away like that."

"Yes, sir, he would at that." He turned to Mann. "Fifty-six-point-five? Who keeps up with their speed in tenths?"

"Rich folks," Mann laughed and put his winnings in his pocket. "Is it cake time yet?"

Mose nodded. Epstein said, "I didn't drive out here to starve." The dog wagged his tail and sneezed.

When the cake, coffee, milk, and hard-boiled eggs were on the porch, Mann said, "Will's headed back to A&M in the morning. He said he'd stop off before he left."

"It'll be good to see him," said Mose. "You gonna keep on doin' yo' practicin' by yo'self?"

"Mostly. I can do my weight workouts at North Texas. We're planning on meeting at a few small rodeos here and there between now and October. Entry fees aren't too bad, and we can use the rides to keep sharp."

Epstein was cutting up the eggs and feeding the pieces to the dog. "What happens in October?"

"Clear Creek County Stock Show. This year they're moving into the big time . . . new arena, first-class roughstock, the best of the best. It's gonna be the real thing."

Epstein had watched Will and Mann ride a few bulls. He said, "I hate to sound like a sissy, but I wouldn't get on one of those bulls for a million dollars a minute."

"There's nothing to it," said Mann.

Mose looked at his grandson and raised his eyebrows.

The city boy cleared his throat and admitted something he'd never told anyone else. "There is if you're scared of bulls."

"Smart folks is," said Mose.

Mann put a bite of cake in his mouth and took his time chewing. After he swallowed, he said, "Poppa's right. Bulls are big, they aren't very forgiving, and they make their own rules." He put another bite in his mouth and talked around it. "But sometimes riding 'em just kinda feels easy."

The three made small talk until Mose stood up and said, "If you boys will excuse me, it's 'bout time for my nap."

Mose was inside the door when Mann said, "This is the third time in the last two weeks you've been out here. What's the deal?"

Epstein pointed at his saucer. "Free cake."

"Right. And what else?"

"I plan on doing my postgrad in philosophy"—Epstein jerked his thumb at the front door—"but I can learn more from that man in one afternoon than I'll pick up in four years of any doctoral program in the nation."

Mann nodded. "He's got it all figured out, that's for sure."

"You mind having me hang around?"

"Nope," he said, grinning, "I can use the money."

"Uncle said you aren't interested in God things."

"Uncle?"

Epstein pointed his fork at the door. "He said call him Uncle."

"Mmm." Mann took a few seconds to push at some crumbs with a fork tine, then said, "Let's lay some ground rules. You're a little weird, but I get along with you as well as anybody I know; *Uncle* obviously likes you, and Dawg thinks you're kin to us . . . so as far as the family's concerned you can move in and live here, but you're gonna have to pull in your horns when it comes to me and God."

"Wow . . . it's a good thing you aren't touchy about it."

"Touchy or not, I was here first."

When Epstein didn't say anything, Mann said, "Too harsh?"

"Nah." Epstein was unscathed. "You're right . . . it's your call. God didn't commission me to force-feed you."

"You catch on quick."

"I got good teachers all around me." He put his saucer down, and the dog went to work on it. Epstein prayed a short prayer, then said, "Can I ask one question?"

"Is this something about God?"

"Yep."

"Why is it nobody else gets saddled with friends who constantly pester them with these kinds of questions?"

"'Cause most *rich* folks know Jews are tenacious, so they don't befriend Jewish orphans."

Mann had to smile. "Will you let it go after one question?"

"Yep." Epstein held his fork where the dog could get to it. "Can you give me thirty seconds on why a kid with a grandfather like that is so angry at God?"

"I'm not angry at God; I'm neutral."

"Why?"

"Sorry, Supe." Mann shook his head. "That's two questions."

"No, it's not. I asked you why in the first question and you didn't give a complete answer."

"You sound like you've been hanging around Missy."

Epstein held his thumb and forefinger a quarter of an inch apart. *"Bisel."*

Mann wasn't smiling when he said, "Then ask her."

The interview was over.

"What're you doing tomorrow?" asked Epstein.

"I'm supposed to help Pat with his yard work, but I could stand to spend that time at Collin Turner's. You?"

"I'm loose."

"Tell you what," said Mann. "How about I call Pat and tell him you'll show up at their place and do the yard work while I get in some time on that electric bull. You get some extra cash . . . I get some practice."

Epstein was thinking. "She'll have chocolate cake there, won't she?"

"You know, for a guy who weighs less than a hundred and fifteen, you sure do eat a lot."

"I think my brain's so powerful it burns the calories off before my body can turn them into muscle." He flexed a bicep barely larger than Mann's wrist. "That's why I decided to become a scholar."

"That's what I figured," said Mann, and went to the phone.

Summer began its annual retreat in early September, and the need for yard work would decline along with the temperature.

On a Monday afternoon, Mann stopped by the Pattersons' to talk to Pat about shifting some of his workload in the office to Epstein. Epstein needed the income and welcomed the extra hours; Mann could use the spare time to hone his bull-riding skills. Pat was agreeable and told Mann to get with Anna and arrange the schedule to suit themselves. Mann was in a good mood when he walked back out to his car. He had his door open when a shrill whistle stopped him.

"You forgot your cake!" yelled Missy.

He shut the door and went back to meet her on the sidewalk. "Thanks. They'd've made me sleep on the porch if I'd left here without it."

"Dawg an' Mose?"

"And Supe. He's practically taking up residence at the house."

"He's never had a brother, Bill, an' his daddy's been gone five or six years. You an' Mose are made to order."

"Yeah, well, as long as he doesn't eat my share of the cake."

She rested her hand on his chest and smiled at him. "You talk real tough, Billy Bull Rider, but you've got a heart as soft as that cake icing."

"Don't tell that to the bulls; it might give them an edge."

She pecked him on the cheek. "I promise."

It was only a matter of time . . . of exercising patience. Moses Washington and Missy Patterson had a father-daughter relationship, so all he had to do was put himself where he could watch her . . . time would take care of the rest. When the white woman stood on tiptoe to kiss the black student, the greenie out on the golf course saw what he'd been waiting three months to see. The philosophy department's office boy was close to the same age Bill Prince would be, and he lived with an old black man who fit Moses Washington's description. It wasn't proof, but it was the next best thing.

Two days later, on a Wednesday, the private line rang in Estelle Bainbridge's office.

"Yes?" said the woman.

"I believe I've found two of them. I need to do some background work to make sure."

"And?"

"Another month."

"And the other one?"

"All in good time. I'll have some questions for these two."

"How will I know you've fulfilled your obligation?"

"I'll get it in the papers and mail you a copy. You can have your people follow up."

"Where are you?"

"You don't need to know that."

"You sound as if you don't trust me."

Her answer was a dial tone.

Seconds later, the phone rang again.

"Yes?"

The man on the phone said, "Sorry, ma'am, he was off the line too soon for us to get an accurate fix. We can put him in the Chicago area, but that's as close as we can come."

"Thank you. You did the best you could."

She had been wise to choose Sheldon Aacock. He called from Chicago to keep her from knowing the location of the two she wanted dead; their actual location could be anywhere between Idaho and Florida. That he mistrusted her spoke well of his craft . . . that he was utterly ruthless was an established fact.

She was pleased, but if things worked out as planned, Sheldon Aacock would not be needed.

Aacock was standing at the curb outside the downtown Greyhound terminal seconds after he put down the phone. He caught a cab back to O'Hare Airport and an American Airlines Boeing 727 to Love Field in Dallas. He was back in Denton before dark.

When the noon get-together was over, Dee Epstein walked into the hall and bumped into Hugh Griffin—literally.

Her notebook was knocked free, and Griffin accidentally caught it on his toe. When he lurched backward the notebook was thrown into the air and landed in his outstretched hand. Dee Epstein saw the miraculous catch, but she was trying to keep from dropping her purse and missed the shocked look on Griffin's face—her brother didn't.

"I'm sorry," she said. "I wasn't watching where I was going."

"No harm done."

"Nice catch." She actually smiled for the first time in weeks.

"I've been practicing." Griffin was smooth . . . acting as if he'd made the miraculous catch on purpose. "May I apologize for the collision by taking you to lunch one day?"

The date request caught her off guard, and when she

hesitated, he said, "That is, if you're willing to date a common agnostic."

She happened to be looking at her brother when Griffin made the crack about agnostics and noticed the way he was looking at Griffin. She said, "I'd love to."

They left it at that, and she said her good-byes.

Michael Epstein followed Griffin to his office and tapped on the open door. When Griffin turned, Epstein said, "I don't want you dating my sister."

"Really? Why not?"

"Simple. You're a weasel."

Griffin's frown became a smirk. "Dee thinks differently."

"What Dee thinks is not the issue here, is it?" Epstein stepped into the room. "I'm her brother, and I won't let you date her."

"You're fifty pounds short of being able to stop me, squirt." Griffin's lip curled, and he took a step toward Epstein. "Go play in the street."

Plastic clicked against plastic as Epstein folded his glasses. He was looking for a place to put them when Mann entered the room. "Hi, guys."

Epstein thrust the glasses at Mann. "Hold these."

Mann ignored his friend and walked past him to Griffin. "You're a faculty member, Mr. Griffin, and this is 'conduct unbecoming.' "

"This doesn't concern you, bro," said Epstein. "Get out and pull the door shut."

Mann said, "Cool it for just a minute." He closed the door but came back to take a mediator's stance between the two men. "Mr. Griffin, you just heard this man say he thinks of me as his brother; that makes Miss Epstein related to me. Now, if I were you, I'd rethink my position. Only a fool would allow himself to be drawn into a fight against two men who feel honor bound to protect their sister."

"You think I'm scared of you two?" sneered Griffin.

"You and I both know you are not." Mann held up a placating

hand. "But I'm equally confident you don't want to cramp your style by ending up with a gap where your front teeth are supposed to be. I suggest a cooling-off period. If we still feel a need to settle this with our fists, we can do it next week over in the gym wearing sixteen-ounce gloves. Either way, here or there, if you start in on one of us, you get both."

The black guy was taller than the would-be philosopher by an inch or two, and Griffin processed a mental picture of what he would look like without his front teeth. He pretended to restrain himself and said, "I'll think about it."

"Good enough," said Mann. He opened the door and escorted a reluctant Epstein into the hall. "Let's me and you get some fresh air, Supe."

The late-September air was good for Epstein. "Where'd you learn to talk like that?"

"Like what?"

"Like some guy from the State Department."

"Well, aren't you the sorry little bigot. Does our two-man Anti-Defamation League allow Jewish members to assume that their black brethren don't know how to use the King's English?"

"Where'd you learn?"

"I read 'Improving Your Vocabulary' in last month's *Reader's Digest*."

"Humph." Epstein went to the next subject. "I didn't need your help back there."

"Right." Mann stopped and faced his friend. "I don't know what you've been smoking, Supe, but being stupid can cause wear and tear on your face. You and I are good friends, and if you and I fought, you'd try not to hurt me. Griffin's a coward; he'd mark you up just to prove he's tough. If you have to fight a coward, you make sure you're holding the difference."

"The difference?"

"In my house, it's a sawed-off hoe handle."

"Uncle's walking cane? You'd use that?"

"Nope, 'cause I don't get in fights."

"Mmm." Epstein pointed back over his shoulder. "You say Griffin's a coward, but you told him you didn't think he was scared of you."

"I told him I didn't think he was scared of *us*. I lied . . . and he knew it. He needed an out."

"I'm not letting him date Dee."

"Boy, you have the IQ of a retarded aardvark." Mann looked disgusted. "Your sister's not going to date him."

"She as much as said she would."

"She won't."

Epstein took thirty seconds to come to the conclusion that his sister was too smart to get hooked by a guy like Griffin. "You're right."

"So, bad boy . . ." Mann was trying not to grin, "what do you plan to tell Poppa?"

"About what?"

Mann patted his feisty little brother on the back. "About walking out of your Bible study and threatening to whip up on a non-Christian?"

Epstein winced. He didn't have an answer. "What would you do?"

Mann looked serious. "I'd pray he doesn't find out."

"You think that's possible?"

"I sure do, provided God strikes me dumb before I get home."

Epstein knew the truth when he heard it, and Mann was laughing loudly enough to be heard by people in downtown Denton.

Epstein left work early and beat Mann to the house in the oak trees. He related the afternoon's events to Mose and was only mildly surprised when Mose failed to react.

They rocked in silence, watching whatever passed in front of their eyes, enjoying the mild weather.

Epstein warmed himself on the solitude shared with his older friend. The old man balanced the hoe handle across his lap and let his memory walk through sixty-plus years of a well-lighted path—a path leading him directly to this porch he shared with an Israelite boy who wasn't much bigger than a thick switch. Every step of the black man's life, large and small, was ordained by Him who calls the stars by name, and as Mose retraced them, he found himself stopping here and there to draw stamina from the wealth of the good times, while using the bad memories to build his resolve.

He was raised by as godly a man as ever there was . . . he was holding the hoe handle Pap gave him . . . the same one he'd used to put down Ced Pommer before Pommer could murder Virginia Parker, thus preserving the line that gave the world Missy Parker Patterson . . . the resulting trip to south Mississippi came about so God could reveal His hand in the saving of Pap by Capt. Gilmer, thus preserving Mose's heritage . . . God took Pap and gave Mose a beautiful and godly wife, then He took their son and gave them a special relationship with a spitfire white child, Missy Parker . . . he went to prison for killing one man and met Sam Jones . . . and came home from prison in time to save Missy by killing another . . . God kept him safe while others died, making him wealthy while others did without . . . then, on a wet night in the Delta, the good Lord gave him a ten-year-old boy to raise, the same way he was raised by Pap. Were it not for the obvious day-by-day intervention of God, he would be looking back on a life of no more consequence than a mist droplet in the wide river of history; however . . . if he could believe his heart, and the counsel of those around him, God was making them ready to watch the waters of history abandon their riverbed and carve a new channel. He would be used in the remaining days of his life the same way he'd been used in all the others—to bring glory to the name of his God.

Finally, Mose said, "Who you reckon needs protectin', you or Bill?"

"Well, if he hadn't been there, Griffin would've done a number on me."

"How 'bout tomorrow?"

"Tomorrow? What happens tomorrow?"

"We don't never know, but in that boy's case"—Mose was pointing toward Denton—"it's gonna be bad."

"Tomorrow? For Bill?"

"Maybe not the day after today, but soon enough. I been thinkin' on what the good Lord's done to bring me to this place, an' it's been more than a body can tell. I can't see no reason for God to have me right where I'm at 'cept to look out for that boy."

"But Bill's grown." *And capable of taking care of himself*, thought Epstein.

"Mm-hmm . . . but he ain't *ready*. Folks that knows 'bout things say my boy's comin' up on a big go-'round."

"How big?" What could happen in the quiet country outside Pilot Hill, Texas?

"That boy gonna be fightin' Satan's demons."

"The real devil?" Epstein had read a little about spiritual warfare. The battle between good and evil was going to rage until the second coming of Christ, but Epstein wasn't expecting to see the front lines.

"Maybe not the devil hisself . . . but his demons, fo' sure. Folks what's rarely wrong think God's fixin' to do somethin'."

"Well, I'll be darned." Epstein eased forward in his chair. Mose Mann did not have an alarmist molecule in his makeup. If the God-fearing old man said his grandson was destined for an encounter with demons, then hell was headed for Pilot Hill—and that meant big trouble for Bill Mann. "That makes Bill the one who's vulnerable. As long as he refuses to choose God, you have to protect him no matter what."

Mose nodded.

"So . . . if this fight you're talking about happens . . . if it's bad," said Epstein, "you might be in trouble."

"I 'magine, but that ain't what worries me. Keepin' that boy alive is all I'm here for."

"When will it happen?"

"Don't make no difference. I just got to make sure I'm ready."

"Then count me in." Epstein sat back in his chair; his mind was made up. God didn't make mistakes, and if He'd given Epstein a friendship with Bill Mann, it was for a purpose. "I don't know how much difference I can make, but if I'm around when it starts, I'll try to help."

"I already knowed that." Mose nodded and smiled. "You took on a big job when you started comin' out here."

"I'm addicted to the cake."

They were quiet until Epstein said, "He's a good man, Uncle."

"He is that," Mose agreed. "He just don't know it yet."

Epstein gave his thoughts to Mose's words, and Mose napped until the dog left the porch and loped toward the driveway; the sound of a fast-approaching car came seconds later.

Mose and his visitor watched Mann's car slide around the long curve, raising dust and slinging gravel.

"He makes it look easy," said Epstein.

"For him, it's easy as sittin' in one of these here chairs."

"He's been looking at old Corvettes," said Epstein.

"That'd be good. If he got one, he wouldn't be tryin' to run it in the ditch."

Mann stepped out of the car and visited with the dog first. When he stood up, he said, "I hope y'all didn't eat all the cake."

Epstein watched his black friend follow the dog to the porch and thought, *Lord, I just volunteered to be the bodyguard of a guy that's taller, tougher, and light-years smarter than I am . . . be kind enough to make me worthy of my role.*

* * *

Epstein's angel listened to the prayer and turned to his companions. *He has embraced wisdom.*

The tallest of the three nodded. *Indeed he has.*

The angel who was entrusted with the guardianship of Bill Mann said, *And none too soon.*

On the second Thursday in October, the noon Bible study was breaking up when Bill Mann stuck his head in Patterson's office door. He was waving a handful of red coupons. "Excuse the interruption . . . tickets for this weekend."

"To what?" asked Dee.

"Another confounded rodeo," said Missy.

Mann grinned and explained to Dee, "Rodeo isn't Missy's favorite sport, but she suppresses her true feelings so she won't sound bitter." He put the tickets on Patterson's desk. "Help yourselves."

"Are you performing?" asked Dee.

"Not performing. Riding bulls."

"Isn't that dangerous?"

Mann chuckled and winked at Missy. "Only for mere mortals."

He was on his way out of the room before Missy could give him a dirty look.

Dee watched Missy stick her tongue out at Mann's back and asked, "One of your favorite people?"

"Only when he's pretendin' to be sane."

Dee was examining one of the tickets. "I've never been to a rodeo."

"Well"—Missy was resigned—"we *have* to go. You want to come with us?"

"Sure."

She held a pair of the tickets out to Epstein. "Supe?"

"Thanks. I'm thinking about asking Bill to teach me how to ride," he joked.

Missy tried to throw the tickets at him, and they fluttered to the floor. Epstein laughed; Missy didn't.

"Was he kidding about how dangerous it is to ride a bull?" Dee asked.

"Humph," Missy snorted. "Imagine a head-on collision between two gasoline trucks . . . it'd be safer to walk through the wreckage with a flaming torch than to get on the back of a bull."

Mann was jogging past the library, hustling to get in an abbreviated weight workout, when he met Hugh Griffin.

"What about that cooling-off period?" asked Griffin.

Mann had decided Griffin was more to be pitied than anything else. He almost smiled at the man. "We're cool."

"Does that *we* include your tough-acting sidekick?"

"Tough-acting?"

"Yeah. Your *brother* was bluffing."

"Not hardly." Mann shook his head. "To hear my grandfather tell it, Supe's 'all wool and a yard wide.' "

Griffin curled his lip. "Sounds quaint, but what does it mean?"

"It means he's the real article, Griffin. You might want to take a second look at him." Mann went on his way and left the pitiable man standing on the sidewalk.

The bull rider was near the PE building when someone yelled, "Hey, Mann, *que pasa?*"

Homero Gonzales was leaning against the wall talking to two striking women.

"Hey, Homer. Not much." Mann walked over. "How 'bout you?"

"*No mucho.*" Homero gestured toward the girls, both blondes. "We're headed down to The Loop for a couple of beers, an' I'm outnumbered. Wanna go?"

"Better not. Got things to do here." Mann didn't drink, and he wasn't going to The Loop with a white girl, but this wasn't the time to say so.

"Maybe this weekend?"

"Can't do it, amigo, I'm doing a rodeo thing at the fairgrounds tomorrow and Saturday."

"You a cowboy now?"

Mann nodded. "Bulls."

"You don't ride on Sunday?"

"We won't know 'til after the Saturday go-round."

"I'd like to see you on a bull."

"Well, if you don't mind sitting by my boss, I can get you a couple of free tickets."

"Is your boss a *gringo*?"

"*Sí*, but he is an *hombre*."

Gonzales held out his hand. "Put 'em on me."

Twenty-six miles away, in Decatur, Texas, a young lady was walking into the showroom at Jason Groves Motors. She was armed with an expensive-looking camera and a serious expression.

The man who met her on the showroom floor said, "Well, you took my advice and pulled your hair back. It looks great . . . and so do you."

"Don't say that. You make me nervous."

The girl's dad smiled. "Sorry. What could I say that will make you calm."

"Is he here?"

"Not right now."

"He told me I could be here at two."

"It's one forty-five, Kim. Relax in my office or grab a Dr. Pepper and roam around the floor. Your choice."

"I'm too nervous to sit. I think I'll go outside."

She went back to the door, rehearsing what she would say

to the dealership's owner, and ran into him. "Oh! . . . Hi! . . . Mr. Groves, I'm Kimberly Kerr."

"Mr. Groves?" The man put out his hand. "And are you the same Miss Kerr who's spent the last five or six years calling me Jake?"

The high school senior hid behind her hands for a moment to regain her composure, then said, "I'm trying to act professional, and you and Daddy are goofing off."

Groves chuckled. "Well, c'mon back here to my office, Miss Professional, and tell me what's on your mind."

She couldn't wait until they were in the office. She offered her camera into evidence and said, "I want to take some pictures at the rodeo . . . some tomorrow, some Saturday and Sunday. Will you pay me for them? I mean, will you buy them if you can use them for advertising?"

Jason Groves was all business. "Do I have to commit before I see the proofs? I mean, a bunch of black and whites of high school goat ropers won't help me sell pickups to real cowboys."

Kimberly turned around and covered her eyes while she took a breath, then turned back to Groves and said, "Okay . . . now listen. I'm going to the stock show this weekend. I'm gonna take some pictures while I'm there. Is it okay if I put together a portfolio of some of the better shots and bring them by for you to look at?"

"Ahh . . . a coldhearted businesswoman. Have a seat." He sank into the chair behind his desk. "I suppose you'll want me to pay for the use of them."

"Are you teasing me?"

"Maybe a little." He winked.

"Well, yes, I want to be paid."

"How much?"

She looked over her shoulder but found no answer. "Uh . . . how about if we look at 'em and see if you like any . . . then decide."

"What're you gonna do with the money?"

"I'm gonna pay my own way through college."

"Well, I *am* impressed." He stood up. "Okay, get out and bring me back some good pictures."

"Yes, sir."

She was in the hall when he yelled, "Kim!"

She stuck her head back in the door. "Sir?"

"I'm riding in the grand entry Friday night, but I don't need any pictures of me. Understand? I won't be there Saturday."

"Yes, sir."

"But we've got our new sign over there . . . when you're looking toward the press box, it's just to the right of chute number six. See if you can get a good action shot with our name in the background."

"Oh . . . I can do that. Thanks, Mr. Groves."

"Certainly, Miss Kerr."

When she was gone, her daddy walked into his boss's office. "Did you tell her that her hair looked good pulled back?"

"Dadgummit . . ." Groves snapped his fingers. "I forgot."

Elmer Kerr said, "Thanks for nothing."

Groves shrugged and sat down at his desk. "How come you're making her pay her way through college?"

"We're not. This is some kind of new independence thing that just came up."

"Oh?"

"Yeah. She'd be her own country if she could."

"Things could be worse."

"Things *are* worse. I want my dollar back."

"What?"

"You heard me. I want my dollar back. You said you'd tell her and you didn't."

"How 'bout if I say it twice when she comes back?"

"Nope. I been telling her all week you'd be more apt to hire her if it was pulled back, and you didn't even notice." He held out his hand and beckoned. "Gimme my dollar."

CHAPTER SEVENTEEN

On Friday, Missy woke up early and spent all day investing her energy in a bad mood. People who aren't asking questions don't want answers—Pat elected to back off and leave her alone.

After supper that evening, the Pattersons were on their way to pick up Dee Epstein when Pat told Missy, "Well, kid, you can keep pouting and ruin the evening for everybody, or you can relax and pretend Christians truly believe God is in charge."

She was looking down, picking at a cuticle. "I don't like for people to tell me not to pout, especially when I'm poutin'."

"Actually," he smiled, "you look just as good frowning as you do smiling. I just thought you might mislead someone about God's sovereignty."

"Thanks ever so."

Silence was the third person in the car until they arrived at Dee Epstein's apartment. Dee was waiting on the sidewalk; Patterson got out to open the car door.

Dee had spent too much of her afternoon at a western-wear store where she spent more than she needed to on jeans and a pair of Justin Roper boots. She didn't know there was a moratorium on smiles. "Do I look like a veteran rodeoer?"

Patterson held the door for her, and Missy slid to the middle of the seat while surrendering a return smile. "Dee, you're one of those people who look good in anything . . . and you look great."

Patterson agreed. "If I didn't know better, I'd swear you grew up in West Texas."

"I can't believe I've lived in Texas all my life and haven't been to one of these things." Dee was beaming.

Neither Patterson nor Missy shared her enthusiasm. Dee didn't notice.

They parked in a neighborhood across from the main gate and were on the fairgrounds fifteen minutes before the rodeo was scheduled to start.

A quarter-mile strip of asphalt led from the front gate to the arena. The flavor of the air at the fairgrounds was a mixture of hotdogs and popcorn swirled with a background of semisweet livestock. If clothes were the only clue, it might be assumed every person at the North Texas Stock Show and Rodeo was born on a cattle ranch. Had Dee failed to check in at the western-wear store, she'd have been one of a only dozen strange-looking people at the stock show not wearing boots.

A surging collection of blue jeans, bright colors, and cowboy hats intertwined in a disordered dance as men, women, and children meandered in the general direction of the arena, sampling the offered entertainment along the midway as they went. Bigger crowds would show up on Saturday and Sunday, but the five thousand folks who wanted three full nights of excitement turned out for Friday night; they seemed bent on using noise to make up for what they lacked in numbers.

Western swing music blared from speakers stationed along the midway. Girls and women sang along with Bob Wills. Scattered couples danced.

Children screamed for parents to "Come look!"

Parents yelled for the same children to "Stay close!" and "Get down off of there!"

A dozen hawkers' voices made themselves heard above the pandemonium.

A group of high school girls dressed in drill-team costumes and fixed smiles wove their way through the crowd. The girls wore matching tennis shoes and carried their white boots to protect them from getting scuffed.

An engine in one of the farm-equipment displays tried to drown out the racket made by the Tilt-A-Whirl.

From somewhere near the middle of the midway, carousel music sprinkled itself on the bedlam.

Pat and Missy stood outside the arena entrance and waited while Dee bought cotton candy and a corny dog.

Dee's selection raised Missy's eyebrows. "A corny dog?"

"Mmm." Dee was grinning. "The man said it was kosher."

Missy had to smile. The young Jewish girl had spent five years under the heavy hammer of trying to provide for herself while bringing up a younger brother, and Michael had years of schooling left. Dee probably hadn't been to anything as festive as a stock show since she was in high school.

Missy told Pat to go find their seats. "Dee an' I are right behind y'all—as soon as I get some cotton candy."

Patterson waved his ticket. "We're supposed to be on the front row, halfway down."

When Missy and Dee got to their seats, the grand entry was just starting. Mose was already there, as well as Homero Gonzales and his blonde *du jour*. Michael Epstein walked up while everyone was standing to honor the colors. As the American flag passed, people cheered and applauded. If there were any flag burners at the rodeo, they exhibited uncharacteristic wisdom—and contributed to their longevity—by exercising restraint.

Dee looked at her brother's feet. "I didn't know you owned any boots."

"Don't," he said. "These're Bill's work boots."

"They look too big for you."

He followed her gaze to his feet. "They stay on pretty good if I cross my toes and keep 'em folded under my feet. You must be thinking about me being too big for my britches."

"There is that," she said.

In the arena, a seemingly endless line of cowgirls, cowboys, current rodeo royalty, former rodeo queens, rodeo performers, the sheriff's posse, citizens of questionable distinction, and politicians of questionable repute trooped up and down ranks of riders until the display became monotonous.

For Mose and the Pattersons, the high point of the procession came when AnnMarie Roberts rode in on Tony. Bill Mann's guests greeted her with applause and whistles. In return, AnnMarie touched Tony with her heel and he pranced sideways for a few feet; she graced her fans with a wink. When the entry was over, four horsemen, one of whom was Morris Erwin, stayed in the arena while the other folks played follow the leader through the exit chute.

Dee watched closely as Erwin and the other three moved away from the chutes toward a small network of metal fence panels on the far end of the arena. "Are they the first act?"

Missy laughed in her face and Dee got tickled. "This is not a circus, girl . . . a rodeo has *events*." Missy pointed at Erwin and his friends. "Those are the pick-up men . . . real good horsemen. They take riders off the bucking broncs an' generally just stay close in case something needs to be done from a horse . . . releasin' straps an' chasin' animals out an' stuff like that. The real action starts down there."

She was pointing to her left, at the business end of the arena, when the PA system clicked on and a born-to-be-broadcast voice said, "Ladies and gentlemen, welcome to the North Texas Stock Show and Rodeo. My name is Link Bledsoe, and it'll be my privilege to be your announcer this evening. Before we get tonight's action kicked off, I ask that you bow your heads with me and let's ask the good Lord's blessings on this time together."

Dee looked at Missy, and Missy reached over to squeeze her hand. "It'll be okay."

The announcer said a long and eloquent prayer and followed it with an explanation of the first event. "Okay, folks, hold on to your seats while these riders try to hold on to theirs. Our first event is bareback bronc riding."

The announcer continued his patter, waiting for the first bronc rider to get settled on his mount and come out of the chute. Thereafter, Bledsoe filled in spots where the action lagged, exchanging banter with a man out in the arena wearing a clown costume. If things got too quiet the clown man would pull his little dog out of a padded barrel and have him do a trick or two.

Trudy Roberts passed with her daddy in tow and stopped to speak to Mose. She held up a stain-covered paper sack. "We're going down to see my bull."

Clark Roberts was in uniform but not on duty. "Morris brought Sweet Thing over here early today. We're not sure he can take care of himself."

Mose slipped out of his seat to kneel by the child, and the three-year-old spoke in confidence to her friend, "He can take good care of himself just fine, but he gets lonesome for me."

Roberts was looking at the child and shaking his head. "I pulled in the driveway a couple of days ago and found him in the yard with her on his back."

"Have mercy, child, what was you doin' on that bull's back?"

"He likes me to rub his hump."

This was news to Roberts. "You've been on him before?"

"Lots."

Roberts rolled his eyes.

Homero Gonzales was fascinated by the girl's disclosure.

Trudy said, "C'mon, Daddy, he'll be impatience."

"I don't think we need to rush, sweetheart. Sweet's not going anywhere."

Trudy turned loose of her father's finger and looked into Mose's eyes. "Will you take me to see Sweet? He's missing me." She held up her sack. "And he's real hungry."

Mose looked at Roberts and the father shrugged. "I'll be close by when y'all get back."

The little girl led with confidence as she and Mose wound their way through the complex warren of fencing behind the bucking chutes. A small city of competitors, stock handlers, and a hundred other people leaned on fences and talked, knelt on the ground and tended to their equipment, or hustled from one spot to another in a determined effort to make sure the rodeo kept happening. Cowboys moved through the crowd, leading their horses.

As the bull tender and her friend moved deeper into the huge shelter behind the arena, soft snorts and the plaintive vocals of restless animals took over from the man-made sounds outside. Mose said, "Smells kinda good in here, don't it?"

Trudy wrinkled her nose. "I think it stinks."

They were in the central alley leading through the long shed when they met AnnMarie. "Hey. Y'all going to see Sweet?"

"Yessum." Mose lifted his hat. "Miss Trudy say he might be missin' her."

"I said he *is* missing me . . . and he's hungry."

"He's right down yonder." AnnMarie pointed. "Turn left in the next alley; Tony's tied up in front of his stall."

"I know where he is." Trudy hadn't come to see her sister.

"Don't go in the stall with him, Trudy. He might not behave with all these other bulls around."

"I know what to do, an' Daddy says I'm not a baby anymore." She tugged on Mose's finger. "An' anyway, Mister Mose won't let me go in."

Mose told the older sister, "We'll be fine," and let himself be led away.

"Good." AnnMarie turned and resumed her walk toward the action. "I'll see y'all later."

The bull enclosures at the North Texas Fairgrounds were technically stalls, but they weren't small, and they weren't made of wood; for that section of the barn where the rough stock was housed, the standards were more stringent. The barn's designers rightly determined that critters who weighed two thousand pounds and earned their keep by being cantankerous should be quartered in pens with eight-foot walls made from heavy-duty four-inch steel pipe; the enclosures were large enough to hold a half dozen bulls with room for them to move around freely. The panels that made up the fronts of the pens could be swung into the aisles to become gates or barriers, thus allowing the holding area to become a changeable maze where stock handlers could easily direct the movement of the varied animals.

Trudy and her escort turned left at the next alley. The paint quarter horse stood three-legged at the far end of the passageway.

By virtue of his status in the world of rodeo, and because Morris Erwin dictated his own terms, Sweet was in an enclosure by himself. He stood near the middle of his stall, facing Tony. When he saw the child, he grunted and moved closer to the front.

Trudy squatted down by the bull and reached in her sack to pull out a wad of wax paper. "You need to eat more if you're gonna be bucking tomorrow." She unwrapped four cattle cubes which were coated with molasses and held two of them through the lower part of the gate. Sweet Thing worked both cubes off the tiny palm and into his mouth. "Mr. Morris says that's all you can have tonight. These other ones are for Tony."

The bull followed her as she moved down to deliver Tony's treat and snuffed his indignation at having to share. With the horse taken care of, she turned to Mose and pointed at the bull. "Pick me up so I can pet him."

"Well, I don't reckon I can pick you up, baby, but I can help you climb." Mose propped his cane against the fence and guarded the child while she worked her way up the makeshift ladder. When she was in place, he held her so her boots rested on one of the rails while she used both hands to rub the bull's neck. The bull moaned his appreciation.

When she felt the bull was thoroughly ministered to, she said, "Okay, that's enough."

Mose helped her down, and she used a short finger to lecture the animal. "You play fair tomorrow. And don't be mean or I won't feed you any more cubes."

She took Mose's finger in her sticky little hand and led him back to the grandstands.

They made it back to the stands in time to watch a young girl wave a camera at the empty place between Missy and Patterson and ask, "Is anyone sitting here?"

Patterson pointed at Mose. "Yes, ma'am, that man coming right there."

"Shoot!" She looked at the seats behind Patterson. "How about right there?"

Hugh Griffin had taken the ticket, but failed to use it. They were left with an abundance of seats.

"I think we've got seats to spare," said Patterson. "Why don't you help yourself?"

"Thanks a bunch." The girl scrambled into the seat next to Homero's girlfriend.

Kim Kerr put the camera to her eye and looked out at her field of view. She would be shooting directly across the area in front of the bucking chutes; the Jason Groves Motors sign was displayed prominently in the background. The only obstructions between her spot and the advertisement were the horizontal railings that bordered the arena. She experimented with sitting, standing straight and stooping; Jake's big sign presented itself perfectly at two different elevations.

The excited professional photographer told no one in particular, "This is perfect," and snapped a picture as a lean deputy sheriff stooped over so his daughter could peck him on the cheek. The man touched his hat brim to the people in front of her and let the small child lead him away.

Kim tapped Patterson on the shoulder and held out her hand. "Hi, I'm Kim Kerr. I appreciate the seat."

Patterson introduced himself and the rest of their group.

The steer wrestling started while they chatted, followed by team roping, then saddle bronc riding. The Denton High School drill team put on their boots to do a routine during what Dee called "halftime."

"What comes next?" asked Dee.

"Calf ropin'," Missy answered.

"Calves? As in baby cows?"

"Not quite babies . . . just small cows."

Dee pointed at the far end of the arena. "Those men on those horses are going to rope babies?"

"They aren't babies, Dee. They're calves."

"Won't it hurt?"

"Usually not."

Dee was holding her clenched fists in front of her face and biting her lower lip when they turned the first calf loose. The cowboy's loop fell over the calf's head, and the cowboy was off his horse and closing in on the small animal when the rope snapped taut; the calf flipped into the air and landed hard on its back. Dee flinched.

The man pinned and tied the bawling animal.

The PA system announced the roper's time, then gave the audience the next cowboy's name and a little of his history.

Seconds later, the gate snapped open again, and the next calf bolted for freedom. The cowboy was a second behind him, swinging his loop, but most of the people within thirty feet of Dee Epstein were not watching the man on the horse.

The pseudo West Texas ranch-raised girl with the dark hair and new boots was jumping up and down screaming at the calf, "Run! Run!" It was the beginning of a modest rebellion.

When the third calf came out, Missy was on her feet laughing and yelling with Dee. By the time the fifth calf was making his run, most of the women and some of the more fun-loving men were standing and shouting encouragement to the calves. Even the more serious western folk enjoy a good time, and when the last calf made his run, everyone in the stands was cheering for what they were calling "the underdogie."

Cowgirls came out next and conspired with their agile mounts to make barrel racing look easy. When they were finished, the announcer said, "Well, folks, it doesn't get any more exciting than what you're about to see next. Our final event this evening is the most dangerous sport in the world . . . bull riding. You boys be getting the racing barrels out of the way, and we'll turn loose tonight's first rider."

While the men were making the bucking area ready, the little man who'd been entertaining the crowd did a few tricks with his dog and swapped banter with the announcer. Minutes later, he took his dog in his arms and fixed his padded barrel so he could get into it quickly. As he was arranging his gear, three more men in bright costumes made their way into the area.

Dee pointed at the new men and asked, "More clowns?"

Missy seemed distracted and didn't answer.

Homero Gonzales leaned forward and spoke over Dee's shoulder, "*Ellos son hombres.*"

She understood part of the Spanish but not the implication. "They're men?"

"No." Gonzales smiled patiently and pointed at the clown standing in the barrel. "*That* is a barrel man . . . a clown." He pointed at the other men who wore the ridiculous costumes and the painted faces. "*Those* are bullfighters . . . tough *hombres*."

Dee didn't understand, but she nodded.

Missy was thinking that bull riding is always the last event on the card because it's the most popular event. It's the most popular event because it's the most dangerous.

Dee's bafflement regarding the clowns was not uncommon. First-time spectators at a rodeo almost always misunderstand the role of the men in the funny costumes—the ones who stay so close to the action during the bull riding.

The real clown is safe in his padded barrel when the bull and rider are turned loose. As often as not, the showman and his little sidekick will come out to amuse the crowd if the time between rides begins to drag. Their act is funny and entertaining, and the crowd always loves it, but the real clown is back in his padded haven before the bucking chute opens.

The other men wearing the clown costumes are not clowns—and they are not there to amuse anyone.

In Texas and all across North America there are two events on the rodeo circuit that take people into heart attack country. One is bullfighting; the other is bull riding. In any one rodeo, the odds of a contestant getting butted, stepped on, gored, or possibly killed are better than excellent—it's practically guaranteed.

Every man who competes in these professions is probably asked once a day why he chooses this way of life. Most of the answers they come up with have something to do with fun, challenge, money, or all three. The average rodeo fan is able to comprehend what would drive a man to match his wits and skill against twenty-two hundred pounds of angry muscle, bone, and horns.

The bullfighters' wild attire and ludicrous greasepaint are camouflage for serious men. Cat-quick athletes with animal in-stincts and the courage of a mongoose, these men are present for one reason—to protect the bull riders. They wear clown regalia, but that's where the fun stops; when the bull explodes out of the chute, what they do looks like entertainment, but it's all business.

To do the job well calls for at least three men—one on either side of the bull's head, and another one nearby to come to the aid of the rider if he gets in trouble, gets thrown, or when he dismounts. The bullfighters want to make sure at least one man is free to attract the attention of the bull when the bull rider gets off.

In those rodeos where they have their own event, bullfighters compete to see who can be the most daring. In simple terms, this means they have a contest to see which man can come closest to causing fatal heart attacks among the spectators without getting himself hurt or killed.

The first rider came out and lasted two seconds before the bull managed to sling him out of position during a tight turn. The rider hung on long enough to get thrown at the top of the next jump. He was splayed out, ten feet in the air, when the bull kicked, hurling the rider into the rails by the bucking chutes. The cowboy was still in the air when the bullfighters moved in front of the bull. They worked the animal away from the crumpled heap in front of the rails and hazed him into the exit chute. People ran to the aid of the bull rider, but he was already getting to his feet. They led him from the arena while Bledsoe reminded the crowd how dangerous bull riding was and began giving the spectators the name of the next rider and his bull.

There were eleven more rides. Missy looked at her feet while the men rode and the crowd cheered.

On the next-to-the-last ride, when the arena was ready, the PA system clicked and Bledsoe said, "Our next bull rider is Bill Mann. Bill hails from right up the road in Pilot Hill, Texas, and this is his first year in rodeoing. For his first ride in big-time rodeo, Bill will be coming out of chute number six on Straight Flush out of the McMillan string. Straight Flush is . . ." Bledsoe continued to ad lib while two stock handlers moved to chute number six to help out with whatever problem was holding up the rodeo.

A minute later, Bledsoe said, "Looks like we're all set. Keep your eyes on chute number six, folks . . . it's Bill Mann on Straight Flush . . . the man against the bull. And here he comes!!!"

Collin Turner told Bill Mann and Will Pierce that only two things can prepare a man for what a bull ride is like. The most realistic would be a bull ride. Letting your friends tie you to a barrel and roll you down a rocky slope might be a close second, provided the boulders try to run you down and trample you.

Straight Flush wasn't a big bull, but that wasn't necessarily advantageous for the rider. Because he was smaller, the bull could move more quickly than most of his larger counterparts. Every time he landed, he was on his way into the air again. The really outstanding bulls were always unpredictable—Straight Flush was good, but he wasn't outstanding. One of his most noteworthy attributes was the gift of being able to snap his body from side to side while in the air, thus ending most rides before they began. The little bull's other major trait endeared him to rodeo promoters almost as much as his athletic ability—he hated anything on two legs, especially bull riders.

Rodeo promoters know something most spectators would hesitate to admit—the onlookers want to see riders get in trouble. When you pit the strength of the bulls, their horns, and their villainous temperaments against the men tied to their backs, you end up with a guaranteed formula for disaster. Having Straight Flush on the card was good for business because the people who were familiar with the bull's reputation knew he was going to go after whoever was in the vicinity as soon as he got rid of his rider.

* * *

The bull was leaving the ground when he came out of the chute. Mann knew Straight would probably snap in the opposite direction at the top of the jump, but he had spent hours telling himself not to anticipate what the bull might do. The world around him was silent. He couldn't hear the crowd's screams. He couldn't see the people. Straight Flush snapped to his right and immediately back to his left more quickly than a hooked fish. Mann stayed in the middle. The bull landed hard on all four legs and left the ground in a hard turn to his left; Mann and his mind went with him. There were no colors in the world; there was only the bull and the abrupt rise, fall, and tilt of the horizon. The bull grunted and heaved, turning hard, landing harder, but the man stayed fixed to his back. A loud horn made itself heard in the man's head, and he waited until the bull was kicking before releasing his hand and rolling free to the bull's right. Straight Flush felt the rider leave his back and wrenched around in the direction his enemy took.

CHAPTER EIGHTEEN

Mann landed on his hands and knees in the sawdust. The bull reversed his turn and was directly over him. The animal's forefeet were on the ground, and from the angle of its legs, Mann figured its rear hooves were still about fifteen feet in the air. Even as he was deciding on an escape route, he could see the animal sweeping his head back to the right, and the young rider knew who the big, bad bull was looking for.

Uh-oh.

Collin Turner's words were in his mind as he started to roll to his left. *If you end up under the bull, start rolling. Get clear, glance over each shoulder while you're gittin' to yore feet to find out where the bull is, and then head for the fence. An' don't be takin' off runnin' without knowin' where he's at. I seen Billy Jack Costello git throwed out in Childress back in '53. He got up an' run right spang into the side of the bull so hard it near broke its ribs. That bull belonged to ol' man Carlson's string—an' he gave Billy Jack "what fer" for tryin' to hurt his "baby."* Mann rolled once more for good measure, and started scrambling to his feet.

He was just coming off his hands when a bullfighter grabbed his belt and arm, yelled, "Git outta here!" and half-shoved, half-threw him toward the arena's eight-foot-high barrier.

He came erect at a full sprint and heard an angry snort from the bull; it was right behind him. He could hear the crowd now, and they were screaming. Another shout from the bullfighter, urgent with alarm, penetrated the thunder from the stands. He felt, or imagined, the hot breath of the bull on his neck. Mann didn't think he could run faster, but his speed increased.

Looking back would only cost him speed—the fence didn't seem any closer—in fact, it looked like it was an additional ten yards away. Bull riders who'd been squatting along the arena fence were scrambling up the railings to get out of the bull's reach. From the corner of his eye Mann saw the pick-up men spurring their horses in his direction. The pandemonium behind him was gathering energy—snorts and grunts from the bull and horses, yells from the riders telling him to run, and shouts by the bullfighters as they battled the enraged bull traveled in slow-motion from his ears to his brain . . . *This is what a war sounds like.* The crowd was on its feet, adding multiplied panic to its screams and yells. The fence was close—almost within reach. The sounds from the crowd increased in pitch—their terror told him he wasn't going to make it. He felt the breath of the bull on his back and made his jump while reaching for an upper rail with his outstretched hands.

His hands closed on the rail third from the top, and he timed the thrust of his leg to coincide with planting his foot on one of the lower rails. His chest slammed into one of the rails, and his face hit the next one up while his body was still moving at sprint speed—the air was emptied from his lungs by the force of the impact. He scrambled up a couple of rails until he felt fairly safe. The crowd cheered with relief, and he turned to check on where the bull was.

Straight Flush knew from past experience that if a rider beat him to the fence the race was over, and the bull lost interest in Mann the second his boot touched the railing. The cowboy-hunter went looking for someone more accessible and squared off with one of the bullfighters.

The bullfighter was amusing and frightening the crowd by trying to hang an old straw hat on one of the animal's horns. The bull was intent on wearing something a little bit more substantial.

"You got out of there pretty quick." Clark Roberts was standing on the other side of the rails. He was grinning at Mann.

"What'd you do the first time you got in front of one of those guys?"

The deputy's smile faded. "You were slow." The rider looked at him for a moment, then both men laughed.

The lawman jerked his head toward the bucking chutes. "You wanta see this last ride?"

Mann was climbing back down into the arena. "Uh-huh. If I got somebody to beat, it'll be him."

The pick-up men hazed Straight Flush to the exit chute, and the announcer said, "Another man from Pilot Hill, Texas, folks. Coming out of chute number five is Will Pierce on Hurry Sundown. Will is another newcomer to the professional ranks, and we're glad he's here. Hurry Sundown is from the Chilton string; he's been out ten times since the last time a rider heard the bell. Here he is, folks, Will Pierce!"

The gate-man pulled the rope, and the bull came out in a rolling right turn and then snapped to his left. While all four of his feet were still off the ground he twisted back to his right and came down with bone-jarring ferocity on his front feet. He was humping his back for the next plunge before his rear feet came in contact with the dirt. It was eight seconds of warfare, but the man on the bull handled it well. When the horn sounded, he released his grip and dismounted to the right, landed on his feet, and folded to the ground. Hurry Sundown knew when the game was over and turned toward the exit chute. Will got off the ground and limped toward the rail. He stopped a few feet short of Mann.

Roberts spoke while Mann watched the bull being hazed out of the ring. "Good ride, hoss. One of the best t'night."

"Yeah. Not bad for a rookie." Mann grinned at his rival.

Will straightened slowly. "Well, it might'a been jest what the doctor ordered for you, ol' buddy," he said between clinched teeth, "I did something wrong on that last jump an' I think I busted one o' my ribs."

Bright and awesome, an angel waited until Hurry Sundown was almost to the throat of the exit chute and appeared in front of him.

The bullfighters and stock handlers watched in amazement as the bull skidded to a halt ten feet short of the chute. Sundown lowered his head and pawed a shovel full of dirt and sawdust twenty feet into the air while letting out a long, questioning bellow. When one of the men slapped him with a hat, the bull pivoted and headed back into the arena. Fuzzy Miller, the closest fighter, grabbed at a horn and missed. Sundown charged through the group of astounded men, bawling and shaking his head.

Mann watched the bull break through the line of tenders and gallop for the center of the arena. Once there he braced his legs and slid to a stop. He swapped ends, looked back the way he'd come, then shifted his gaze and shook his head. He was looking at Will Pierce.

The pick-up men were jogging their horses out to haze the stubborn bull back to the exit chute; he was holding up the show. Cowboys were spotted along the railing around the arena, some watching the bull, others talking to friends in the stands. The horsemen took no notice of Will and his friends.

Mann watched as Sundown pawed the earth and waggled his horns. The bull blew into the dirt and bellowed. *Uh-oh—thirty yards of clear ground between three men and a bad bull isn't as much as I'd ask for.* Without taking his eyes off the bull, Mann called over his shoulder, "Clark, come over here and get Will."

Roberts was already over the railing; he'd been watching the bull too. "I got 'im."

The people in the immediate vicinity—the ones who could see Will was injured—were on their feet. Men were yelling instructions. Women were holding their hands over their ears and screaming for someone to help the three men. Young children were clutching at their parents' legs.

It was time for Bob Pierce to intervene.

He started to move forward and realized that his wife's hand was locked on his arm. He slipped his fingers under hers, lifted her hand, and put his lips next to her ear. "I'll be back in a minute."

When she heard his voice, his wife turned her eyes on him and said simply, "You bring that boy"—she was pointing at the arena—"with you."

He winked without smiling, nodded, said a businesslike, "Yes'm," and stepped down through the crowd toward the fence.

Nudging people aside, pushing gently but firmly, Pierce tried to make his way toward the rails. The crowd was intent on the action in front of them, and few people noticed the man brush by them—they noticed less that his lips were moving in a silent, one-sided conversation with an unseen Person.

Next time he'd buy tickets on the front row.

Roberts had one of Will's arms over his shoulder and was helping him hobble to the fence. If the bull decided to charge and Will couldn't climb, the deputy would need help to get him over the barrier.

Sundown chose that moment to erase all speculations about his intentions. Someone in the stands watching the three cowboys saw what was coming and yelled, "Look out!!!"

The bull was already running—digging at the dirt like a race-horse, straining to accelerate.

Mann sidestepped to put himself in the bull's path.

The pick-up men spurred their horses, but they were too far away to help.

Bill Mann took three steps toward the charging bull and slipped off his hat.

In the stands, a well-groomed forty-five-year-old woman turned away from the scene and bowed her head. *Lord God in Heaven, God of the impossible, spare this brave boy and our son.*

On the other side of the arena, Missy Patterson closed her eyes and whispered, "You are our strong fortress, Father, our very present help."

Bob Pierce stopped halfway to the railing and began to pray more earnestly.

Mann held his arms apart and yelled, "Whoa, bull!"

Sundown's eyes went wide with fear. He braced all four legs and made his third panic stop in the last thirty seconds, sliding in a shower of dirt and sawdust to within three feet of Bill Mann. Mann stepped out of a cloud of suspended silt and dust and slapped the bull on the nose with his hat. "Git yourself where you're supposed to be."

The bull recovered and whirled toward the exit. The stands were silent for long seconds, then the clapping started. Just clapping at first, then yells and whistles.

Mann used his hat to knock some of the dust off and walked over to check on his friend.

Bob Pierce went back to get his wife.

Missy and SuAnne Pierce collapsed into their respective seats and thanked a gracious God for His intervention.

The crowd watched Bill Mann talking to his friends.

When her husband reached her, SuAnne said, "We owe that boy."

Her husband had tears in his eyes. "That *man*."

She took his arm and said, "C'mon. They'll take him back there behind the chutes."

Will tried to put his bull rope over his shoulder.

"Watch it there, old son," Roberts cautioned. "Don't be twisting around like that, you could stick a hole in your lung."

"Here." Mann put out his hand. "Gimme the rope, Will."

Will grimaced and extended the hand with the rope in it. "I never broke a rib before. If I was choosin', I think I'd rather have this happen to one o' y'all."

They were under the nearest public-address speaker when it blared, "Folks, the judges tell us that ride was worth eighty-four points for Will Pierce, the cowboy out of Pilot Hill, Texas. Let's have a big hand for Will and our other riders."

"Boy, you're gonna be the one to beat now." Mann grinned at the boy who was concentrating on breathing without causing himself pain.

"Congratulations, Will," Bledsoe announced. "That puts an end to the bull riding for tonight with Will Pierce in the lead by two points. You folks come back here tomorrow night for the second round, and we'll see who's gonna be leading for the final go-round on Sunday. Be sure and be here." Bledsoe continued with his description of what would take place in Saturday night's events while Mann and Roberts accompanied Will toward the chutes.

They went through the gate under the press box and stopped by a beat-up wooden bench. Roberts eased Will to the wall and stood between him and the press of behind-the-scenes people and horses making their way back and forth in the passageway.

"Throw that gear on the bench, Bill. I'll prop Will up against this pole while you walk over yonder and get the EMT guys."

Will was starting to turn pale. "I don't need any help. I can—"

"Yeah, right." Roberts shook his head disgustedly then grinned. "Boy, you need to act like you've got some sense. If your rib is busted, then you need to get it fixed before somebody bumps into you and pokes it through your gizzard." He turned back to Mann, "Tell 'em I said to bring a stretcher. Okay?"

The messenger was already on his way. He raised a negligent hand as he walked off. "Yes'r. We're hurrying."

Mann weaved between people and animals for a dozen steps and almost ran into the two uniformed paramedics; he knew the one in front. "Hey! I was just coming to get you guys. Where you going?"

The Denton firemen continued on their mission, and Mann turned to fall in step with them. Tommy Perrin, the taller of the EMTs, was a graduate of Pilot Hill High School. His partner was Tommy Thompson from Denton.

"Hey, Bill. You're late, boy." Perrin was the spokesman for the two-man team. "Somebody said Will bunged up a rib. That right?"

"Aw, he's not hurt," kidded Mann. "He got cold feet when he thought about going up against the real riders tomorrow night. I'd say he's trying to bow out of this thing gracefully."

They kept moving the short distance through the crowd, arriving to find Roberts and Will as Mann left them.

"Mann here says you're fakin' it, Will." Perrin was watching the injured rider's face as he spoke. "Which side are you pretendin' it's on?"

Will didn't change expression. "Tommy, this ain't comfortable by a long shot—and if you make me laugh I'll tell my mom you did this yourself."

Tommy nodded silently, unrolled a blood pressure cuff from the box on the litter, and put it aside. "I reckon that'll serve to keep me quiet for a week or two." He pointed at Little Tom. "Roll it in close an' let's strap it to him in the vertical an' then tilt him an' the litter back to horizontal. We might can keep down the movin' an' bendin', whatcha think?"

"I like it. Gimme a second to drop this baby."

They collapsed the litter, strapped Will to it while he was still standing, and with the help of a few bystanders they moved him from standing to lying without his having to bend at the waist. By the time they had the wheels down, the rider's parents were at his side. Will was appreciably paler.

"What ya'll doin' down here? I'm fine. Ain't I, Tommy?"

Bob Pierce spoke so his wife could hear. "Everybody knows you're gonna be fine, son." He moved aside to let the woman behind him step forward.

The lady looked down at her oldest child, took in the fact that he didn't appear to be in extreme danger, and smiled at him. "It is not necessarily mandatory that a rodeo be this exciting, is it?"

She touched the sleeve of her son's shirt with a trembling hand, then looked at the senior medic over her granny glasses. "Is he all right?" Her expression was the "don't-lie-to-me-boy" one Tommy had seen once or twice in the seventh grade.

"He's fine. He's gonna be sore tomorrow, but that's all."

She backed a step. "You drive carefully, Thomas."

She was the only person on the planet who called him Thomas. "Just like haulin' eggs, Miz Pierce." He grinned at her.

"SuAnne," she corrected.

He grinned at her and blushed. "Yes'm . . . SuAnne." He looked at SuAnne's husband. "We'll see ya'll at the hospital, Bob."

The man lifted his hand and nodded at the retreating uniform.

The EMTs merged into the crowd, and the Pierces turned to Bill Mann. Bob put out his hand. "Thanks."

Mann smiled. "Sure."

SuAnne Pierce looked for a long time into the young man's eyes. Bill Mann had been her son's best friend for eight straight years—the two boys slept at each other's houses, worked together at the feed store, and ate whatever was in her refrigerator, on her stove, or in her pantry. When words failed her, she kissed him on the cheek and patted him on the arm.

He took off his hat and ducked his head.

The couple turned and walked in the direction of the midway. They were silent for several seconds, seemingly oblivious to the people they were passing. Her first words were, "I was worried."

"Mmmm. We were both worried, hon."

"He looked okay, didn't he?" She was better after seeing the boy, but it didn't hurt to get some assurance.

"He looks great. I mean it." They walked for a few seconds. "I'll call Alan to come down and look at his chest. The ER guys can do it, but Alan looks at ten a day. I'd like him to see the X-ray before Will leaves the hospital." His voice had less edge to it now that they knew the boy was better.

The excitement was over, and Mann was using his hat to knock off as much dirt as he could.

"What bull'd you draw for tomorrow?" asked Roberts.

"The best there is." Mann grinned. "Mr. Sweet Thing himself."

"Boy, if you can stay on that bull, he'll win the whole thing for you."

Mann's grin was broader. "You got that right."

*   *   *

The Pierces were in the midway, dodging people. Bob turned to his wife. "How old was he when he was in the seventh grade . . . uh, Miss SuAnne?" He drawled her name in a poor imitation of the fireman.

"How old was who? Will?" She looked at him.

"No, not Will. Tommy. How old was he?"

She spoke without looking at him, "Oh, twelve or thirteen; everybody in the seventh grade is twelve or thirteen, I guess. I don't remember. Why?"

"Did it ever occur to you that he might've had a crush on you?"

"Thomas Perrin?" She pondered for a while, then said, "No." She sounded preoccupied.

"You never had any indication that he was attracted to you?"

They were walking through the crowd on the midway, heading to the parking lot. People spoke to them—they spoke back. They traveled some distance before she responded.

"I didn't say that."

"Huh? You didn't say what?"

She turned to wave at a lady in a denim shirt with blinking lights on the sleeves. When she turned back her expression was noncommittal. "What you said . . . I didn't say that."

"Humph. If all the people I tried to get information from were as wily as you are, we wouldn't have a prison population problem."

She was wide-eyed with innocence. "You should be ashamed. I just finished answering your questions about that boy, and you're ready to incriminate me." She sniffed then said, "Lawyers are all alike."

He took her arm as they stopped to wait for a wagon to pass. "You don't fool me, blondie." He was using his Perry Mason voice. "I saw the way he looked at you."

"I'll have you know I have that effect on a lot of men." Her nose tilted up. "So there!"

"Ahhh!" He was winning. "So he did have a crush on you."

"He most certainly did not, Mr. District Attorney. And I resent your saying so." She waited while he unlocked her car door. He pulled the door open and held it while she sat down. She turned to look up at him. "He was madly, unreservedly, head over heels in love with me." She was giggling when she pulled the door closed.

They were almost to the hospital when he asked her, "What on earth do you do for a man who saves your son's life?"

Bob Pierce didn't know he was holding the answer.

CHAPTER NINETEEN

Hmm?"

Someone was speaking to her, but she couldn't quite understand what the person was saying. She strained to make out the words. The voice spoke again, loud enough to wake her, and her eyes came open in soft darkness.

"What?"

She lay still for a moment, alert and listening, then propped herself up so she could see over the pile of man and pillows on the other side of the bed. Pat kept the alarm clock on his side because she habitually overused the snooze button—it was four in the morning. The edges of their bathroom door bled a rectangular halo of dim light, illuminating the familiar shapes in their bedroom. All was quiet. She and Pat were alone.

But who had spoken to her?

She rested her hand on Pat's back and whispered, "Are you asleep?"

He grunted something into one of the pillows without waking.

She was not a light sleeper, and what she had heard was no dream.

She swung her legs out and sat up on the edge of the bed,

carefully surveying the darkness around her, listening. The room was cool and still. Somewhere in the distance a neighbor's dog barked. She wasn't sure why she was awake—she couldn't bring herself to wake Pat, and she couldn't stay in bed.

She pulled on Pat's terrycloth robe and was at the door of their bedroom when she paused. Prompted by an afterthought, she eased open the drawer in her bedside table and took out a small revolver. Holding the gun next to her leg, she moved to their bedroom door and flipped on the light in the den. Nothing. She tiptoed across the den and into the entry foyer; the bathrobe drug the floor; the tile was cold on her bare feet. The front door was locked . . . nothing on the front lawn but moonlight.

Within a few minutes, she'd made a cursory search of every room in the house, checked the garage, and stepped outside to look in the backyard. More moonlight. The neighbor's dog was silent.

The figure she faced when she stepped back into the house gave her a short-lived start; her reflection looked back at her from a full-length mirror mounted in the back hall. She stared at herself for a moment then snorted, "Humph. Well, Lord, I guess You woke me up for a good reason, but it sure wasn't to fight off a mirror." She slipped the pistol into a pocket of the robe and padded into the kitchen.

Pat would not be up for another hour or two, so she puttered around the kitchen, readying the coffeemaker and unloading the dishwasher.

Minutes later, the percolator's job was done, and she was on the way to the den and her favorite chair with a steaming mug of coffee. She put the cup on a nearby table with her Bible and was in the middle of curling her feet under her when the voice spoke the words that had waked her: "Be ready."

The start she'd gotten from her reflection in the mirror was nothing—she went rigid, her hands braced on the arms of the chair. Even as her eyes swept the room, she knew she would not see the speaker. Three seconds later, she realized she was sitting still when she needed to be moving. Five seconds after that she was snatching up the phone in the kitchen and dialing a number from memory. Holding the pistol and dialing at the same time was awkward, but that was how it had to be.

The man she was calling might not consider himself a valuable resource, but he possessed firsthand knowledge of what could happen after an invisible being tells a person to "Be ready." Hearing what he had to say might prove vital to Missy Patterson.

Saturday morning in Moores Point was just like any other for A. J. Mason. He was at his kitchen table, reading his Bible and waiting for a pan of water and coffee grounds to boil. He picked the phone up on the second ring. "Hello."

"A. J.?"

Until she started Mrs. Smith's kindergarten, Missy spent most of her days in the Moores Point pool hall watching her granddaddy and his friends play dominoes. When she was three years old, one of the regulars dubbed the girl's voice "a buttermilk baritone." No one had a voice like hers. "Mornin', Missy. You out at the lake?"

"No, sir. I'm at my house."

The girl had never called him before daylight. "Gettin' started kinda early, aren't you?"

She offered a desperate prayer against what she was sure would be Mason's response, then told him why she had called. "I just heard the voice."

The warm confines of Mason's kitchen seemed to chill, and he could feel the hair on his forearms stiffen.

Twenty-three years earlier, in 1945, Missy was a skinny seven-year-old—Mason, a quiet-seeming grandfather with a soft spot for children, especially Missy. On a Sunday morning in June of that year, Mason walked out of church to hear a voice tell him to "Be ready."

There was no one near him when he heard the words, and he wrote the message off to an overactive imagination.

That same day, as he was lying down for his afternoon nap, he heard it again—the same voice conveying the same two-word message: "Be ready."

Shortly thereafter, when Mason went for his Sunday-afternoon ride, he carried along two rifles and a shotgun.

Three hours later, he was standing in the center of the Cat Lake bridge, engaged in an incredible struggle—a battle—and he was the only person holding a gun. In the space of a few minutes, using all three guns, he shot and killed twenty-some-odd cottonmouth water moccasins—snakes whose bodies were being used by demonic beings in an orchestrated assault on Missy. Because of God's direct intervention, Mason and the girl survived unscathed.

Fifteen years after the incident on the bridge, the messenger's voice came to him in the predawn hours, speaking the same two all-important words. Later that day, he carried a deer rifle and shotgun out to Cat Lake and saved the girl again. During the second conflict, which proved to be no less bloody than the first, he had to help kill a man he'd known for thirty years.

"Have you got a gun close by?" he asked.

His question told Missy that God's answer to her urgent prayer was *It's starting again, honey, and you're right in the middle.*

She sighed, "Yes, sir—got it right here in my hand."

"Do you have your back to a wall?"

She mentally slapped herself on the wrist and backed against the wall by the phone. "I do now."

"Okay. Now . . . were you awake when you heard it?"

"Not the first couple of times, but I was just now. I was sittin' in the den."

"Tell me what you heard."

She gave him a detailed account of what transpired, and waited.

He took a few seconds to weigh what she'd told him then said, "Sounds just like what happened to me, baby."

"So it was an angel, wasn't it?"

"Yep." There was no doubt in his mind or tone. "An' if what's happened in the past is a guide, you can know he's warnin' you to be ready to deal with what's comin' from at least one demon."

Missy had been trying to prepare herself for what the man was going to say—mentally resisting the inevitable. Hearing his assurance that she was destined for an encounter with a demonic being was like taking a body blow with a large mallet. He could hear her take a deep breath. Her words, when they came, were emphatic. "A. J., I do not want this."

Mason understood. The words from one of Martin Luther's old hymns coursed through his mind. *His craft and power are great, and armed with cruel hate, on earth is not his equal.* Only a fool would relish an encounter with a satanic being.

He looked at the saucepan full of boiling coffee and used it for an excuse to say, "Hang on just a minute. I'm gonna put down the phone an' pour me a cup of coffee."

He put the receiver on the counter by the sink and filled a mug half full of the black brew. He moved to the window and held the cup against his chest as he prayed silently, *Lord, You an' I know You could've picked anybody You wanted to handle what's comin'. I ask that You'd give me the words that will show this young girl how special it is that . . . of all the people on the earth . . . You chose her.*

He picked up the phone and said, "You still there?"

While he was pouring his coffee, she'd been digging in her heels. "I am, an' I still do not want to do this."

"How come you called me, then?"

She could feel her face get hot. "It seemed like a good idea at the time."

"Mmm."

"What do you think I ought to do?" she asked.

"Well, I think it'd be a good idea for us to pray."

"You go first."

"Fine . . . an' you need to keep your eyes open." He bowed his head. "Lord, we got no idea what You're gonna bring us, on this day or any other, but we know You've warned this woman, an' we have to figure that whatever comes will be bad. I pray, Lord, that You would make her strong an' watchful, an' that You'd see fit to protect her an' them she's near. Amen."

Missy had been listening and thinking while Mason prayed. When he finished, she cleared her throat and said, "Father, forgive me for not comin' to You first. I don't know what it is You have in mind for me, an' I don't know when it's comin' . . . I just know I want to do what's pleasin' to You when it gets here. Lord, there's so much to pray for . . ." She stopped again and used the sleeve of the robe to do double duty on her nose and eyes; she wasn't saying what she felt.

Silence came and went over the phone. The old man was weighed down by recollections of the past tragedies and horrors portended by the voice she'd heard. The girl's mind was occupied by memories of the same events, and she could feel her knees beginning to shake. Finally, she said, "Lord, I don't like anything about this. I'm not all that good with a gun, an' I'm . . . I'm . . . uh, just me. Why would You choose somebody like me for somethin' like this?"

Mason waited for the girl to ask for God's help, but the request didn't come. When the line stayed quiet, he asked, "Are we through prayin'?"

"I guess . . . for now."

Mason said, "Amen."

"Well . . . what do you think I ought to expect?" she asked.

"Gimme a minute." Mason leaned against the kitchen

counter and lowered his head, using his free hand to push his glasses up and pinch the bridge of his nose as he said a second silent prayer, *Lord, I'm not sure what's goin' on in this child's heart . . . but You are. I ask that You would see fit to bring her close to Yourself . . . give Your angels charge over her protection, an' hide her under Your wing. Amen.*

If there were words to help her without upsetting her even more, they eluded him. He settled his glasses back in place. "You were there both times it played out for me, Missy. If this is about you havin' to stand against one or more demons, you've got your work cut out for you. Demons don't give no quarter . . . you need to start right now an' figure it's gonna be as bad as a person can imagine . . . an' expect it to be worse."

"I guess I knew that, but I wanted really bad not to hear it." She was having a hard time getting her breath. "What do I do first?"

"Well, keepin' that gun close is a good idea, but prayer is the most important thing," He looked at the darkness on the other side of his kitchen window and asked, "Have you got all your house lights on?"

"Not yet."

"Well, when you get off of the phone, get 'em turned on."

"Yeah, I thought of that. What about things I might not think of?"

He knew Missy had been handling guns all her life. He also knew she'd never shot at a man. "If this plays out like it did for me, you've already figured out you're fixin' to be standin' in the middle of hell on earth. That means you need to be gettin' your teeth set for havin' to do some shootin'—it could be a man or an animal or both. It'll help if you get it fixed in your mind that when a demon takes over the body of some animal or human, it's not a man or an animal anymore—it's God's enemy, an' you're His right hand . . . an' the only way you're gonna be able to get it stopped is to break its legs or cut its spine."

"Okay." Involuntary tremors were taking control of her body. "A. J.?"

"Mm-hmm?"

The quaking in her body worked its way into her voice. "I'm shakin' so bad, I couldn't hit the inside of the house."

"That ain't something you got to worry about . . . God ain't askin' you to be accurate. I always figured God called on me back yonder 'cause I'm a shooter, but when it comes right down to it, all He's lookin' for is the person who'll stand where He tells 'em to. You just get yourself ready . . . God'll take care of where any bullets go."

Her mind stepped away from the man on the phone, and she whispered her next question to the empty kitchen. "Why is this comin' to me?"

He said, "God's gonna be there, Missy. He says He is."

His words brought no comfort. "He was there the last three times the shootin' started, A. J., an' we lost a good man every time."

Mason needed to get her thinking about something that would steer her away from uncertainty. "How many guns you got in the house?" he asked.

She took a ragged breath and shuddered. "Two or three handguns, maybe two rifles, some shotguns."

"Are those shotguns loaded?" he asked.

"Yes, sir," she sniffed. "Buckshot."

"Good. I'd scatter them around where I could get my hands on one quick like."

"I thought about that." She dried her eyes again while mentally picking places where she and Pat would put the weapons. "You think that'll be enough?"

"Honey," he grimaced, "I hate to tell you this, but when this gets kicked off, one of them .50 caliber machine guns wouldn't make the difference. God's already decided how it's gonna come out; He's just lettin' you have a part."

She thought A. J. would encourage her, but she felt as if she were caught in an emotional undertow. "How long do you think it'll be before it starts?"

"Well, for me, it all happened the same day I heard the voice, but I had a few hours both times . . . to get ready, I mean. What you'll need to do is keep a gun in your hand or next to you 'til it's over . . . an' it wouldn't hurt to keep some extra cartridges in your pocket."

"Okay." Her voice was trembling, but she didn't have to take notes; plans for keeping guns near at hand were forming in her mind.

"Where's Pat?"

"Still asleep."

"Mmm. Well, wake him up soon's we get off the phone. He needs to be gettin' his head clear."

"Okay. Anything else?"

"What's on your schedule today?" He was trying to see the future.

"Normal stuff. Pat will putter around here most of the day; I'd planned on goin' shoppin'. If nothing happens, we'll see Jeff an' Ceedie tonight . . . at . . ." Her voice trailed off for a moment, then came back in a harsh whisper, "Oh . . . great . . . please, God . . . You can't be lettin' this happen."

"Missy? Are you okay?"

"I just remembered. We're supposed to go to the stock show rodeo tonight."

Mason's mind filled itself with imagined opportunities for calamity at a livestock show; there were too many animals, powerful animals. "Do you have to be there?"

"Yeah. Pat an' I promised the young man who works in his office that we'd be there to watch him compete . . . last night and tonight." She didn't want to say Bill Mann's name over the phone, but A. J. would know who she was talking about.

A. J. did know, and he dreaded hearing the answer to his next question. "Compete how?"

"He's a bull rider." She looked at the sink, thinking that spitting might take the bitter taste out of her mouth.

"Lord, have mercy on us all." The old man's worst fears were confirmed. "What're the chances of gettin' him to stay away from there tonight?"

"Somewhere between zero an' none, I guess, but I'll talk to him." The probability that she was facing a battle with demonic forces, coupled with multiplied memories of Bill's unflagging contempt for the things of God, brought her frustration to the forefront and made the edges of her words sharp. "We've met this kid's granddaddy, an' that old gentleman has tried to reason with him, but the boy's too confounded stupid to hear him."

Mason had made two trips to Denton over the past couple of years—once with Missy's parents, once by himself. On both trips, he spent almost the entire time with the old fellow they called Mose Mann.

"Is the granddaddy gonna be at the rodeo?" he asked.

"Yep. He's gonna be sittin' with us."

Mason's face hardened. In spite of the social conventions of the Deep South, Mason and Mose Washington were long-time friends. The idea that a stubborn kid would allow himself and Mason's good friends to be exposed to danger rankled him. He said, "Well, you can't take anything for granted, but I think you've just figured out where the trouble's gonna start."

"What about the folks out here?" she asked. "Do I tell 'em what I heard?"

"I think that'd be a good idea." A. J. and FBI agent Jeff Wagner had been on the same side in a gunfight, and he'd had opportunities to visit with the sheriff and Clark Roberts. "Jeff knows how to handle himself good as any, an' that sheriff an' deputy should know what to do. It'd be best to let them in on what's happenin'."

"You're right." She nodded. "An' Jeff has been through this before."

"That's right. An' if what I hear's true, that sheriff's deputy ain't no slouch."

"Yes, sir. He's tough."

They'd said almost all they could say, but he wasn't ready to let her hang up.

"One last thing, Missy."

"Yes, sir?" The conversation had taken a lot out of her, and she was ready for a break.

"I want you to think over what I'm fixin' to tell you." He paused for a moment, then said, "You an' me don't know exactly what's comin', but we know God picked you to deal with it before He created the earth. You been right in the middle of two of these—really three, if you count Dillworth—an' they've shaped your choices for your whole life. You've always been different, Missy . . . practically fearless . . . I've watched you face up to the kind of things that would run a brave man out of town. There ain't been a day in your life when you weren't headed toward something bigger than what the rest of us are lookin' at." He paused, then spoke emphatically. "I don't know what's gonna happen out there, but it makes all the sense in the world that He'd choose somebody special to handle it. That'd be you."

Half the people in the Western Hemisphere had spent the summer telling her she was special—and she was fed up with it. "Is that all?"

Mason heard the defiance in her tone and chose to save his breath . . . she wasn't defying *him*. He said, "Yeah, I reckon that about does it."

She hung up without saying "Good-bye."

She woke Patterson and told him what she'd heard. He was on his feet seconds later. "You were wide-awake?"

"Sittin' down for my quiet time."

She told him what had transpired during the past five minutes, including a condensed version of what Mason said. While she talked he dressed. He put on a dark blue windbreaker, then took a twin of Missy's pistol out of his shirt drawer and dropped it in his pocket.

"We'll go see Mose."

"Is it too early?"

"No."

As soon as Patterson was ready, they called Mose and told him they were on the way to his house.

He didn't even ask why.

———

Mason was ten or twelve hours from Denton, Texas . . . too far to stand next to the girl but close enough to pray. He finished his Bible reading, then picked up his cup and walked down the hall toward his bathroom. Five minutes later, he was moving his electric razor in slow circles on his face, following the movement with his eyes, seeing nothing . . . trying to pray for the girl.

He'd been standing in this same spot the last time he heard the voice. Now, eight years later, the only words he heard were in his own mind . . . from one of his favorite scripture verses, 1 Samuel 14:7. "Do all that is in your heart," Jonathan's young armor bearer told his master, "turn yourself, and here I am with you according to your desire." Mason's prayers felt weak to him, but the Lord says His words will not return to Him without accomplishing that for which He sends them. *Turn yourself, and here I am . . . turn yourself . . . here I am . . . here I am . . . here . . . here.*

When he finished shaving, he picked up a small, round brush and watched whisker clippings accumulate in the sink as he cleaned around the razor's cutting edges. *Turn yourself . . . and here I am with you . . .*

He walked into his bedroom to get his wallet, keys, and pocketknife. He settled the wallet in his pocket, staring into his dresser's mirror; an old man, bent and honed by old age, stared back—neither saw the other. It was at least twelve hours from his house to Denton, Texas. He went to his gun rack, praying,

Lord, if You want me by that girl's side, You'll have to pick me up and put me there.

Minutes later, when he left the house, he was carrying his Bible and a Winchester pump shotgun, 12-gauge.

CHAPTER TWENTY

The dog was on the porch to greet Missy and Patterson. Mose served coffee in the kitchen while they waited for Mann to get dressed. When Mann came to the kitchen, Missy mentioned that his left eye was puffy.

Mann waved away her concern. "It's nothing . . . probably got bumped during the dismount last night." He grinned. "Will would swap places with me . . . I imagine he slept sitting up last night."

He poured his coffee while Missy began relating her morning's experience.

When she finished, Mose said, "Well, it don't surprise me none . . . an' I guess the same goes for you. We been lookin' for it since late May."

Missy didn't tell him she hadn't spent the summer expecting to get called into a fight with the forces of darkness. She looked at Mann. "You're stayin' pretty calm."

The young man who wasn't interested in angels was concentrating on stirring sugar into his coffee. "Sorry. I know you're upset, but none of this makes sense to me. If angels are really warning you, why can't they fight the battle?"

Missy sat back and took a breath.

When Mose stood up, Mann's eyes followed him. "Did I make you mad?"

"No-no. I'll be right back." The others could hear his footsteps as the man made his way to his bedroom. He was gone less than a minute, and when he came back he was carrying an ancient revolver in his belt.

Mann looked at the old gun and asked, "What're you gonna shoot?"

"Whatever comes down the pike." Mose took his seat and picked up his cup. "We ain't speculatin' anymore; we fixin' to get in a fight."

Mann let his eyes move around the table, looking from one person to the next. All three were looking at him. "You're all carrying guns, aren't you?"

Missy said, "Dadgum right," and Pat nodded.

Silence followed.

Mann left the table to warm up his coffee and leaned against the kitchen counter. "The three of you have been my family for almost half my life. You haven't held anything back for yourselves . . . not a dadgummed thing." The people at the table waited while he stopped to sip his coffee and arrange his thoughts. "There is no kid in the world—black or white—who feels any more loved than I do . . . and I'm grateful, but . . ." He put his cup down, rested both hands on the counter behind him, and looked at Missy. "But you're expecting me to believe we're in some kind of danger because of something that could have been a dream . . . or your imagination. I'm really and truly sorry . . . *really* . . . but I don't think I'm being stubborn, and I don't want to disappoint you . . . and I care whether or not you get mad at me." He shook his head slowly. "I believe we'll always be in danger from the Bainbridges, but I cannot believe any of this angel talk is . . . is real."

Missy knew trying to convince him would use precious time and probably be an exercise in futility. She nodded and said, "I know."

Mose was noncommittal.

Patterson said, "I understand."

Mann touched Missy's arm when he took his seat at the table. "Thanks."

Patterson addressed himself to Mann, "Mose and Missy and I need to talk about what we're going to do, and I think it would be wise for you to sit in on the planning in spite of your skepticism. If we're wrong, all you've lost is a little sleep. If we're right, you'll be more prepared. What do you think?"

"You're right," agreed Mann.

The skeptic moved back and forth between the table and the kitchen while the other three talked, listening to their conversation with half an ear while he baked biscuits and kept coffee cups filled. The believers spent their time trying to plan for an attack that might come at any moment, from any quarter. The dog split his time between Missy and the biscuit baker.

Thirty minutes into the session, the planners found themselves immersed in "what if" scenarios that forked and branched like cracks in a shattered mirror.

Mann was arranging bacon in the frying pan when Missy pushed her chair back from the table and stood up. "Y'all, this is ridiculous. We keep talkin' about goin' to war, but we don't know any of the who, what, when, where, an' how's that're waitin' on us. An' if that's not enough . . . all we've got are these little .38 peashooters." She pulled out her snub-nosed pistol and frowned at it. "I'm the best shot in here, an' I'd have a hard time hittin' the floor with this thing." She put the pistol down by her coffee cup and turned away. "This is foolishness."

The three men watched as she walked into the living room.

Patterson rubbed his chin and traced in figure eights on the tabletop with his fingertip. Mose massaged the arms of his chair and frowned. Mann brought the pot over and topped off their coffee cups.

Patterson took a sip of coffee and said, "She makes a good point."

"Uh-huh"—Mose raised his finger like a teacher stating an important fact—"but not like you think."

"No?"

"Not by a long shot." Mose shook his head and stood up. "We been goin' the wrong way." He walked to the living room door and said, "Step in here, Missy."

When the girl was seated, Mose said, "You was right 'bout the foolishness. We been wastin' our time tryin' to figure out what we needs to do, when what we should'a been doin' is prayin'."

"I've already prayed," said Missy.

"Then you prayin' the wrong way, child, or you wouldn't be so put out."

Her tone was too curt when she said, "You'd be put out too if you were as scared as I am."

The words were on their way before she gave a thought to where they were going. Her eyes went immediately to Bill Mann; he was watching her and patting the place where she'd hit him for speaking harshly to Mose.

She took a deep breath, her hundredth in the last few hours. "I'm sorry, Mose."

"Never mind that, girl."

She couldn't remember a time when she had been disrespectful to him. Her handgun lay on the table in front of her, and she picked at the checkering on the pistol grip with her fingernail. A tear spilled onto the table, and she beckoned to Mann, "Hand me a napkin."

He put one in her hand and she blotted her eyes. "You're right. I've been spendin' my time bein' mad, an' I need to pray." She frowned. "An' I've been mad 'cause I'm scared. Is it okay to be scared?"

"Lemme read us somethin', then we can talk some 'bout bein' scared." Mose's new Bible was only nine months old and already showed signs of use around the edges. "Thus says the Lord,

'Let not a wise man boast of his wisdom, an' let not the mighty man boast of his might, let not a rich man boast of his riches; but let him who boasts boast of this, that he understands an' knows Me, that I am the Lord who exercises lovin'kindness, justice an' righteousness on earth; for I delight in these things,' declares the Lord." He let the words hang for a moment then said, "We done clean forgot what our job is. Missy, me an' you talked 'bout this a million times when you was growin' up—we supposed to spend our time knowin' God an' makin' Him known; He takes cares of the rest . . . *all* the rest." He closed the Bible and rested his hand on it. "We'd do better to turn loose of what *we* wants . . . an' start thinkin' about what *God* wants."

"I don't understand." Missy looked at Pat then back at Mose. "Will thinkin' about what God wants help me know this is gonna turn out right?"

"It sho' will, if you get yo' mind right. I was named after the Moses in the Bible 'cause he was God's man for the time, but he got started slow. He had everything goin' for him, but he balked when God chose him 'cause he didn't know God good enough— but when he put his hand to it, it turned out real good. God didn't have to come down hard on David 'cause David spent the whole time he was a boy, thinkin' on how to know God better. When that giant poked fun at God's folks, didn't nobody in that whole army have to tell David what needed doin' . . . that child stepped up an' done it."

The room was quiet. The day's first redbird twittered shrilly, and Missy stood up and walked to the front door. The bird called again, and Missy pushed the screen door open. "I'll be back in a minute."

She stood on the porch, her silhouette showing up against the hint of daybreak. The men ate biscuits and bacon and drank their coffee in silence.

The Moores Point Café opened at five o'clock, and Mason's coffee was waiting for him at his regular table. He was unfolding his newspaper when Van Hobbs slid into the chair opposite him and offered the older man his regular greeting.

"Mornin', Mr. A. J., ready to go for a ride?"

Mason was shaking his head before the question was out of the man's mouth. He took a sip of coffee and got busy with his paper. "Maybe tomorrow."

Hobbs came home from World War Two and started a one-man crop-dusting operation. In the years since the war, his business expanded; he bought more airplanes and hired two pilots to help him. For the past ten years, he had used his profits to finance a respectable farming operation. The easygoing pilot's offer to take Mason up in one of his airplanes was a standing joke, but the old man's response never varied. Mason hated the thought of getting off the ground.

The waitress took Hobbs's breakfast order, and the two men drank their coffee in silence until Mason happened to think that the agriculture flying was over for the year. He said, "How come you're flyin' today? The cotton's all ready to pick."

Hobbs was engrossed in his own newspaper. "Gotta take one of the planes out . . . get new wing rigs installed. Got an empty seat, but nobody's got the urge to ride along."

"Mmm." Mason lost interest.

Three cups of coffee later, Hobbs stood up and said, "Well, don't ever say I didn't offer to show you the Lone Star state."

Mason put his cup down slowly. "The what?"

"Texas." Hobbs grinned. "I'm heading out to Weatherford. You could've had a bird's-eye view of Texas for free."

"How close'll you be comin' to Denton?"

Hobbs shrugged. "I'll be going north of Dallas . . . probably fly right over Denton."

"Does Denton have an airport?"

"Yep, and an old grass strip north of town called Hartlee Field."

"What time would we get there?"

Hobbs grimaced. "I'm real sorry for baitin' you, Mr. A. J. I gassed 'er up before I came to town, and I've gotta leave as soon's I can see . . . that means you don't have time to pack anything. Maybe next time."

Mason stood up and pointed at the front door. "I need one thing out of my truck, an' I'll be ready to leave. What time will we get there?"

Hobbs looked at his watch and shrugged. "We'll stop in Texarkana for gas . . . probably be in Denton before noon."

Mason said, "I'm ready when you are."

When Missy came back into the kitchen, she said, "I've been tryin' to do this by myself."

"An' so have the rest of us, but that's behind us."

"What do you think I should do?"

"That's just it, child. This ain't 'bout what you gonna do . . . it ain't never been 'bout you . . . it's 'bout what God's gonna do. You go to yo' house an' get on yo' knees an' thank God for whatever's past an' whatever's comin' . . . an' leave the rest to Him."

One question continued to resonate through her mind. "I can't figure out why He'd pick me."

"I've seen how you live yo' life, baby, an' God ain't never made a mistake yet. We all been comin' to this day since 'fore the earth was here. It goes back past you an' me, past Pap even. God's been gettin' us ready for a long time."

"But why *me?*"

"Have mercy, child, you *listenin'*, but you ain't *hearin'*." He was frowning. "You got to turn loose of that thinkin' 'bout yo'self. The good Lord ain't never give us a chore to do without givin' us the wherewithal to do it, an' He never will. He just calls us to step up an' do the confounded job."

She looked down at the handgun. "Even with a pea-shooter?"

"Oh, yes, baby." Mose smiled. "Lemme see that shooter."

She passed the gun to him and he opened the cylinder. The bullets dropped into his palm and he stood them in a line on the table. "Five cartridges . . . same number as them smooth stones that young boy—that chosen one—took up agin' that giant."

The young woman let the words sink in, then pushed away from the table and stood up; the men stood with her.

Her moves were deliberate; she took the bullets, one at a time, and slipped them back into the .38. When it was loaded, she closed the cylinder and smiled softly at her almost-daddy. "I guess that's what I've been needin' to hear."

Mose and Mann walked their guests outside. Mann and the dog followed Pat and Missy to their car. The sun wasn't quite up, but alternating layers of vivid red and bright blue said it was on the way.

Mann looked at the horizontal streaks of color and said, "My dad used to say, 'Red sky in the morning, sailor take warning.' "

Pat paused and looked at the coming daylight before sliding behind the wheel and said, "I guess that makes it official."

At nine that morning, Pat took one of the shotguns and walked into the hall. "I'm going to put this one by the front door."

"Mmm." Missy crossed the den and stood in front of a wide bookcase, searching the rows of books until her eyes fell on the spines of a pair of identical volumes. The book she pulled off the shelf first was fairly nondescript—a medium-blue hardcover, slightly larger than a college dictionary. She put it aside and reached for its twin. The second book was decidedly more unique—a hole as big as her finger was centered in the front of the book, just under its title . . . *Things to Come*. She sighed as she traced her fingertips over the cover's fabric, letting the rough, black flecks on its surface tickle her fingertips.

In 1958, during the second of Missy's three clashes with satanic beings, a demon-crazed college boy, a young man masquerading as a Christian, fired a pistol at her from less than three feet. The damaged book—owing to God's direct intervention—took the bullet meant for Missy's chest. She touched the cover's surface to her face and let her cheek move across the rough specks of burned gunpowder, remembering.

Without thinking, she closed her eyes and sank slowly to her knees; her chin touched her chest and the bookcase became an altar as she whispered, "Lord, people have been tellin' me I was special ever since the first time You called on A. J. to save my life. I may be lookin' forward to havin' to use a gun today, an' You an' I both know I can't shoot like A. J. I beg You, Father . . . I implore You . . . in what You have chosen for me to face . . . that every action I take would bring honor to Your name. Lord God in Heaven, give me only that Your power would be perfected in my weakness. Amen."

She took one of the books to the kitchen and pulled open the drawer where she kept a few small tools and some single-edged razor blades.

Missy spent most of the morning reading her Bible and praying. Pat prayed and read as well and got up every thirty minutes or so to walk through the house. They had sandwiches and iced tea at noon, and she was cleaning off the table when the doorbell rang. They looked at the kitchen clock first, then each other. It was almost one, and they weren't expecting company.

Pat said, "Better let me open it."

She nodded and followed him toward the door.

When Pat opened the door, Missy heard A. J. Mason say, "Boy, I sure hope you got a gun in that other hand."

Pat took his right hand from behind the door and showed the pistol to Mason. "Come in, A. J." When Mason stepped across the threshold Pat nodded to his left. "I think you already know my wife."

"Hello, A. J." Missy was standing six feet to the side with a shotgun snugged against her shoulder. The gun's barrel was pointed at a spot just left of the door; Missy's finger was resting on the trigger guard. "You're just in time for dinner."

Mason nodded his approval. "You're a little perkier than you were the last time I talked to you."

"Yes, sir. Mose had a little talk with me right after you did. It wasn't easy, but he finally got the message across." She stood the shotgun against the wall behind a drape, then linked her arm in his and started for the kitchen. "Well, you didn't have time to drive. Did God send you out here by Angel Express?"

"Caught a ride with Van Hobbs, an' I 'preciate God gettin' me out here so quick."

"You rode in an airplane?"

"Mm-hmm, an' next time I'll be comin' on that Super M."

"Super M?" asked Patterson.

"Tractor." Mason winked.

Missy took her friend's hand and squeezed it. "I stood on Mose's front porch this mornin' an' prayed to God that He'd send you."

"Well, He sure done it." Mason put the only thing he'd brought to Texas on their coffee table—his Bible. "Let's call Mose an' get me a handgun."

CHAPTER TWENTY-ONE

The thunderstorms promised by the dawn came in at mid-afternoon and left just before supper. Mason sat by himself on the covered patio and watched the weather move northeastward. He'd spent most of the afternoon with Mose; since getting back to the Pattersons' house, he'd sought solitude—content to sip an occasional cup of coffee and read from his Bible. He passed on supper.

Patterson finished eating and stepped outside to ask Mason if he wanted more coffee.

Mason ignored the offer. "This rodeo place . . . is it covered?"

"Yes, sir. Brand-new indoor arena—doubles as a show barn—first class."

"No mud?"

"No sir. Everything's covered or paved with blacktop."

"It's a big rodeo thing then . . . lots of people."

"Probably ten thousand tonight, depending on the weather. It's not in the class with Fort Worth or Houston, but it's big."

Mason stood up, taking his empty cup with him, and went over to stand by one of the stone columns at the edge of the patio.

After waiting long minutes in silence, Patterson opened the back door and stepped inside the house. He looked back at Mason and said, "We'll leave in a few minutes."

The old man didn't turn; his eyes were fixed on something Patterson couldn't see. "I'm ready."

Patterson, Missy, and Mason drove straight to the fairgrounds; Dee would meet them at their seats.

Every person who'd been at the fair the night before brought a friend, including the midway barkers. The drugstore cowboys were out, flanked by women wearing tall hair and rhinestones—glitz and glimmer, noise and lights. Las Vegas was in Texas.

They were almost to the arena when they saw Mose standing near a concession stand. He was holding a cup of coffee and watching the crowd move by.

Mason looked at Mose's coffee. "Any good?"

"Not good as mine," said Mose, "but it's tolerable. Can I buy y'all a cup?"

"I got it." Mason looked at Missy and Patterson. "Y'all want coffee?"

Missy shook her head, but Patterson contradicted her. "That'd be good, thank you. Both of us."

Missy looked at her husband first, then at Mason. "I'd like that."

Mason ordered the coffee, and the high school girl who waited on him asked where he was from.

"Miss'ippi."

"I thought so." The girl's cheeks dimpled and she patted him on the hand. "You talk just like my granddaddy. You know where Rolling Fork is?"

"Yes'm. Been there a time or two."

She brought the coffee, and Mason, who had wasted too much of his life minding his own business, said, "Honey, I need to ask you somethin' important."

"What?"

"If you died tonight, would you go to Heaven?"

"Sure as shootin'," with softer dimples and a warmer hand pat. "I accepted Christ when I was nine years old. How 'bout you?"

"Yes'm. I was a little older, but He got it done. How much I owe you?"

"It'll be seventy-five cents. We have to charge a lot 'cause it's the fair."

Mason handed her a twenty-dollar bill and said, "Keep the change, hon. Buy yourself somethin' nice."

She could hear something he wasn't saying. "Are you okay?"

"Just about perfect." He winked at her, and she watched him walk over and hand cups to a young man and woman. The black man with them said something and they moved away.

They were approaching the arena's east entry ramp when Patterson stepped clear of the pressing crowd. The other three followed, and the four gathered in a small circle by one of the grandstand's metal pillars. Patterson held his cup up, "He said, 'Do this in remembrance of Me.' "

Without hesitating, his companions held up their cups. The four said, "Amen," and a camera flashed.

"Hi, y'all." Kim Kerr came from behind her camera. "Have you got room for me to sit with y'all tonight?"

Missy took the girl's arm and moved to the ramp going into the arena. "If we don't, we'll just scroonch up."

Dee was waiting for them by their seats. Hugh Griffin walked up as they were settling in.

Patterson introduced Griffin to Mose and Mason. The old men were both gracious and reserved. They shook his hand firmly and looked him in the eye—Washington was warm enough; Mason remained cool and aloof. The academician from California had seen pictures of men like the two—men dressed in starched khakis, their shirts buttoned at the neck—time had stooped their backs but not their backbones.

Mason leaned close to Missy and asked, "Where's Jeff an' Ceedie?"

"Jeff's in Washington. I told Ceedie not to come."

"Good. How 'bout the sheriff an' that deputy?"

"Don't know about the sheriff. Clark'll be here."

As if waiting to be announced, Clark and Trudy Roberts chose that moment to make their entrance. Roberts was in civilian clothes—straw cowboy hat, starched shirt and jeans, and flat-heeled Ropers; his badge was pinned to his belt in front of his holster. Trudy went straight to Mose so she could show him what she had in her sack.

Patterson stood to make the necessary introductions. Griffin shook hands with Roberts first and stepped back.

When Mason put out his hand, Griffin watched the deputy take off his hat. "Good to see you again, A. J." He swept his hat to include the others in his greeting. "We're glad you're here."

"It's good to see you too, son." He looked at Roberts's pistol. "Lotta sidearm."

Roberts looked down and rested his hand on the gun. "Biggest I could find." He let his eyes sweep the arena. The sawdust surface was carpet smooth and smelled faintly of fresh cedar and livestock. The gate under the press box was swinging open in preparation for the grand entry. "Big enough to stop a grizzly."

"That ain't gonna make the difference," said Mason.

"Yes, sir, I know . . . but I don't think He'd have me leave it at home."

Griffin heard the comment and wondered, *Who wouldn't have a deputy sheriff leave his pistol at home?*

Trudy had the waxed paper out, showing off her cattle cubes. "Mr. Erwin says two cubes won't hurt him any."

"Well, I'm right sure he'll be pleased to see you."

"Me too. Daddy told me a thousand times not to ask you to walk with me. Why'd he say that?"

Mose smiled and stood up. "I reckon he wants you all to hi'self."

"Oh, he's not goin'. My momma's down there somewhere." She pointed toward the chutes. "She said she'd take me. Will I see you after?"

"After?"

"After the rodeo."

"I hope so, baby. I'd like that."

Their brilliance found its source in Him whom they loved and worshiped.

They were facing outward, standing in a loose circle around their humans, alert, listening and watching. When Roberts and his daughter walked away, one of those who remained looked at the child's angel and said a single word: *Vigilance*.

The child's angel said, "Yes, my leader. For Him who sits upon the throne and for the Lamb."

Link Bledsoe came over the PA system and asked the men to remove their hats so they could pray. He said another well-read prayer, then told everyone who the first bareback rider would be.

Kim Kerr took photos. Griffin engaged Dee in one or two short conversations; the remainder of their group was quiet. Homero Gonzales hadn't showed.

Michael Epstein got to his seat while the steer wrestling was in progress. He sat down behind Mose and said, "Sorry I'm late. Anything going on?"

Mose shook his head. "Been quiet." He glanced to his left and saw a red-faced Millie Clark marching toward them with Trudy snuggled in her arms. He watched the way Millie planted her heels as she threaded her way through the crowd and added, "'Til now."

"Old age is making my dadgum brain soft." She was fuming, talking loud enough to be heard ten rows up.

The child was clinging to her mother's neck. She was covered with dirt and sawdust, clutching her paper sack; tears were drying on her cheeks.

"You okay, baby?" Mose asked.

"He wasn't behavin' nice. I was bein' nice an' he tried to butt me."

"Daddy always said there's no such thing as a pet bull. He was right." Millie's anger was becoming the fear of what could've been. She was beginning to tremble.

Missy eased over and said, "You wanna sit down?"

Millie tried to take a steadying breath. "Maybe in a minute."

Bledsoe announced the first rider's score and started his spiel about the man coming out of chute number two.

Clark Roberts was nodding and speaking to people, working his way down the wide aisle toward his wife. Millie saw him, and her lower lip began to quiver. He started talking before he got to them. "AnnMarie told me Sweet was acting up. Are y'all okay?"

Trudy held her arms out to her father. When he took her she buried her face against his neck.

Millie took his free arm and held it; she was trembling again. "I wasn't paying attention . . . not close enough. I mean, who expects . . ." She shuddered. "She was trying to get her sack open . . . had her head and shoulders between the bars . . . leaning into Sweet's stall. I untied Tony to move him closer to the water, and he jerked free—probably to get at the sack." She shed her first tear and reached out to touch her daughter. "The stupid horse got his nose between the rails and knocked her out of the way at almost the same instant Sweet hit the rails where she'd been standing." She closed her eyes and held a shaking hand over her heart, forcing out the words. "I thought he got her . . . he hit the rail . . . hard enough to bend it. If Tony hadn't . . ."

The crowd around them watched as she leaned against her husband's chest and sobbed.

The men on the front row stood so the family could sit down.

Trudy was frowning. "He not stupid."

Ten minutes later, Trudy was sitting on Mose's lap and retelling the story. Millie recovered almost as quickly as her daughter, and Missy introduced her to their group.

During a lull in the arena, things grew relatively quiet around them at the moment Trudy told Mose, "Tony was nice."

"He was nicer than Sweet, honey," said her mother, "but knocking you fifteen feet down the aisle when he snatched at the cubes is not nice."

"Tony wasn't snatchin'." Trudy frowned and wiggled out of Mose's lap. She put one fist at her waist. "Tony was heppin' me."

"Okay." Her mother brushed at the child's hair. "He was helping."

The child held out the crumpled sack. "He handed me back my sack when you picked me up."

People in the near vicinity knew the Robertses, and they'd been listening to the account of what happened. A few smiled at the little girl's tale.

Millie took the sack and stared at it. The last time she'd noticed it, it was lying in the dirt outside Sweet Thing's stall.

In the aftermath of the bull hitting the fence, she had run to the child and scooped her up. Trudy cried loudly, mostly out of fear and anger. She was holding the child against her, patting her back, comforting her, saying, "It's all right, baby, it's all right now. Mommy's got you."

The little girl abruptly broke off her crying in the midst of a long wail, sniffed, and said a soft, "Thank you," as if talking to someone who approached her mother from behind.

Millie had turned to find Tony standing quietly at her shoulder.

She squeezed the child close and carried her out of the stall area. "You're so welcome."

Clark Roberts reached for the girl's hand. "Tell me about Tony handing the sack to you."

People several rows up were leaning forward to hear what the child would say. Trudy was unperturbed. "When Mommy picked me up, he rolled it over with his nose an' picked it up an' handed it to me. He was very behavin'."

Millie was holding a hand over her mouth and shaking her head; new tears wet her cheeks. "He . . . wouldn't . . . do . . . that."

"Would too," argued her daughter.

"He picked it up with his mouth?" asked Roberts.

"You're bein' silly, Daddy," the little girl giggled. "You know horses don't have fingers."

A few people wondered at the spunky little girl's tale; most just smiled.

Mason listened to the child's story without moving. At its conclusion, he leaned back and looked at Mose. Mose pursed his lips and nodded imperceptibly. Clark Roberts and the Pattersons were staring across the arena at nothing.

Bucking animals and tenacious riders came and went. Minutes passed.

Mike Epstein caught Mose's eye and asked, "Did I hear that little girl right?"

Mose nodded. "You understand?"

"Yes, sir. Mostly, I guess."

Dee listened to the exchange then asked her brother, "Understand what?"

"You don't want to hear it."

"I do too."

"An angel or angels intervened for the kid . . . pushed her out of the way."

Dee watched for eight seconds as a man rode a horse that didn't want to be ridden, then said, "You know, it's more likely I could stay on one of those horses for an hour than carry on a conversation with you that doesn't eventually lead to our having to talk about God."

"Whew!" Epstein's shoulders sagged, and he used a hand to smooth the thick mustache. Dee could be blunt, brilliant, and brittle, all in the same breath. "Is it that bad?"

"Only all the time." She softened her words with a wink.

Missy heard Dee's words, but she didn't see the wink. She turned in her seat and propped her arm on Dee's knee. "Tell him you love him."

"I beg your pardon."

"Do like you're told," Missy said gently. "Tell your brother you love him."

"He knows I love him."

"I think you an' I should take turns being stubborn. I'll go first." Missy shook the girl's leg with her elbow. "Tell your brother you love him, or I will make a scene."

Dee smiled and looked at her brother. "I love you."

Epstein was grinning. "I love you too."

Missy said, "All better," and turned back to the rodeo.

The Denton High School Drill Team was marching into the arena. Their boots looked great.

*   *   *

Pretty girls were riding fast horses around the barrels in the arena when Morris Erwin pulled his horse near the rails in front of Millie Roberts. "Where's AnnMarie?"

Millie pointed in the direction of the chutes. "Down there with Clark. Why?"

"Sweet's cuttin' up some. I figured to have her keep Tony close to him 'til we get him back in the trailer."

Millie left Trudy sitting by Mose and stepped across the aisle to Erwin. "Morris, if Sweet comes back in my yard again they'll haul him off in the renderin' truck. I mean it."

Erwin said, "I'll talk to you later," and rode off. Two minutes later he was leaning from his horse and talking earnestly to Berg Vaughn, the arena director. He left Vaughn to find AnnMarie.

When he found AnnMarie she was behind the chutes holding Tony's reins. Sweet Thing was nearby in a holding pen.

"I brought Tony up here because Sweet's actin' cantankerous."

"You did good." Erwin pointed at the arena. "I already talked to Berg. As soon as they get the bulls in the chutes, I want you to come out in the arena with us. Sweet can see Tony from out there, an' it might keep him steady."

"What do I do?" She'd never been in the arena while an event was going on.

"You don't do anything—nothing; Berg made that real clear. If the pick-up men go to work, you an' Tony stay out of the way. If a bull comes down there by us, you take Tony as far from him as you can get. Y'all ain't out there for but one thing, an' that's to keep Sweet settled an' stay clear of everythin' else. Understand?"

"For gosh sakes, Morris. You could've said all that in three words. I'm not an idiot."

"Naw"—Erwin's smile was dry—"you're a thirteen-year-old smart aleck." He turned his horse toward the arena. "Keep that paint away from trouble."

"Yeah," she mocked, "we sure don't want any of your precious animals to get hurt, do we?"

Erwin ignored her.

* * *

When the bull riding started, Missy closed her eyes.

Some of the bull riders got off easy, some were thrown hard, but only one had to be carried out of the arena by the two Tommys.

Missy opened her eyes when Bledsoe said, "And coming out of chute number three, Bill Mann of Pilot Hill, Texas. Bill rode Straight Flush all the way to the bell last night. Tonight he's comin' out on one of the best bulls in rodeo, Mr. Sweet Thing himself, a Brehmer Cross out of the Morris Erwin bucking string . . . two thousand pounds of horn and muscle." The people who knew rodeo cheered as much for Sweet as for Mann. Neither the bull nor the rider heard them. The announcer talked and Missy watched the gate man. The gate man watched the rider.

Sweet Thing's performance was worth the price of admission, and Bill Mann rode him all the way to the horn . . . but very few would remember the ride.

No one would forget what happened afterward.

CHAPTER TWENTY-TWO

The horn sounded, and Mann grabbed the end of the bull rope. On the next jump, as Sweet kicked, he released the rope, pulled his hand free, and rolled to his right. Sweet felt Mann's weight shift and twisted hard in the same direction. The bull got his head around in time to butt the rider under the chin, and Mann landed in the dirt.

Fuzzy Miller was the bullfighter nearest the action and saw Mann take the blow. He darted in to help Mann to his feet and pushed him out of the way while keeping an eye on Sweet Thing. The ride was over and Sweet was turning in the direction of the exit chute.

Sweet Thing was a favorite on the rodeo circuit, a ton of tough competitor without an ounce of meanness in him. Fuzzy slapped the bull affectionately on the shoulder and told him, "Good ride, ol' buddy, good ride." The big gray bull shambled toward the exit with Fuzzy as an escort.

Brent Travers picked up Mann's bull rope and jogged to catch up with him. He handed him the rope and walked a few steps with him. Mann nodded at something he said and kept walking.

Travers slapped the rider on the shoulder, told him the same thing Fuzzy told the bull, and turned back to his business. Fuzzy was waving at him, yelling, "C'mon, Brent, we got—"

Travers's arms were coming up, and his mouth was opening to yell, but it was his eyes that communicated the warning. Fuzzy whirled back in time to take the bull's horn in the center of his chest. The blow lifted him off the ground. He cartwheeled in the air—a full, slow-motion revolution—and landed in the dirt in front of the bull. He was bloody from his nose to his waist . . . and still as death.

Bill Mann, unknowing and unmoved, was weaving slightly, progressing steadily in the direction of the perimeter fencing, dragging his bull rope.

Wild Bill Sanders and Brent Travers, the two remaining bull-fighters, were closing in on the bull. Sweet might choose to do further harm to the man who was down, and it was their job to get control of him. They intended to do just that.

Erwin watched his bull hit the fighter and cursed. All four pick-up men touched their heels to their horses and moved out.

Erwin looked back at AnnMarie and said, "Take Tony down there by the exit chute an' see if Sweet'll follow 'im."

"Yes'r." AnnMarie and Tony moved off at a lope.

Mann stopped ten yards short of the fence, dropped his bull rope, took off the straw hat, and brushed at his chaps with it. People were split between those yelling at him to run and others who were stunned by his bizarre behavior. He heard the noise the people were making but attached no significance to it—people were always making noise. He looked behind him.

A bull was standing on the other side of the arena, looking at someone who was splayed on his back in the dirt. The bull stepped back from the body, shook his horns, then let out a half-sigh half-snort. As the sound resonated in his chest, the huge head swung slowly to his right and Sweet Thing looked directly at Mann.

Mann picked up his rope, coiled it carefully, and slapped it on his chaps to knock the dirt off. He turned toward the fence again, and Missy jumped up and climbed to the top of the railings. She held on with one hand and gestured wildly with the other, yelling for him to hurry. He looked at her without changing his expression or pace.

Wild Bill and Travers were shouting and waving their hats in an effort to entice the bull to follow them toward the exit chute. The mounted men moved in closer and slapped their ropes against their legs to get him started.

The bull didn't move.

In the background a voice on the public-address system urged the men in the ring to move faster.

Grant Sanders—Wild Bill to rodeo people—was the more experienced of the two fighters, and something about the bull's eyes was worrying him. "Somethin' ain't right here." He was muttering to himself, but Travers heard him.

Travers was watching the animal's eyes because they would always telegraph the animal's next move. The bull was intent on something behind the two men.

A fixed gaze by an animal in the midst of so much activity was not natural. Travers wanted to see what was attracting the animal, hoping it might prove to be something they could use to their advantage.

Turning his back on a bull this close was tricky, but he snapped his head left for a glance behind him. In that first instant, he did not believe what his glimpse told him. Mann was barely moving—almost meandering along on the far side of the arena. A man in a long-sleeved shirt converged on the rider. He would need a wide window of opportunity to get Mann safely to the fence.

"This ain't good!" Travers had a feeling that the bad part of the fight was yet to come.

"Yep! He's zeroed in on 'im, ain't he?" Sanders hadn't missed a thing.

"I'm gonna git closer." Travers was on his toes, bouncing and weaving, moving directly in front of the bull.

"Easy now, Brent," warned his partner. "He don't act like he's buyin' it."

The fighter stepped in, talking to the bull. "Okay, ol' son, let's me an' you do us a little dance here"—he was a foot from the bull's nostrils—"an' give them cowboys a chance to head for th' drink stand." He slapped the bull across the eyes with his hat and kept bouncing sideways toward the exit ramp. The bull flinched, glanced only briefly at Travers, and turned his attention back to the man shuffling slowly in the direction of the fence.

In the stands, several people watched the bull's eyes as he watched the disoriented youngster. The two men in the clown clothes between the boy and Sweet Thing were shouting and waving their hats in an attempt to herd him toward the exit chute. The four pick-up men moved in and slapped their ropes against chap-covered legs to get him moving. The bull seemed unaware of all but one person.

The right-hand judge, Caleb Lacey, was jogging out to help Mann. Two bull riders who had been watching from the side of the arena followed.

When the bull didn't move, the pick-up men changed tactics; three of them were swinging their ropes, shaping the loops. Erwin sent his loop out, and it settled over the horns of the bull; the second loop was right behind it. Both men dallied the ropes around their saddle horns and backed their horses to take up the slack. The third rider was moving into position behind the animal, his own loop already swinging. He was waiting for the bull to pick up a back foot so he could "heel" him. With the brute's head under control they could put the bull anywhere they wanted him if they could get a rope on one back leg.

Before the front riders could take up the slack on their ropes, the bull shook his head and one of the loops fell in the dirt.

Erwin let his rope go slack while he waited for his partner to get back in the play. Roping yourself to a one-ton bull while you're on a half-ton horse is a good way to get your horse hurt.

Mann turned in time to see the bull shake off the rope and watched the two bullfighters dancing in front of the animal. The man lying on the ground hadn't moved.

Caleb Lacey got to Mann's side and took his arm.

Sweet Thing took a step toward the two men.

Missy said, "That's it."

Patterson, Mose, and Mason apparently agreed because they were getting out of their seats.

Dee was confused. "Are they leaving?"

Her brother stood up and said, "Not yet."

"Where are they going?"

Epstein pointed at the figure out in the arena. "To get him."

Patterson was climbing the fence. The older men were slower, but they were right behind him.

Dee Epstein stood up and grabbed her brother's arm. "You aren't going out there while that bull's loose."

Epstein pulled away. "I'll be back."

Mason and Mose were making good progress. Patterson was almost to the top of the fence, but Missy wasn't waiting. She hoisted herself over the top rail and jumped. She rolled once and grabbed her lower leg.

Patterson was kneeling by her a second later. "What happened?"

"My ankle!" She had to yell to be heard over the screams from the stands. "Go! Go! I'm comin'! I'll crawl!"

Patterson shook his head. "If you're out there, there'll be two people to protect. Wait here."

Mose and Mason stopped near the couple and Patterson said, "Pull her over against the fence."

"No!" she was crying. "*I'm* the one He told to be ready. He told *me*!"

"Be still, Missy," Mose ordered. He nodded for Mason to take her other arm, and they dragged her to the fence.

She pushed herself to a sitting position and looked at Mose. "Why did this have to happen now?"

"'Cause God got somethin' else for you. For now, He 'spects you to watch an' pray." He left her. Seconds later Michael Epstein climbed down the fence; he was carrying Mose's cane in both hands like a rifle, looking neither right nor left.

Clark Roberts was standing on the stairs to the press box when the ride ended. He watched Fuzzy get hooked, and when the bull slipped the pick-up man's rope, he started down the stairs. He pushed his way through the crowd and was at the ramp to the grandstand when Missy jumped into the arena.

The second pick-up man threw his rope again, and the bull ducked his head. The man cursed and Sweet started forward.

Erwin knew where Sweet was going. There was no way he could stop him, but he could slow him. He let the rope tighten and reined his horse back. The bull didn't slow. If he knew he was dragging a horse, it didn't show.

* * *

Caleb Lacey watched the bull separate from the cluster of bullfighters and pick-up men and stopped. Mann kept walking—oblivious and helpless.

Erwin swung his horse up and out, thinking to pull the bull off line, and the bull began to run. Lacey moved to meet him.

The bullfighters were sprinting, chasing the bull, yelling and waving their hats.

Lacey had ridden over a thousand bulls before he retired, and he knew how much harm this one would do if it got to the boy. He planned to stop its charge, or at least slow it, without getting killed.

He changed his grip on the clipboard he was holding, snapped his wrist, and launched it Frisbee-fashion at the bull's face from twenty feet. The clipboard was still in the air when Lacey followed it in.

The clipboard bounced off Sweet's nose. An instant later Lacey dodged under the blunt horns and threw his weight at the animal's right leg. The judge hit the front of the leg as it was moving forward; the bull stumbled slightly, and when his left front foot came down again it was square in the center of Lacey's aluminum clipboard. The uncontrollable skid turned the bull. He stumbled, lost his footing, and went into the dirt on his knees.

Erwin took advantage of the moment and backed his horse, hoping to keep the bull down. It didn't work, but it distracted the bull. Sweet scrambled to his feet and charged the horse. Erwin threw the rope clear and let the bull chase him to the exit chute. At the last moment, the bull turned away from the chute and started back toward the people near the fence.

Patterson and the two old men had guns under their shirts, but if they fired and missed, they would most certainly hit someone in the arena. The three of them got Mann and started back the way they'd come.

*   *   *

AnnMarie Roberts could see her daddy in the stands, pushing by people, rushing to get where he could help.

Morris Erwin was back in the arena, circling between her and the ongoing fight.

Mose and the other men helping Bill Mann were almost to the fence.

The bullfighters sprinted to a spot between Sweet and the people at the fence and turned to face the bull.

A small man carrying a stick left the side of the arena and walked in the direction of the bullfighters.

The bull was running, gaining speed.

Sanders was shouting at Travers, "He ain't gonna slow down for us."

Travers had time to yell, "What're we gonna do?"

"Try to not get killed!"

The bull charged between them and they each grabbed a horn. Sanders was knocked aside; Travers was dragged a few yards.

The bull didn't slow.

Mann and his rescuers were at the fence.

The last line of defense was twenty feet from the railings—the skinny little guy with the stick.

Mose was moving up behind Epstein, yelling, "Stab him in the face!" Michael Epstein nodded and as the bull bore down on him, he presented the stick like a bayonet-equipped rifle. The charging bull lowered his head and Epstein dropped to his knees. At the last second the man lunged forward, thrusting one end of the stick into the bull's face while trying to ground the other.

The bull's momentum drove the wooden spear deep into his nostril and his head followed the weapon into the dirt—his nose dug in, and his momentum upended him. He cartwheeled, doing a half-rotation in the air, and came down on Mose and Epstein.

Grunting and bellowing, Sweet lashed out with his legs and horns, struggling to right himself. He regained his feet and backed away from the two men in the dirt. When the men didn't move, he jogged in a tight circle as if looking for the source of the next attack.

Bob Pierce was at the front of a small wave of people who were coming over the fence to help.

Morris Erwin moved his horse in to crowd the bull away from the people, and Sweet hooked it. The horse screamed and ran from the fight. Sweet charged into a cluster of people near Mann.

AnnMarie leaned over Tony's neck, nudged him with her heels, and said, "I guess it's our turn, boy. Let's get closer."

Some unknown number of people were mixing into the tumult at the fence. Cowboys and spectators, ranchers and grocery-store clerks were stepping into the war . . . moving the injured to the side or trying to boost them up the fence.

AnnMarie watched Sweet find the man he was looking for. She gripped the pommel with one hand and booted the horse, crying, "Go!" Tony was running at a full gallop within three strides.

She closed in on the battle and watched the bull bunch his muscles to hurl himself into the crowd of people. She leaned over the horse's neck and yelled, "Hit 'im, boy!" And that's what Tony did.

They careened into the side of the bull, driving him bodily away from the action. Sweet turned on Tony and tore a V-shaped wound in his shoulder forward of the girl's right knee. The horse grunted and almost went down. AnnMarie turned the horse and waited while Sweet tried to find Mann again. She could feel Tony trembling.

"It's okay, boy, it's okay," she whispered. When the bull charged again, she and the paint met him just before he pinned Mann to the fence.

The horse fell, and she rolled clear in time to hear her daddy's voice yelling, "Get out of the way!"

Clark Roberts was sprinting along the grandstand aisle. He wasn't sure what he was going to do when he got to the battle; he prayed as he ran.

People saw him coming and started shouting and jerking people out of his way. As he closed in on the area immediately above the conflict, he saw the bull charging toward several people at the base of the fence. Before Sweet could hit the people, Tony and AnnMarie hit him, and the bull went into the fence without harming anyone.

Roberts continued to yell, "Get out of the way!" While sprinting through the crowd.

Onlookers jumped out of his way. He chopped his steps, timing his move, and pushed off with his feet as he grabbed for the railings directly above the bull. He scrambled up the rails like a lizard and was in the air, his body moving to horizontal, when the world slowed.

He pulled on the upper rail with both hands and looked down on the bull. As his body was clearing the top rail he reached for his pistol with his free hand and looked at the place he wanted to land.

His body continued to rotate; he was coming down perfectly, right against the bull's left side. Particles of sawdust stood out against the black coloring around the bull's neck; a splintered piece of wood protruded from its nostril. Roberts let his left hand touch the bull while he was still in the air, coming down in front of the bull's hump. He used the bull to steady himself . . . when his toes touched the ground, he pressed the barrel of the gun against Sweet Thing's side, tilting it to aim at his heart, and pulled the trigger. As soon as he heard the concussion, he remembered Pat Patterson telling him about being attacked by demon-controlled animals . . . he couldn't stop the bull with a heart shot.

The first shot staggered the bull. When Sweet regained his footing, Roberts triggered the gun again and broke the animal's front leg. The bull collapsed on top of him and began thrashing and bellowing, trying to regain his feet. Roberts was pinned and helpless.

Mason came from nowhere. He dropped to his knees next to Roberts and held his hand out for the big pistol. Roberts slapped it into his hands, and Mason used one shot to sever the bull's spine. The jerking and twisting stopped.

Morris Erwin was there within seconds. He knelt by Sweet's head and rested his hand on his neck. The bull blinked his eyes and Erwin turned to Mason. "My bull ain't dead yet, mister."

"I'm real sorry about this," said Mason. "You want me to do it?"

Erwin shook his head, and Mason handed him the gun. The bull watched his owner put the muzzle between his eyes and sighed. People who could see what the man was going to do turned away. Erwin said, "You were a good bull," and pulled the trigger.

When he knew Sweet Thing was dead, Erwin stood up and looked at the aftermath of the storm. Injured people were being helped by their friends . . . Millie and Trudy were in the stands, both were crying . . . people were watching Erwin . . . the brand-new arena was as silent as an empty church. He tossed the pistol into the dirt by his bull and said, "He was the gentlest animal I ever knowed." He looked at Sweet again then walked away.

AnnMarie stood close by holding Tony's reins, speaking calming words to the horse; she and the horse were trembling. Erwin stopped long enough to look at the horse's cut and say, "He'll be okay," and kept walking. He got several steps away before he came back to tell the girl, "There ain't a man in here could've done any better'n you did tonight." He took off his hat. "An' I'm real proud to call you my friend."

The paramedics were loading Fuzzy onto a stretcher. Two off-duty firemen had another stretcher and were running toward the group by the rails.

Dee Epstein was in the dirt with her brother's head in her lap. She was holding his broken glasses in one hand and pushing the hair out of his eyes with the other. A broken piece of hoe handle and an old boot lay near his leg.

The fireman stopped and knelt by the girl and her brother.

They were too late.

Missy crawled to where Mose lay and was kneeling over him. "Mose?"

"I'm here, child."

She took his hand. "You're hurt."

He smiled without opening his eyes. "Don't feel too bad."

"What do you want me to do?"

"Where's that boy at?"

She looked over her shoulder. "He's comin'. Pat went to get him."

"I needs to talk to him."

"He won't remember what you say, Mose. He took a lick on the head."

"Then you can remember what I say an' tell him when he's right. Understand?"

"Yes'r." She watched his chest rise and fall, then said, "Mose?"

"I'm still here, child."

"I never got to thank Junior for savin' my life."

"Mm-hmm."

"When you get to Heaven, would you tell Junior I 'preciate him savin' my life?"

He smiled again. "That's the first thing I'll tell 'im."

"An', Mose?"

"Mm-hmm?"

"Would you . . ." She stopped to get her breath. "Would you tell him I love him?"

"He always knowed that, baby. An' he sho' loved you."

She sighed.

"Baby?"

"Sir?"

"I'm fadin'." He lifted a finger. "I want you to tell that boy God's been linin' out somethin' for him to do for a long time. Folks has lived an' died so God can show him He's got a plan for his life. You understand?"

"Yes'r."

His brow wrinkled. "Lots o' folks has lived an' died so that boy will know he's special . . . me an' you an' him was chosen. I want you to remember that, an' I want you to tell it to him. Hear me?"

"I'll tell him."

"That's good."

"Mose?"

"Yes, baby?"

"I love you, Mose."

"I know, baby." He smiled again and died.

Mason was there in the next minute; Pat and Mann were right behind him. They found Missy holding Mose's hand.

Mason took off his hat and knelt on one side of the girl. Pat stood near with Bill Mann. Mann brushed absently at the front of his shirt.

Missy beckoned to Pat. "Bring him over here by me."

She signaled for Mann to kneel by Mose, and he let her put his hand on the old man's chest. "I'll have to tell you this again when you can understand what I'm sayin', but you need to know you heard it here first."

Mann responded with a blank look.

Missy put her hand on top of the young man's and said, "A special thing happened here today. Before he died, Mose said to tell you that you an' me an' him were chosen . . . We're special. I promised him I'd tell you. Understand?"

Without changing expression, Mann reached out with his free hand and brushed at the sawdust on Mose's face, and said, "Okay."

CHAPTER TWENTY-THREE

Late on Sunday afternoon Missy stopped by her house to pick up the dog and drove out to the house in Pilot Hill. Pat was waiting at the hospital; they'd follow as soon as Mann was checked out.

She sat in the car with her right leg propped in the passenger's seat—in no rush to be in Mose's house without him.

The dog asked to get out, and she opened her door. Leaves, loosened by the season and knocked down by Saturday's storms, blanketed the yard and drive. The dog made a circuit of the yard as she watched, moving at an old man's pace, while Missy breathed the tree-filtered air; the cats and birds were absent. After his territory was carefully inspected, the dog went up the front steps one at a time, sniffing each one. He stopped at the front door, looked it up and down, then backed away and came back to stand by the car.

"Okay, okay. Lemme get my stuff." She worked her way out of the car. She'd used crutches more than once in the past, and getting her purse, book, and crutch under control only took a moment. When she was fully loaded, she said, "C'mon."

She stood inside the front door and used the crutch to hold the screen door open for the dog. He backed away.

"He's not comin' home, Dawg," she spoke as she would to a friend. She said the next words to herself as much as to the dog. "I had him for thirty years, an' you had him all your life, but he's gone now, an' he's not comin' back."

The dog's ears flapped when he shook his head. He backed another step.

"Let me know when you change your mind." She let the screen door slam.

The doctor told her the cast would speed her recovery and diminish the chances of re-injuring the ankle. The pain pills he'd given her were at home in the trash. If she kept her leg elevated, she could tolerate the throbbing.

She put her purse and book on the coffee table and lowered herself to the couch. Pat had spent the night at the hospital with Bill; she and the dog sat in the den all night by themselves. She put her head back and closed her eyes.

A voice said, "You should've listened to the dog."

The speaker stood in the kitchen door. He was black, medium height, slender. In his hand was a small automatic pistol. She'd never seen a real silencer, but she watched movies and television. He said, "The dog knew I was here."

"What do you want?"

"I want to know when Bill Mann will be home."

She didn't change expression, and he took a step toward her. "I'm a professional killer and I'm good at what I do because I enjoy it. You will eventually tell me what I want to know because you want to—but the motivating factor is the crucial thing here. I'm giving you one chance to speak without being motivated."

She couldn't function as well if she were shot in the knee. "They'll be here in a few minutes, I think. Bill's getting checked out of the hospital."

"They who?"

"My husband and Bill."

"Move slowly." The automatic didn't waver. "Use one hand . . . take your purse by the bottom and let its contents spill carefully onto the table."

She slid forward and did as she was told. When her revolver slipped out, he said, "You Texas women are a different breed. Use the crutch and push the gun to the end of the table."

She complied, and he picked it up. "I saw you in action at the rodeo last night. You're the kind of person who would carry a firearm."

"What now?"

"Now, we wait."

"The Bainbridges sent you here."

"One Bainbridge, actually. Congresswoman Bainbridge paid me to find Mose Washington, William Prince Jr., and the white man."

His confession was a death sentence for Missy. "How'd she know where Mose an' Bill were?"

"You weren't listening. She doesn't know where they are . . . she doesn't know where I am."

"You went to Cat Lake."

"I did."

Missy frowned. "How can she not know where you are?"

"Congresswoman Bainbridge is not someone I deem worthy of trust. I took my money and told her I would let her know when the contract was fulfilled. After this evening, I intend to find that white man and then disappear for at least ten years."

"Whatever she paid you, we'll pay you more—double even. Tell her Mose and Bill are dead. Take her money and ours and quit for good," she reasoned. "If you haven't told her they've been found, you can tell her they're both dead."

He shook his head. "Honor among thieves."

"You're not possessed, are you?"

"By demons? You must be joking." He smiled for the first time. "Is anyone?"

"The woman who hired you is."

Aacock didn't believe her and said so.

He only took his eyes off her for a second at a time, watching her as if she were a snake. She closed her eyes and prayed, *Lord, You have promised that You are my stronghold an' shield, my very present help in time of trouble. Father, if we are to live through this, it will be because You choose to stand between us an' this man.*

She opened her eyes and the dog pawed at the screen door. When no one moved, he coughed. He'd bark next.

Aacock said, "I don't want to hurt an animal, but I will. Does he bite?"

She knew the dog had attacked a gang member in Chicago for threatening Bill Mann. "I've never even heard him growl."

He held the automatic by his leg and walked over to let the dog in.

Dawg pranced in with his tail held high—no hesitation, no hackles, no furtive looks. For the first time in his life, he passed on having the girl rub his ears. He waited until the man resumed his place by the kitchen door and lay down a few feet away. When settled, he kept his head up instead of resting it on his paws and turned a steady gaze on Missy.

"Let us pay you more money—whatever we have—all of it," Missy was speaking earnestly. "Just leave us alone."

Aacock shook his head without speaking.

Missy bowed her head and closed her eyes.

When she looked up Aacock was watching her. "You have a reputation as a religious woman."

She had to ask. "Can I tell you about Jesus?"

He pointed at her crutch. "Only weak people need those."

"You're so wrong, an' He's so real."

Her preaching brought out the worst in him. He leaned near and read the title of her book. "*Things to Come.* More Christian propaganda?"

She took the book, put it in her lap, and rested her hand on the cover. "The things of the future were set by God before time." The confidence in her tone was a missed warning.

"Am I supposed to care?"

Missy bowed her head again and closed her eyes.

Aacock said, "I asked you a question."

When Missy looked up she had tears in her eyes. "Jesus Christ died so you could live."

Aacock, who rarely lost control of his emotions, was tired of hearing about Jesus. He spurted a chain of profane words to lend credence to his chosen stance and sneered, "I don't *want* to live."

"I know," said the girl.

She looked at the dog. He was waiting . . . his feet under him . . . his unblinking eyes fixed on hers.

"Good dog," she whispered.

She said it so softly that Aacock assumed she was praying with her eyes open. He caught the movement on his left and turned toward the threat.

The dog was in the air when the killer's silenced gun coughed. The bullet hit the dog in the chest, and the animal's body struck the man, knocking him back a step. He was near recovering when an explosion slammed him into the wall.

The woman was still sitting on the couch. The book she'd been holding was on the floor in front of her—a tattered mass of paper. It looked to Aacock as if someone had used the pages to cut out paper dolls. The woman was holding a smoking pistol. Aacock used his last thought on earth to wonder why someone would let a child cut up a perfectly good book.

Patterson and Mann found her sitting against the wall, holding the dog's head in her lap. Her gun was on the floor by her leg.

She smiled up at them and said, "I wish you could've seen him. It was beautiful."

Patterson knelt by her. Mann picked up her pistol and went to check Aacock's body. Missy inclined her head toward the dead man. "The yardboy from Cat Lake."

Patterson nodded. "I figured. Let me get you to a chair."

"In a little while." She smiled down at the dog and smoothed one of the long red ears. "He was so magnificent."

Mann was kneeling over the killer. "We're in trouble."

"Nobody's in trouble," she said.

Mann frowned at her. "They know where we are . . . where I am."

Missy traced her fingernails through the dog's slick coat. "Nobody knows where you are." She told them why.

Neither man spoke as she related what Aacock told her. When she finished, Mann said, "The Bainbridges will find out as soon as the police trace who this guy is."

"They can't trace someone that doesn't exist."

Both men looked at her.

"Hello!" called a lady's voice. Someone was in the front yard.

Mann looked out the window. "It's Will . . . his mom and dad are with him." He turned and looked at Aacock's body. "What're we gonna do?"

"The smartest thing under the circumstances." Pat walked to the door. "We're going to run it right down the middle."

Will was taking his time getting out of the car. SuAnne Pierce was coming up the steps with Bob on her heels. "We didn't know if y'all would have chocolate cake yet, so we brought two. C'mon, boys."

Patterson stepped out and stood between her and the door. "Have a seat on the porch, and let me get Missy and Bill."

"Nonsense." She stepped around him and across the threshold. Missy and Bill were standing between her and the body, but she saw it. Her mouth came open then clamped shut. She backed onto the porch.

Bob Pierce looked at her face and took her arm. "Sweetheart?"

"Have her sit down, Bob," said Patterson. "She's had a shock."

Pierce guided her to a chair.

Patterson stuck his head in the door. "Bill, I need to ask you something."

Mann was handing Missy her crutch. "Tell them the whole thing," he said.

SuAnne had yet to speak when Pierce turned to Patterson. "What's going on?"

"You need to take a look in the living room," Patterson said, "then I want you to come out here and let us tell you a story."

Thirty minutes later, Mann, Missy, and Patterson watched as Bob Pierce finished digesting what he'd heard. SuAnne Pierce was holding *Things to Come*. Someone had cut away a place inside the book, a carefully carved recess that would hold a small five-shot revolver. Will was sitting quietly by his friend.

Bob Pierce sat back and ran his fingers through thinning hair. "I became a lawyer because I believed in the law. I became a district attorney because I want to see criminals punished." He paused and rubbed his hand on his leg. "I'm getting old now, and I often see more justice outside the courts than in. If the powers-that-be get that body, I don't think Bill will last a week."

"What do you suggest?" asked Patterson.

"You've thought about this longer than I have. Do you have any plans?"

"I do," said Missy. "I say we bury him in that low spot about a hundred yards behind the house."

Bob and SuAnne Pierce exchanged a knowing look. She smiled and repeated his question to him. "What on earth do you do for a man who saves your son's life?"

Bob stood up. "Where're the shovels?"

Michael Epstein was buried in Dallas on a beautiful Monday afternoon.

Tuesday they buried Mose and his friend. A slow, soaking rain started at noon and lasted until midnight—classic funeral weather. Mann sewed the dog into a soft blue blanket, and the people watched as he lifted him like a baby and placed him on top of Mose's casket.

Morris Erwin stood under the awning, watching the rain and visiting with some of those who lingered after the service. Millie kissed him on the cheek, and Trudy hugged his neck. He recognized A. J. Mason and spoke.

The two old-timers pulled aside, and Erwin wondered out loud why a bull would go crazy.

"I can explain it," said Mason, "but you won't understand it 'til you understand somethin' else."

"What's that?"

"Well," Mason cleared his throat, "I spent more'n seventy years mindin' my own business, but I'm changin' in my old age, an' I need to ask you somethin'. Do you know for a fact you'll go to Heaven when you die?"

"Do you?" asked Erwin.

Mason said, "Yep," and told him how he knew.

Patterson was back in his office on Wednesday. Griffin was waiting for him.

They stood at the window and looked at the coming fall colors. Griffin didn't see them. "What would possess a man like Mike Epstein to do what he did?"

Patterson remembered Missy's descriptive phrase for what the dog had done. "It was beautiful, wasn't it?"

Griffin thought back to the skinny kid kneeling in front of the charging bull and started to protest. As his memory added to the clarity of the image, he drifted away from the window. At the door, he stopped and said, "Yeah. It was breathtaking."

━━━━━━

On the Thursday after the rodeo, Missy answered her doorbell, and Dee Epstein said, "I didn't know where else to go."

Missy gathered the girl close and said, "I'm honored that you chose to come here."

━━━━━━

Kim Kerr walked into Jason Groves's office and plopped down in a chair. When he looked up she handed him a manila folder.

"What's this, kid?"

"Eight-by-tens of the rodeo."

He hefted the folder. "Not very many. How much is all this gonna cost me?"

The girl shrugged.

He flipped open the folder and picked up the first picture. He looked at it for a second then showed it to her: an eight-by-ten glossy. "Nice. Four people toasting with paper cups."

"I like it."

"Mmm."

The next. "This is cute . . . a little girl kissing a man."

"It's her daddy."

"Mm-hmm." Leading Kim to think he might buy her pictures was a mistake.

The next picture was of the two old men in the "toasting" picture. They were sitting side by side—a black man with a white shadow. It was a study in the lean-jawed, unrelenting determination that made the West what it was, but the men weren't even wearing western shirts. Groves looked at it and put it aside without comment.

When he saw the last photograph he stared at it for a long minute, then rose slowly out of his chair. He glanced at Kim and went back to the photo study. He took a magnifying glass from his center drawer and walked to the light from the window. "You took this?"

"Yes, sir." She was looking down, busy watching herself click the tips of her thumbnails against each other.

"It hasn't been monkeyed with or anything like that?"

"No, sir."

He carried the picture back to his desk and picked up his phone. He was dialing when something occurred to him. He held the receiver against his chest and said, "You and I kid around a lot, Kim, but this is serious. Promise me you took this."

She looked up at him. Two giant tears, one on each cheek, were leaving wet trails on her face. "I took the picture, Jake."

———

Two weeks later the cover of *Life* carried Texas to the world. The cover editor wanted to retouch the photo, but the photographer was adamant—as is or nothing.

The top of the picture showed a lean man clad in a straw cowboy hat, long-sleeved western shirt, blue jeans, and cowboy boots vaulting a high fence. He was moving away from the camera; his body was horizontal—his legs straight, his heels together. His left arm was on the rail, his right hand was moving for his gun.

The bottom third of the black-and-white photo depicted a battle zone—men engaged in a life-or-death struggle.

Centered in the picture was a huge advertisement for an automotive dealership.

The peculiar thing about the picture was the man's firearm. Contrary to the law of gravity, it was waiting in midair just above the holster for the man to put his hand on it.

The photographer parceled out the rights to the picture— the hat, shirt, jeans, holster, belt, boot, and firearm companies all wanted a part.

Kim Kerr's college education, her trousseau, and her brand-new two-door hardtop were all paid for.

———

Mann answered the phone. "Feed store."

"Hi. You want a good sandwich for dinner?"

"What time?"

"As soon as you get here."

"Is it okay if I bring Will? He hasn't eaten in almost an hour."

"Always."

"We'll be there at noon."

"Great."

The young men who walked into the Pattersons' house were dusty from hats to boots. Missy took one look and said, "We're eatin' on the patio."

They laughed and helped her move the food outside.

They were well into the meal when she told Mann, "We have a present for you."

He sat back. "Is it better than food?"

She said, "Just a minute," and went into the den. When she came out she handed him the hoe handle.

He stood up and turned the stick in his hands. It was totally restored—no evidence of splintering, no cracks. "It's perfect."

"Good."

"How'd you do it? I thought it was gone."

"I had help." She patted Pat's arm.

Patterson was pleased with the result. "The pieces fit together like they were machined."

"It's the most special present I've ever gotten."

"We're really glad you like it."

With the meal over, Mann and Will were leaving when Mann said, "Would you do me a favor?"

"Of course," she said.

He held out the hoe handle. "Would you keep this here for

a while? I'll be moving around in the Air Force, and I don't want to risk losing it."

"We'd love to have it here." She pointed across the room. "It'll fit just right over there by the fireplace."

Readers' Group Guide Questions

Chapter 1: Share a time when you experienced the protection of God's guardian angels.

Chapter 3: Describe a person you know who, like Jimmy Palmertree, has an "uncanny ability to 'read' people."

Chapter 4: Has there ever been a time when you knew it would be to your advantage to *not* know something?

Chapter 4: Would you, like Mose Junior, be willing to give your life to save another person? Why? Why not? Or would it depend on the circumstances and/or person?

Chapter 5: There was a moment when Pat touched Missy's arm and quoted part of one her favorite Bible verses, saying, ". . . yet with gentleness and reverence."

Have there been times when you *knew* what someone was telling you was right, but you still didn't like it? Explain.

Chapter 7: Parker wanted to say more to young Mose, "but the words were trapped behind his emotions."

Has this ever happened to you? Explain.

Chapter 8: Crawford could look back on a specific time when he'd asked Jesus to be his Savior. Can you? Would you be willing to share your experience with the group?

Chapter 10: Mose & Harley were caught in the grips of a tornado . . . "the inside of the storm was a portrait of evil in motion." Describe something similar you have experienced.

Chapter 11: On his deathbed, Pap gave Mose his blessing. Consider the blessing you might give your children/grandchildren. Are you willing to share it with the group?

Chapter 12: Hugh Griffin was offended by Pat's and Missy's praying before a meal. Have you had a similar experience? What was your response? Was Griffin's reaction justified? Why? Why not?

Chapter 15: Do you agree with the statement, "I submit that a man will readily abandon a lie that can profit him nothing, if by doing so he might evade a hideous death"? Why? Why not?

Chapter 18: Bob Pierce asked the question, "What on earth do you do for a man who saves your son's life?" How would you answer him?

Chapter 22: During the frantic moments with Sweet in the arena, what role do you imagine yourself playing?

Chapter 22: In this chapter we read one man's words before he took his last breath. What do you want your last words to be? Whom would you have hear them?

Acknowledgments

Hundreds of skilled and caring people have given of themselves to bring this work to fruition. Only a few of them are mentioned here.

Were it not for my editor and his wife, Gary and Kim Terashita, I would still be cooking books on my computer while hoping and praying for an opportunity to see them in print. Man has yet to craft the words that would adequately communicate what those two have done on behalf of my writing.

The folks at FaithWords and Hachette Book Group have treated me as if I were an honored guest in their home—their penchant for hospitality is exceeded only by their pursuit of excellence on behalf of my books. Special thanks to Cara Highsmith, Gary's editorial assistant, who guards, encourages, and promotes my work. Those same thanks to Brynn Thomas, Jana Burson, Preston Cannon, Harry Helm, Linda Jamison, Kathie Johnson, Norm Kraus, Chris Murphy, Bob Nealeigh, Lori Quinn, Renee Supriano, Jodie Waldrup, Kaye Wright, and Rolf Zettersten.

To my publicist, Jeane Wynn of Wynn-Wynn Media, LLC . . . my thanks for a stunning job.

Durene White has invested long hours making sure that the writing in this book—as well as almost everything else that comes off my computer—is coherent. In any place where my meaning seems murky, rest assured that I failed to take her advice. Deanna Campbell and Paul Polk framed the questions for the Readers' Group Guide and critiqued the book . . . a huge help. Our friends Bob and Amanda Bailey from Yazoo City, Mississippi, have poured prayers, support, and encouragement on this effort. Our children and their spouses, Cody and Helen, Ron and Aubrea, and James and Kelli have never ceased to shore me up. To Diane and Tommy, Cheryl and Doug, Richard and Durene, Tesh and Alexa, Jim and Joan, Gene and Louraine, Lloyd and Deanna, Bill James, our Sunday night study group, the ladies in Nan's BSF class, and people too numerous to name . . . thank you for your fervent prayers. And to Betty Aden, my sister-in-law and life-long friend, thanks for carrying the message of my work to your part of the Western hemisphere.

Sincere thanks to Mrs. Myrna Lazenby, vice-president of The Lamar County Historical Society, who answered my many questions and gave me invaluable insight into the yesterdays of Purvis, Mississippi, and The Great South Mississippi Tornado. She was also kind enough to bring to my attention the historical society's *The Purvis Tornado of 1908*, a comprehensive collection of photographs of the tornado's aftermath along with selected eyewitness accounts.

Allan Hammons of Greenwood, Mississippi, gave me a tour of his antique photographs of the Mississippi Delta and took his valuable time to answer my questions about the cotton gins of years ago. Thanks, Allan.

In the thirty-first chapter of *Proverbs*, King Lemuel gives us an inventory of the characteristics of a godly wife. I don't know if the king had a woman in his life like the one he described, but his word picture is a portrait of my Nan. Were it not for her, you would not be reading these words.

And above all . . . God gives me day-by-day proof that He is exceeding abundantly gracious beyond all I could ask or think by letting me express my deep appreciation to those named in these acknowledgements, to those of you who have taken the time to read this book, and to the many who prayed.

Thank you.

Get the whole story in

Books One and Two of the

BLACK OR WHITE CHRONICLES:

ABIDING DARKNESS

and

WEDGWOOD GREY

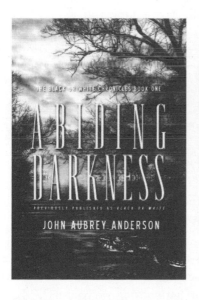 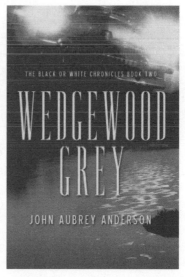

Pick up *Abiding Darkness* in mass market paperback

July 2007 and *Wedgewood Grey* November 2007.